THE MARIGOLD CHAIN

A RESTORATION NOVEL

Stella Riley

Copyright © 2012 Stella Riley
All rights reserved.

ISBN-13:978-1517099206
ISBN-10:151709920X

Cover design by Ana Grigoriu-Voicu, books-design.com

CONTENTS

	Page
PROLOGUE	1
THE CIRCUS	2
One	3
Two	14
Three	26
Four	40
Five	56
Six	68
THE DRAMA	80
One	81
Two	89
Three	103
Four	117
Five	127
Six	138

	Page
Seven	148
Eight	162
Nine	177
Ten	183
Eleven	203
Twelve	215
THE SONG	230
One	231
Two	242
Three	255
Four	267
Five	281
EPILOGUE	296

PROLOGUE
LONDON September 1665

Silence, heavy as a funeral pall, hung over the stifling heat of London. And because it had scarcely rained since April, the stench rose sickeningly from the filth in the gutters and from the accumulated refuse, noisomely rotting in the laystalls. The closely-gabled streets, empty of carriages and drays, carts and stalls, devoid of their usual bustling throng, echoed eerily with the hurried footsteps of those rare souls intrepid enough to venture abroad; shops were shuttered, taverns closed and on Cheapside, once a busy thoroughfare, grass grew between the cobbles. Like the ghost of some interminable Puritan Sunday, death had cast its greedy shadow over the City.

And while the plague reigned in London and claimed a hundred thousand souls, the Court invested Oxford with brittle brilliance and stayed to celebrate Christmas.

PART ONE

THE CIRCUS

Oxford, January 1666

*'We have ventured our estates
And our liberties and lives,
For our Master and his mates
And been tossed by cruel Fates
Where the rebellious Devil drives
So that not one of ten survives.
We have laid all at stake
For his Majesty's sake,
We have fought, we have paid,
We've been sold and betrayed
And tumbled from nation to nation:
But now those are thrown down
That usurped the Crown,
Our hopes were that we
All rewarded should be
But we're paid with a Proclamation.'*

ONE

It was the first of January in the year of our Lord sixteen hundred and sixty-six – the year for which so much had been balefully prophesied – and, in Oxford, the sun was shining. Thin, feeble rays fell from a pale, translucent sky and touched the rime-encrusted trees with hard, gleaming beauty. It was cold; too cold for snow and the ground was like iron from a succession of fierce frosts. Today, the parties of courtiers still in exile from plague-stricken London and usually to be seen riding on this open stretch of common were absent, and the clearing was deserted save for the noisy inhabitants of a rookery, a girl sitting motionless on the stile and a sturdy four-year-old playing with a dog of uncertain lineage but unquestionable stamina.

'Here, Aggie! Here!' called the child, rushing in pursuit of his errant pet.

A chill wind whipped the branches of the trees and set them dancing in a wild aerial ballet. The girl on the stile shivered and caught the folds of her cloak more closely around her. In doing so, she was forced to relinquish the broken strings of her hood which instantly blew off her head releasing a flood of pale red hair to lift and fly behind her. She made a half-hearted attempt to recapture it and then, resigning herself to remaining hoodless, jumped down and set off to follow the child who had wandered further than she liked.

'Aggie's runned off,' he observed. 'Gone to caught rabbit.'

The girl shook a strand of hair from her face. 'So he has,' she agreed in accents faintly but unmistakably French. 'He is quite faithless and a disgrace to his name. Though how your Papa could suppose a name like Agamemnon suitable for any dog, I'll never know.'

'I want to play in my house,' said the child, tugging at her cloak. 'Come on, Crowie!'

The girl grinned suddenly. The way Tom said it, her own name sounded even sillier.

'Very well. Come, then.' And she took his hand as they followed the direction that Aggie had taken along the edge of the copse.

They could not have been more than half a dozen steps away from the hollow oak that Tom called his house when they saw the horsemen; four of them, riding easily along from the far end of the clearing, their voices ringing on the crisp air.

'Look,' said Tom, unnecessarily. 'Is it the King, Crowie?' His one brief sight of Charles 11 had had a profound effect on Master Tom, with the result that he now expected to discover his monarch in all manner of unlikely locations.

'No, petit. Not the King. Some of his friends, perhaps.'

They were closer now; three extravagantly dressed in velvet and lace with sweeping plumes in their hats and the fourth, some little way behind, older and more soberly attired but with a precision that proclaimed the soldier. There was a sudden burst of laughter and a light, pleasant voice said clearly, 'Optimism and ambition are wonderful things, Daniel. But if it's a wager, you're welcome to try.'

One of the group – presumably the aforementioned Daniel – broke away and, drawing his sword, brandished it laughingly. 'Nice of you! But twenty guineas says I can unseat you.'

The gentleman to whom his remark had been addressed also stopped.

'Done,' he said. And pulling off his coat, he flung it with lazy accuracy at the still, soldier-like figure some few yards to his left. Then he too drew his sword.

'They're having a war,' announced Master Tom with relish. Then, 'I like the brown horse best.'

The girl smiled and kept a firm hold of his hand. Since the gentlemen were obviously not in earnest, there was no reason why the child should not watch and, here at the edge of the trees, they were far enough off to escape notice.

It could not have lasted more than ten minutes but it was worth every freezing second. Worth it just to watch the horses - one a glossy chestnut, the other a magnificent black - and still more so to see the economic control which enabled their riders to manage them with only one hand and the pressure of their knees. And the swordplay was pure joy. The blades exploded together, ringing, chiming and hissing, wielded with supple dexterity; but where Daniel's play showed neatness and the occasional flair of the well-taught, his dark-haired friend was possessed of an easy brilliance that enabled him to press a constant and fast-moving attack whilst maintaining a light-hearted commentary on his opponent's technique.

'Nowhere so busy a man as he there was, and yet he seemed busier than he was,' he recited. 'Oh no – not the feint you picked up in Scotland! It never works, you know ... better to try the German style. You must have learned something from Rupert. Oh bravo!' And he parried a deceptive thrust with an agile twist of his arm.

It was perhaps fortunate that Daniel also had a sense of humour.

'Some of the ditch shy are, yet can lie tumbling in the mire,' he retorted. And concluded with an accompanying sweep that should have caused his adversary to fall as he attempted to parry it. Instead, Daniel's blade met empty air as the other man dropped low to one side before returning to the saddle in the same fluid move, his point immediately darting inside Daniel's weakened guard only to withdraw again.

'Surprise is the essence of attack – and for God's sake, keep your guard up. I don't want to stick you by mistake.' The bantering voice ceased abruptly as his point was parried and immediately threatened, 'Well done. That nearly worked. But those who sow the wind, you know ...' And with one sharp, turn of the wrist, Daniel found himself disarmed.

For a second there was silence and then, kicking his feet clear of the stirrups, the other man slipped from the saddle, saying invitingly, 'Come on. Get down and pick it up. Let's see how out of practice you really are.'

Daniel shook his head, laughing a little. 'I don't think so. And anyway, the bet was that I'd unseat you – and there you are on the ground.'

'But no thanks to you.' The dark-haired man picked up Daniel's sword. 'If you want this back you'll have to come and get it.'

'Blast you, Alex – I know what you're like!'

'Meaning you'd prefer something a bit easier?' He turned back to their other companions. 'How about it Giles? You'll be gentle with him, won't you?'

The man wearing exquisite grey velvet said calmly, 'Hold me excused. I've no desire to work up a sweat just now. Give Danny his sword back, Alex. The horses are getting cold.'

'You're no fun.' Alex looked back at Daniel. 'If you won't come down, your sword stays here - like Excalibur.' And he drove Danny's sword into the frozen ground.

'No!' Daniel dropped quickly from the saddle and made a dive for his maltreated blade. 'You're a bloody maniac, Alex.'

'So they say.' Alex advanced smiling. 'Disarm me or put me on my back and the bet stands. Refuse to try and you lose by default. That's fair, isn't it?'

'Just do it, Danny,' sighed the man in grey, 'or we'll be here all day.'

Daniel shrugged and hurled himself at Alex, his sword sweeping hard at the other man's blade. Alex parried, pivoted and, with another almost invisible twist, sent Daniel's sword spinning and Daniel himself backwards on to the hard ground with a thud.

Alex grinned, head on one side. 'You should have recognised that one. It's the second time I've used it in ten minutes.' Then, sheathing his own sword, he held out a hand to Daniel and hauled him to his feet. 'Pay up - and let's go. Before Giles gets cross.'

Grinning, Daniel pulled a handful of coins from his pocket and slapped them in Alex's hand. 'You can buy the ale,' he said. 'I'm cleaned out.'

Then, laughing, they re-mounted their horses and it was over. The grey-clad man and the soldier cantered up to join them, coats were donned and they were off.

Tom gazed wistfully after them, then twisted his head to look up at the girl. 'I liked that, Crowie. I wish they'd do it again.' And filled with the spirit of emulation he galloped round in circles until he came to the tree-house and vanished inside it. Aggie emerged panting from behind a bush and followed him.

The girl hugged her mantle round her and glanced anxiously at the sky. Another ten minutes, perhaps, and then she must restore Tom to his Mama. She walked a little way along the edge of the copse and, finding a tree with a conveniently situated branch, hoisted herself on to it, aware that the prospect of abandoning freedom to return to her own home was even less palatable than usual. She sighed, stirring reluctantly, and then was still as a sound reached her ears. The drumming of hoof-beats approaching rapidly from the west of the common. As soon as they came into view she recognised the horses; they were racing, three of them almost neck and neck with the big black ahead by two lengths.

They thundered towards her down the open stretch, riders crouched low with coats and feathers flying – and then it happened. Drawn by the noise, Tom's small figure came rushing out into the clearing, out past the safety of the trees and straight into the path of the oncoming horses.

'Tom!' The girl gave a strangled cry of warning and threw herself forward in an attempt to reach him whilst knowing already that it was too late. Fear made her clumsy. Her foot became entangled in her cloak and she measured her length on the ground with a force that knocked the breath from her body so that she could do nothing but watch as the great sable horse bore down on the tiny figure of the child.

But she had reckoned without the ingenuity of the blue-coated rider. He could have had no warning but he put the split second he did have to good use. Making no attempt to alter his direction, he rode on, allowing his horse's forelegs to miss Tom by inches whilst leaning down to swoop on the child and hoist him clear of the ground by means of his stout collar.

Sick with relief, the girl closed her eyes and let her head fall on to her arms. When she looked up again, all four horsemen were trotting back towards her with Tom perched high in the grip of his rescuer and chattering away with all the blissful unconcern of the very young.

'I'm not frit,' he announced boastfully. 'I like horses. Please can I have it to hold?'

The man laughed. 'Well, if you're sure you're not frit ...' And he handed the reins into Tom's inexpert grasp. 'His name is Caesar. If you want to be his friend you should talk to him.'

Obediently, Tom transferred the dangerously slackened reins into one chubby fist and patted the gleaming black neck. 'Hello, Caesar. I'm Tom.'

And the man laughed again. It was a curiously infectious sound and, looking up, the girl received a confused impression of long, lightly-curling black hair and a pale, fine-boned face alight with amusement.

Then she realised that one of the party had dismounted and was offering his hand.

'Let me help you,' he said, taking her arm. 'You've had a nasty shock.'

She glanced up and liked what she saw. Fair hair framed a face set with intelligent dark grey eyes and a firm mouth, oddly at variance with his languid tone.

She nodded. 'Yes. I – I thought he was going to be killed.'

'Which he very nearly was,' remarked a cool, pleasant voice. But perhaps you'll take better care in future.' The blue-coated gentleman had ridden up and was passing Tom down to her.

Too surprised to reply, she took the child without a word.

'Crowie, did you see? I rode on the big horse. I rode it myself!'

She held him tight and managed a weak smile. 'Yes. Yes, I saw.'

Tom inspected her with interest. 'Was you frit, Crowie? I wasn't.'

'Of course you weren't. And now I daresay you'd like to ride my Bess, wouldn't you?' It was Daniel who spoke; red-haired, freckled and grinning with cheerful sympathy.

'Yes – oh yes!' cried Tom. 'Put me down, Crowie. I'm too big to be held.'

She shook her head. 'I don't think --'

'But I want to!'

He wriggled so much that she had to release him but directed a rueful smile at Daniel.

'It's simply that I would prefer he didn't think he has only to court death under the hooves of a horse in order to be offered a ride on it.'

He laughed. 'Don't worry – I'll talk to him. And by the time you've stopped shaking, we'll be back. Here, Giles – toss him up.'

With a half-mocking lift of his brows, the fair-haired man lifted Tom and swung him up in front of Daniel.

'He'll be quite safe, you know,' he told the girl as she watched them canter away. 'And it's better that he should see this as an adventure rather than have nightmares.'

She considered this. 'Yes. I daresay you're right.'

Then, a little reluctantly, she turned to Tom's saviour and found herself impaled on a pair of curiously light blue eyes … like polished steel over-laid by the merest sliver of aquamarine and rendered all the more striking by the dark lashes framing them. They rested on her with a glint of satire and a strange intensity that, just for an instant, made her forget to breathe.

'Oh,' she thought. He was probably the best-looking man she had ever seen - and possibly the most intimidating.

'Well, Mistress?' The charming voice was edged with impatience.

Acutely aware that her hair was straying in all directions and her gown and cloak adorned with fragments of mud and twig, she felt the blood rise to her skin and set her teeth, lifting her chin stubbornly.

'I wished to thank you, sir,' she said carefully. 'Had you not been so quick-thinking, Tom could have been badly hurt or even killed. I – I'm very grateful to you.'

'Yes,' came the bland reply. 'You should be. As a nursemaid, I wouldn't say you are a roaring success, would you?'

'Short of chaining him to her wrist,' objected the fair gentleman, 'it's difficult to see what she could have done.'

But the girl had recovered her composure and needed neither defence nor to explain herself. Brown eyes resting kindly on her mentor, she said, 'Don't worry. I understand perfectly. It gave you a fright as well and you're not quite yourself yet.'

The blue gaze widened a little and, glancing round, the gentleman surprised a grin on the face of his soldier companion seated patiently some few paces behind.

'You hear that, Matt? My nerves are all to pieces.'

'That'll be the day,' grunted Matthew tersely.

The younger man laughed and turned back to look at the girl. 'If that remark was designed to put me in my place, I'm afraid it was wasted,' he told her gently.

'I can see that, ' she shrugged. 'But thank you for pointing it out.'

It was perhaps fortunate that Daniel chose this moment to return and lower Tom to the ground. The girl took his hand and reminded him to say thank you. With an engaging smile, the little boy did as he was bidden and insisted on being lifted up to that he could give each horse a last pat. Giles bowed elegantly over the girl's hand and climbed back into his saddle, while the dark-haired man showed his impatience by encouraging Caesar to fidget.

'Are we finally ready?' he asked. 'Wonderful!'

'Oh, shut up, Alex,' said Daniel amicably. 'What's the hurry?'

'The hurry,' said Alexander Charles Deveril, crisply, 'is that I've no mind to allow Caesar to take cold in this wind. The rest of you may be happy to linger – but I'm going.'

And with that he wheeled his horse round and was off down the common at a gallop, leaving the other three to watch with something akin to resignation and the girl with admiration mixed liberally with disapproval.

'G'bye! G'bye!' shouted Tom, waving with all his might as they rode away. And then, 'Those mens were nice, Crowie – 'specially the one with hair like yours.'

She laughed. 'Yes, petit. Very nice.' But in her mind there lingered nothing but the image of a piece of brilliant horsemanship and a pair of worryingly compelling ice-blue eyes.

* * *

Much later that evening, Mr Deveril faced a very different lady across the meagre width of her hired parlour and listened whilst she spoke in tones of calm finality.

'I'm sorry, Alex, really I am – but I've made up my mind and there's nothing you can say that will make me change it.'

'No? Well, let's see if I understand you correctly,' he replied with equal calm. 'You're saying that you intend to marry Graham Marsden – a man more than twice your age – purely in order to gain social and financial security. Is that it?'

Lady Sarah Courtenay eyed him sulkily. 'Yes. But there's no need to put it like that. It sounds horrid.'

'Precisely.'

'No! It isn't at all horrid – it's perfectly reasonable. David has been dead for two years now and, even though I like my life the way it is, it can't go on. I haven't any money at all – and I hate being poor. It's all very well being a widow if one is a rich widow. As things are, I have no choice but to marry.' She spread her hands and smiled with artistic witchery. 'Surely you see my position. It's much the same as your own, after all.'

He did not reply immediately but simply gazed at her in apparent meditation. Lady Sarah knew that she was worth looking at and was entirely aware that the new gown of Lyons silk was an excellent foil for her silver-gilt curls and the exact cornflower blue of her eyes but something in Alex's face made her experience an unfamiliar moment of doubt.

'Well?' she demanded, tired of the silence. 'It's true, isn't it?'

'Yes,' he said slowly, 'it's true. I, on the other hand, won't be putting myself up for sale.'

'Oh! I'm not!' An angry flush stained her ladyship's exquisite cheeks and her fingers toyed irritably with the sapphire pin at her breast.

'Aren't you? Then how would you describe it?'

'As – as a marriage of convenience!' she retorted defiantly.

He laughed. 'Yes. I can see how convenient it would be for you. But what does Marsden get out of it?'

Her brows arched in astonishment. 'Why - me. He adores me.'

'I see. And you? Do you adore him?'

This was not quite how Lady Sarah had planned it but she rose to the occasion, the cornflower eyes misting. 'You are unkind, Alex. You know how I feel.'

'I thought so, certainly,' came the deliberate reply. 'But you've got to admit that it seems somewhat odd that you can marry Marsden, yet love me.'

Sarah's brow cleared as if by magic. She crossed to his side and tucked a hand through his arm whilst bestowing a dazzling smile upon him.

'My dear one – of course I love you. How can you doubt it? And if I were rich – or you were – why, there could be no question! But as things are ... well, it isn't as though you could possibly marry me yourself, is it?' she asked reasonably.

'Isn't it?' There was a faintly disquieting note in his voice but his face was unreadable. 'And what if I were to ask you – now? If I offered you hand, heart and name, would you give up your fine plans to be with me?'

She sighed wistfully and shook her head.

'Dearest, if only I could – but it isn't possible. You must see that. One can't live on air – and we both have expensive tastes. I like beautiful things and you – well, it can't be denied that you like the card table. So there you have it. I need a rich husband - and you, my sweet, should get a wealthy wife.'

Without warning, he freed himself from her and dropped into a chair, his expression openly sardonic.

'I could not love thee, dear, so much, loved I not … money more?' he quipped. 'If I had a fortune you'd love me forever - but since I don't, I'm a luxury you can't afford. Is that it?'

A shadow of annoyance crossed the lovely face and the equally lovely shoulders shrugged elegantly.

'One must be practical. And provided we are careful, it need make little difference to us – unless you are determined to be difficult?'

'Difficult ? *I*? But do go on. Exactly how is your marriage to make no difference?'

Sarah eyed him with irritable misgiving. There were times when Alex was as provoking as he was attractive; times when she half-regretted that she was not yet ready to dispense with his extremely satisfying attentions. She summoned the aid of her most seductive smile.

'Surely you don't need to ask? As long as we are … discreet … there's no reason why you shouldn't visit me from time to time,' she explained delicately.

He did not speak for a moment and his face remained impassive.

Then, with something akin to interest, he asked, 'Are you serious?'

'Of course. Why not? It's the perfect solution.'

'You don't think it's a bit like eating your cake and having it?'

She laughed. 'And what's wrong with that? All one needs is a little ingenuity.'

'So it would seem.'

She looked searchingly at him in sudden doubt but before she could speak he went on, pleasantly contemptuous, 'So. I don't qualify as a husband but you're willing to retain me as your lover; and Marsden, having no appeal for you apart from his money, is to be given horns. It's a charming notion, my dear, and no doubt I should be flattered – but unfortunately, I'm not. In fact, the only certainty it arouses in me is the knowledge that you are a bigger whore than I thought. Not that I've anything against whores – quite the opposite! But, as a general rule, I prefer them honest.'

Eyes snapping with fury, Sarah leapt up stamping her foot.

'How dare you! How dare you speak so to me!'

Alex looked her up and down, his face rather pale.

'It's not very difficult. My only surprise is that you duped me so thoroughly before – for I never really knew you, did I, Sarah? I never guessed what a selfish little bitch you really are.'

She controlled herself with a visible effort.

'You're just jealous. No one speaks to me that way, Alex. And by tomorrow, you'll sorry for what you've said and be back here on your knees, apologising.'

His brows rose. 'I wouldn't bet on it, if I were you.'

'You forget how well I know you. And you were quite content to be my lover before – so why not after? Why cut off your nose to spite your face? It isn't as though Graham Marsden is a friend of yours, is it?'

He gave an odd little laugh. 'You're missing the point. Firstly, I find the thought of cuckolding anyone – friend or no – singularly repellent. And secondly, I expect you, if you love me at all, to love me exclusively and irrespective of material considerations. If I ask too much ... let us kiss and part.'

Swallowing an angry sob, Lady Sarah said petulantly, 'You are unreasonable! I thought you loved me!'

Quite without haste, Alex rose and, taking her hand, raised it to his lips.

'Did you, my sweet?' he asked dryly. 'So did I.'

And turned and left.

TWO

The Acorn tavern was hot, noisy and crowded, but Mr Deveril seemed oblivious to its warm, cheery chatter. Pushing his way carelessly to the counter, he demanded a bottle of eau-de-vie and, when it came poured a glass and downed it in one.

'Alex! Where have you been? We've been waiting for you.'

With unnecessary force, Alex dislodged the hand clasping his shoulder and swung to face its owner.

'Have you? Why? You must have other friends.'

His colour rising, Daniel Fawsley met the unpleasant blue gaze squarely.

'We have,' he replied tersely.

'Then go and join them. You and Giles ought to be able to manage without me for one night. And I,' announced Alex conversationally, 'intend to get extremely drunk. Preferably, in blissful solitude.'

For a second Danny scrutinized him, his lips pressed tightly together. Then, 'Hallelujah,' he said, turning on his heel and walking away.

Throwing himself back into his chair, he stared at Giles Beckwith with unaccustomed gloom and, lifting his tankard, drained it before he spoke.

'Next time,' he said feelingly, 'you go. He says he's going to get drunk – which, if you ask me, will be a public service.'

'Ah.' Giles rested his fingers together and surveyed the shadowy corner where Alex sat alone with his bottle. 'Then I think he would be better doing so at home. If he's in one of his moods, he'll look for someone to offend. And everyone doesn't know him as we do.'

'Oh Lord!' Danny grimaced. 'You're not suggesting we try to get him home by force, are you?'

'No. I'm not. It may have escaped your notice, but I am wearing my best coat.'

Danny raised one quizzical brow. It amused Giles to pose as a fop, but to Danny's certain knowledge he was the only man who stood any chance of wrestling Mr Deveril and winning.

'What I am suggesting,' continued Giles placidly, 'is that one of us should go for Matt.'

Danny leaned back and folded his arms.

'What you're suggesting is that I go for Matt.'

Giles smiled. 'Unless you'd rather stay here and keep Alex out of trouble?'

'Well I wouldn't!'

'No. I didn't think you would.'

Danny was justifiably indignant. 'Damn it, Giles – you know what he's like. How many times has he made you want to hit him just by the way he looks at you?'

His friend laughed. 'It's a bit extreme perhaps – but I take your point.' He paused as Danny got up. 'So be a good fellow and make it quick, will you?'

When Danny left the tavern, Alexander Deveril was broaching his fourth shot of brandy. He leaned back, chin on chest, legs stretched out and ankles crossed. One hand was plunged deep in his pocket while the fingers of the other were loosely curled about the goblet. There was nothing in his attitude that spoke of danger and to the casual observer he merely appeared to have left sobriety behind him and be verging on sleep.

Mr Beckwith was not deceived. They had grown up together – in France and in many army camps and battlefields since then – and though the indulgence in drink was a fairly recent innovation, the wild moods were not. In recent years, when anything had really hurt him, Alex had developed a talent for finding and making the most unforgivable remark. With a faint sigh, Giles crossed the room to stand looking down at him from the other side of the table.

Alex did not move but the lowered lids lifted and the light, compelling gaze fell full on the other man.

'Oh hell,' he said. 'Enter Sir Righteous, full of good intentions and dressed to kill. Danny-boy called up reinforcements.'

Giles sat down. 'Do you want to talk?'

'Why? Are you lonely?'

'I was referring,' said Giles patiently, 'to whatever has occurred in the last four hours to induce this epic fit of sulks.'

Alex drained his goblet, filled it and drained it again.

'If you enjoy catechisms and confessions,' he said at length, 'you should enter the priesthood. Alternatively, go and find somebody else to mother. I don't need you.'

'A fact for which I'm duly grateful,' retorted Giles, signalling for the potboy to bring him more ale. The low-ceilinged room was hazy with pipe-smoke and the blast of icy air that came in with a small party of finely-dressed gentlemen was refreshingly welcome. He glanced back at Alex and noted that his cheeks held a betraying flush and that the bottle was more than half empty.

'Do you suppose that one bottle will be enough?' he asked casually. 'Or is this the beginning of a crapulous week?'

'For Christ's sake!' The pewter vessel cracked down on the table. 'Haven't you anything better to do? You are neither my brother nor my keeper and my moods and habits are not your business. So stick with Danny who has no nasty vices to offend you or go home to your embroidery – but leave me alone!'

The flush that sprang to Giles' cheeks had nothing to do with drink.

'My pleasure, I assure you. I doubt you'll find you can drown your inadequacies in eau-de-vie – but if there's any chance it will take the edge off your bitching tongue, I'll buy you an anker.' And he walked away before the infuriating boredom in Alex's face drove him to violence.

Alex watched him go and then, delicately, he began to sing.

His serenade passed unnoticed. The trio of latecomers, having progressed by degrees from mannerly tipsiness, were fast approaching a state of cupshot roistering. Glasses were raised to the King, to each other, to a speedy return to London and to their respective ladies. At this last, a large gentleman, splendidly attired and equipped with swarthy good looks but marked by the ironic finger of Fate in a manner not instantly obvious, rose swimmingly to his feet.

'To Sawah,' he pronounced. 'May she soon be wedded, bedded and bored.'

The younger of his companions frowned as he grappled with what he considered a vital point.

'Can't say that,' he objected. 'She ain't exactly a bawd, old fellow.' He thought about it. 'Ain't exactly a rose of virtue neither – merry widow and all that. But you can't call her a bawd.'

'I don't know why you don't give it up, Gresh,' said the other man. 'Every time you visit her it costs you a fortune.'

The swarthy gallant waved a dismissive hand and subsided into his chair.

'I can afford it. Gave her a sapphire pin only this morning and last week it was a pearl necklet. Twuth is that she'd not mawy Marsden if I were fwee.'

'Roses out-red their lips and cheeks
Lilies their whiteness stain
What fool is he that shadows seeks
Who might the substance gain?'

sang Alex Deveril softly, his gaze fixed reflectively on a point some two feet above the swarthy gentleman's head.

Gloom, meanwhile, had settled on the third member of the trio.

'Damn war,' he groaned. 'Damn plague, too. Between the two of 'em, my profit's down by half this last year. Don't know how you manage it, Gresh. You're the only one who ain't suffering.'

Lord George Gresham gave an immense hiccup that rocked the table.

'I have good contacts and good information, Wobert. And a first-class Captain.'

'Hm! Well, if we don't beat the Dutch soon, I'll be a ruined man. Can't understand it. In Cromwell's day our Navy was the best there was – and now look at it. All to pieces!'

'The pwoblem,' said Gresham derisively, 'is that it's being wun by Sandwich, who is a wogue and Wupert, who is a fool.'

Confused, the quiet young man looked hard at him.

'Woo who?'

'Wupert!' repeated Gresham, irritated. 'Wupert of the Whine. A man, Fwedewick, only fit to be a widing master.'

Robert nodded, but Frederick remained unconvinced.

'Can't say that,' he recited. 'He's supposed to be pretty good with a sword too.'

Robert stared at him pityingly.

'What good's that? You can't lead the fleet like a cavalry charge. He needs strategy.'

Gresham snorted. 'Stwategy? Shouldn't think Wu – that His Highness knows what it means. Look at how he lost the war with Cwomwell! Spent his time wushing about on fool's ewands – he and those young idiots who followed him calling themselves cavalwy. And wemember Bwistol? He suwendered it against the King's expwess orders. Why, the fellow's not even bwave! And now --'

He stopped abruptly as a hand closed like a vice on his shoulder and, jerking his head round, found himself impaled on a piercing, blue gaze.

'Good evening, my lord,' said Alex, his tone pleasant but his smile markedly less so. 'You talk too much.'

Gresham spluttered. 'Damn it, sir – who the hell do you think you are?'

'Merely one of the 'young idiots calling themselves cavalry'.'

His lordship's face became rather red.

'Weally?' he asked, with what should have been freezing dignity.

'Weally,' echoed Alex unkindly.

Lord Gresham turned from red to puce.

'You're dwunk,' he said furiously. 'You don't know what you're doing.'

'I'm drunk,' agreed Alex, 'but as for the rest – we'll see.' He crooked his fingers round one red velvet lapel and drew Gresham easily to his feet. 'A not-particularly wild guess would suggest that while Prince Rupert was fighting for his King, you were sitting safe by your hearth; that later on you were quick to ingratiate yourself with your snuffling Puritan masters and that five years ago you performed the same volte-face in favour of Charles Stuart. And you ... you are the snivelling little runt who calls Rupert a coward?'

His lordship closed his mouth and raised an arm only have it fall useless to his side from a swift, hard chop to the wrist. Then his collar was seized in strong, fine-boned fingers and savagely twisted.

'If you are sensible,' said the playful voice, 'you will admit yourself mistaken about His Highness and then drink his health. You and your friends.'

'A-and if I don't?'

Dark brows rose over eyes filed with malicious invitation. 'Do you really want to find out?'

'I say!' bleated Frederick with an attempt at bravery. 'You can't really --'

'Of course he won't!' snapped Gresham. And then realised his mistake.

From across the room, Giles watched with a certain detached interest. But when he saw his lordship clawing frantically at the fingers slowly tightening his collar, he decided that it was time to intervene. Quite without haste, he strolled across the room marvelling that so few people appeared to have noticed the incident. By the time he reached the little group, however, it was attracting rather more attention – for Robert had joined in the fray and was trying, so far without success, to break Alex's grip. Gresham's breath was coming in wheezing gasps and perspiration beaded his brow. Giles stepped forward and tapped Robert on the shoulder.

'Allow me,' he said politely.

Robert retreated thankfully and, as he did so, Alex turned his head. Giles did not hesitate. With a small, satisfied smile, his fist shot out to take Alex on the point of the jaw and send him reeling back amongst tables and benches. He went crashing to the floor and was still.

Giles stood over him, absently rubbing his knuckles and then looked up to meet Danny's astounded gaze.

'You took your time,' he drawled. And, looking beyond Danny to Matthew Lewis's enigmatic countenance, 'Sorry, Matt. It couldn't wait.'

Matt walked forward and looked thoughtfully on Alex's prone figure. 'How many times did you have to hit him?'

Giles smiled. 'Would you believe once?'

Matt grunted. 'He'll be well into his altitudes then. I'd best get him home.'

'Yes. In a minute.' He turned back to Gresham who had collapsed in his chair and was massaging his throat and choking spasmodically. 'I should point out, sir,' said Giles with unusual crispness, 'that I prevented Mr Deveril from strangling you for his sake rather than yours. With his reasons for wishing to do so, I am in complete accord. And, that being so, I must insist on a full retraction of your slanderous attack on Prince

Rupert's valour and leadership – both of which are above reproach. Should you refuse, I shall have no alternative but to serve you in a similar manner to that of my unconscious friend here. Well?'

Lord Gresham had suffered a very trying fifteen minutes. He did not doubt that Giles was capable of carrying out his threat and one look at the faces of Danny and Matt was sufficient to inform him that they too would be delighted to manhandle him.

'Oh vewy well!' he said with the nearest thing to a snap he could manage. 'I take it back – and do not doubt that His Highness has many excellent qualities. Satisfied?'

'Not especially,' replied Giles coldly, 'but it's an improvement.' He picked up his lordship's glass and put it in his hand. 'Now get on your feet and toast the Prince's health.'

Gresham glared but saw no help for it. He hauled himself out of his chair and jerked up his glass as ungraciously as he dared.

'Pwince Wupert – his health.' And he drank.

'Prince Rupert!' echoed a mixed chorus of voices.

'And God bless him,' added Matt.

* * *

Alex came round with a crashing headache, a jaw as stiff as last week's bread and total recollection. With practised ease, Matt used his most uncommunicative front to prevent an eruption and it worked perfectly until he was forced into a refusal by a demand for brandy. His first flat denial was met with a dangerous silence but, standing his ground, Matt remarked that ale was easier on the liver and had the added advantage of being cheaper. Ten minutes later he was allowed to have his way – but not graciously.

And that was just the beginning. He stayed through the initial stages while Alex, sprawling in a chair, consumed his first jug; and, then, thinking nostalgically of night marches in wet weather, judged it safe to go out for a time.

When he came back the scene showed little change. Alex did not look up but sat motionless and apparently relaxed, mug clasped in one lax hand. The black hair was clinging in untidy dampness to his brow and the lawn shirt was crumpled and sweat-stained. Matt stood in the doorway where the hot, stale air hit him like a blow and assessed the situation. Then he walked to the window and, pulling back the curtains, threw it open.

Bright, merciless daylight spilled into the room and an icy blast blew over Mr Deveril producing an involuntary shiver. He looked round.

'Close it.' That was all. But his tone implied more than a death-threat complete with ritual.

Matt stared phlegmatically back without replying. With a lithe, violent movement that overset his chair, Alex rose swearing, lurched across the room and slammed the casement shut with a force that cracked two of its panes. Matt grinned sourly.

'Man, you've a way to go yet,' he said. 'You've still got the use of your legs.'

As expected, he was awarded a dirty look.

'Blame the ale. It's damned slow.'

Matt retrieved the velvet coat from where it lay on the floor and hung it up. Then he poured himself a mug of ale and sat down.

'It's fast enough – unless there's a shortage I've not heard about.' And then, because he had certain private suspicions which he'd be happy to have proved right, 'And if it's that bad, I doubt you'll find three days concentration will improve it. Why not find yourself a woman?' And he waited for the explosion.

It did not come. Instead, his mouth curling unpleasantly but in much the same tone as one saying 'Pass the salt,' Alex said, 'All women are whores.'

Matthew was imbued with a certain satisfaction for, in his opinion, a few days of rank discomfort would be small price to pay for an end to Madam Sarah's hold over Mr Deveril. It was just a pity that, after a youth which had held no opportunity for more than passing dalliance, Alex should fall in love for the first time at the age of thirty with a rapacious beauty of doubtful reputation. 'So if he wants to stay cupshot for a sennight, he's welcome this once,' thought Matt, cynically. 'I'll have a few myself just to celebrate.'

But, despite these heartening reflections, there is nothing very pleasant about being cloistered with an ill-tempered drunk and when, after a day of unnatural silence his attempts to persuade Mr Deveril to put some food in his stomach were met with an epitome of double-edged wit, Matt removed himself instantly and without a word, leaving Alex humming gently beneath his breath.

He came back, of course, because a few heated words were not enough to sever a bond forged over fifteen dangerous yet often hilarious years that he would not have missed for anything that he could think of and which made him remain now from what he insisted was habit. So, having walked off his temper in the cold air, he returned and was instantly rewarded. Still at the table, head pillowed on his arms, Alex was asleep. Mr Lewis nodded to himself and tiptoed out again.

It was some two hours later when Giles Beckwith ran lightly up the stairs, rapped at the door and received no answer. Having good reason to suppose that there was someone within, he waited for a moment and then knocked again, this time more loudly. After a moment he heard Alex's voice, a trifle blurred but otherwise composed.

'Who is it?'

'Giles. Open the door.'

'Why?'

'I want to talk to you.'

'Why?'

Mr Beckwith was aware of intense irritation.

'Oh for God's sake – don't be an ass!'

That did the trick. The tumblers clicked and the door swung wide on the point of a sword. Coatless and disorderly, Alex examined his friend with an impersonal stare. Giles looked back, cool but cautious.

'Is that really necessary?' he asked, indicating the bright ribbon of steel.

'Yes. I thought it might persuade you to just turn around and go.'

'It hasn't,' said Giles simply. 'We need to talk. But not like this.'

'Why not? Scared?'

Giles looked from the perfectly steady blade to the expressionless face above it.

'Hardly,' he said. 'You aren't sober enough to present a problem.' And then threw himself swiftly to one side at the sword drove at his throat. Hitting the doorpost, he grabbed the velvet coat from where it hung and used it to protect his hand as he caught at the flashing steel. He gave it a hard, downward twist and, abruptly, Alex let go. For a second they faced each other, both breathing rather fast, then Giles spoke, his voice icily quiet.

'Do that again and you'd best hope to make a thorough job of it.'

'Or what?'

'Or I may forget our past friendship.'

'My God! How will I survive?' mocked Alex, smiling but pale.

The grey eyes hardened with something akin to disgust.

'I don't think I care.'

'That's the spirit! So is that all you came to say?'

'No. I thought you might have sobered up and be ready to talk.'

'You should have known better.'

'As you say. Where's Matt?'

'Out.'

'In other words, you've exceeded even his patience.' Giles paused briefly, and then, 'I presume we owe this epic tantrum to Sarah Courtney?'

Suddenly bored, Alex turned away and dropped into a chair.

'Presume what you like – just don't expect me to listen.'

'I don't,' came the blunt reply. 'But if you're sulking because I hit you, accept that I did it before you choked the life out of that pompous fool and ended up in front of a magistrate.'

'It wouldn't have come to that.'

'It could very well have come to that. You were drunk and in a foul mood – and capable of just about any kind of lunacy.' He paused. 'You're out of control, Alex. A spoiled brat taking your ill-temper out on everyone around you and plunging into whatever kind of dangerous stupidity occurs to you next. I'm just glad that Rupert isn't here to see you.'

Alex came to his feet like an uncoiling spring.

'That's enough. You can chew on my failings till you choke – but not here. I don't want sympathy, brotherly love or nauseating bloody morality – and I don't respond to the magic name of Rupert being banged over my head. So go and mourn my decaying senses with Matt and Danny. They'll agree with everything you say – which should comfort you – and I'll be left in peace, which should suit everybody. Shut the door on your way out.'

Giles gazed across at him, his expression taut and cold. Then he threw down the sword so that it went clattering and sliding across the floor.

'Go to hell,' he said. And left.

* * *

A little while later when Matthew returned he found Alex at the window, his fingers pressed hard on the ledge and his face glacially composed. Matt took one look and suffered the rare sensation of being out of his depth.

'Thinking hard, Matt? Difficult, isn't it? The wrong word now could spell catastrophe.' Alex's voice was brittle and, when he turned Matt saw that the blue eyes were at their most impenetrable.

'Aye. Who woke you?'

'Giles. Thoughtless of him, wasn't it? But cheer up. I'm going out.'

Matt eyed him sardonically.

'On two hours sleep in as many days and no food to speak of? They'll be finding you in some gutter.'

'Perhaps.' He crossed to the mirror and inspected his reflection with a wry grimace. 'Oh God – Faustus reborn. I need a shave. And a clean shirt.'

'And a bloody good wash.'

Alex turned, smiling a little. 'Well, then?'

Matt did not respond but he did go in search of hot water. Nearly an hour later when Alex was washed, shaved and changed, he was still presenting an aspect of dour silence. Alex picked up his hat with its trailing white plumes and walked to the door, his face thoughtful. He laid a hand on the latch and then turned back.

'Matt?'

'What?'

A hint of colour touched the flat pallor of his cheeks.

'It's not easy, I know – but it will pass. Until then, don't let me ...' He hesitated a little. 'I'm aware that I'm often my own worst enemy. But bear with me – if you can.'

Matt scowled.

'I'll do my best,' he said gruffly. And then, 'If you go to Ashton's house, you'll probably meet Mr Giles there.'

'Ah.' Alex met his gaze with one of limpid innocence. 'Then I should be in for an interesting evening, shouldn't I?'

And was gone.

THREE

It was close on five o'clock when Alex let himself out of the house and the wintry dusk was almost complete. He walked swiftly in the direction of the Acorn and was nearly there when, cutting down a narrow passage, his ears were alerted by sounds of a scuffle round the corner ahead of him. He checked his pace and moved silently to the end of the wall.

It was too dark to see details but the overall picture was plain enough and Alex stifled the first impulse to laugh that he had felt in three days. What he had heard was nothing more that the ensuing struggle as an inexpert young man attempted to embrace an unwilling young lady. As Alex turned the corner, she dealt her admirer a ringing box on the ear and, as he stepped back to try and capture her arm, followed it up with a well-placed kick on the shin. The young man released her, cursing, and bent to rub his afflicted leg. Strangely, the girl remained where she was, watching him.

'Damn it all, there's no need to cripple me!' he expostulated.

The girl said something Alex couldn't quite hear and the fellow replied with, 'Well, I didn't think you meant it. And it's not as if you don't know how I feel about you. But I suppose I should have guessed how it would be.'

'Indeed you should,' said Alex, his voice quivering slightly.

The girl stiffened and pulled her hood more closely about her face while the young man straightened so quickly he banged his elbow against the wall.

'Who the devil are you?' he gasped, clutching this new injury.

'Call me the Voice of Experience,' returned Alex. 'And I'm appalled by your clumsiness. Don't you know better than to maul a girl in a draughty alley? And if you must do so, you'll find it helps to decide beforehand the way your attentions are likely to be received. When uncertain, a wise man always protects his flank by taking the lady's hands – so!' And before the youthful pair had any idea of his intention, he had imprisoned the girl's hands and pulled her against him to hold them behind her back.

'I say! What the --'

'Watch and learn,' reproved Alex. 'You'll find it worthwhile. Now, where was I? Ah yes. One hand should suffice – now darling, don't struggle – and with the other you may lift her chin.' He smiled fleetingly into the girl's startled face, very little of which could be seen for her enveloping hood, and then bent his head till his mouth found hers.

Hovering uncertainly, the young man watched in astonishment, his mouth opening and closing as he formulated and discarded a variety of objections. He was naturally reluctant to lay hands on a fellow wearing a sword, but he knew he ought to defend his companion, who was fighting to free herself. Only then, in the seconds he spent hesitating, she stopped struggling. He watched in rising indignation as her hands, now released, showed no inclination to attack but slid up the gentleman's arms to his shoulders and on till they clasped each other around his neck. And Alex, finding both arms suddenly free, used them to gather the girl still closer. It was more than their outraged spectator could tolerate and he surged forward to grasp the audacious gentleman's arm.

With an easy action, Alex shrugged him off but retained his hold on the girl. Startled and somewhat unsettled by the surprising depth and sweetness of her response, he was more than a little tempted to kiss her again in order to find out if he'd imagined it. But, even as the thought occurred, her hands disentangled themselves from his hair and moved to pull her hood more closely around her face again. Slowly, Alex released her murmuring softly, 'Well ... that was unexpected. But extremely enjoyable, I must say.'

Then, removing his hat, he swept a deep bow that encompassed both the girl and her would-be swain and said, 'It seems we've all learned something tonight.'

And with that, continued on his way, leaving the stunned pair to stare wordlessly after him – one with sulky anger and the other with shaken and confused blankness.

* * *

Having spent a pleasant hour in the Acorn without starting a fight, Alex duly made his way to James Ashton's house just off St John's Gardens whence he had been invited for a bachelor supper to be followed by a little gaming. Had he not been in need of a distraction, it is unlikely that he would have availed himself of this invitation for he did not particularly like Ashton. They had first met in Paris at the beginning of 1651 but James, though some five years older, had let his father go alone to Worcester and then sat out his exile in safety and comfort, living off the relatives of his despised French stepmother. Beyond this, Alex knew only that Ralph Ashton had lost his life in a Royalist conspiracy before the Restoration and that his widow, having returned to Oxford in 1660 with her stepson and young daughter, had followed him shortly after it.

He was admitted by an untidy manservant and had hardly removed his hat when his host was upon him with what was surely misplaced affection. At thirty-five, James Ashton was already putting on flesh and his ruddy, heavy-jowled face bore the marks of soft living and over-indulgence.

'Deveril, m'dear fellow!' he boomed, heartily pumping Alex's unresponsive hand. 'Glad you could make it. It'll be quite like the old days in Paris.'

Since Alex had only been fifteen years old at the time, he could not imagine to what old days James might be referring. Contenting himself with a lift of one ironic brow, he allowed himself to be ushered into the parlour.

'Two friends of mine, Deveril – Bob Colne and Sam Hassall,' said Ashton, before moving away in response to a discreet gesture from his servant.

Alex bowed and murmured a polite greeting whilst scanning the rest of the company. He looked at Giles and their eyes met and locked. Then, excusing himself from the two merchants, he crossed the room and bowed to him with exaggerated courtesy.

'As you see, I decided to leave hell for another time and come here instead. It's likely to be a fairly similar substitute.'

'It will be if you have anything to do with it,' returned Giles coolly.

Alex smiled self-deprecatingly. 'I do my best.'

'Oh Lord!' muttered Danny, ruefully. 'If that's the way of it, I've a good mind to go home.'

'And miss all the fun? Alex would never forgive you. He's suffering and is very kindly making sure that we all get a share.' Giles turned back to Alex. 'Have you a special treat in store – or is this a mere run-of-the-mill occasion?'

Alex smiled slowly. 'An element of suspense is always fun, don't you find?'

Of the two remaining guests, Alex was surprised to find one faintly familiar, though from where he could not recall. The other, however, was instantly and ludicrously recognisable. Sardonic blue eyes met astounded hazel ones and Alex bowed mockingly to the young man whose dalliance he had so effectively disrupted earlier in the evening.

Richard Stavely looked back, scarcely able to believe his bad luck and too shocked to bow in reply. An angry flush surged up to the roots of his hair and he thought of a number of things he would like to say but could not without looking even more foolish than he already did. On his way across the room, Alex paused briefly beside him and murmured, 'I won't tell if you don't,' before moving on.

The gentleman on the couch, whose face Alex had as yet been unable to place, showed no signs of being pleased to see him. In fact he seemed extremely nervous and closely resembled a startled rabbit. Alex repressed a grin.

'Allow me to introduce myself. I'm Alexander Deveril.'

The gentleman swallowed convulsively. 'Frederick Iverson.'

'Mr Iverson. Have we met before?'

There was a short pause and then, 'No. That is – can't say we met exactly. Never introduced, you know.'

'Ah. More in the nature of an ... encounter ... perhaps?'

'That's it,' was the grateful reply.

'When and where?'

This brought the rabbit look back with a vengeance.

'The Acorn – night before last. I was with Gresham.'

'Oh God – yes!' Alex gave a crow of laughter. 'You were the one who said that Rupert was quite good with a sword.'

'Yes,' said Frederick, brightening at this evidence in his favour. 'Didn't think you'd remember.' He thought for a second and then added naively, 'Didn't remember much myself.'

Alex regarded him with mild reproof.

'I remember it,' he explained, 'because it is the most thundering understatement I've ever heard. Oh – stop shaking. I'm not going to hurt you. I save that for bombastic idiots.'

Frederick stared at him, fascination mingling with budding respect. Then, standing up in a rush of confidence, he held out his hand as Alex took it, said, 'Tell you what – good thing if you had strangled him. He's a Bad Man.'

Alex frowned slightly. 'That's interesting. You must tell me more – another time. I think we're being summoned in to supper.'

They were and it proved to be both unimaginative and poorly cooked, with the result that everyone drank a little more than usual. The talk was also besieged with pitfalls, due mainly to a seating arrangement that placed Colne and Hassall together at the end of the table where they could and did conduct a conversation which excluded everyone else and Giles and Alex exactly opposite each other where they indulged in spasmodic sniping. Danny, uncomfortably situated beside Giles, hovered between laughter at the absurdity of it all and fear that one would push the other too far.

By the time they rose from the table some two hours later, everyone was a little the worse for wear and Alex was fast approaching his most volatile state.

Retiring from the dining-room, the party moved back to the parlour where a number of small tables had been set out and the dresser stocked with squat, dark green bottles and glasses. The Rhenish wine which had been served through supper had given place to brandy … and devilish bad brandy at that, thought Giles putting down his glass almost untouched.

As soon as they entered the room, Colne and Hassall headed for the remotest of the tables and, producing a well-used tarot deck, settled down to a serious session of tarocco. Danny, anxious to keep Messrs Beckwith and Deveril apart, chose Giles as the more amenable of the two, rounded up Richard Stavely and proposed a game of gleek, neatly leaving Ashton and Mr Iverson to take care of the other half of his problem.

They solved it by suggesting that they also make a three at gleek, to which Alex agreed with a noticeable lack of enthusiasm, expecting to be bored.

He wasn't and the reason was perfectly simple. He could not lose. No matter what he drew or discarded, the result was always the same. He won. And after the first hour he began to find it funny, for it was nothing to do with expertise or intellect – just pure, unadulterated luck. The cards were running his way and it seemed that nothing could stop them.

Frederick took his losses in good part but Ashton grew steadily less jovial as, coin by coin, his money moved across the table and finally he came abruptly to his feet, refilled the glasses and proposed they change the game.

Alex smiled with maddening understanding.

'What did you have in mind?'

'Dice,' replied Ashton. 'Maybe these three will join us?'

At the magic word 'dice', Danny's eyes brightened and he promptly forgot all his sterling resolutions and started pushing tables together.

Alex smiled down at Mr Beckwith. 'Take the bank, Giles?'

'I might. But if all you want is the opportunity to break me, I'm sure we can arrange something.'

'Generous,' mocked Alex. 'But sufficient unto the day and all that.' He indicated the table. 'Shall we?'

As luck would have it, it was Danny whose throw won him the dubious privilege of the first bank. He gaily emptied his pockets on to the table and the game opened on a guinea stake. At the end of an hour when Ashton threw for the bank and won, Danny was still an easy winner but Mr Stavely, having lost consistently, had declared himself at beggar's bush and dwindled into a glassy-eyed observer.

Ashton smiled for the first time in half an hour and opened his bank on a stake of five guineas. Giles favoured him with a long, cool stare, called a main and won. The smile faded but Ashton need not have worried. On his second throw, Alex challenged the bank and took it.

'Stake fixed at five,' he announced. 'Giles?'

'Seven,' called Giles. And turned up a deuce and a four.

The game continued. Alex's luck was still in and the heap of coins in front of him gradually increased. By the time the clock struck ten, Mr Iverson (now Freddy to everyone) had joined Richard on the periphery and Ashton, becoming grimmer by the minute having lost more than he could afford, was writing vowels to cover his losses. At this stage a wiser man would have withdrawn but James Ashton was gamester enough to indulge in the belief that his luck must turn. However, as the evening wore on and he wrote more and more notes, he began to feel frightened. He called, threw and lost. Again.

'It seems time another took the bank,' he muttered, looking at Giles and Danny. 'What d'you say?'

Mr Beckwith raised his brows with faint hauteur. 'As the rest of you wish. For myself, I am satisfied.'

'So'm I,' agreed Danny, blinking owlishly. 'But then, I'm devilish drunk. Are you drunk, Alex? Giles isn't. He don't care for the brandy.'

Mr Deveril greeted this piece of tactlessness with a laugh. His collar was loosened, his hair disordered, and the effect of the brandy was evident in his too-steady gaze and less than steady hands.

'Yes, I am undoubtedly drunk – but it's immaterial.' He looked at Ashton. 'There's some three hundred in the bank. Will you throw for it?'

Ashton hesitated but only for a moment.

'Yes, damn you, I will.'

'Wonderful. After you.'

Ashton threw a five and a four. Unhurriedly, Alex cast a four and a six, then sat back in his chair.

'You lose,' he said flippantly. 'Satisfied?'

Ashton banged his fist on the table.

'No, I'm not! You hold too many of my vowels.'

With an expression of distaste, Mr Beckwith moved as if to get up. Alex looked at him, the pale eyes glimmering strangely in the candlelight.

'Don't go, Giles. We have arrived at the high point of the evening. Mr Ashton isn't satisfied. You should sympathise.' He looked back at his host. 'So. You haven't the money to try another throw. Pity.'

Ashton glared at him and cudgelled his brain for inspiration. And then it came to him; an idea so wild and wily that it stopped his breath. He slopped more brandy into his glass and laughed.

'I've a stake for you – if you've the stomach for it.'

Alex smiled. 'Name it.'

Ashton laughed again. 'M'sister.'

There was a sudden silence.

'Would you mind repeating that?' asked Alex softly.

'My sister. Step-sister if you want to be pernickety. When m'father married his Frenchie widow, her Frenchie brat came along with her. She's got a dowry of eight hundred pounds from her mother. I'll stake her hand in marriage against your bank – three throws to decide.'

Silence was succeeded by uproar in which Danny, Richard and Freddy all spoke at once. Out of this, Richard emerged triumphant – largely because in lurching to his feet he overset a chair.

'You – you're mad!' he shouted.

'Mind your own business,' snapped Ashton. And then, to Alex, 'Well?'

'Can't do it,' announced Freddy positively. 'Can't stake a lady.'

'I'll stake what I choose.'

Danny wagged a solemn finger at Alex.

'Wouldn't take him if I were you,' he advised. 'You haven't seen her. Might be a hag.'

Freddy blinked, much impressed by this logic, and then shook his head regretfully.

'She ain't,' he said simply. 'But that's not the point.'

Ashton was losing patience.

'Enough! Will you cover, Deveril – or haven't you the nerve for it?'

Alex's eyes had never left Ashton's face. He raised one brow and said, 'My friend, I have the nerve for more or less anything.'

It was all Giles had been waiting for.

'This is absurd,' he said coldly. 'Ashton – you can't toss your sister into the pot like a handful of coins. Her dowry isn't yours to dispose of and she can't be made to marry anyone just because you're in debt. As for you, Alex, are you too drunk to realise how utterly stupid you're being?'

Alex laughed a shade wildly.

'Oh I realise, sweetheart. I'm just not sure that I care.' He turned to Ashton. 'Produce your stake. I'll take you.'

Ashton relaxed and summoned his servant.

'Fetch my sister,' he ordered.

The man goggled.

'But – it's late, sir. Miss Chloë retired some hours ago.'

'Then wake her up. Go to it – hurry!'

The man gave up and went out.

Richard Stavely, who had stood through this discussion in a trance-like stupor, suddenly roused himself to protest.

'You've no right! It – it's disgusting and I won't let you do it!' And, stepping valiantly forth, he tripped over the fallen chair and measured his length.

Danny and Freddy inspected him with professional interest.

'Looks like he's knocked himself out,' observed Daniel.

'Out cold,' corroborated Freddy cheerfully. 'Pity.'

And, pleased to find themselves in agreement, they drank a toast.

Waiting for Ashton's sister to make an appearance, Giles informed Colne and Hassall that it was time they left and, since his tone brooked no argument, they gathered up their cards and departed, muttering.

When they had gone, Giles made another attempt to make Ashton and Alex see sense. Ashton ignored him. Alex leaned back in his chair, whistling; then, like the others, he turned and, unlike them, remained seated as the door opened and a girl came in.

Daughter of Ralph Ashton's second wife, Marguerite, Chloë Herveaux was just twenty and though, as Freddy had said, she was not a hag, neither was she precisely beautiful. Of medium height, fine-boned and slender, she had grace and a certain distinction which was nothing to do with her shabby dress. But her face was one of character, rather than loveliness. Narrow, arched brows were set above dark brown eyes, wide and intelligent; her nose was short and straight, her lips firm, her chin determined. And the long hair falling down to her waist was unfashionably straight and the colour of newly-beaten copper.

She stood quite still, hands clasped loosely in front of her and surveyed the company. Her glance lit upon Freddy and a tiny smile touched her mouth.

'Good evening, Mr Iverson,' she said, as calmly as if it was perfectly normal to be roused from bed at midnight to attend her brother's bachelor evenings.

Freddy bowed politely. 'Servant, Mistress Chloë.'

The dark gaze transferred itself to Giles, widened, moved quickly to Daniel and on to Alex where it stayed for a moment. Mr Beckwith's brows rose sharply and Mr Fawsley frowned as if trying to place her. Mr Deveril looked back at her with interest but no other discernible expression. She restored her attention to Giles, who swept her an elegant bow.

'Mistress Ashton ... we have met before, I think. But perhaps you don't remember?'

'Yes I do,' she averred. 'Only I don't know how to address you. And my name is not Ashton – it's Herveaux.'

'My apologies.' He smiled engagingly. 'My name is Beckwith. And this Mr Fawsley – and, over there, Mr Deveril.'

She directed a brief smile at Danny, passed over Alex and curtsied to Giles. Then she turned to her brother and her eyes became quite blank.

'Well, James? What am I doing here at this hour?'

For a second, Ashton had the grace to look embarrassed but he conquered it.

'You're here,' he said slurring his words a little, 'because I've chosen to stake you.'

'Plait-il?'

'I said I've staked you. You're to be my pledge in a game of dice.'

She stared at him uncomprehendingly. 'If this is some sort of joke – '

'It's not. But if I win, nothing changes as far as you are concerned.'

'That's no comfort,' she said coldly. Then, 'And if you lose?'

He reached for his glass to avoid looking at her.

'Your hand and marriage portion go to the winner.'

There was a long silence during which Chloë's expression changed to one of blistering contempt.

'I see. And to which of these ... gentlemen,' she gestured swiftly round the room, 'goes the delightful opportunity of winning me? Not all of them, surely?'

'No. Only one,' said Alex, coming slowly to his feet. 'Myself.'

Giles saw her composure crack – but only a little. A sudden flush stained her cheeks and the small capable hands clenched over each other; then she drew a long breath and was in control again.

'Ah well,' she said, in apparent resignation. 'One cannot have everything.'

Her eyes wandered past him and perceived the recumbent form of Mr Stavely, as though for the first time. Her brows rose.

'Why is Richard lying on the floor?'

Freddy and Danny exchanged warning glances.

'He's tired,' said Freddy.

'Thought he'd take a nap,' added Danny helpfully.

'Oh? I had thought it must be the brandy. But perhaps it's better than usual?'

Giles swallowed a laugh and began to feel a certain admiration.

Ashton, meanwhile, was becoming belligerent again.

'Enough of this piffling talk – it's wasting time. Shake the bones.'

'One moment,' interrupted Chloë. 'Do I have any choice in this?'

'No,' snapped her brother.

'Yes,' said Giles. 'Of course you do.'

She looked at him enquiringly.

'You can't be bartered in this way against your will. It is quite reprehensible. So if you wish to halt this lunacy now – all you have to do is say so. And I will see to it that your decision is respected.'

His reward was an unexpectedly charming smile.

'Thank you.' The smile disappeared as she turned to look at Alex. 'And you ... Mr Deveril, wasn't it? We don't know each other and my dowry is no great fortune. So why would you accept a wager of this kind? Or are you just as drunk as my brother?'

Alex made an expansive gesture, swayed slightly and said grandly, 'Drunk or sober, wager or dare, I never refuse a challenge.' And dropped back into his chair.

She looked at him and sighed.

'Oh dear. That doesn't sound like promising husband material, does it?'

Alex laughed and reached for the brandy.

She ignored him and, turning back to Giles, said 'So. I may refuse to take part in this charade ... and stay here. And trust that my brother, having conceived this original idea, does not seek to repeat it on another occasion when I may be less fortunate in being offered protection.'

'There is that,' Mr Beckwith admitted reluctantly.

'Yes. I am not inclined to rely on it. Of course, if Mr Deveril loses, it may happen again anyway. And next time the gentleman concerned may be an ancient, or poxed, or – worse still – one such as my brother himself.' She eyed Ashton dispassionately. 'All things considered, I think I prefer to take my chance now. At least when he is sober, I imagine Mr Deveril is usually in full possession of his faculties.'

'Much obliged to you, Marigold,' slurred Alex, raising his glass to her.

Chloë ignored him again and looked across at her brother.

'Very well. Throw your dice, James. I consent.'

'Wait.' Giles frowned. 'I won't ask if you know what you are doing. I can appreciate your situation only too well. But are you sure this is wise?'

She shrugged easily and said with an effort equally invisible, 'No. But it's clear that I'd be very stupid to stay here.'

'You don't know Alex.'

'You don't know my brother. And this, believe me, is the last straw.'

Brown eyes met grey and then Giles acknowledged defeat.

'Do you at least have somewhere to go?'

She nodded, 'In the morning. Little Tom's family will take me in for a time. His mother knows how things are in this house.'

'Well, then. If you are quite decided, I shall take my leave. I'm afraid that I derive no amusement whatsoever from games of this sort.'

She smiled again, but this time it was tense, automatic.

'No. I understand.' She held out her hand. 'Goodbye – and thank you.'

He bowed and gallantly kissed her fingers.

'Au revoir, mademoiselle. I shall hope to meet you again in more pleasant circumstances.' And before she could reply, he turned, nodded perfunctorily to his host, and left.

Chloë faced her brother. 'Well? What are you waiting for?'

Alex, who had watched all this in dreamy silence, suddenly laughed.

'What indeed?' He reached for the dice-box, shook it, and threw.

Freddy peered at the dice. 'Five and four,' he announced.

Ashton followed suit and cast a six and a deuce.

'First throw to Mr Deveril,' said Danny boisterously. 'Take a wager, Freddy? I'll lay ten guineas on Alex.'

'Can't,' said Freddy morosely. 'And I wouldn't take you if I could.'

Alex grinned and threw again – a three and a five. Ashton replied with a pair of sixes.

'One all,' sang Danny.

Mr Deveril picked up the box for the last time and threw.

'Quatre trey,' called Freddy, not to be outdone. 'Shouldn't have much trouble beating that.'

It was evident that Ashton thought so too. What his sister thought was less obvious but her knuckles glowed white with pressure as she watched him make the deciding cast. He threw; Freddy and Danny craned over to count the spots, then, 'Quatre deuce,' shouted Danny. 'Alex wins!'

Ashton sat still, frowning at the dice as if staring at them would change the outcome. Then slowly lifting his head, he met Alex's eyes, and saw, behind the haze of intoxication, pure contempt.

Very carefully, Alex rose and made Chloë a deep if unsteady bow.

'Madam, I have won your hand in fair play. Will you come with me?'

Shock drained the blood from her skin.

'N-now? You want me to leave with you now?'

'Naturally. You just shaid – said – you couldn't stay here.'

'I know. But I didn't expect … I thought that in the morning …' She stopped and then said desperately, 'It's the middle of the night!'

'Nowhere near it, m'dear. Not much past eleven yet.' Rocking slightly, Alex held onto the back of his chair and offered her a rare, genuine smile. 'So will you come?'

Her colour returned and a sort of madness took hold of her.

'Yes, sir. If you wish. Are we going now?'

He nodded, half laughing.

'Then I will get my cloak,' she said calmly and went out of the room.

In the short time she was away, Ashton stared at Alex with bleary hatred but no one spoke. Then she was back, her cloak draped over her shoulders and a small bag in her hand.

'I am ready,' was all she said.

Ashton glared at her from beneath lowered brows.

'Then go – and good riddance! But don't think you can come crawling back here!'

She surveyed him distantly. 'I won't crawl and I won't come back,' she said flatly. 'I would sooner starve in a ditch.' She looked at Alex. 'Shall we go?'

He smiled again and scooped up coins and promissory notes haphazardly into his pocket. 'Upon the instant. Let's shake the dust of these unhallowed halls from our feet and take to the road.'

And followed by Danny and Freddy, he threw an arm about her waist and swept her out of the house, singing as he went.

FOUR

Out in the street the fresh air hit them with instant effect. Alex reeled and Chloë had to exert all her strength to keep him upright. A glance behind showed that Danny and Freddy were having similar problems with each other.

Mr Deveril's balance returned and he gazed abstractedly at the sky.

'Then if thou'lt have me love a lass, let it be one that's kind
Else I'm a servant to the glass that's with Canary lined,'

he declaimed happily. And then, 'Are you kind, Marigold?'

Chloë looked at him, torn between laughter, exasperation and something she couldn't put a name to.

'Sometimes,' she grinned. And, as a shiver ran down her back, 'But this isn't the time to discuss it. Or to recite poetry either.'

'Quite right,' applauded Daniel.

'Philistine,' said Alex vaguely, starting to walk.

'What I want to know,' said Freddy, 'is where we're going.'

'That's easy,' replied Danny. 'Home.'

Alex stopped so abruptly that Freddy cannoned into him.

'No, we're not,' he said positively. 'I'm going to be married.'

Chloë's heart gave a sickening lurch, then resumed its usual beat as she realised how impossible it was.

'Are you?' asked Danny with interest. 'Congratulations.'

Freddy shook his head. 'Can't be done.'

'Why not?'

'Need a parson – middle of the night – all asleep,' came the succinct reply.

'Then we'll wake one,' decided Alex.

Chloë found her tongue as last.

'If you were intending to marry me,' she said carefully, 'I don't think it's a very good idea. You – we don't know each other and --'

'No. So we won't be disappointed.' The blurred voice was faintly bitter.

'But you should think about what you're doing! You can't want to be married – not just like that, anyway! And --'

'I won your hand – and that I shall have,' said Alex doggedly. 'I don't ask you to love me.'

Chloë viewed this demonstration of unexpected lucidity with resentment.

'I know that – but I prefer to wait. Perhaps,' she added cunningly, 'I may marry you tomorrow.'

'No. Tonight.'

'But – even if were possible – it's ridiculous. You're drunk!'

'Frequently, darling.'

'And tomorrow you'll feel differently.'

'So?' His face assumed an expression of total obstinacy. 'Don't argue. You can't run off with me then refuse to marry me. It isn't done.'

'Quite right,' said Danny, re-entering the lists. 'Ought to get married right away.'

'If you can,' added Freddy, faint but pursuing.

'You are all as bad as each other,' announced Chloë crossly. 'You can't wake a priest at this time of night and expect him to marry you.'

'Watch me,' grinned Alex. And then, meticulously, 'And I'm not going to marry a priest. I'm going to marry you.'

Danny dissolved into a fit of giggles and communicated them to Freddy. Alex remained, swaying slightly, his eyes fixed on his proposed bride.

'Well, aren't I?' he asked with a particularly charming smile.

Something recognised, but as yet totally uncomprehended stirred inside Chloë as she met those quizzical silver-blue eyes ... and, swept for a moment to a realm way beyond common sense, she gave way to it.

'Yes. It would seem that you are. But it would still be best to wait till -_'

'No, it wouldn't,' laughed Alex, sweeping her along with him. 'Now – who knows where we can find a parson?'

Freddy thought. 'Chaplain – St John's College,' he offered.

'Excellent. Lead on – we follow.'

So, not without difficulty, the little party made its way across St John's Gardens, led by Mr Iverson. Progress was both slow and noisy and Chloë felt very doubtful that all three gentlemen would retain their senses long enough to arrive at their destination – which, in her opinion, would probably be a good thing.

However, her hopes were dashed when they all came safely to the Reverend Morland's little house. And then the fun really began for, when their imperious hammering brought no result, they started clamouring and hallooing up at the windows. Chloë perched resignedly on the edge of a water-butt and decided she had lost her senses to be there at all.

Eventually a light showed at an upper window which was then thrown up to disclose a night-capped head.

'What the – what is going on?' demanded a thin, querulous voice.

'Come down and find out,' invited Mr Deveril.

'I will do nothing of the kind! What do you mean by waking me at this hour? Is someone dying?'

'Not that I know of. I want to get married.'

'You what?' spluttered the cleric.

'I want to get married,' repeated Alex obligingly. 'Come down.'

'I most certainly will not. You're drunk, sir!'

'I know. Ah well, if you won't come down – I'll have to come up.' And so saying, he seized the thick creeper which enveloped the house and began to climb.

Chloë decided that it was time to intervene.

'Mr Deveril – if you break your neck you won't be able to marry anyone.'

Alex peered down from a couple of yards up.

'I'm quite safe.' Hanging one with one hand, he took his hat off and tossed it to her. Then he started to climb again, accompanied by a duet of advice from below and recrimination from above.

He had almost reached the window when there was a sharp crack as a branch snapped under his foot. 'Damn!' he said cheerfully. There was a scuffling sound as he searched for a new foothold and found it. Then he was nose to nose with the Reverend Morland.

The Reverend retaliated by trying to close the window.

'Now, now,' reproved Mr Deveril, grabbing the casement. 'Where's your Christian spirit? I am a branch to be plucked from the burning. Pull me in.'

'You are an ill-conditioned and cupshot nuisance – and you can go back the way you came.'

Alex looked down and shut his eyes quickly as the earth rushed up to meet him.

'Not entirely true,' he said weakly. 'Not at all, in fact.'

And just as Chloë opened her mouth to shout, the Reverend disappeared from view as Alex dived head first through the window. There was a loud crash, then a voice said furiously, 'Get off me, sir. You are sat on my stomach!' Upon which Danny and Freddy burst into howls of laughter.

A few minutes later the door opened to reveal Mr Deveril, dishevelled but otherwise unhurt, and behind him the meagre figure of the Reverend Henry Morland, clutching a robe over his outraged person. Daniel and Freddy wandered in, leaving Chloë with little alternative but to follow, while they manoeuvred the protesting cleric into the parlour. Freddy lit a branch of candles and everyone blinked in the light.

' …. and moreover I shall complain to a magistrate. Your behaviour is iniquitous! I have never been so scandalised in my --'

'Enough,' interrupted Alex. 'I don't want a sermon – I want to be married.'

'And I tell you it's outside the canonical hour and therefore impossible!'

'Let's hope,' said Mr Deveril silkily, 'that you are mistaken.'

Chloë sprang forward. 'It might be best if you let me explain. Sir, the situation is a trifle … peculiar. This gentleman,' she indicated Alex, 'has won my hand at the gaming table and --'

'What? Do I hear you correctly? He won you?'

'Yes. And so --'

'From whom did he win you?'

'From my brother. Mr Iverson will confirm?'

Freddy nodded solemnly.

The Reverend looked inexpressibly shocked.

'You poor girl! This is barbarous – Sodom and Gomorrah! But you are safe now, my child. None can force you against your will whilst I am here!' he announced heroically.

Chloë lost a little of her assurance.

'Ah – yes. Thank you. Only it is not quite so ... you see, I ... er ... I agreed to it.'

A number of conflicting emotions warred with each other in the worthy gentleman's face and he appeared beyond speech.

Alex laughed. 'Well done, Marigold. At least you've stopped him talking.'

'Oh be quiet!' snapped Chloë, incensed.

'Hussy!' cried the cleric. 'Abandoned Jezebel!'

Alex advanced with intent. 'Will you marry us?'

The Reverend Morland squeaked as a hand grasped his shoulder, then meeting a glittering blue stare, he capitulated.

'Yes. I w-will,' he quavered. 'You deserve each other!'

'We thank you. Now go and dress. I'm damned if I'll be married by an unfrocked parson.'

So eager was he to be rid of his unwelcome guests, that the Reverend excelled himself. In rather less than ten minutes he was back, wig and stock askew but otherwise presentable and gripping his bible. Outside, the church clock was striking twelve.

'Very well,' he said irritably. 'Let us proceed.'

Chloë's face was the colour of parchment but she drew off her cloak, smoothed the long rose-gold hair with hands that shook only a little and stood before the cleric. Alex ploughed an erratic course to her side and dropped his arm across her shoulders.

'Dearly beloved,' began Reverend Morland in a tone more properly suited to an exorcism, 'we are gathered here in the sight of God ...'

And fifteen minutes later they were out in the street again with the door slammed and securely bolted behind them. With a sense of complete unreality, Chloë looked down at the heavy and over-large signet ring which adorned her left hand and then at the man who was now her husband. Mr Deveril appeared to be in rapt contemplation of the rime-encrusted trees glinting in the moonlight.

'A Froggie would a-wooing go, "Heigh Ho!" says Rowley,' he sang.

To the tune of childish rhymes, they made their way back to Brewer Street and by the time they arrived outside Mr Deveril's door, where Danny and Freddy took a blithe farewell, Chloë doubt that she could have gone any further. The difference between helping Mr Deveril and carrying him was now minimal and she guessed that her brother's brandy was about to have its usual effect. She propped him against the wall, groping in his pocket for a key which she eventually found and used to open the door.

'Cock-a-doodle-doo! My dame has lost – has lost ...'

Chloë grinned, replaced the key and, shouldering her burden, surged across the threshold. Alex detached himself and stormed the stairs, reciting.

'The King of France went up the hill with forty thousand men!' His impetus wore out after the first five steps and he remained poised with indecision.

'The King of France came down the hill and ne'er went up again.' He turned round and sat down. 'I can't.'

Chloë started to speak and then stopped as a door opened above and light spilled down the staircase. 'Is that you Mr Alex?'

'Matt? I thought you'd be asleep,' said Alex hazily.

'Did you?' asked Mr Lewis, descending the stairs. 'I doubt there's anyone who'd sleep through the din you were making.' And then he stood still, looking at Chloë with dawning recognition.

Alex smiled and allowed himself to be assisted up the stairs, saying dreamily, 'Matt ... my old, old friend. Tell Sarah will you?'

'Tell her what?'

The blue eyes opened briefly.

'Tell her I'm married,' he replied, with surprised simplicity. And then, eluding Matthew's grasp, slid peacefully to the floor.

* * *

Alex awoke to a sensation of knives grinding inside his head. He groaned and tried to halt the painful process of returning consciousness by rolling over and burying his head in his arms. His mouth felt as though it was full of sawdust and his stomach full of bile.

'Mr Deveril?'

The soft-voiced enquiry struck him like a clarion and he groaned again in what he intended as a negation.

'Mr Deveril? It's only a headache, you know – you're not dying.'

Stung to indignation by the unfeeling nature of this remark, Alex replied with a muffled curse.

'Don't be vulgar,' said the voice, warm with barely repressed laughter. 'That's no language for a gentleman.'

'Go away,' he muttered.

'No. It's past two in the afternoon and I have a tisane here which will make you feel much better – but you must sit up.'

'I don't want to sit up. I want to be left alone.'

'Don't be a baby.'

This was the last straw. Alex opened his eyes and gingerly turned to face his tormentor. A waterfall of hair, gleaming rose-gold and a lot brighter than he thought necessary, dazzled his vision. He shut his eyes for a moment and then, blinking, looked again; brown eyes, flecked with amber. There was something familiar about them too – something he felt he ought to be able to remember but could not.

'Who are you?'

Amusement gave way to reproach. 'You don't know?'

'I wouldn't ask if I did.' He sat up very cautiously. 'God – my skull's split.'

'You shouldn't have drunk the brandy,' said Chloë severely. 'Mr Beckwith had more sense.'

'He would,' replied Alex acidly. A strange fact communicated itself to his impaired faculties. 'We are sitting on the floor. Did I sleep here?'

She nodded, grinning.

'Why?'

'Mostly because you passed out - but also because I had your bed. Drink this.' She handed him a mug.

Alex sniffed it suspiciously. 'It smells disgusting.'

'It tastes disgusting too,' she told him cheerfully. 'But it truly will make you feel much better. And it's your own fault, after all.'

'I know. I shouldn't have touched the brandy,' recited Alex, preparing to swallow the mixture. 'Just tell me one thing; why did you sleep in my bed?'

Chloë watched him tilt the mug to his mouth and grimace as he tasted its bitterness. 'But where else should I sleep? We are married.'

The timing was perfect. Caught with a mouthful of tisane, Alex spat, spluttered, dropped the mug and began to cough. Chloë thumped him helpfully on the back and then, when the choking subsided, passed him a handkerchief.

Alex mopped his eyes and then sat quite still, turning the dampened linen thoughtfully in his fingers. Finally, he said, 'Would you repeat that?'

Chloë experienced a pang of misgiving.

'I said that we are married.'

Looking up, his eyes bloodshot but disconcertingly intense, Alex considered her.

'Now that,' he remarked, 'is news.'

She met his gaze stubbornly. 'You've forgotten. I thought you would.'

His mouth curled unpleasantly. 'You were right. I can't, after all, be expected to recall all my careless excursions into matrimony.'

Just for a second, with a lurch of her stomach, she almost believed him. Then misgiving became irritation and she said, 'Can we discuss this sensibly?'

'I doubt it.'

'Look,' said Chloë crossly, 'you could at least try to be helpful. I know it was a mistake. I knew it at the time and I tried to stop you – but you would have it. And so here we are. The question now is what we're going to do about it.'

Alex stared at her. Then, on an explosion of breath and with less than his usual grace, he got to his feet and extended a hand to her.

'Well for God's sake let's begin by getting off the floor. My head is pounding and my bones feel as though somebody's taken a cudgel to them. So if you want me to think, I'll need a chair and a gallon of water.'

Accepting his hand, Chloë rose and followed him to the table. Silently, she poured water from the pitcher and put it in front of him before sitting down. Alex drank, clutched his head for a moment and then looked at her.

'My recollections of last night are, to say the least of it, imperfect. Remind me.'

She looked back at him, her hands clenched tight in her lap.

'James Ashton is my step-brother and you must have won more than he could afford to pay because he ended the night by staking me – or rather my hand in marriage and my dowry.'

Alex's face showed nothing. 'Presumably my luck held or you wouldn't be here. What then?'

'Oh then you insisted we be married immediately – so you climbed the wisteria and sat on the Reverend Morland. He wasn't happy. He said we deserved each other.'

Mr Deveril's sense of humour wasn't working and the blue eyes frowned in an effort of memory.

'Did I force you to it?' he asked bluntly.

Chloë coloured a little but her gaze did not waver. 'No. Or not in the way I suspect you mean it.'

'Well I suppose that's something. But why the hell did you do it? You can't have wanted to marry me.'

The flush receded leaving her rather pale and her voice, when she spoke again, held more than a trace of constraint.

'I let James stake me because it was a chance to get away from him and seemed the lesser of two evils. And no, of course I didn't want to marry you. I expected to stay in the house last night and throw myself on the charity of friends this morning. I didn't bargain for you being so bull-headed or Freddy Iverson and your friend Mr Fawsley encouraging you in your madness. I thought that you'd sober up and regain your senses and that we could come to some arrangement that didn't involve marriage. But none of that happened.'

'So I gather. But still ... you agreed to it.' It was not a question.

Chloë hesitated and decided that the best form of defence would be attack.

'Yes. Well, marriage would be a necessary snag if you were to acquire my dowry, wouldn't it?'

She was subjected to a long and trying scrutiny.

'Acquit me,' he said coldly, at last. 'I'm not a fortune-hunter, looking for a rich child-bride. How old are you, by the way?'

'What do you think?'

He considered her. 'Sixteen?'

She drew herself up. 'Certainly not. I'm twenty.'

Mr Deveril was not impressed. 'Well, you don't look it.'

'No?' She returned his gaze. 'Well, you don't look as if you'll see thirty-five again – but I suppose that's the brandy.'

Alex stared at her. Then, 'Oh God!' he said with a smothered gasp. 'You mistake me. I'm not usually crapulous more than four days out of seven.'

Chloë remained unmoved.

'Oh. But I could hardly be expected to guess that, could I?' And meeting his eyes, saw the very real laughter there. She grinned back. 'I must say, you're taking it better than I expected.'

'Practice, they say, makes perfect,' he replied absently. He rose and walked away from her, running his hands through his hair. 'Doubtless I was given your name but I've forgotten it.'

'It is Chloë. But I was becoming quite used to Marigold.' She looked at him thoughtfully. 'If you are willing to forgo my rather small fortune, we don't really have a problem.'

Alex leaned against the mantel and folded his arms.

'You are offering me a divorce?'

The narrow brows rose in surprise.

'No. We don't need a divorce. The marriage is only on paper, so what we need is an annulment. It should be quite simple.'

The ice-blue gaze rested on her sardonically.

'It would be quite simple if you hadn't spent a night in my bed.'

'But no one knows that,' she said calmly. 'However, if you think it necessary, we can ... provide substantiation.'

'Ah.' He smiled. 'You're suggesting we rely on medical evidence to dissolve the bond between us by proving it a marriage *nisi accedat copula carnalis*?'

'If that means it hasn't been consummated, then yes.'

'I see. Excuse me asking,' he said delicately, 'but *can* we rely on it?'

She frowned irritably. 'Again – yes.'

Mr Deveril smiled with what Chloë personally considered to be infuriating admiration and said, 'That's comforting. Unfortunately, however, it may not be enough.'

'Why not?'

'I imagine you are a Catholic?'

'Yes. What of it?'

'Simply that I'm not. Which poses not one problem but two – and I doubt we'll find that provision has ever been made for cases such as ours. If that's so, the theologians and canonists will be able to use us as an excuse for interminable debate. In short, it will take time.'

'Oh,' said Chloë.

'Oh,' agreed Alex. 'Which brings us to what we are going to do in the meantime. Is Ashton your only relative?'

She nodded. 'Unfortunately. The only good part is that he's not blood-kin.'

'So I presume you don't want to go back?'

'Never in this life.'

'Do you mind if I ask why?'

Wanting, if possible, to avoid this conversation, Chloë said evasively, 'You know him.'

'Not well - but as much as I care to,' replied Alex. 'And I imagine the reasons why I dislike him aren't the same as yours. Well?'

She sighed and, realising that she was going to have to say something, decided that it might as well be the truth – distasteful though that was.

As dispassionately as possible, she said, 'He put a roof over my head because it suited him to have an unpaid house-keeper. And I wouldn't have minded that if there had ever been enough money – but there never was because he either drank it, spent it on whores or gamed it away. We couldn't keep a maid-servant more than a week because he tried to bed them and then hit them when they said no.' She paused briefly and, when she resumed, her voice was completely without timbre. 'Recently, it's been worse. He can't afford the whores and ... and I've had to bolt my door at night.'

His eyes hooded and unreadable, Mr Deveril contemplated the faded gown with its signs of careful mending, then the impossibly straight spine and the tilt of her chin, both which told him that sympathy would not be welcome. Finally, with an almost imperceptible nod, he said, 'Will you excuse me for a moment?'

Rising, he reached for his coat and rifled through the pockets till he found a handful of crumpled paper. 'Thought so,' he murmured. And then, opening the door, shouted, 'Matt?' – only to discover that Mr Lewis was just outside, sitting on the stairs, whittling.

'What the hell are you - - ?' began Mr Deveril. And then, with intense irritation, 'Give me some bloody credit, Matt. She's a child, for Christ's sake! What did you think I was going to do?'

'Make bad worse – same as always,' retorted Matt. He stood up amidst a shower of wood-shavings and looked through the open door at Chloë. Then, apparently satisfied, said, 'What did you want?'

A hint of colour touched the flat pallor of Alex's face and the flash of temper vanished as quickly as it had come. 'These are Ashton's notes of hand from last night. Take a look and see what they amount to, then go and tell him I want them honoured by the end of the week. Oh - and tell him I've married his step-sister but warn him against paying us any bride-visits.' A hard smile curled his mouth. 'Frighten him a bit, if you like ... or even a lot.'

Matt's seamed face brightened. 'Reckon I can manage that.'

'I don't doubt it,' returned Mr Deveril absently, waving him on his way.

As soon as the door closed, Chloë said baldly, 'Why did you do that?'

'For fun,' he said flippantly. And then, catching sight of her expression, 'Don't read too much into it. I frequently do things I don't have to. Now. Where were we?'

She was starting to wonder how often Mr Deveril said what he really meant – but wisely refrained from asking and said instead, 'You were trying to decide what to do with me.'

A very different smile lit his eyes. He said, 'Not the best way of putting it - but yes. And I have a suggestion. I will make discreet enquiries about the possibility of an annulment, meanwhile you will continue to reside here with all the appearance of wifely permanence. All, that is, save one.'

Chloë looked up, a sudden light in her eyes. '*Nisi* something *copula carnalis*?'

'That's the one. You've a good memory.'

'Only for vital implications.' She hesitated. 'Since you don't want either me or my eight hundred pounds, I can't imagine what possible benefit such an arrangement might be to you.'

'You don't need to. And don't be so cynical. Call it a matter of chivalry.'

She gazed back in rapt fascination. 'Chivalry? Really? That's nice.' Then, shaking her head, 'I'm sorry, Mr Deveril – but I don't believe you.'

His expression remained enigmatic and his voice pleasant as he said, 'That, of course, is your privilege.'

'I suppose it wouldn't have anything to do with Sarah, would it?' she asked thoughtfully. And was given ample time to regret the question.

Finally, he said, 'Who told you?'

She swallowed. 'You did. At least, you asked Mr Lewis to tell Sarah you were married. And when I told him I had no intention of holding you to it, he said I'd be doing you a favour if I didn't tell you so just yet. So I thought ... I just thought the two things might be connected.'

He did not speak but the look in his eyes was no longer either enigmatic or pleasant. Recognising that she had made a major tactical error, Chloë saw nothing for it but to plough doggedly on.

'What I'm trying to tell you is that, if you have an understanding with Sa – with any other lady, you need not feel honour bound to terminate it because of me.'

'Am I,' he asked sweetly, 'supposed to be grateful?'

'No. You're supposed to tell me if you are betrothed – or the equivalent.'

Faster than she would have thought possible, he was across the room and leaning his hands on the chair-back beside her.

'You are either very tactless or indulging in a fit of female curiosity – or both. But you should have stuck with Matt. You might have found him easier game.' He drew a sharp breath. 'I won't be interrogated or discussed – in fact, I've a strong dislike of both. Do I make myself clear?'

Chloë said weakly, 'I was trying to be helpful.'

'Well, don't. I can arrange my life without outside assistance. And though I'm obliged to you for the Self-Denying Ordinance, I'm not particularly impressed by sacrificial gestures. Especially when they're unnecessary.'

Rather pale but capable once more of meeting fire with fire, Chloë said witheringly, 'I see. Do I applaud, say thank you or cast myself down the nearest well?'

'The choice,' replied Mr Deveril, coldly, 'is yours. What you not do is make any more attempts to organise my existence. Our marriage, as you said yourself, is only on paper.'

She suddenly felt rather angry.

'You don't need to remind me — and you needn't be afraid that I shall try to change it. With an annulment pending, your privacy and your bed are both quite safe from me.'

Alex raised one mocking brow and surveyed her from head to foot until she flushed to the roots of her hair.

'My dear girl,' he said carefully unlocking each syllable, 'I don't need your assurance of it. You won't invade my privacy because you won't be given the opportunity; and as for my bed ... I believe it's usual to wait until you are asked.'

* * *

The meal, which Matt shared with them, was not a success. Mr Deveril delivered an acid diatribe on the subject of well-meaning interference to which neither of his listeners felt any desire to contribute. Chloë began by envying Mr Lewis his ability to let it flow over him without showing any more reaction than a deaf-mute and ended by wishing she could sink into the floor. When they had finished eating, she rose thankfully to clear the board only to be pressed back into her seat by Matt's large hand on her shoulder.

'Sit down, Mistress,' he said tersely. 'I'll take care of this. You might as well stay there and see what you've taken on.' He glanced at Mr Deveril and added, 'Ashton was out. I'll maybe try later.' And picking up the plates, he stumped out.

Chloë was left uncomfortably facing her husband who, mercifully, had stopped talking and was watching her sardonically.

'Well? Are you lost in admiration of my loquacity or debating whether or not to fly the coop?'

'Neither,' she returned shortly. 'If you really want to know, I was thinking a tongue like yours could start a small war.'

The blue eyes lost their baleful gleam. For a moment, Mr Deveril contemplated her in silence and then, against all expectation, he said, 'I apologise. I don't suppose the situation is any easier for you but at least you've retained a sense of proportion. It was unfair of me to reward it with ill-temper.'

Chloë smiled a little. 'Perhaps it's a bad time?'

'You could say that. At the moment, it feels like total bloody disaster – most of which is entirely my own fault. The only consolation is that I rarely make the same mistake twice ... unless you favour polygyny?'

'Only,' she said firmly, 'when I can't get cloves.'

His brows soared and he said amicably, 'I'd say you've a fairly smart mouth of your own, Marigold. However – let us address the practicalities. As you'll have realised, this is a lodging house so the accommodation is somewhat limited but I believe we can get round the problem. You take my room, Matt will remove to an empty one on the floor below and I'll occupy his. That should preserve the proprieties without letting the world know what we're about.'

'We aren't going to tell anyone, then?'

'Not unless we must. I may eventually have to confide in Giles in order to stop him trying to knock my head from my shoulders, but --'

He stopped as the door opened and a lady came in. She was beautiful – tall, dark-haired and graceful. For a moment, Chloe wondered if this could be Sarah but a glance into dark-fringed blue eyes assured her that it could not.

'Hello, Ju. Welcome to Pluto's den. What brought you? Feminine intuition or a message from Matt?'

Lady Julia Blanchard laughed and shook her head.

'Wrong on both counts. I met Freddy Iverson.'

'Iverson?' repeated Alex vaguely. And then, looking at Chloë, 'He was a witness?'

She nodded. 'Yes. Mr Fawsley, also. Mr Beckwith left before the game.'

'Bristling with disapproval. Yes. I can imagine. Oh – this is my sister, by the way.' He turned back to her ladyship. 'So. You know everything and it's all true. This is Chloë.' And, closing his eyes, he rested his chin on his chest, apparently relinquishing all interest.

Fortunately, my lady knew better than to let it bother her. She walked over to Chloë, smiling warmly but with faint anxiety. 'Alex is determined to be difficult – which as you may have already gathered is by no means unusual. I am Julia Blanchard and I came especially to meet you. It's too much to expect that Alex should recognise the awkwardness of your position so I thought perhaps you might make do with me.'

The kindness was unexpected and Chloë felt herself grow pink.

'Thank you. It is rather awkward. I only wish I could explain how it happened.'

Alex opened one eye. 'Don't put yourself out. I daresay Julia understands perfectly – or thinks that she does.'

He sister's response to this cryptic utterance was to put out her tongue.

'Go to sleep. You look like a two-day-old corpse. And, of course I know how it happened. With you, how do such things ever happen? You were monumentally drunk and that's all it takes when you're in a wild mood.' She returned her attention to Chloë. 'Did you bring your things with you or must you go back for them?'

Chloë shook her head. 'I have what I needed for over-night and a spare gown. But that will have to do because I don't intend to set foot in that house ever again.'

Somewhat to her surprise, Julia accepted this without question.

'I don't blame you. If Alex had behaved as your brother has done, I'd never willingly have seen him again either – assuming I hadn't already killed him.' She paused. 'Let me help. You are smaller than I – but no doubt we can contrive something. Now don't argue – just get your cloak. You must come home with me right now and we'll get to know each other and leave Alex to sleep himself into a better mood. He won't even miss us.'

Chloë glanced at her somnolent husband.

'Yes he will. The same way he'd miss an aching tooth.'

And had the satisfaction of seeing his lips twitch before Julia swept her away.

FIVE

Being both practical and intelligent, Chloë had never supposed that her curious half-marriage would be easy, but what she had not expected was for Alex to create a state so negative as to resemble fighting a curtain. There were no difficulties or unpleasantnesses, no quarrels, no scenes; in fact, there was nothing tangible at all. It was smooth, civilised and about as substantial as living in a cloud.

On the fourth day, he presented her with a wide, gold wedding band and reclaimed his signet ring in a manner so crushingly bright as to rob the gesture of any significance it might have had. At this point, Chloë was tempted to seek advice from Mr Lewis; that she did not do so was due less to Mr Deveril's embargo on such discussions than to the fact that Matt (though quite kind in his taciturn way) was keeping her at arms' length in a way that discouraged confidences. Then, towards the end of the week, Mr Lewis presented her with a purse containing eighty-five pounds and told her that her step-brother had paid up and Mr Alex said she was to take the money and buy anything she needed – at which point, Chloë decided she really didn't know what to think.

During the third week in January, news that France had declared war on England caused a flurry of excitement that touched Chloë not at all. For her, the days fell into a pattern in which her path rarely crossed that of her husband. Alex was out a great deal and she seldom knew where he went; likewise, if he got colossally drunk, she did not know it – though she suspected he didn't and wondered if the shock of finding himself married was responsible. Left very much to her own devices, she spent a lot of time with Julia and her husband Sir Thomas, and the three of them were soon on the best of terms. Indeed, Lady Julia's only complaint was that Chloë, acutely aware of the ambiguity of her position, flatly refused to enter the little society that flourished amongst the exiled courtiers; and when all her persuasions met with the same stubborn denial, Julia said that their return to London would change everything and temporarily gave up.

It was only then that Chloë realised the full implications of her marriage; that Alex's residence in Oxford was but a temporary measure and that he moved in circles quite outside her own limited experience.

From Danny and Freddy who, having taken a liking to each other, often visited as a pair, she learned a little about Mr Deveril's activities – largely because Danny was a participant in most of them. Without embarrassment, he recounted details of a number of ludicrous wagers – from riding backwards down the High, to removing the weathervane from a particularly inaccessible church steeple. Alex, it appeared, was bent on living dangerously.

It did not take Chloë long to notice that Mr Beckwith was conspicuous by his absence and, since no one seemed to find it worthy of comment, she steeled herself to ask Mr Deveril. Then, encountering him on his way out with his right arm resting picturesquely in a sling, she changed her mind. It wasn't the time to take any silly risks – and she probably wouldn't get an answer anyway.

Less than half an hour later Mr Fawsley arrived and, finding that he had missed Alex, was just about to leave when Chloë pounced on him and bade him come up and talk to her. Danny groaned, brushed imaginary sweat from his brow and limped painfully up the extra flight. Chloë shut the door behind him and eyed him severely.

'I knew it. You've been fighting with Mr Deveril.'

He dropped into a chair. 'Not me. I've got more sense.'

'Then what,' she asked sceptically, 'have you done to your foot? And why is Mr Deveril wearing a sling?'

'Cabbages,' grinned Danny.

She sat down. 'Cabbages?'

'That's it. A whole cart-load of them, at the side of the beadle's house – and Alex bet me that he could plant more of 'em on the roof than I could.'

'I see,' sighed Chloë. 'And?'

'I scored five then lost my balance, came down at full gallop and missed the cart. Aye – you can laugh but I've got a cursed sprain and it hurts like hell.'

'Then you are well-served for you might have broken your leg. Do I take it that Mr Deveril has broken something?'

'No – but it should have been his neck,' replied Daniel, pushing a fiery strand back from his brow, 'He put up seven and was just on his way up with the eighth when the beadle came out. God, but he was furious! There he was, cursing like a goblin and then he started shying cabbages up at Alex who was still on the roof, laughing himself silly.'

'Go on – or let me guess. Mr Deveril threw them back?'

Danny nodded. 'He did.'

'I wish I'd seen it,' said Chloë. There was comfort in the idea of the intimidating Mr Deveril playing pitch-and-toss with a cabbage. 'How did he fall?'

'The wilder the goblin's throws became, the more determined Alex was to catch them. In the end he lost his footing, rolled sideways on to the cart and dislocated his shoulder. The leech put it back and said he was damned lucky to come off so light – but Giles says he's always had a charmed life.'

Never slow to seize an opportunity, Chloë made her second pounce of the morning. 'I'm glad you mentioned Mr Beckwith. I've been wanting to ask about him.'

Danny looked uneasy. 'Oh?'

'Yes. He never comes here – and no one mentions him. Do you know why – or must I ask Mr Deveril?'

Unease became alarm. 'Not unless you want your head bitten off. They're in the middle of some quarrel or other. It started the day after we met you in the fields with young nipperkin and it's got steadily worse since. Giles won't talk about it and I daren't ask Alex.'

Chloë frowned. 'But they're friends, aren't they?'

'Oh yes. Have been for years – long before I knew either of them. They were both mercenaries, you know.'

'No, I didn't know. You've fought with them, then?'

'In Sweden, six years ago. It was only a short campaign but Prince Rupert said that, with a bit more experience, Alex would make a first-rate captain one day.'

Chloë thought for a moment and then said, 'I should have thought three weeks long enough for two grown men to sulk – and if it isn't, they need help.'

Mr Fawsley levered himself to his feet.

'Oh no,' he said firmly. 'If you don't know better than to interfere between those two, I do! There'll be no reasoning with Alex just now because being incapacitated makes him irritable. And if you're lunatic enough to look him in the eye and tell him he should have thought of that before, I'll wash my hands of you.'

Chloë grinned. 'I'm not entirely stupid.'

'Good. Look – take my advice and leave well alone. I've had three weeks of living betwixt the devil and the deep – but I know from experience that if you get between them and all that happens is you draw their fire.'

The brown eyes reflected intense speculation.

'When did you last see Mr Beckwith?'

'Giles? This morning. I met him on the High – said he was going to Tom Blanchard's.' He stopped abruptly as Chloë got up and reached for her cloak. 'Where are you going?'

'To see you out and then for a walk in the park.'

'No you're not. It's snowing. You're going to try and catch Giles.'

She laughed and shrugged. 'There's no reason why I shouldn't call on Julia. I often do. Perhaps you'd like to escort me?'

'Well I wouldn't,' said Danny frankly. 'I won't have anything to do with it.'

'You could wish me bonne chance.'

'I could and I do. Good luck – and goodbye. And for the Lord's sake, don't tell Alex you've been discussing it with me.'

'I don't intend to tell him anything.'

Danny eyed her with pronounced misgiving. 'What, then?'

'I'm not sure,' she admitted. And added cheerfully, 'Je m'en fiche.'

* * *

The snow was lying six inches thick in the streets and more swirled down from the sky in great, soft flakes. It covered the houses and colleges with gleaming grace and bathed the town in rare tranquillity.

A large flake settled on Chloë's nose and she brushed it off, smiling. Her hands and feet were icy, but she did not notice as she slipped and slid happily along the riverside. She watched a group of boys enjoying a snow-fight and felt foolishly regretful that, being technically an adult, she could not join in. She dwelt for moment on the alluring picture of cooling Mr Deveril's temper with a well-placed snowball and then decided that in that sort of contest, as in most others, he would probably win.

Lady Julia, ravishing in blue silk and talking all the time, swept Chloë through the hall. 'My dear, I have told you over and over – only unmarried girls wear their hair down. You really should curl it and put it up.'

'My hair won't curl.'

'Not at all?' demanded Julia sceptically

'No. Or not in any way that's the least use. It wilts.' Chloë spread expressive hands. 'So there you have it. Curls are out. If I must wear it up, it will have to be braids and a pound of ironmongery.' Then, entering the parlour, she found herself face to face with Giles Beckwith and remembered – as she had not done before - how very self-contained and elegant he was. She also noticed his slight frown.

As for Giles, he saw a torrent of rose-gold hair falling over a shabby green gown and brown eyes full of sudden doubt. Banishing his frown, he bowed and said, 'Mistress Chloë. It's a pleasure to see you again. I trust you are well?'

'Perfectly well, thank you.' She hesitated, glanced briefly at Julia and added, 'I suppose you know that I – that I'm --'

'That you're married? Yes.'

Giles had received a garbled version of the midnight wedding from Daniel and then a rather more lucid one, based on Chloë's own account, from Julia Blanchard. It had made him feel rather ill – mainly because he blamed himself for walking away instead of staying to control the proceedings. It had also made him want to throttle Alex. His next thought had been to go straight round to Mr Deveril's lodgings to find out how things were with Chloë and if she needed help … but he hadn't done it because he'd known that if he had, he probably would have throttled Alex.

Chloë smiled wryly at him. 'It wasn't part of the plan.'

'No.' Giles realised that he couldn't say the things he wanted to say in front of Mr Deveril's sister. 'I regret that I've been unable to call. Alex and I aren't exactly on visiting terms at the moment. But if I can be of any assistance to you – at any time – I hope you will tell me.'

'Thank you.' She paused, 'Actually, there is something. I thought if someone - meaning myself - poured a little oil on the troubled waters, you and Mr Deveril might overcome your differences.'

'I fear it might take more than that,' he replied a trifle grimly. And then, 'Alex doesn't know what you're doing, does he?'

'No.'

'And nor do I,' said Julia. 'Giles – have you and Alex quarrelled?'

'Something like that. I thought you knew.'

She shook her head. 'No one tells me anything! But it's not past mending, is it?'

'I don't know. I suspect that, this time, it just may be.'

Julia sat down. 'I'm sorry. He said something unpardonable, I suppose?'

'In the years we've known each other he has probably said a hundred things that were unpardonable,' replied Giles placidly. 'If that were all, it wouldn't matter.' He picked up his hat and turned it between elegant fingers. 'You must excuse me, ladies. I won't discuss it.'

'Well that makes two of you,' said Chloë gloomily. 'If you are going, will you escort me home?'

Julia blinked and Mr Beckwith, who had not been prepared for it either, bowed.

'I'd be honoured,' he said.

Chloë turned to her sister-in-law. 'You'll forgive me, Julia?'

Her ladyship shrugged. 'Would it make any difference if I didn't? I take it you only came to talk to Giles and haven't finished with him. He has my sympathy!'

*

Walking down the street, her hand firmly clutching Mr Beckwith's sleeve, Chloë appeared deep in thought. When she finally looked up, it was to find the dark grey eyes resting on her with a mixture of amusement, wariness and something she did not recognise. Then he smiled.

'How does it feel to be Mistress Deveril?'

'Strange – and all the more so when I'm addressed that way. I wish you would call me Chloë. Danny and Freddy both do.'

'Do they? Well, perhaps their position is less equivocal,' he replied evasively. 'How are you finding Matt?'

The straight nose wrinkled thoughtfully.

'I think the word is cautious.'

'Ah. He would be, of course. I would guess your marriage came as a not-unpleasant shock and he's reserving judgement until he knows you better.' He paused and steered her around a minor snowdrift. 'A taciturn specimen, our Matthew – but you can trust him absolutely.' He stopped again, this time to choose his words, 'I don't imagine it's easy living with Alex?'

'You're wrong,' responded Chloë trenchantly. 'We co-exist in perfect harmony.'

Mr Beckwith was somewhat taken aback. 'You do?'

She gave him a sardonic smile. 'Yes. It's quite simple when you only meet in passing on the stairs or at meals. And the conversation, of course, is never allowed to impinge on the personal. It's uncommonly difficult to quarrel about the flavour of the soup or whether it will thaw by the end of the week.'

'I see. Do you want to quarrel?'

'Not necessarily. But I'd like to reach some sort of ordinary understanding.' Chloë took a moment to remind herself not to say too much. If she let the annulment out of the bag, Mr Deveril would have her head on a plate. 'The only things I know about him are what Julia or Danny have told me. I don't even know how old he is!'

'He's thirty – a couple of years younger than myself and a couple of years older than Danny.'

'Well he's currently behaving like a ten-year-old.' She looked up at Giles. 'Did you know he and Danny are careering around Oxford indulging in student pranks?'

He nodded, frowning a little. 'There's been some talk.'

'I know. I offered to mind little Tom as I used to - but as soon as his mother knew I'd married Mr Deveril, she more or less showed me the door. And that's why I thought,' concluded Chloë deviously, 'that you might be able to help.'

The frown vanished and he laughed. 'No you didn't. You thought I'd tell Alex that all is forgiven and stay around to hold his hand.'

'And won't you?'

'No. What in particular is worrying you?'

'Apart from the fact he could break his neck? The possibility that, thanks to him, Danny or Freddy could break their necks, too.'

'I doubt it will come to that. However ... what tactics have you tried so far?'

'None. I was hoping you might suggest something.'

'I suggest that you leave well alone,' he said, unwittingly echoing Daniel. And then, without warning, 'Why did you marry him?'

The brown eyes widened and became blank. 'For his money?'

'He hasn't any – or not a great deal, anyway. Try again.'

Chloë ran her hand absently along a window-ledge, scooping up snow and watching it fall to the ground. Then, as they turned into Brewer Street, she stopped walking and looked into his face.

'You were there. You know why. I told you at the time.'

'You did,' agreed Giles slowly, 'but it doesn't explain why you went through with the midnight wedding. No one has told me that Alex forced you. Did he?'

'No.'

'Then why?'

'I don't know!' she said, unable to find a good answer. 'It was as if I couldn't do anything else - like rushing downhill very fast and not being able to stop!'

'Ah. Yes. Alex has that effect on people.' He paused again, not sure how much to say. 'He is unpredictable, provoking and wild. Unfortunately, he is also charming, clever and physically attractive. It would be easy, I imagine, to become ... dazzled.'

Chloë's colour rose a fraction.

'You forget that I'm twenty years old, half-French and very practical.'

'My dear, I know it,' he replied dryly. 'But you wouldn't be the first.'

Afterwards, Giles could never decide if she had understood or even heard him. While he spoke, she had been gazing abstractedly down the street and then, turning abruptly to face him, she somehow slipped on the snow and would have fallen had he not caught her. Deftly holding her in steady hands, he set her back on her feet and was startled by a sudden gasp of pain.

'Oh – my ankle! I've twisted it,' she said with another agonised breath.

In view of recent history, Mr Beckwith could not forbear casting a suspicious glance into her face. He discovered that it did indeed look rather pale and instantly felt guilty. 'Can you walk?'

She winced and but said, shakily, 'Oh yes – if I can just lean on your arm?'

'Don't be a martyr.' Scooping her easily into his arms, Giles strode down the street to her door. Then, entering the house, he bore her up the stairs.

Chloë's heart was beating a fierce tattoo and behind half-closed lids, she wondered – since she knew what awaited upstairs - what she was going to do when they got to the top. Giles pushed the door open with his shoulder and then checked on the threshold.

Just in front of the fireplace stood Mr Deveril, one arm in a sling and the other resting casually on the mantelpiece. He had discarded his coat but the lawn shirt was immaculate, the long hair burnished and orderly and his expression bland.

'Well, well. Sir Galahad, I presume. Is this a social call?'

Chloë saw the need to remove herself before her duplicity became common knowledge. 'Mr Beckwith – thank you very much, but I think you should put me down. Now.'

His attention clearly riveted on Alex, Giles did as she asked, saying coolly, 'Hardly. I'm here because your wife needed help.'

The emphasis on those two words spoke volumes and Alex raised his brows while the ice-blue eyes remained fixed on Giles' face. With one quick glance, Chloë ascertained that neither man was paying her the least heed. Edging backwards to the door, she removed the key and had shut and locked it behind her before either of them realised what she was about. Then she retreated a couple of steps, key clutched to her chest, and allowed herself to breathe again.

The sound of the key turning in the lock, loud in the tense silence of the room, must have roused them. She heard Giles' voice. 'What the --?' and the sound of hasty footsteps. Then the latch of the door rattled as he tried to open it. Chloë swallowed and sank weakly down on the top step of the stairs.

'Chloë! What the devil do you think you're doing?' Mr Deveril's voice, edged with impatience.

'Sitting on the stairs,' she said.

There was an ominous silence. Then, 'Are you going to unlock this door?'

'No.' She drew a deep breath. 'Since I couldn't bang your heads together, I decided to shut you in.' She half-wished she could see their faces and then was glad that she couldn't.

'Why?' asked Alex.

'Your wife,' said Giles acidly, 'wants us to kiss and make up.'

There was another silence.

'If you were thinking of the window,' offered Chloë helpfully, 'it's no use unless you can fly. The door is the only way out – and I have the key.' She eyed the stout oak frame gratefully.

'You could put your shoulder to it,' said Alex to Giles, 'or your foot. Or we could call Matt.' The light voice was curiously strained.

The next instant the passage reverberated as the door received and withstood an explosive assault from within.

'That two-handed engine at the door stands ready to smite ... but it won't work,' said Mr Deveril. And raising his voice, 'Matthew!'

Before he spoke, the door on the lower landing opened and Mr Lewis looked up at Chloë from the bottom of the flight.

'God rot it. What's to do?'

'Matt?' Mr Beckwith's voice, unusually crisp, drifted down to him from behind the closed door. 'She locked us in.'

'And we'd like to be let out,' added Mr Deveril. 'So "with forced fingers rude" make her give you the key. We won't mind if you have to use force.'

'And get a move on,' cut in Giles curtly, 'before we get a full rendition of Lycidas.'

Matthew stared at Chloë incredulously.

'You've not locked Mr Alex up with Mr Giles?'

She nodded. 'Not the cleverest solution perhaps – but the best I could manage at short notice.'

'You daft lass – they'll kill each other.'

'They won't. Mr Deveril can't use his arm. His right arm. So Mr Beckwith won't touch him, will he?'

Mr Lewis eyed her mistrustfully. 'Will you hand me the key?'

'No. But I'll make it easy for you to give up.' And she calmly slipped the disputed object into her bodice. 'Voila!'

Very slowly, Matt's face split into a broken-toothed grin.

'Damn me, Mistress,' he said, his tone at complete variance with his expression. 'Damn me ... aren't you taking a terrible risk?'

Chloë grinned back. 'You tell me.'

They surveyed each other amicably.

'Two massy keys he bore of metals twain - the golden opes, the iron shuts amain,' declaimed Alex obscurely.

'Oh for God's sake!' snapped Giles.

Matthew addressed the closed door. 'She's put the key in her bosom.'

Sudden, total silence. Then, 'She's what?'

'She's put the key in her bosom,' repeated Matt. 'Do you want me to get it out?'

He was answered, incredibly, by a crow of laughter.

'Oh Matthew! Check and mate,' said Mr Deveril unsteadily.

Matt and Chloë exchanged glances.

'It's your call,' he shrugged. 'I'm going out.' And he went.

'Chloë.' It was Giles voice, quivering slightly. 'I believe I'm going to strangle you.'

With some difficulty, Alex stopped laughing.

'And since I have only one good hand, I'll let you. The only question is – do we sink our differences long enough to obtain that satisfaction?'

A second passed, then two, three. Chloë strained her ears.

'It's tempting,' responded Mr Beckwith carefully. 'You wouldn't rather call her bluff? Or wait to see what she tries next?'

'Not really. Unless you'd like the rest of Lycidas?'

'I wouldn't. In fact, I give you fair warning, Alex – if you inflict another word of Milton on me, I'll throw you through the window. Sling or no.'

And suddenly they were both laughing. Chloë listened for a moment, smiling, and then – unable to wait any longer – fished for the key and opened the door. Giles was resting his brow on the heel of his hand, his shoulders shaking and Mr Deveril was leaning weakly back in a chair, his expression brighter than she had ever seen it.

Together they became aware of her and together, after one significant shared glance, they advanced towards her. Chloë looked back with mingled satisfaction and wariness.

Mr Deveril said regretfully, 'I don't think you should strangle her, Giles. It lacks finesse.'

'You may be right. But she said she'd sprained her ankle, you know.'

'Did she? Did you?' The light gaze rested on Chloë.

Wariness became mild alarm. 'Yes – but it's much better now.'

'Are you sure? One shouldn't neglect these things. Perhaps we ought to put something cold on it?' he asked of Giles.

Mr Beckwith nodded. 'I take your drift.'

'Oh no, you don't!' Chloë made to remove herself from harm's way – but too late. A pair of firm hands dropped on either shoulder and held her captive.

'Definitely a two-handed exercise,' remarked Alex. 'Shall we go forth together?'

And forth they went, despite Chloë's struggles which, though weakened by laughter, were by no means negligible. Each with an arm about her waist, they lifted her off the floor and carried her, protesting all the way, down both flights of stairs and into the street. Then, turning to a point where the building described a corner, they stopped.

Ruffled and breathless, Chloë made one last bid for freedom – and failed.

'You wouldn't!' she said. 'Not in there. It must be three feet deep!'

Mr Deveril gazed consideringly at the snowdrift and then, in the same manner, at his bride. 'Easily. Possibly more. What do you think, Giles?'

'Undoubtedly more,' drawled Mr Beckwith. 'It's perfect.'

'In that case,' said Alex, 'what are we waiting for?'

And with infinite care, they delivered her deep into the heart of the drift.

SIX

From the reconciliation, there arose a number of surprising and diversely effective consequences. Mr Beckwith returned to the fold, Mr Deveril stopped playing fast and loose with his limbs and his wife caught a chill.

For Chloë, Giles was a welcome addition to their small circle. She found him a stimulating, witty companion and, while by no means blind to his good-looks and charm, was able to simply enjoy his company. That it was otherwise for Mr Beckwith, she had no means of knowing.

For inside a single hour, Giles had discovered that here was a girl with whom he could all too easily fall in love – and the knowledge was as bitter as it was precarious because, of all women, this one was forbidden. She was married – though as yet probably only in name - to his oldest friend. And need not have been had he acted differently.

Mr Deveril continued to spend a good deal of time in the company of his friends but his demeanour glittered a little less than before and Chloë, in the grip of a head cold of epic proportions, could only be grateful. She was grateful, too, for the profound effect her prosaic affliction had on Mr Lewis.

Coming upon her the following morning, complete with pink nose and streaming eyes, the inimitable Matthew had appeared to undergo a change of heart. From a stance deliberately non-committal, he grew, in the space of ten minutes, actively partisan. Suddenly 'Miss Chloë' instead of the formal Mistress, she was shooed back to bed and there served with a mug of butter-ale which she found decidedly nasty but which, she was assured, would instantly alleviate her sufferings. And indeed, after a day spent largely in slumber, she was sufficiently recovered to view with loathing another hour spent in her bed.

Secure in the expectation of undisturbed seclusion, she decided there was little point in dressing but she slipped a robe over her night-rail and dragged a brush through her hair before sitting down in front of the fire. Within ten minutes the inactivity was proving too much for her and she prowled restlessly about the room. She was at the window, observing that there were distinct signs of a thaw, when a tap at the door heralded Matt bearing a tray.

She smiled placatingly. 'I felt better so I got up for a while.'

Matthew grunted and stared disapprovingly at her bare feet.

Chloë glanced guiltily down and said, 'I haven't any slippers – but I'm not cold. Tomorrow I'll be perfectly well again.'

'Tomorrow you'll be in bed for a week,' retorted Matt. 'Come back to the fire, you daft lass.'

And Chloë, who had not been kindly scolded since she was fourteen, was glad that her nose was already pink and blew it determinedly. She sat down and Matt dumped the tray unceremoniously in her lap, saying crossly that he thought she might be hungry.

'Thank you. It was kind of you to take the trouble, Mr Lewis.'

'It's no trouble. Just be sure you drink the butter-ale,' he said. And, with an oblique look, added, 'I reckon you'd better get used to calling me Matt.'

It was the beginning of a curious friendship in which little was said but much understood for, in healing the breach between Alex and Giles, Chloë had taken a load from Matthew's mind and he was grateful. So when, on the next day, she asked him to find her something to do, she received a slow, wicked grin which, half an hour later and surveying an immense pile of mending, she had no difficulty in interpreting.

'You're sure,' she asked sardonically, 'that you couldn't find anything else?'

Matt rubbed his chin thoughtfully. 'Not unless you'd maybe like my things as well. But I thought you'd prefer to start with Mr Alex's.'

Her brows rose. 'Does he have anything left to wear? Do you?'

'Not much.'

'I see. I did wonder why he was in such a hurry to be married. Now I know.'

Beginning with two coats, each needing no more than a button, she set to work and, by the time Matthew appeared with her dinner, the pile was considerably diminished. After she had eaten, she set about restoring Mr Deveril's shirts and when Mr Lewis came back for the tray, she asked him how on earth they had managed before.

'Poorly,' responded Matt, sitting down to watch her.

Chloë tilted her head. 'Wouldn't you like to learn? Despite all the graces the convent taught, this is the only one I was much good at. Sister Thérèse said I'd been sent to her as a punishment.' The brown eyes twinkled engagingly. 'Do you think I'm a punishment, Matt?'

'I think you're a sauce-box,' grinned Matthew, 'and that's just as well. What I don't need are vapours and hysterics. Mr Alex is enough fireworks for anyone.'

Chloë stopped work. 'I know he can be wild ... but he's not stupid, is he?'

'He's sharp as a Puritan's nose. It's a pity he don't use it to manage his life.'

She looked down at her hands. 'I shouldn't have given way to him that night - I know that. But I don't know what to do about it.'

'What do you want to do?'

'I don't think I know that either.' She met his eyes. 'Not that I have much choice.'

'Then you'd better wait it out. It'll not hurt either of you and, if there was any harm in it, I'd say it's been done by now. Wouldn't you?'

Chloë hesitated, unsure of his meaning and therefore acutely wary. Then, shrugging slightly, she said, 'Probably – but you'd know that better than me. You've been with him a long time, haven't you?'

'Nigh on fifteen years,' said Matt. 'Since Worcester-fight.'

'Tell me,' was all she said.

For a moment, she thought he was going to refuse but then, nodding tersely, he began.

'The Scots raised an army in '51 to win the King's throne back. When His Majesty brought Captain Harry with him – Mr Alex's father – I joined him because I'd fought alongside him before.' Matthew paused, remembering. 'He'd a small troop of horse and he'd brought Mr Alex along – fifteen years old, the image of his dad and near as tall. Captain Harry was that proud of him. I mind him bringing the lad to me and saying, "My son, Matt – Alexander Charles Deveril. D'you think we can make a soldier of him?" And he laughed.'

'And did you?' asked Chloë.

'Aye. Took to it like a flea to fur, he did – for all it wasn't the best of campaigns.' Matt's face darkened. 'The Scots wouldn't fight and Leslie didn't make 'em.' He moved as though to spit and then thought better of it. 'When it was all over bar the shouting, Captain Harry grabbed Mr Alex's bridle and shoved it in my hand, telling me to get him out of there and to safety. And he rode off.' There was a short silence broken only by the crackling of the flames. 'He never came back.'

Chloë stirred and, avoiding all the trite remarks she might have made, said, 'So where did you and Mr Deveril end up?'

'Paris by way of Felixstowe and the Hague. It was a black time. We were cold, hungry and ragged and there was no one we dared trust. Those months changed Mr Alex. By the time we reached Paris, no one would have taken him for a lad of less than sixteen – which was just as well since we'd only one trade we could ply.'

'Soldiering?' asked Chloë.

Matthew nodded. 'We fought in this campaign and that until '54, when we went back to Paris – which is where Mr Alex met Mr Giles again.' Matt grinned sourly. 'We'd timed it well. Lord Southampton had arrived to meet King Charles about a group of Royalist gents calling themselves the Sealed Knot. Not that we knew that till later and by then the three of us were bound for London. For the next four years we lived disguised as poke-noses, passing information and doing what we could to save loyal folk from discovery. They were good years, too, in spite of the rope being ready to drop round your neck any minute. Then that turn-coat Willys sold Cromwell's spymaster a list of names and we had to leave in a hurry.'

Chloë laughed. 'Was there ever a dull moment?'

'Not as I recall. We fought Sweden under Prince Rupert – that's when we picked up Mr Danny. Then in no time at all, Cromwell died and King Charles came back to his throne and by September 1660 we were in London again. And that,' announced Matthew crossly, 'was when our troubles really started!'

'Shouldn't it have been the other way about?'

'It should – but it wasn't. I doubt Mr Alex has mentioned his Cousin Simon?'

She shook her head. 'No.'

'His father was Captain Harry's younger brother and, while the Captain fought for the King, brother Robert didn't commit himself till he could come down on the winning side. He joined Cromwell after Marston Moor and by the mid-fifties he'd made himself useful enough to be granted all the sequestrated Deveril property ... most of which ought to have gone to Mr Alex.'

Chloë drew a breath of dawning comprehension.

'And which he expected to regain when the King came home?'

'Aye – and he'd a right to expect it. Only it didn't work out that way. Uncle Robert died in '59, just in time for his son to see which way the wind was blowing. While Mr Alex was still in Sweden, Simon crossed to Hamburg along with Roger Palmer and while the King's head was filled with Madam Barbara, he made his peace, all manner of promises and heeled himself in with the Duke of York for good measure. By the time Mr Alex got back to England, Cousin Simon was assisting York in the Navy Office and so high in favour there was no shifting him. He wouldn't give up the land and, having accepted his vows of loyalty, the King couldn't take it from him.'

'Wasn't there was some sort of Proclamation?' asked Chloë, frowning.

'Words on paper,' snorted Matt. 'So Mr Alex was left with nought but a draughty run-down place in Southwark and no means to put it to rights. He'd have gone back to France but that the King was full of soft words and promises – like always. At first, he was angry and then he grew bitter; and because, for the first time in ten years he hadn't got a job to do, he took to the bottle. Not every day but too often for his own good.' Matt stopped and leaning forward, poked the fire with a vicious jerk. 'And then he met Sarah Courtney.'

'Ah.' Chloë met his gaze thoughtfully. 'You don't like her.'

'I can't abide her,' replied Matt roundly. 'She's a selfish, conceited, conniving harpy and, but for her, Mr Alex would have gone selling his sword again last year.'

'Does he love her?'

Matt shrugged. 'Maybe. He thought he did, at all events.'

'Enough to marry her, perhaps?'

'Small chance of that!' snorted Matthew.

'Why not? If she loves Mr Deveril --'

'You don't know her, lass. She loves two things – herself and money. Mr Alex is a fine-looking young man from a good family but he ain't rich. That makes him suitable as a lover but no use at all as a husband.'

'Oh,' said Chloë weakly. 'I hadn't realised it was … that Mr Deveril was … I thought that he and Sarah were …' She stopped. 'Say something, Matt – before I make an even bigger fool of myself.'

He grinned. 'You thought what a nice, well-brought up girl would think. Sarah's something else. She's going to marry Graham Marsden on Friday. He's sixty-odd if he's a day but worth more than a shiny shilling.'

'Does Mr Deveril know?'

'He knows, all right. I've got an idea she told him, then suggested that the two of them just carry on as before.'

'That's … not very nice.'

'No, it isn't. My guess is Mr Alex told her goodbye and then got so drunk that he almost killed a man, quarrelled with Mr Giles and married you.'

Chloë accepted this evaluation without a blink but her expression sharpened a little. 'And you thought I'd make a nice, temporary safeguard?'

Matthew looked somewhat disconcerted. 'Something like that.'

'But given the choice, you'd prefer to see him a mercenary again?'

'Unless things change – aye.'

She nodded slowly and fixed him with an owl-like stare.

'What you're really saying,' she suggested, 'is that he needs an occupation.'

A glimmer of approval lurked in the black eyes.

'Now that,' he agreed, 'is exactly what I'm saying.'

* * *

When Friday dawned, the promised thaw had become a reality and the exquisite carpet of white had melted into an untidy piebald slush. Water dripped sluggishly from the rooftops and gurgled dirtily down the gutters and, away from the cobbles, the ground had the consistency of gravy-sodden bread. Chloë, on her first outing for almost a week, stepped carefully while casting dubious glances at the menacing sky and then, regretfully curtailing her expedition, headed back towards Brewer Street.

For the past three days her mind had been occupied almost exclusively by Matt's revelations. Two points in particular obsessed her. One was the problem of finding suitable employment for an out-of-work mercenary and the other, the possible reasons for Mr Deveril choosing to keep her with him. With the first of these, she made no progress whatsoever; with the second, she eventually decided that there was really only one conclusion. That Mr Deveril's reasons for wishing to maintain the fiction of wedlock were much the same as those of Mr Lewis.

She had barely entered their lodgings and not even removed her cloak when Matt walked in and stood looking at her with dour foreboding. He said, 'We've got a problem. He says he's going to the wedding and I'm not convinced it's just to dance.'

'Oh.' Shades of potential disaster crowded Chloë's mind. 'How do we stop him?'

'Short of banging him over the head? I don't know. But I don't want to involve Mr Giles if I can help it.'

'No.' A pause and then, hopefully, 'We could lock him in. It worked before.'

'The mood he's in? We can't afford the breakages.'

Her heart sank still further. 'He's been drinking?'

'Only a bottle or two. He won't pass out any time soon.'

'That's a pity.' Chloë thought rapidly. 'How long have we got?'

'Not long. He's downstairs taking a bath.'

She walked to the window and stood looking out, fingers resting lightly on the sill. Then, turning, she gave a rueful smile.

'Get the butter-ale ready. I'm going for a ride.'

The black eyes narrowed and then widened incredulously.

'You're going to take Caesar?'

'Well, I don't imagine Mr Deveril is planning to walk to church. Not in this mud.'

Matt shook his head worriedly. 'He'll be too strong for you. There's none but Mr Alex ever rides him.'

Chloë grinned weakly and refrained from telling Mr Lewis that she hadn't ridden a horse since she was fourteen. Instead, she said, 'I know. So I should think Mr Deveril will come after me, wouldn't you?'

'There's no doubt about it,' said Matt grimly. 'Lass – he'll fillet and bread you!'

'Probably,' agreed Chloë. 'But at least he'll be nice and clean and properly dressed for it.' And, with apparent irrelevance, 'I think it's going to rain.'

* * *

It was undoubtedly going to rain. In fact, it was already beginning to do so in large, spasmodic spots as Chloë and Caesar reached the edge of the common and the skies promised a deluge to come.

Taut as a bowstring with strain, Chloë thankfully left the town behind her. Matt had been right. Caesar was strong, disliked strange hands and, ridden side-saddle, was almost impossible to manage. The muscles of her arms and shoulders ached with the effort of controlling him and her hands were numb and bloodless from the tourniquet of reins she had been forced to twine around them. Breathlessly, she spoke soothingly in Caesar's ear and hoped that Mr Deveril arrived before his horse succeeded in breaking her neck.

She was out in the middle of the clearing when she heard the sound of hoofbeats borne on the wind. Throat tightening, she turned her head and looked; a horseman riding ventre à terre. Mr Deveril. And then the heavens opened.

Alex approached in a haze of flying mud and came to a slithering halt beside her. He had discarded his sling, she noticed, and the rain was fast ruining his beautifully-feathered hat. Below that she was careful not to look.

'Get down,' he said.

She looked then and saw that, though his mouth smiled, his eyes were furious. Chloë's insides lurched unpleasantly. She ignored it as best she could and raised her eyebrows.

'I'd rather not. It's wet. Did you know that your hat is moulting?'

There was a brittle pause. Then his teeth gleamed as he said, 'Should I be surprised? I thought it was part of the plan.' And dropping from the saddle, he said again, 'Get down.'

And this time, with her nerves vibrating like wires, she saw no alternative. She slid unassisted from Caesar's back and arrived up to her ankles in freezing slush.

Without a word, Mr Deveril put the reins of both horses in her hands and began the process of changing saddles. Chloë watched in growing irritation while the rain weighed down her cloak, plastered strands of wet hair to her cheeks and began to trickle down her neck. She had been prepared for discomfort. But there were limits – and this unnerving silence was beyond them.

She said, 'What's wrong? I can't believe that you're lost for words.'

Unmoved, he continued tightening the saddle-girths at Caesar's side. 'There's no hurry. I've a number of things to say to you. Later.'

Chloë swallowed. 'Monologue, then. It's a pity everybody tiptoes round your feelings. It gives you the idea you can do what you like.'

'It's a pity,' returned Mr Deveril, 'that no one taught you to heed a warning the first time it's given.' In the brief glance which was all he gave her, the silvery eyes sliced into her like a knife. 'The last thing I need is another bloody nursemaid.'

'That's true!' Chloë's smooth, wet face flushed with annoyance. 'What you need is a straightjacket! My goodness - if you'd only use your brain instead of letting your stomach take over, we wouldn't be out here getting wet. And if you can't keep away from a woman who obviously doesn't want you, then it's because – despite all the melodramatics – you haven't got the backbone!'

Rain dripped steadily from the brim of Alex's hat. His face was white with temper and a pulse throbbed in his jaw. 'You'd be wise not to continue taking advantage. If a man spoke to me like that, he wouldn't still be standing.'

'Don't hold back on my account.'

'I don't hit women. Not even silly schoolgirls with ideas beyond their capabilities.'

'I got you here, didn't I?' Chloë met his hard stare with one equally challenging. 'Do you really think I did this for my own amusement?'

'Well is certainly isn't for mine!' snapped Mr Deveril scathingly. And with barely contained savagery, he threw her up into the saddle, hurled himself astride Caesar and set off homeward, leaving her with no choice but to trail in his wake.

The return ride was extremely unpleasant. Rain continued to fall heavily and mud flew against Chloë from the hooves of her borrowed mare and from those of Caesar, whose pace, though fast, was never enough to leave her completely behind. She rode on, grimly bedraggled and chilled to the bone – and preferring both to the tongue-lashing she suspected lay ahead of her.

When she drew rein in the stable-yard, Mr Deveril had already dismounted and stood waiting for her. He lifted her down with hands that bit like a steel trap and, holding her elbow in the same manner, marched her silently into the house.

As they gained the top of the first flight, Matthew emerged from his doorway. The lined, brown face was inscrutable as ever and only his prompt appearance betrayed his anxiety. Chloë met his gaze with one equally expressionless. Mr Deveril walked past him without a glance.

'See to the horses – and make sure Caesar is properly rubbed down.' He flung the command over his shoulder in a tone Mr Lewis had only ever heard on the battle-field and knew better than reply to.

Upstairs, Alex closed the door, leaned against it and hurled his sodden hat across the room. Then, folding his arms, he stared at his dripping wife with rigidly controlled temper.

'Next time you have an insane desire to risk your neck by interfering in what is none of your business – do it without placing my horse in like danger. You may consider it a justifiable hazard but I don't.'

Chloë looked back, too cold and wet to think up anything clever. It seemed the last straw that, while she got soaked and looked awful, Mr Deveril got soaked and looked no less attractive than usual. She unclenched her teeth, felt her nose begin to prickle and sniffed despairingly.

'I'm sorry. I thought it would be all right.'

The ice-blue eyes flared dangerously.

'Don't lie. I'm not a fool and neither are you. You knew exactly what you were doing. You wanted to stop me making an appearance at Sarah's wedding, so you did. On present showing, you'll be doing my breathing for me in a month. On the other hand, though today the method was probably your own, the idea originated from Matt. Didn't it?'

She jumped and the drips that were forming pools around her accelerated their passage. One droplet made its way down the side of her nose, now decidedly pink, and she smeared it aside with the back of her hand.

'If you want to blame anyone,' she said between chattering teeth, 'blame me.' And unable to hold his gaze any longer, she peered down at the strings of her cloak which her frozen fingers had manipulated into a knot.

For a second, Alex remained quite still, watching her. Then, 'Oh hell!' he said. And, moving with suppressed violence, pulled off his coat, tossed it away and closed in on her. 'Hell,' he said again, 'and damnation.'

Brushing aside her stiff, unskilful hands, he busied himself with the tangled strings. And suddenly, without looking, Chloë knew that the crisis had passed.

Mr Deveril demonstrated his superiority by quickly undoing her cloak and casting it after his coat. Quite without warning and as much from released tension as from cold, Chloë began to shiver. The blue eyes travelled impersonally over her from dripping rose-gold hair to soggily clinging hem.

'Turn round,' he said.

Chloë blinked. 'W-what?'

He sighed. 'You're soaked to the skin and likely to take inflammation of the lungs if you stay that way. Turn round.'

Her cheeks flamed and her voice, when she spoke, was an unlovely squeak.

'My lungs are quite healthy – and I can manage, thank you.'

Patience snapped and became sarcasm.

'If you think that, at a time like this, I'm likely to be mad with lust I can only think that you rate your attractions rather too highly or have forgotten the vital implications. Now – turn round!'

And helped by his hands on her shoulders, she did.

With head bent and senses totally disordered, she felt him unlace her gown and slide it from her arms to lie in a heap around her ankles. The shivering intensified.

Alex untied the tapes of the petticoats and they joined her gown on the floor. Then, leaving her clad only in her shift, he threw open the closet, pulled out a heavy chamber-robe and thrust it in her hand.

'Take off your chemise and put that on.' His mouth twitched almost imperceptibly. 'I won't look.'

Feeling that this wasn't the time to argue, Chloë watched him turn his back and did as she'd been told. When she signified her readiness, he came back to her holding a towel.

'Now sit down.' He indicated a chair beside the fire and, with ruthless efficiency, proceeded to dry her hair.

Under his hands, the blood began to circulate again in Chloë's limbs and warmth returned slowly. When he had finished, she took the towel and wound it round her head like a turban.

'Thank you.' She viewed him consideringly. 'Should I offer to return the favour?'

'Only if you're prepared to have your bluff called.'

'And if I am?'

'You'd be disappointed. I don't,' he said, 'have any petticoats.' And went out.

Left alone by the fire, Chloë stared thoughtfully down at her hands. There seemed to be at least three Mr Deverils and when you never knew which one you'd meet next, it was not a help.

Rather desperately, she picked up a brush and started to disentangle her hair.

PART TWO

THE DRAMA

London, the Channel, Holland & Tunbridge Wells February to August, 1666

*'Now the times are turned about
And the Rebels race is run.
That many headed Beast, the Rout
Who did turn the Father out
When they saw they were undone,
Were for bringing in the Son.
That fanatical crew which made us all rue
Have got so much wealth
By their plunder and stealth
That they creep into profit and power;
And so, come what will,
They'll be uppermost still:
And we that are low
Shall still be kept so,
While those domineer and devour.'*

ONE

The Court, having been detained at Oxford throughout January by the birth, three days after Christmas, of Lady Castlemaine's fifth (and allegedly royal) bastard, finally returned to London at the end of the month and settled, bickeringly, into its habitual domicile of the palace of Whitehall.

On February the tenth, his Britannic and Protestant Majesty, King Charles the Second, made reluctant response to the French proclamation of the previous month and declared war on his Gallic and Catholic Magnificence, King Louis the Fourteenth. The announcements of both sovereigns, being little more than token gestures, passed largely unnoticed by the English populace – who feared the Dutch more than they feared the French and a further out-break of the pestilence more than either of them.

On the twelfth, Alexander Deveril and his half-French titular wife, together with Messrs Beckwith, Fawsley and Lewis, left Oxford unregretted and unregretting behind them and followed in the wake of the Court. Giles returned to his lodgings in King Street, Danny to his uncle's home in the Strand and Mr Deveril and party to his house hard by St Mary Overie in Southwark.

The house at first sight was daunting. Built in the previous century of patterned brick laid between bands of silvering wood, it stood in a small wilderness that had once, long ago, been a garden and behind high, crumbling walls through which one passed by means of an exceedingly rusty gate. It was a large, projectoried building, gabled and irregular with high, twisting chimneys and dark leaded windows. Finial capped dormers peered down from above corbel-mounted oriels and below these, the ground floor boasted wide, square-ended bays between two of which stood an imposing portal topped by a badly weathered cartouche. Chloë stood amidst the weeds of many seasons and viewed it with a sinking heart.

Inside it was worse. Layers of dust mantled a vision of sparsely-furnished and decaying grandeur and the light, dimly filtering through smeared and grimy windows, touched fraying brocade curtains, balding Kurdistan rugs and festoons of cobwebs on the panelled walls. It was gloomy, forbidding and cold.

Alex stared at it as though he were seeing it for the first time and then turned to Chloë, who was.

'Oh Christ!' he said with an unheard-of ring of feeling. 'I'd forgotten what a mausoleum it is. Do you want to go and stay with Julia?'

'While you and Matt stick pins in the curtains and sweep the dust under the carpet? No, thank you.' She peered at a particularly large cobweb strung between the carved beams of the ceiling. 'I think you must have spiders the size of bats.'

'Probably. If you move the webs, the house falls down.'

'Let's hope not,' grinned Chloë. And then, 'I'll need help. Can we afford a strong, healthy girl?'

'Just about. The question is, will we find one who can cope with you and Matthew?' He held up a warning hand. 'No – don't say it. I can guess.'

At which even Matt cracked a smile.

* * *

On the following day Mr Lewis produced a sturdy, smiling damsel named Naomi and possessed of a head of hair that would, as Mr Deveril pointed out, make her an asset to anybody's cornfield. All that mattered to Chloë was that her new handmaiden was industrious, capable and willing. Within four gruelling days, assisted by Matt, they had removed every vestige of a cobweb, swept the house from top to bottom and washed all of the windows. And in the uncompromising light of day, Chloë made an unexpected discovery.

The house was beautiful. Shabby and neglected, bereft of many of the pieces of furniture and paintings that had once graced it, the structure itself, when clean, revealed a variety of exquisite features in nearly every room. Initials twined with lovers knots in her bedchamber; the wide hall and broad, oak staircase; the dining parlour with its carved beams and double linen-fold panelling; and the graceful parlour, its ceiling painted in muted reds and blues and where, pulling down a moth-eaten tapestry from above the fire, Chloë found a stucco over-mantel depicting Persephone at the birth of Spring. Around it in silver tracery were the words, 'Thou art fairer than the evening air, clad in the beauty of a thousand stars.'

When shown this, Mr Deveril whistled appreciatively and ran one finger delicately over a semi-naked dryad. 'Why did I never see this before?'

'Because someone with terrible taste hung a poor representation of the Battle of Jericho in front of it.'

Alex looked closely into the face of Persephone.

'Be grateful. If it's valuable – and I think it may be - it would probably have gone to provide cannon for the King. Like everything else.'

Chloë said, 'The words round the edge. Is that poetry?'

'Marlowe,' said Mr Deveril absently. 'Brighter art thou than flaming Jupiter when he appeared to hapless Semele, more lovely than the monarch of the sky ... and so on and so on.'

Chloë opened her mouth, closed it again and then said, 'How do you do that?'

'Do what?'

'Remember endless screeds of poetry.'

He turned from Persephone, shrugging slightly.

'Fifteen years of moving around, living in army billets.'

'I don't follow.'

'Aside from drinking, whoring and gaming, reading is the only leisure activity left to you,' he said impatiently. 'So I read such books as came my way and when there were no new ones, I read them again.' He paused. 'You look surprised. No doubt you thought I was more the drinking, whoring and gaming type – in which, of course, you would be mostly right.'

* * *

Having cleaned the house, Chloë enlisted Matthew's help in removing sundry items of furniture from rooms she did not need for use in those she did. In this way, four bedchambers were made habitable and the parlour granted a degree of comfort that had seemed unthinkable only a few days earlier.

For nearly a week they lived on dishes from the cook-shop before Chloë, tiring of this arrangement, took the notion to invade the hitherto unused kitchen and take over the catering herself. Without informing

Mr Deveril, she decided to make her culinary debut on a day when Giles and Danny were bidden to supper and, assisted by a faintly dubious Naomi, she made her preparations.

At first all went well and Naomi, waiting at table, served a well-roasted goose and a spicy rabbit hash. The trouble, when it came, was caused by a mutton pie which perished unsampled when the oven burst mysteriously into flames. Hopeful of rescuing the pie, Chloë threw open the oven door then, scorched and coughing, hastily kicked it shut again; and dislodged an avalanche of soot from the chimney.

It dropped into the fire, releasing clouds of smoke, formed a black crust on a simmering pot of fricassee and filled the air with gently descending flakes which came tenderly to rest on the fruit tartlets, on the dish of cheeses and on Chloë. By the time the dust finally settled, the entire kitchen appeared to have been showered with volcanic ash and Naomi, arriving to find her mistress black-faced and choking in a room laden with smoke, uttered a hearty shriek and ran for help.

Within seconds Mr Deveril was in the doorway, closely followed by Giles and Danny. He checked on the threshold and then strolled on, blue eyes interestedly inspecting the damage, before coming to a halt by the table. He gazed down on the spotty tartlets and then across at his equally spotty wife, standing like Dido among the ruins of Carthage.

'"The blasted hearth laid low in horrible destruction." Does anyone,' he asked unsteadily, 'fancy a sooty tart?' And gave way to laughter.

Two days later, Mistress Jackson was installed in the kitchen.

* * *

Balked of employment in this field, then magisterially despatched by Mr Deveril on a tour of silk-mercers and milliners in the company of his determined and energetic sister, Chloë retaliated by bending her fertile brain to an enterprise of a very different nature suggested by the cost of dress materials.

The state of declared, if not actual, war between England and France showed every sign of hitting fashionable Londoners where it hurt most. Prices were already rising and Lyons silk and Nantes velvet were being bought in enormous quantities before the expected scarcity became a reality. Chloë, bullied by Julia into paying thirty pounds for length of figured brocade, shuddered and then bombarded her companion with a series of detailed questions on the types, qualities and origins of every fabric she saw.

Born of her impending annulment and Mr Deveril's straitened circumstances, a fascinating idea had taken root but she took her time before tentatively broaching the subject with her husband. His reaction was irritatingly predictable – a mixture of amusement and impatience. It was a pipe-dream, a fantasy, a flight of schoolgirl romance, he said. It was impractical, foolish and probably impossible. Chloë demanded reasons and was given them in a stream of concise and numerically listed points; then, warming to his theme, Alex subjected her to a relentless inquisition from which she emerged battered and depressingly aware of her own ignorance but fundamentally unconvinced. She sought information in Tom Blanchard's small but well-stocked library and then, rejuvenated, took her problem to Matthew. And Matt, after a long and persuasive discussion, reluctantly agreed to make enquiries.

Strangely, it was in Mr Fawsley that she found her first real supporter. Danny had offered his services as guide and mentor in the intricate ways of the City and with this aim in mind, called for her on the morning of Shrove Tuesday and found himself escorting her on a tour of the wharves between Blackfriars and Dowgate. Standing on Queenhithe and uncomfortably aware of language colourful enough to make a sailor blush, he was moved to remonstrate.

'This isn't a part of London that ladies visit,' he announced. 'Let's go.'

Chloë removed her gaze from the Betsy-Rose whose holds were disgorging a multiplicity of barrels and tarpaulin-covered boxes and looked absently at Daniel.

'There's no need to be embarrassed,' she said. 'I'm not listening. What's a fishmonger's daughter?'

'Never you mind,' frowned Danny, taking her arm in a firm grip and leading her back in the direction of Thames Street. 'Why on earth did you want to come here?'

'Research,' said Chloë. 'I'm considering making a little investment.'

The frown faded and he looked suddenly interested. 'In what? Shipping?'

'In a way. I've a dowry of eight hundred pounds and it seems a pity not to put it to work. I thought I might perhaps buy a cargo.'

'And sell it where?'

'Tangier. The garrison there might be glad of a few home comforts the Navy doesn't provide, don't you think? Then on to Genoa for velvet and Tunis for silk and home for a nice profit.'

Danny looked faintly disappointed. 'Why not the East?'

'Or the moon?' grinned Chloë. 'Because everything has to start somewhere. But today the Mediterranean, tomorrow - - '

'Russia,' said Daniel dreamily. 'China, the Indies.'

'Why stop there?'

'I daresay I shan't,' he replied simply. 'Since I was old enough to make sense of them, I've always loved maps and books about far-flung places. Places I want to see for myself ... places so different from here that you can hardly imagine them.'

'You're serious,' she said slowly. 'I didn't think you were serious about anything.'

'About this I am.' The cheerful, freckled face showed rare determination. 'And one day I'll go – you'll see.'

* * *

On the first day of March, Matt sought out Chloë and informed her that he had found a Captain – one Nathaniel Pierce – who was willing to undertake her commission for a return of forty per cent. Two hours later the three of them sat facing each other in Chloë's restored parlour.

Their discussions, arduous and complex, were made lengthier by the Captain's tendency to digress or reminisce every second or third word; but eventually they reached agreement on all the major points and drew up lists of items and quantities to be purchased for the outward voyage to the English garrison at Tangier. It was decided that this part of the venture should be handled jointly by Captain Pierce and Matt with Chloë taking care of all finances and paperwork. The proposed route was to take The Black Boy on from Tangier, through the pillars of Hercules to Genoa where Pierce would buy velvet and any other materials he considered to be of the right quality and price. From there he would sail down the coast of Italy to Naples for tortoiseshell and perfumes, then across the Tyrrhenian Sea to Bizerta for oranges, figs, almonds and silk and back home with all possible speed. He hoped to sail within a fortnight and return by the middle of August. Matthew was plainly sceptical.

'There's Dutchmen in the Channel and Frenchies further south. How do you plan on avoiding trouble?'

The Captain tapped his nose.

'There's ways. The Black Boy is fast and well-armed for a merchantman. And we carry a full set of flags. You can leave that part to me – it won't go amiss. We were at war with the Dutch last year as well but I still ran half a dozen trips into La Rochelle – and that was trickier by far, I can tell you!' He laughed and settled back in his chair. 'Not but what they didn't nearly have us one time. I remember it like yesterday. There we were, out in mid-channel ... '

Chloë and Matt exchanged glances while the Captain droned happily on; then, seizing her opportunity when he paused for breath, Chloë asked quickly, 'Do many English merchant ships sail the Channel these days?'

'Not many, Mistress Deveril. But a few do – and do it successfully. Sam Vine, for one ... and I'd give a lot for a look at his holds. He sails the Arabella for Lord Gresham – but you don't make his kind of money by running another man's business, no indeed! I'd stake my right arm he's either smuggling or breaking bulk.'

'Breaking bulk?' queried Chloë.

'Aye, Madam. Selling a portion of his cargo on his own account – like my Lord Sandwich was caught doing with captured prize ships last year. I'll go bail Vine is such another. A young friend of mine – a slip of a lad merely – sailed with him one season and told me that there was a strange air aboard the Arabella. Secretive, he said. Then, the next voyage, he didn't come back. They said he'd been lost in a heavy sea ... but I always wondered if he'd learned things he wasn't supposed to. Vine's a chancy bastard to cross – if you'll forgive the expression, Mistress.'

Chloë forgave the expression, smothered a yawn and began tactfully moving the Captain towards the street. Just less than half an hour later, when the door closed behind him, she leaned against it laughing weakly while Mr Lewis sank down on the foot of the stairs.

'Rot me,' said Matt bitterly, 'if I ever met a set of pipes so full of wind. The man's got a tongue like a fiddler's elbow. Aye – it's all very well for you to laugh. You haven't got to go shopping with him.' He eyed her sourly. 'Not but what his clack won't have its uses once he's away to sea.'

Still laughing, Chloë sat down beside him. 'How?'

Matthew favoured her with an acid grin.

'No one in their right mind is going to take him prisoner. He'd talk 'em to death.'

She leaned forward and buried her head in her arms.

'I know,' she said unsteadily. 'I know. But I just hope I never have to introduce him to Mr Deveril.'

Matt's eye brightened perceptibly and he drew a long breath.

'Now that,' he said wistfully, 'is a sight I'd pay money for.'

TWO

With reluctance, Chloë undertook the task of acquainting Alex with her plans and was relieved to find them met with nothing more than a slightly derisive shrug and a very firm order not to visit the docks or have anything to do with anyone of the maritime persuasion unless Matthew was at her side. Then, with his usual efficiency, he fulfilled the legalities that placed Chloë's dowry at her disposal and calmly withdrew his interest.

Sitting in front of a pile of lists and accounts in the small room she had appropriated as a sort of office, Chloë stared irritably at her neat columns of figures and wished Mr Deveril would achieve consistency. One could, at a pinch, come to terms with the temperamental wildness coupled with occasional, effortless charm - or the clever, frequently acid tongue and the rare, irresistible smile. One could even get used to the demonic good-looks. But not when the demon displayed traits of endearing humanity ... such as laughing himself silly over a ruined dinner.

There was worse to come. On the day The Black Boy sailed for Tangier, Mr Deveril strolled into Chloë's ordered sanctum and informed her that she was going to Court.

'And don't tell me you've nothing to wear. I've seen the bills.'

Chloë opened her mouth to point out that she'd ordered only two gowns, one of which she was currently wearing and instead heard herself say weakly, 'If you don't mind, I'd rather not go at all.'

Alex shook his head, his mouth curling pleasantly.

'This isn't an invitation, Marigold – it's a royal command. The King is curious, so you're going to Whitehall – powdered, perfumed and dressed to kill – to satisfy him.'

'What do you mean – he's curious? About what?'

'About you - or rather us - and why we want an annulment.'

Her eyes widened. 'How does he know about that?'

Impatience stirred. 'How do you think? I told him. We want an annulment and Charles is the person best-placed to help us get one.'

She turned this over in her mind for a moment and then said, 'It's probably another stupid question but ... do you actually know His Majesty?'

'Yes. I won't pretend he's an intimate acquaintance but I've known him since Worcester and I can assure you that he's not at all frightening.'

Chloë felt like shouting, 'Not frightening? He's the King, you idiot!' But said dryly, 'I'm glad to hear it. And the whole court isn't frightening either, I suppose?'

He shrugged. 'It's a run of the mill occasion with, I presume, all the usual faces. The worst it's likely to be is tedious.' His expression became the one which usually heralded one of his more outrageous statements. 'And only think – if we're lucky, His Highly Susceptible Majesty will take such a fancy to you that we'll find ourselves sundered in record time so you can be Queen of the May.'

She eyed him witheringly. 'In that case, how can I refuse?'

'Just what I've been trying to tell you,' said Alex. 'You can't.'

Later, en-route in hot-footed panic to see Lady Julia, Chloë wondered whether Mr Deveril was in a greater hurry than previously to have their union annulled – and, if so, why. She also finally and with reluctance admitted to herself that it wasn't what she wanted. She told herself it wasn't that surprising. For the first time in years, she was happy. She had a home she enjoyed caring for, friends she valued and a small business venture she hoped would prove profitable. She had every reason to be happy. It was nothing at all to do with the difficult, charming man who had just talked her into what might well be the most terrifying evening of her life.

Lady Julia, as it turned out, was not impressed.

'So?' she asked calmly. 'I told you it wouldn't be possible for you to hide yourself away here in London. I'm only surprised that it's taken Alex so long to do something about it.' She laughed. 'Don't look so scared. There's nothing to worry about.'

'There's nothing to worry about,' agreed Chloë sourly, 'except that the only gown in any sense suitable is that green brocade you made me buy. And it isn't finished yet.'

'Is that all? We can soon change that. Come on – smile! Lots of girls would give their eyes for this chance.'

'Well that just shows how unworthy I am. I've got my priorities all wrong.'

But on the following evening, at the end of an unusually careful and lengthy toilette, her feelings underwent a slight adjustment as she studied her reflection in the glass. One couldn't deny that a bit of effort paid dividends and it seemed that Julia had been quite right about the disputed brocade. Dark green and richly glowing, it proved an excellent foil for what Chloë privately considered the undue gaudiness of her hair and seemed to enhance the whiteness of her skin. After long argument, Julia had also had her way on the cut of the gown and, though it still seemed rather revealing, Chloë had to admit that it showed her shoulders to advantage.

The puffed, elbow-length sleeves ended in falls of the same creamy lace that edged the bodice and, gathered into the deep point of the waist, the full skirt whispered slyly as she walked. Chloë's only lingering reservation was – between tight-lacing and a daring expanse of décolletage – what might happen if she indulged in unwary movement.

After ten minutes of unaccustomed indecision, common sense prevailed and she relinquished any notion of curls. Instead, she created an intricate halo of woven plaits and confined the surplus in a delicate, filigree caul. The result was elegant if rather severe and Chloë was moderately pleased.

If Mr Deveril was impressed by the transformation he made no comment on it, although the pale gaze narrowed a trifle as it rested on her ... and if Chloë was disappointed by the omission, she did not show it. At any event the thought, if it existed at all, lasted only a second. After that – and not for the first time – she resigned herself to the fact that some people had a whole battery of unfair advantages.

Although immaculately saturnine in black velvet, with a sapphire order glowing on his breast, Alexander Deveril's magnificence had little to do with his clothes. It came from the high cheekbones, the sculpted mouth, the ice-blue eyes fringed with thick lashes, the casually elegant posture ... and the long, loosely-curling hair, gleaming with the blue-black sheen of a raven's wing. Chloë sighed and reflected that no amount of time spent in front of her mirror was ever going to compete with that.

Alex smiled with his habitual ambiguity and, taking her cloak, dropped it neatly about her shoulders. Then, tucking her hand through his arm, he said, 'Relax. It's a reception – not an execution.'

Chloë was spared the necessity of finding an answer by the advent of Matthew's head around the door. 'The carriage is here,' he said and fixed her with an unwinking stare meant, she thought, to convey encouragement. She smiled weakly at him and he withdrew.

Mr Deveril picked up his hat and said cheerfully, 'Boot and saddle, my dear. We're off.'

The air of breezy anticipation clung to him all the way to Temple Bar, manifesting itself in a stream of mostly disrespectful information about Whitehall and its inmates that Chloë might have found funny had she been listening. Swinging left into the Strand, the carriage was briefly lit by the flare of a link-boy's torch and, taking advantage of it, Alex directed a quizzical glance at his wife's rigid profile.

'I hope,' he said annoyingly, 'that you've brought a clean handkerchief.'

Chloë turned her head and, beneath the smooth rose-gold braids, her face was pale with fright. She said flatly, 'I wish you wouldn't be so bright. If you wanted to be helpful, you'd tell me whether any enquiries you may have made about the annulment have caused it to become common knowledge or if it is still a well-kept secret. If I'm likely to be asked any awkward questions, it would be nice to be fore-warned so I can sharpen my tongue and my elbows.'

For a minute, Alex continued to look at her. Then, with a sigh and a shrug, 'All right. You want to know if I've begun attempting to free us both; the answer is yes. You want to know how these attempts are progressing and the answer is that they are going as you would expect – that is to say, slowly. And you want to know if the people you will meet this evening are so far unaware of our intentions- again yes. I hope.' His mouth curled slightly. 'Stop worrying. Everything will be fine. Dull, but fine.'

The coach bumped into the brightly-lit yard of Whitehall and Chloë regarded Mr Deveril irritably. 'I'm glad you think so.'

The blue eyes grew thoughtful.

'I know what it is,' said Alex. 'You haven't any jewels.'

Some colour came back into her face.

'Don't be ridiculous,' she snapped. 'I don't care a fig for such things!'

'No? What a pity,' he said regretfully, slipping one hand into his pocket. 'Then you won't want this.' And hanging from the long, shapely fingers was a golden, topaz-studded chain, whose centre supported a delicate, tawny flower cunningly wrought. A marigold.

Chloë stared at it and felt her breath leak away. That was the trouble with Mr Deveril, she thought. One minute he was being thoroughly aggravating and the next he did something ... something like this. Very slowly, she looked into his eyes, her breathing still erratic and her wits scrambled.

Mercifully, he did not appear to expect an answer. As the coach drew to a halt, he untied the strings of her cloak and fastened the pretty thing around her neck with a gesture entirely prosaic.

'Not, of course, that you required further adornment,' he said placidly, 'but it is a matter of confidence. There.' He leaned back to inspect his handiwork. 'The perfect finishing touch. Don't forget to avoid lonely antechambers. Shall we go?'

It was astonishing that, for the first time ever, something in his voice calmed and encouraged her. Chloë's heart resumed its usual rhythm and she allowed him to hand her down from the coach.

'I don't know what to say – except thank you, of course,' she said shyly. 'I'm not sure I deserve it. It's very beautiful.'

Mr Deveril removed his hat and swept a flourishing bow.

'Then you undoubtedly do,' he replied with an indulgent gallantry clearly not meant to be taken seriously.

Inside was a blaze of lights and a bewildering press of people, not all of them of the haut monde. Whitehall, once the property of Cardinal Wolsey and now, thanks to the addition of Inigo Jones' banqueting-hall, the largest palace in Europe, covered twenty-three acres and comprised a maze of galleries, courtyards and some two thousand rooms. Anyone with the right of entry could walk in to watch the King at dinner or catch the eye of some influential personage in the Stone Gallery; and, since many took advantage of this privilege, the Palace was inevitably crowded.

Having separated her from her cloak, Alex conducted her through a complicated route of corridors and stairs, greeting people as he went but stopping for none. Crossing the second gallery and answering Chloë's unspoken thought, he said, 'They should supply maps. It's a warren built for rabbits by rabbits … but here we are. It's a pity that Parliament chose to send the late King to his execution from the Banqueting Hall for it means that, not unnaturally, the present King has a dislike for the room. But possibly you consider this one well enough?'

Wordlessly, Chloë nodded. The creative genius responsible for the great painted ceiling might not have been Rubens but it was masterly enough to endow its vivid, cloud-borne figures with vigorous majesty, while the huge tapestries that covered the walls depicted scenes of equal grandeur and triumph. The splendour of Solomon, the might of Samson and the patience of Moses looked down with lofty eminence in the dazzling light of several hundred candles; and below and between, the glittering flower of English nobility eddied and swayed amidst the crystal and gilt, linked by rank and wealth and fashion.

Chloë stared, blinked and stared again. Then, swallowing resolutely, she looked up at her husband.

He said cheerfully, 'Cosy, isn't it? Like a bushel of pretty sugared almonds jostling for position in the same exquisite dish. Only much of the sugar is actually arsenic and most of the kernels are rotten. But fear not – for here are Giles and Danny. Bread-crumbs amongst the marchpane.'

There was a faint question in the straight line of Chloë's brows but she turned to meet Danny's open-mouthed gaze.

'My God!' he said. 'I'd hardly have known you. What have you done to your hair?'

She frowned. 'I'd ask you the same question if I were not on my best behaviour.'

He grinned. 'Sorry. I meant to say that you look wonderful. What do you think, Giles?'

Mr Beckwith thought a number of things he could not possibly say; such as the fact that the severely upswept hair revealed an unsuspectedly pure line of cheek and jaw ... and that simplicity suited her in a way that made every other woman in the room look tawdry. He smiled and bowed gracefully over her hand.

'I think you look charming,' he said lightly. And to Alex, 'You'll present her?'

Mr Deveril's expression was seraphic. 'What else?'

'That,' said Giles, 'was what I was wondering.'

'Oh ye of little faith!' came the reproving reply. And, drawing Chloë with him, continued unhurriedly across the room before coming to a sudden halt.

Chloë glanced sharply in the direction of his gaze. It appeared to be focussed on the couple approaching them. A couple widely dissimilar; the lady young and ethereally fair and a gentleman whose face, below his modish wig, bore the look of ill-health.

'Why Mr Deveril – what a charming surprise! We'd begun to wonder if you hadn't done something dreadful and been forced into horrid seclusion.'

The lovely creature was speaking and the significance of her words was not lost on Chloë in whom suspicion became certainty. She glanced fleetingly at the gentleman and then her attention was claimed by Alex, his bow just a fraction too low and his voice a little too mellow.

'Lady Marsden – your most humble servant. Sir Graham – allow me to offer my felicitations. My warmest felicitations.'

Sir Graham bowed and smiled gently at Chloë. 'I thank you. But it seems I should return them – for I understand we are in like case.'

'Are we?' The silver-blue gaze expressed mild alarm, transferred itself to Sarah and on to Chloë. Then, delicately, 'I don't think so.'

'What Graham means,' sighed Sarah, 'is that, like us, you are recently married.'

'Oh. I see. And you have been longing to meet my wife. Quite.' He performed a belated introduction and then turned again to Sir Graham. 'You must forgive me. My acquaintance with your bride is of such a ... long-standing nature ... that I had forgotten that mine is a stranger to you.'

The older man's smile retained its kindly unconcern as he kissed Chloë's hand and asked if it were her first visit to Court.

'Indeed, it is. She is a country girl – a rose freshly-plucked.' Alex smiled beneficently at Sarah and, as she opened her mouth to speak, addressed himself once more to Sir Graham. 'I daresay you would recall my wife's step-father – Ralph Ashton?'

'Yes, indeed. Her mother also,' nodded Sir Graham. 'She was very charming.'

Sarah looked avidly at Chloë. 'Your marriage was such a surprise – we are all quite curious. Did Alex woo you with poetry and sweep you off your feet?'

'Not quite,' said Chloë, finally managing to get a word in. 'He took care of the poetry and I did the rest.'

'Oh. How ... original.' The cornflower gaze widened, drifted briefly to Alex and then back again. 'One hears such stories ... of card games, for instance.'

'Rumours always lie. It was dice, actually ... followed by a midnight wedding. Chloë, you see, was so eager that she didn't even wait to ask if I could support her. Impractical ... but winsome, don't you think?'

Chloë thought that it was time someone gave Mr Deveril a dose of his own medicine. She looked into his eyes and with a languishing sigh, said, 'But it isn't always possible to be practical. You were so strong and romantic and ardent. And so very, very dr—'

'Determined,' supplied Alex with faultless timing. His apparently affectionate arm gripped her waist like a steel band. 'And you were unable to resist me. There's no need to be coy.'

Lady Sarah smiled maliciously.

'Indeed, no. I assure you that I understand perfectly – and am all admiration for your fortitude. The singularity of your position must be most trying. One can only hope,' she finished sweetly, 'that Alex has not proved a disappointment.'

Chloë was getting tired of her ladyship's little innuendos. Opening her eyes very wide, she said, 'Goodness me, no! How could he?' And felt the arm around her quiver as if Mr Deveril, damn him, was trying not to laugh.

'How indeed?' replied Sarah, as though she could have named a few things. And then, smiling full into Alex's eyes, 'And how fortunate you are, my friend, in acquiring so devoted and ... innocent a wife.'

'Am I not?' came the bland response. 'Undoubtedly a pearl amongst women. And talking of pearls – I've been admiring yours. A wedding gift, perhaps?'

Sarah flushed and her fingers stole to her throat.

'No – or not from me,' said Sir Graham. 'But perhaps from your first husband, my dear...?' He looked at her fondly.

'Yes.' It was said with a sort of curt defiance. 'David gave them to me.'

A slow smile lit Mr Deveril's face. 'Yes? He obviously had excellent taste. I doubt if even Lady Gresham has anything finer.'

One glance at her ladyship's face was enough to inform Chloë that this seemingly harmless observation was more in the nature of a Parthian shot. Fortunately, however, Sir Graham plainly understood it no more than she did herself. He took his wife's hand and prepared to move on saying, 'I think you almost as fortunate as I am myself, Deveril – and I hope you will be as happy.'

'Or even,' said Sarah, with a glittering glance between her lashes, 'half as happy.'

From the edge of the room, Mr Fawsley watched them and then made his way across to Chloë and Alex. They did not appear to notice him. Alex's eyes were cool as glass and Chloë's held a furious glint as she said, 'If you ever do that again, don't count on my support. Sir Graham is a nice man who's done you no harm – and, with a wife like that, he doesn't need extra troubles of your making.'

'I knew it,' said Alex. 'You want to take him home and brew him a posset.'

'Stop trying to turn the tables,' snapped his wife. 'Since you plainly know where she got those pearls, it was presumably from you.'

Too shocked to keep his mouth shut, Danny said, 'God, Alex – you didn't, did you? I thought you had more sense!'

Irritation flared in the light eyes and Mr Deveril said blightingly, 'Firstly, Daniel, it's no business of yours. And secondly, I'd be grateful if you would both stop jumping to conclusions.'

Chloë swallowed and said, 'Oh. Well ... even if it wasn't you, you were still wrong to bring it up just then. And in future don't use me to score points.'

'I wasn't aware that I had. But tell me ... how may I 'use' you?' The dark brows lifted slowly. 'There must be something that isn't prey to that tediously restricting moral code of yours – else why did I marry you? And why – more interesting still – did you marry me? I'm sure you have a useful, practical reason that I haven't been privileged to hear yet.'

He waited, the bright gaze resting scathingly on her face. Chloë stared back unflinchingly but said nothing. Alex laughed.

'My point, I think.' He turned to go, then stopped. 'And you needn't concern yourself over Sir Graham. When a gentleman marries a whore he expects these little inconveniences. And, though I've plenty of faults, hypocrisy isn't one of them.' And he walked away.

Uncomfortably and in silence, Danny offered Chloë his arm. Then, clearing his throat, 'Chloë, you know – he doesn't mean half of what he says.'

She turned her head, her eyes focussing slowly on his face.

'No. And he doesn't say half of what he means.'

Only partly understanding, Danny felt a sudden spurt of anger.

'Perhaps not. But it's no excuse for what he said about your marriage. I was there and if anyone was at fault, it was Alex. He's got no right to blame you.'

Chloë smiled and shook her head.

'That isn't what he was doing. But if he had, it would have been true. He was drunk – I wasn't. As it is, he was saying something quite different and he may be right about that as well. That's the trouble.'

Feeling distinctly out of his depth, Danny tried to think of something to say and failed. Fortunately, he was spared the need. The room fell silent as the royal party came in.

Like the Red Sea before Moses, people fell back leaving a passageway down the centre of the chamber and, hastily copying those around her, Chloë spread her skirts in a deep curtsy. It seemed to last a long time. Her muscles tensed with strain and began to ache and the sight of the tiled floor, which was all she could see, became monotonous. Cautiously, she raised her head. After all, if the King could invite her out of curiosity, surely she was entitled to a little of her own. So she looked up and, between the shoulders of the lady and gentleman directly in front of her, saw the unmistakable figure of Charles Stuart.

She remembered him more clearly than she had expected - though, of course, no man she had ever seen was quite so tall. And he had really changed very little save in his dress, which was naturally finer than that of the beggar-King he had been six years ago in Paris. Chloë watched him critically and did not immediately observe that the dark, heavy-lidded eyes had turned in her direction and were dwelling on her with lurking amusement. When she did observe it, she was too surprised to react properly and before she realised it, had grinned, blushed and suddenly seen what it was about him that was considered so attractive.

Then the talk broke out afresh and, helping her to rise, Danny said ruefully, 'Oh hell. Look who Alex is with now!'

Chloë looked and perceived a slightly-built gentleman of moderate height whose wig and apparel represented the zenith of fashion. His shoes were high-heeled and beribboned, his breeches edged with lace and his braided coat a wonderful confection of yellow shag-silk. Chloë stifled a grin and raised tolerant eyes to his face. Fine-boned and set with grey-blue eyes, it was not unpleasing save for its faint effeminacy and expression of languid boredom. There was also, she thought, something vaguely familiar about it.

'Who is he?' she asked.

'That,' came the ominous reply, 'is Simon Deveril – Alex's cousin. And they hate each other's guts.'

'Oh.' Chloë felt rather cheated. Matthew had prepared her for a species of villain but, beside Alex, this exquisite gentleman was no more than an over-dressed mammet. 'I'm disappointed. What do you suppose they're talking about?'

'I'd rather not know,' said Danny. 'Look – there's Lady Julia.' And, having steered her purposefully over to her ladyship's side, he made good his escape.

Resplendent in cherry taffeta, Julia eyed Chloë with approval.

'Very nice. Rather stylish, in fact.' She examined the marigold chain. 'That's pretty. From Alex?' And, when Chloë nodded, 'Good. Does he approve of your new sophistication?'

'It's a little hard to tell. I think so.'

Julia sighed. 'Tiresome, isn't he? And annoying, since he knows very well he should stay at your side tonight and not go trying to provoke Cousin Simon. Oh yes – I saw him – and whatever he was up to, it had nothing to do with family affection or even common civility. It never does. But never mind.' She smiled and gestured with her fan. 'I'll present you to Barbara Castlemaine.'

'Over my dead body, Julia,' stated Mr Deveril crisply from behind them.

Startled, her ladyship turned swiftly, saying, 'For heaven's sake – lower your voice. She's the King's mistress! Haven't you any tact?'

'Not much,' replied Alex carelessly. He laid Chloë's hand on his arm. 'You'll have to be content with meeting his Majesty. His influence may be a thought less blatant but his manners are infinitely better.' And with a coolly dismissive smile for his sister, he led Chloë away.

'Why,' she asked mildly, 'don't you like Lady Castlemaine?'

'For a number of reasons,' came the unhelpful reply, 'which will soon become apparent, I imagine.'

Chloë glanced at the flaunting redhead whose low-cut gown made her own appear positively decorous.

'It's apparent already,' she said cheerfully. 'And I'd have thought she was just your style.' Which was how it came about that the first time the King saw Mr Deveril with his bride, the blue eyes were brimming with suppressed laughter.

Alex bowed and presented Chloë in the correct manner. She sank into her best curtsy and wondered if His Majesty intended to chide her for her earlier lapse in etiquette.

She need not have worried. Charles Stuart was a cynic and an inveterate womaniser but he was also extremely good-natured. Taking her hands, he raised her easily from the reverence and favoured her with his lazy smile.

'We are pleased to welcome you to Court, Mistress,' he said in a voice every bit as beautiful as Mr Deveril's, though much deeper, 'and hope you are pleased to approve us.'

Looking up, Chloë met the mischief in his eyes and found it impossible not to respond.

'Thank you, sire. But if Your Majesty is gracious enough to show approval to one who, by birth, is half French, how could she fail to grant hers to you?'

'My dear, if all the French were like you, I believe we would not be at war.' The King turned to Alex. 'I see why you have been keeping her such a secret and I sympathise – but I'm afraid it won't do. We shall expect to see her frequently at Court in the future.'

Mr Deveril smiled. 'A command, sire?'

'Not at all,' responded Charles promptly. 'A mere request which you will be pleased to grant since it comes from your sovereign. And now you may remove yourself for a few minutes. Your lady wife will not miss you – and neither shall I.'

'That's what I'm afraid of,' said Alex resignedly. He bowed and left them.

Chloë was left looking up at her King. He offered his arm and said with uncanny intuitiveness, 'You did not wish to come. I wonder why? Something to do with the ambivalence of your position, perhaps?'

She spread expressive hands. 'Something like that.'

He nodded. 'Alex informs me that he is making enquiries into the possibility of having your marriage annulled. I don't imagine that he's done so without your knowledge and consent. Am I correct?'

'Perfectly correct, sire.' Wondering if he was about to tell her the thing was done, her insides lurched unpleasantly.

'I see.' The dark eyes examined her thoughtfully. 'You realise it is quite likely that the final decision may well rest with me? And that being so, I have just one question I desire you to answer.' The harsh lines of his face dissolved into another magnetic smile. 'I need hardly say, I hope, that this entire conversation will remain wholly confidential.'

Chloë eyed him with hypnotic interest. 'All of it?'

'All of it,' Charles assured her. 'You may therefore speak quite freely. Are you in any particular hurry to be set free?'

She thought for a moment, debating how deliberate his choice of phrasing might be. 'Why no, Your Majesty. I do not believe so. Is there some difficulty?'

The wide mouth curled with perceptive amusement.

'Merely that I am not entirely convinced of the unsuitability of your marriage. I've a suspicion it may be rendering Alex a trifle less ... erratic. But I should be sorry to inconvenience a lady and since I fear it may be some time before I can come to a conclusion, I wished to discover if such a delay would be ... displeasing to you.'

Chloë drew a long unsteady breath. She thought again of the house, of her ship on its voyage to Tangier; she thought of Matt and Danny, Giles and Julia. And though she knew the where the danger lay and how great it was, she resolutely ignored it.

'N-no, sire. It wouldn't displease me at all.'

'Ah,' said Charles gravely. 'I hoped that might be the case. But enough – I will exert myself and present you to the Court. Whom would you most like to meet?'

There was only one answer to that. Chloë looked at the small, wistful-eyed lady sitting almost alone at the end of the room.

'If it is not an impertinence, sire, I would very much like to meet the Queen.'

THREE

In the latter half of the month, Chloë made four visits to Whitehall but mercifully none of them were marked by the nerve-blasting occurrences of the first. Catherine of Braganza, after a rather distrait beginning, proved both sweet-natured and shy. Chloë promptly disregarded her royal status and set out to befriend her.

Of Giles she saw very little but his manner remained one of friendly aloofness and so, together with Matthew, Danny continued to be her closest companion. They danced, laughed, talked and pored over endless charts and works of geography, all of which resulted in a close friendship and a rapport of unusual proportions. Chloë found how much more there was to Daniel than high-spirits and a sunny disposition and Danny understood a good deal more about Chloë than she was ever to realise.

Towards the end of the month Queen Catherine fell ill and, after twice failing to get in to see her, Chloë had to content herself with sending little posies of early flowers — products of the unseasonably mild weather and so far unspoilt by the lack of rain. On Easter Sunday she attended Whitehall chapel with Lady Julia to hear a sermon of more than ordinary length and dullness preached by the Bishop of London; and on Easter Monday, having no engagements, she dressed simply, left her hair loose and planned to devote herself to household matters.

Finding herself deserted save for Naomi and Mistress Jackson, she decided to inspect the linen and make a preliminary assault on the mending. Alone in the linen-cupboard, she spared the odd thought for Mr Deveril and Danny who, having challenged each other to some highly suspect activity referred to as 'shooting the bridge', had set off with Mr Beckwith in tow as a reluctant witness. Chloë concluded that it was as well she didn't know what they were doing since she had better things to do than spend her time wondering which of them would come back with a broken bone or cracked head this time.

Downstairs in the parlour she sat, chin in hand, contemplating the fruits of her mission and trying to summon up some enthusiasm. It wasn't easy. She sighed, threaded her needle and impaled the first of a pile of napkins with a savage stab. Then she was saved by the bell. A gentleman to see her, said Naomi, agog with curiosity. A Mr Simon Deveril. After a long pause, Chloë shut her mouth and told Naomi to admit him and bring refreshments.

Exquisite as ever, Simon Deveril entered the room and crossed, gently effervescing, to her side. 'My dear Cousin – I am delighted to meet you at last! And you will not mind if I call you Cousin? It's what you are, after all.' He took her hands and saluted each of them with impeccable artistry.

Chloë smiled politely and reflected that this Mr Deveril plainly had all the graces. Her hands were retained and he stepped back to survey her.

'I'm afraid I grew positively weary of waiting for someone to introduce us. It is not often that one acquires such a charming new relative – and so unexpectedly. But dear Alexander is always so precipitate ... I tremble for him often, I promise you ... though in this case one cannot blame him. Nor even for wilfully keeping us apart as he has been doing.' He released her hands in order to shrug elegantly. 'The poor fellow does not like me, you know. I grieve to say it – but so it is.'

Fascinated by his verbosity and wondering if he could not outshine even Captain Pierce, Chloë achieved a sympathetic smile. 'What a shame. Why ever not?'

'He believes – quite mistakenly, you understand – that I wronged him,' replied Simon plaintively. 'Indeed, he has become utterly obsessed with the idea and I can only hope you will help him to outgrow it.'

'Then aren't you running the risk,' said Chloë, unable to resist the temptation, 'that poor Alex may throw you down the steps?'

He shuddered delicately. 'I sincerely trust not. I do so dislike violence.' And then, 'I take it that he is not, at the moment, at home?'

Chloë smiled, indicated a chair, and watched him sit with due deference to his lilac velvet. 'No. But I expect him back quite soon.'

'Really?' he replied languidly. 'I shall not pretend to be sorry to have missed him – and must congratulate myself on the aptness of my timing.'

As Naomi bore in a tray of wine and small cakes, a sudden suspicion darkened Chloë's mind. 'Shooting the bridge' they had said. There was only one bridge and Simon had either crossed it or passed by it on his way to Southwark. If Alex was there and Simon had seen him, then he had known she was alone. She supposed that, under the circumstances, that might be considered reasonable; she, however, found it decidedly underhand and resolved to make it plain to Cousin Simon exactly where her loyalties lay.

'You are under a misconception, Cousin,' she said rather more acidly than she intended as the door closed again behind the maid. 'You will stand a much better chance of effecting a reconciliation with Alex if you visit his house when he is in it. And I must own that I feel it would be more appropriate.'

Simon raised his brows. 'Dear me! Are you asking me to leave?'

'Not at all. But you should understand that there can be no question of my discussing my husband with you.'

He sipped his wine and surveyed her over the rim of his glass.

'I see. How delightfully wifely of you. Alex is fortunate to have … won so fair a prize. I do so admire women of principle – and the Court, as I feel sure you've noticed, is full of ladies renowned for their lack of them. Which reminds me.' He paused slightly and then went on, 'Sarah is dreadfully worried about poor Alex. It is quite absurd, of course, but it seems she feels his rather sudden marriage is a tragic mistake and all her fault.'

The brown eyes became quite blank. 'Oh?'

'Yes.' Simon looked a little anxious. 'How difficult this is … one hardly knows what to say.'

'Then perhaps it's best to say nothing,' she suggested. 'Have a cake.'

He sighed. 'My dear, please believe that I have no wish to distress you but equally I should like to set Sarah's mind at rest – and my own. Also, and not to put too fine a point on it, if she is likely to confide in others, you might prefer to be aware of what she is saying.'

Again, it sounded reasonable enough – except when you considered what you knew of Lady Sarah or admitted that you were starting to dislike Cousin Simon. Chloë maintained her remote expression and said distastefully, 'Very well. Say what you came to say.'

Simon drained his glass and set it carefully down.

'Not so very long ago, Sarah and Alex were ... close friends. I understand that they only quarrelled when Sarah announced her intention to wed Sir Graham in preference to Alex himself. Of course, she did her very best to soften the blow ...'

'I'll bet she did,' thought Chloë savagely.

' ... and she also, very sensibly in my opinion, advised him to make a wealthy marriage of his own. But she says that what he in fact did was to become so violently drunk that he – forgive me – accepted you as a stake in a game of dice and, having won, proceeded to marry you whilst in the same condition. It's utter nonsense, of course. Even Alex wouldn't behave so foolishly. But the poor, dear girl thinks he did all this in a flood of despair – for which she can't forgive herself.'

He was watching Chloë closely and she knew it. After taking the time to mentally apply a pleasingly vulgar epithet to Lady Sarah, she met his gaze and smiled brightly.

'I'm inclined to agree with you. It is nonsense. And if Lady Sarah really cares about Mr Deveril, it's not a tale she will repeat. You can assure her that, as always, he knows exactly what he's doing and I am possessed of a wealth of sympathy and understanding. In fact, I suggest she confines her concern to her own husband.'

He smiled back, gently incredulous. 'So there's no truth in it?'

Chloë sat very still and kept her eyes on his to avoid any impression of mendacity.

'Only that my brother did insist Mr Deveril play him at dice before he would give him my hand in marriage. But that,' she explained with nonchalant finality, 'is just an old family custom. Have a cake.'

Simon accepted the plate she offered and, with it, a change of subject. Chloë asked if the Queen was yet well enough to be told of her mother's death and he replied with easy suavity and a description of Court mourning.

Soon after that he left and she was very glad to see him go. She sat down again and picked up her sewing, a tiny preoccupied frown creasing her brow, but it was a long time before she set a stitch. She was just laying down her second napkin when the sound of the bell heralded the arrival of another visitor. Chloë sat back and waited. This time Naomi looked both flushed and flustered.

'Another gentleman, Madam,' she said in breathless but congratulatory accents. 'He says he's the Duke of Cumberland.'

'Does he? Then I expect he is. You'd better show him in.'

Naomi took a deep breath, opened her mouth and then changed her mind.

'Yes'm.' She bobbed a curtsy and withdrew.

Puzzled, Chloë grinned at her retreating back and, smoothing her hair with one perfunctory hand, rose to meet her second unexpected visitor of the morning.

The door opened and a man came in. Exactly what Chloë had expected, she was not sure but nothing had prepared for the reality. He was the tallest man she had ever seen and of magnificent physique, with all the aura one imagined in a hero of romance. His dark wig was elaborately curled and his garments richly sombre but, more than these, it was his face that commanded her attention.

The gentleman was not young and his face was one of decision and character, proud and beautifully sculpted, broad of brow and cleft of chin with a long straight nose from which harsh lines ran to a full-lipped mouth. The eyes, set beneath strongly-marked brows were large, heavy-lidded and dark - not unlike the King's, thought Chloë. Especially when they glinted with lurking amusement as they were beginning to do now.

Suddenly recollecting herself, Chloë flushed and curtsied.

'Your Grace ... I am so sorry ... I wasn't expecting ... ' And stopped helplessly.

The gentleman swept the floor with the plumes of his hat in a swift, deep bow and the smile in his eyes grew teasing.

'Six feet four inches,' he supplied helpfully in a deep voice which, like her own, was faintly accented. 'Two inches taller than the King.'

For a second she stared at him and then, with a grin, recovered her voice.

'Thank you, sir. I was wondering.' She hesitated and then said, 'We haven't met so I imagine you were hoping to see Mr Deveril. I'm afraid he is out at present – Naomi should have told you.'

'I believe she may have been trying,' replied the Duke regretfully, 'but I think she was a little over-awed. I sometimes do that to people.'

Chloë laughed. 'So I've noticed.' She wondered if it was a condition he could inspire in Mr Deveril, then came to the sad conclusion that it was unlikely.

'I did call to see Alexander,' the gentleman went on, 'and it is a matter of some importance. Perhaps you can tell me where I might find him?'

'Not exactly. He went out some time ago with Mr Beckwith and Mr Fawsley to 'shoot the bridge' – if that makes any sense to you?'

His Grace threw back his head in a deep, full-throated laugh.

'Then I imagine you can expect him back soon in need of a change of clothes.'

Chloë raised enquiring brows. 'Oh?'

'It's ebb-tide, ' he told her, 'and a small boat sailing under the bridge gets sucked through like a cork and spat out on the other side. They call it 'shooting the bridge' – and usually end up taking a swim.'

'Or splattered against one of the archways?' suggested Chloë.

'There is always that possibility.'

She drew a long breath. 'Let's hope not. Meanwhile, perhaps you'd care to wait?'

He bowed slightly. 'If it would be no trouble, I'd be glad to do so. But it seems you are busy.' He indicated the mound of linen.

'Yes – and very tedious it is when you've no one to talk to.' She smiled up at him. 'I'd be grateful if you'd sit down – I feel at a terrible disadvantage.'

The wide mouth curled attractively.

'It doesn't show – but thank you.' And swinging the silk-lined cloak from his shoulders with a panache worthy of imitation, he tossed it over a chair-back and sat down, placing a flat leather box on his knee. 'My sister Sophy says that when I'm on my feet, it's like talking to a bean-pole.'

Chloë glanced up from her mending.

'And does she often talk to bean-poles?' Then coloured right down to her collar, unable to understand what it was in him that had caused her wits to wander twice in ten minutes. 'I'm so sorry. I don't usually make inane remarks – but it's been a peculiar morning.'

The Duke did not seem to mind. He said, 'It's some time since I saw your husband. Have you been married long?'

'Three months.' Her colour receded a little and she hoped it was not the start of a second inquisition. 'Do – do you know Mr Deveril well?'

The dark eyes rested on her enigmatically.

'Moderately so. A difficult young man of more than usual ability. And a good soldier.'

Chloë looked up again, needle poised. 'You've fought with him? Under Prince Rupert, perhaps?'

His teeth gleamed in a faintly wolfish grin. 'What do you know about Rupert?'

'Not a great deal. Only that Matt says he's the best cavalry leader in the world and that he must be an exceptional person if Mr Deveril respects him. I wish - - '

'Yes?'

She bent her head and continued to sew, aware of a need to be careful.

'I wish I could meet him,' she finished lightly.

There was a brief silence, then his Grace said, 'You might be disappointed. Or is it to control Alexander's excesses that you want him?'

The needle stopped again. Plainly, she hadn't been careful enough.

'No! No – it's just that we think, Matt and I, that he needs an occupation and I thought that His Highness might perhaps be able to help.' She stitched on, thrusting away a ridiculous impulse to confide in this sharp-witted stranger.

The Duke opened his box then closed it again, laying a sheaf of papers on the lid. He produced a narrow piece of charcoal and turned it in his fingers.

'Rupert deals in warfare. Do you think Alex would be willing to leave you after so short a time?'

'Yes,' said Chloë baldly without looking up.

The charcoal made contact with the paper. 'And you wouldn't mind?'

'No.' She thought and then added, 'I don't like waste.'

'Neither do I,' the Duke replied, his eyes on his work. 'But there are many different kinds – and it's sometimes difficult to distinguish the temporary from the permanent.'

Chloë stared at him, frowning, and caught a darkly studious gaze before it dropped back to the paper.

'You mean,' she said, struggling to understand, 'that Mr Deveril is wasting more than his talents?'

She received a small, abstracted nod.

'What, for example?'

'That's a question you had best ask yourself.' The charcoal made a number of bold, sweeping movements.

'I am asking it,' returned Chloë, 'but you are the one who seems to have the answers.' She pushed her needle jerkily through the material. 'I just wish you'd share them with me.'

'Very well.' The Duke stopped what he was doing and fixed her with a disconcertingly piercing stare. 'It seems to me that if his three-month bride is still thinking of him as Mr Deveril, he's also wasting his opportunities. D'accord?'

Chloë's hand slipped and the needle jabbed her finger. She sucked it, shook her head and said, 'Au contraire. Mais c'est une bien idée.'

His Grace raised one ironic brow and shrugged faintly before returning to his paper. There was a long silence broken only by the sound of charcoal on paper, then he said bluntly, 'There's no need to look so uneasy. I'm not going to pry. And I'll even manage to give Alex a little something to occupy his mind – as it happens, that's why I'm here. But he won't be able to discuss it with you so you'll need to accept that fact.'

The colour seeped back into Chloë's face and she gazed at him eagerly.

'You have work for him?'

'Yes … well, the truth of the matter,' said the Duke, looking suddenly discomfited, 'is that I'm not - - ' And stopped as sounds of disturbance reached them from the hall; crisp footfalls approaching the door and the clear, unmistakable tones of Mr Deveril. His Grace gave a rueful grin. 'Too late,' he sighed and, laying aside his box and papers, rose from his seat.

The door opened and, still speaking, Alex walked in followed by Giles.

' ... and taking it all in all, he was damned lucky not to be sucked up into the pumping mechanism and sent to Trinity House in a pipe! The day Danny - - ' He came to an abrupt halt and stood staring at Chloë's visitor, light eyes wide with shock.

'Sir!' He saluted smartly. 'I had no idea - - '

'Obviously,' said Duke easily and achieved instant silence. 'Don't disturb yourself. I could have sent word – but I preferred not to.'

An unpleasant, sinking sensation gripped the pit of Chloë's stomach and she eyed her guest with foreboding as he greeted Mr Beckwith with a slow, infectious smile. Giles bowed deeply and said, 'As always, it is a pleasure to see Your Highness.'

That did it. Chloë stood up, drawing three pairs of eyes. She looked directly at her new acquaintance. 'You said,' she observed accusingly, 'that you were the Duke of Cumberland. You did say that?'

'I did – and I am,' he replied placatingly. 'It's just not a title I find much use for except as a jest to old friends which was all I intended today. Unfortunately, it misfired somewhat – due completely to Alex's ill-timed absence - but having announced myself as Cumberland, it seemed a bit difficult to tell you that I'm also Rupert Palatine.'

Chloë was not noticeably comforted. 'My sister, Sophy,' she thought dismally. Sophia, Electress of Hanover, of course. And what had she said? Something stupid about bean-poles.

'But I talked about you ... and, what's more, you encouraged me to do it!'

Rupert grinned. 'Yes. I enjoyed that. You were very complimentary.'

Chloë glanced at her husband and saw that laughter wasn't very far away. It was too much. She restored her attention to the King's first cousin and lost her head.

'Yes,' she said indignantly, 'I was. But I'll know better next time.' And watched in disgust as all three gentlemen dissolved into mirth.

Giles was the first to recover and, moving towards her with the warmest expression she had seen in his face for a long time, said evenly, 'I think it would help if you began again. Sir, I have the pleasure to present Mistress Chloë Deveril. Chloë – allow me to introduce His Royal Highness, Prince Rupert of the Rhine and Bohemia, Count Palatine, Duke of Cumberland, Earl of Holderness and joint commander of His Majesty's Navy.'

Chloë curtsied. 'It is an honour to meet you, sir,' she said. And resolutely bit back one final piece of levity.

Prince Rupert, nobody's fool, bowed and supplied it for her.

'And we are delighted, Mistress Deveril. All of us. I hope I'm forgiven,' he continued pleasantly, 'but in case there is any lingering doubt, perhaps you'll accept this as a small peace-offering.'

Chloë took the paper from his outstretched hand and stared down at it in silence, the smile dying on her lips. The stillness dragged on until, torn by curiosity, Giles and Alex crossed to see that it was she held; and then they too looked without speaking.

It was a sketch, a mere line-drawing, but exquisitely and intuitively executed. The face was Chloë's and yet not. Hers was the long, smooth hair, backswept on one side of her face and falling straight as a curtain on the other and hers the delicate profile etched clear as a cameo against it. The high tapering brow, the short aquiline nose and the pure line of cheek and jaw were hers; but to the portrait as a whole, Rupert had added qualities from within that perhaps only Giles recognised.

The face, gracefully tilted on the slender curve of the throat, looked with downcast eye at something which the beholder could not see. Long, curling lashes shadowed the cheek with an illusion of serene purity and though the nose and chin retained their strength and character, the mouth had acquired a warmth and sweetness that made Giles look away. It was only Mr Deveril who understood, as Rupert had perhaps intended, that in style and composition, it was the face of a virgin saint.

Alex looked slowly across at the man whose brain and military skill he admired above all others and silver-blue eyes met the heavy-lidded Palatine gaze in mutual speculation. Then, almost imperceptibly the Prince shrugged, causing a tremor of unwilling amusement to tug at Alex's mouth.

It was left to Chloë to break the silence.

'It's beautiful,' she said shakily. 'But it's not me.'

'Yes it is,' said Giles shortly, then walked away to the window, a faint flush staining his cheeks.

Rupert cast a swift, appraising glance at his back and then smiled at Chloë. 'Not as you see yourself, perhaps. But you must allow the artist a little licence.'

She knew that her nose was pink but for once didn't really care and pulling out a handkerchief, she blew it defiantly. 'Yes. Well. Would the artist be good enough to sign it?'

The dark brows soared and he laughed.

'I'd be delighted! Our family doesn't usually get to sign its masterpieces,' he said, as he scrawled his name at the foot of the picture. 'In the old days, my sister Louise used to have Honthurst sign her work because his name fetched a better price.'

Chloë received the paper carefully and smiled at him.

'Thank you. It – it's the greatest compliment anyone ever paid me and I shall treasure it always.'

The Prince flashed a sardonically enquiring look at the silent Mr Deveril and, seeing it, she said quickly, 'I'll leave you to complete your business – but perhaps Your Highness would join us for dinner?' And, waiting only for His Highness to signify his acceptance, she fled.

Giles turned back from the window and looked at his former chief.

'Shall I go too?'

'No.' The easiness which had characterised Rupert for the last hour fell away like a sheared fleece, leaving him crisp and commanding.

'Sit down, gentlemen. I have a task which I hope won't prove beyond you. Indeed, I selected you in view of your past experience and your ability to keep your mouths shut. The matter we're about to discuss is both grave and secret – which is why I have come here in person and without, I hope, anyone being aware of it. It's vital, both for the success of your mission and for your personal safety, that no one suspects what you are doing. I don't offer you payment – only a challenge and an element of risk. Do I have your support?'

There was no doubt in the faces of either of his listeners.

'Certainly,' said Giles.

'As always,' said Alex, 'you need not have asked. What do you want us to do?'

The Prince reached out, dropped the pile of papers on the table between them and laid his outspread fingers on them.

'Unless I'm greatly mistaken, the Navy is at the mercy of a dangerous and high-skilled enemy agent. I want you to catch him.'

Mr Deveril's eyes opened guilelessly wide. 'On the premise that it takes one to know one? Yes. Well, we'll try not to disappoint you.' And to Mr Beckwith, 'You'll have to buy a new knife to hide beneath your cloak, Giles. You can't enter the best spying circles with outmoded accoutrements.'

Rupert was not amused.

'Stop trying to be funny and listen. You know – or you should do – how serious the political situation has become and how crucial is it that we seal the course of the war this summer. We are no longer at war merely with Holland but also with the French. The French fleet is small but its locations along the coast make it a force to be reckoned with. Their main base is Toulon but there are detachments at Brest and La Rochelle. If Holland and France mounted a simultaneous attack, England could find herself facing the Dutch to the north-east with the French nipping her backside from the south. Holland also has an alliance with Denmark and I have just heard that she made peace with Munster on the eighth. In addition, I'm told that – despite rumours to the contrary – Sweden has concluded an agreement with France. You have only to add that, as usual, we're critically short of money and the Navy is in debt to the tune of more than a million pounds and you'll perhaps appreciate why the last thing we can afford at this stage is a network of spies and saboteurs.'

Giles stirred thoughtfully. 'You said ... unless you were mistaken. I gather that means the evidence is negligible?'

His Highness nodded. 'With the exception of two minor incidents which I'll come to presently, the evidence – if you can call it that – is just a collection of costly organisational blunders. You'll find reports on each of them here.' He tapped the pile of papers. 'I suggest you both read them thoroughly at a later date. But if you want an example of the type of thing I'm referring to, let's consider the battle of Lowestoft last June. Having put the Dutch to flight, our fleet gave chase with the Duke of York's ship, the Royal Charles, leading. Like myself, James had been on deck for some eighteen hours so when the worst was past, he gave orders for the pursuit to continue and retired to his cabin. His flag-captain did the same and the ship sailed on under the command of John Harman. During the night, Harman received orders via Henry Brouncker that he was to slacken sail and abandon the chase – which he did, followed by the whole fleet. Next morning, with the enemy well past our reach, it turned out that the Duke had given no such order. It had been a fabrication of Brouncker's own and, not surprisingly, it cost him his position in the Duke's household.'

'Just that?' said Alex dryly. 'No further reprimand?'

'No. The matter was raised in Parliament but Brouncker was never brought to trial.' Rupert paused and then went on, 'For the rest, we come to a staggeringly large amount of trivia. The kind of thing one puts down to mismanagement, coincidence, poor workmanship, accident, carelessness or even plain, old-fashioned bad luck. It's only when you add it all up that it starts to look as if we're either jinxed or the target of sabotage. When you read the reports you'll see how many messages are delayed or incorrectly delivered; how many of our supplies are misdirected, damaged or lost in transit – or even never sent at all; and how many time-consuming accidents appear to occur in our dockyards. But what convinced me that all these incidents were part of an organised campaign were the two events I mentioned earlier.'

He flicked through the heap and extracted two sheets of paper.

'Three weeks ago a fire broke out in the store-house at Harwich. Fortunately, Silas Taylor and his lads quenched it before it did much damage and I filed a report of it in my collection. After all, fires do break out from time to time – and especially when the weather is as dry as it's been recently. So I thought little of it until last week when another fire broke out at John Longrack's timber-yard ... and this time our arsonist friend wasn't so clever.' Rupert leaned back in his chair. 'It was the day after that little shower last week and he must have had trouble getting the wood to take so he crossed the yard and fetched some pitch. That was when he was seen by someone who thought he was pilfering. When it became plain what he actually was doing, our ham-fisted friend set up a hue and cry instead of quietly knocking him on the head. The result was a mad chase three times round the timber-store before somebody stopped it by releasing a loaded platform of logs.' He paused and added triumphantly, 'The fire-raiser was one Joseph Cotterell – and he'd been employed at Harwich at the time of their fire.'

Alex rested his fingertips together and regarded the Prince over them.

'I was about to say that we could start with him ... but something tells me that we can't.'

'You can't,' agreed Rupert. 'When the logs came down he was rolled out like pastry. Sadly, you're going to have to start on a much wider field.'

'How wide?' asked Giles.

'If all our troubles are connected, there must be one man in charge of operations and, from the diversity of his activities, he has access to a fairly extensive range of Naval matters. There are a number of people of whom this is true and it's possible to identify them.' Rupert pulled a folded sheet of paper from his pocket. 'To the best of my knowledge, all of their names are on that list. I hope so anyway.'

'So do I,' said Alex, his eyes skimming down a column of some twenty names.

Rupert grinned and stood up, stretching.

'So there you have it. If I'm wrong, I'll be grateful if you prove it. If not, I want a name backed by indisputable evidence. And most of all, I want the man.'

'When do you join the fleet?' asked Giles.

'A week today. Albemarle and I are taking up our command at the Nore – though I doubt we'll put to sea for a while. Any further information of the kind you have there will come to you by way of Hayes, my secretary – you can trust him absolutely. And when I've gone, if you need official backing, you'd best go to Lord Arlington. But don't let him override your judgement.'

Mr Deveril looked up from the list, his eyes perfectly guileless.

'This list of Naval know-alls is incomplete,' he said gently. 'One hesitates to mention it – but Your Highness does not appear to be on it.'

Rupert looked back, irritation mingling with amusement.

'My Highness is thirsty,' he said. 'So why don't you apply your scintillating wit to something useful - and go and open a bottle.'

FOUR

Monday, April the twenty-third was a day of public rejoicing as befitted the feast day of Saint George and the anniversary of the King's coronation. For Alex and Giles, a week into their list and so far achieving nothing but an awareness of the scale of the task, the day was notable only for the departure of Prince Rupert and the Duke of Albemarle for the Nore.

Having read and re-read Rupert's notes, they still had no real clues to follow but knew that the Naval Office in Seething Lane contained information pertaining to most related matters. Alex duly despatched Mr Lewis to keep an eye on it while he and Giles began on the Naval Commissioners. Mr Beckwith went off to Chatham to investigate Peter Pett and Alex checked out Sir Thomas Harvey.

Both of them drew a blank, the first of many. But Matthew, placidly keeping his finger on the pulse of the Naval Office, was able to offer a piece of advice.

'If that Clerk of Acts isn't on your list, he ought to be. His name's Sam Pepys and I doubt there's much goes on in the Office that he don't know about.'

At the end of a week Mr Deveril had found out a good deal about Mr Pepys but none of it indicated any dealings in treason.

'He's honest,' he told Giles with a grin, 'in the only ways that matter to us. In other respects, he's a lecherous old goat. You'd be amazed what that man can do in a moving carriage or even in a doorway. And he's got women all over London – respectable matrons too because he doesn't seem to fancy the common harlotry.' He laughed. 'Even if our Samuel had the inclination to try a little sabotage, I doubt he'd find the time.'

Giles smiled, then leaned back in his chair and closed his eyes.

'Fortunate fellow. I often think,' he said languidly, 'that I must be missing something. Cross him off then – and Chicheley too while you're about it. He's in love with his work – cannon, saker and culverin. Who's next?'

Alex struck out the two names. 'Four down, sixteen to go. Christ! This could take months.'

'True. I should think though, that we might cross off York and Albemarle. It's hardly likely to be either of them and every little helps.'

'All right. Fourteen then. At this rate, it will still take us nearly two months.'

Mr Beckwith sighed and opened his eyes.

'Have you ever thought,' he asked, 'that it might not be any of them?'

Alex looked back reflectively.

'Have you ever thought that it might be someone employed in one of their households?'

Giles closed his eyes again.

'I have been trying,' he complained gently, 'not to think of it.'

* * *

Whitehall was still officially mourning the death of Luiza Maria of Braganza and, in addition to the usual trappings, the Queen had ordered that the ladies of the Court should dress their hair plainly and discard their patches. For those accustomed to, or dependant on, such aids this was a hardship of no mean order and a good many tongues remarked on the interesting fact that certain accredited beauties – notably my lady Castlemaine – looked a good deal less striking because of it.

To Chloë, whose only concession to cosmetics was the skilful darkening of her lashes and whose hair, by comparison, was always dressed simply, it made little difference. However, she had come a long way from the girl who, four months ago, rarely spared a thought for her appearance. A latent instinct for colour warned that her hair, which appeared garish against most bright shades, would render pastels insipid and that she must therefore choose very carefully. Most greens suited her, as did the darker hues of turquoise, and a cream and amethyst shot silk proved moderately pleasing. But Chloë knew there was one colour that would do more for her than any other and the period of Court mourning gave her an excuse to try it.

The resulting creation, a dramatically simple gown of supple black satin, was everything that she had hoped; indeed, it was more, for it even produced a reaction in Mr Deveril. For the very first time, the ice-blue gaze rested on her as if it saw more than the usual, mildly tedious responsibility. There was even, thought Chloë incredulously, an element of approval in it.

'My God,' said Alex at length. 'If Rupert was here, he'd be drawing you as Circe.'

And despite the mocking tone, she knew it was a compliment

She also knew, from the stares and turning heads at Whitehall, that it was not prejudiced – a thought which should have pleased her a great deal more than it did.

Less pleasing still was the unhealthy pallor of the Queen's face. Like Chloë, Catherine also wore black but, unlike her, it did not suit her and though her smile was a warm as ever, she looked tired and wan.

At the other end of the room, Lady Sarah Marsden dismissed her own personal little court and moved with all the graceful intent of a praying mantis towards Mr Deveril; and Alex, seeing her coming, neither advanced nor retreated.

'Well, my dear.' The kitten's eyes were bright with speculative amusement. 'Your wife is making progress. Your doing, I suppose? But you've a long way to go, I think, before she's more than merely presentable.'

'Jealous, Sarah?' he enquired pleasantly.

She laughed and shrugged elegant shoulders.

'Of the object of a drunken carouse? Hardly!' Her eyes trapped his and held them. 'She has nothing that I lack – or could not have if I wished.'

'She has a brain.'

This shaft missed its mark altogether. Sarah raised her brows and said, 'Really? I noticed that, since she couldn't be a Court beauty, she's decided to set up as Court Jester – but a brain? And if she had, what good would that be to you?' She smiled sweetly. 'You always used to have mundane requirements but high standards. So the last thing you want is a wife whose looks are no more than passable but who has the potential to shake your self-conceit.'

'The woman who could do that,' he remarked agreeably, 'hasn't been born yet. Something I fancy that we have in common.'

Again, his meaning escaped her and flicking open her fan she said, 'We've many things in common, Alex. In fact, we're very alike, you and I.'

'No. You may be like me – though I don't see how – but I, thank God, am nothing like you.' His glance strayed around the room. 'I don't see your devoted spouse here tonight.'

She looked up into the cool, impassive face and said in a tone limpid with innocence, 'No. He's in the country. He won't return until Saturday.'

The pale, translucent eyes widened. 'Sarah! You're not, by any chance, propositioning me, are you?'

And her ladyship, who – for the first time in her beautiful life – was doing just that, dropped her fan. Alex grinned and, with a smooth bow, retrieved it. 'You can't imagine how flattered I am.'

With an effort, she pulled herself together while the ambiguity sailed over her head.

'And so you should be – if it were true. As it is, I'm merely offering you the chance to admit you were wrong in your attitude to my marriage and to escape the tedium of your own ... for which I feel partly responsible.'

'You're too kind. Do you think I deserve it?'

'Probably not,' she replied with superb confidence. 'But I'm willing to give you the benefit of the doubt. Tomorrow evening I shall be alone. If you call, I will receive you.'

Mr Deveril turned the fan pensively between his fingers.

'You have a fascinating view of my character that is entirely your own,' he told her gently. 'I don't change my mind from minute to minute. And I myself hardly change at all.'

'Even to admit when you're wrong?' Faint irritation crept into Sarah's voice. 'Everything you said that day was out of pique. You didn't mean any of it.'

'Sadly,' mourned Alex, 'I'm very much afraid that I did.'

A purely natural flush touched the rose-petal cheeks.

'Including marrying that sandy-haired schoolgirl? Don't be so foolish!'

He sighed. 'Why does no one ever believe me?'

'Because you only talk for effect,' she snapped. 'Don't you realise that half the men in this room would give a fortune for what you're refusing?'

'Then I suggest,' smiled Alex, extending the fan on outstretched palms, 'that you offer it to them.'

For a second Sarah stared at him with utter disbelief and then, seizing her property, stalked off without a word.

Chloë, meanwhile, had been prised from the Queen's side by Cousin Simon who, it appeared was consumed with a burning desire to present her to his patron. Bluff and good-natured but totally lacking his brother's subtle charm, James, Duke of York received Chloë warmly, bestowed on her five minutes of amicable and wholly unexciting conversation and then bade her 'go and dance with this fancy popinjay of mine'; which, being a sort of royal command, she did.

It was when they left the floor that she found herself confronted by Lady Sarah Marsden, her hand on the arm of a swarthy gentleman in red and her eye lit by a vengeful gleam. Simon greeted them with every sign of affectionate pleasure.

'Sarah, my dear! How perfectly ravishing you look. I simply don't understand how Marsden can bear to tear himself from your side.'

She smiled and spread her hands resignedly. 'Oh – business. The estates, you know.' And, turning her attention to Chloë, 'I have just been telling your husband how fortunate he is. Poor Graham is forced to be away from me a whole week.'

Chloë received the implication with a blank stare.

'Oh? What a shame. But I expect he enjoys the rest and the change of air.'

The cornflower eyes narrowed a fraction and, instead of replying, Sarah chose to look up at her escort with a charming blend of coquetry and contrition. 'Oh George – how thoughtless I am! You don't know Mistress Deveril, do you?'

Dark, insolent eyes moved lingeringly from Chloë's face to her décolletage and back again. 'I haven't had that pleasure.'

Sarah's mouth curved happily. 'Then allow me to present you. My dear,' she said to Chloë, 'this is Lord George Gresham.'

And that, thought Chloë, explained a lot. Court gossip said George Gresham was not only notorious rake but also extremely rich.

He kissed her hand with unnecessary warmth.

'Charming,' he murmured, 'quite charming. But then, Devewil's taste always is.' Which made everyone smile but Chloë who was busy wondering how she could get away from the bad company into which she had accidentally fallen.

'Mistress Deveril,' Sarah was saying kindly, 'is still very new to our life here so we must help her all we can. I vow Alex is so neglectful that he doesn't deserve so devoted a wife.'

Chloë looked back reprovingly.

'Not neglectful, my lady – merely trusting. He knows, you see, that he can.'

George Gresham was unused to being ignored by little ingénues and he had, moreover, a score to settle with Mistress Deveril's husband. He said, 'Weally? But perhaps he has had no worthy wival. I wonder who might appeal to you, Mistwess? My lord Rochester, perhaps?'

'Or Prince Rupert,' suggested Simon, re-entering the lists with a vengeance.

If Chloë hesitated, it was only for a second.

'I haven't the pleasure of the Prince's acquaintance. And then, in my simple, rustic way, I find I'm more than satisfied with my husband.'

'Such loyalty,' cooed Sarah. 'Aren't you jealous, George?'

Lord Gresham smiled and his eyes caressed Chloë thoughtfully.

'I am never jealous,' he replied. 'I am merely filled with a devouwing cuwiosity to know Mistwess Devewil better.'

The submerged unpleasantness of the conversation was beginning to annoy Chloë but she still thought of and discarded three possible answers before saying brightly, 'How nice. You must come to supper some time. All of you. And then we can all get to know each other better. Including, it goes without saying, my husband.' And was rather pleased with the silence she produced.

A hand touched her elbow and she turned to find Mr Fawsley's blessedly friendly face at her side. He greeted her companions politely but without any enthusiasm and said, 'I've been looking for you everywhere, Chloë. An old friend has turned up and I promised to take you to him.'

'Oh? Who is it?' she asked eagerly while her eyes flashed signals at him.

'Wait and see,' he replied obediently. He bowed stiffly to the others and placed Chloë's hand on his arm saying, 'If you will excuse us?' And promptly led her away.

'Who is it?' she asked again as they moved out of earshot. 'I suppose there is someone?'

'Never mind that,' said Danny shortly. 'What you do think you were doing with that precious trio? You should know you can't trust Simon – and Sarah and Gresham are downright trouble-makers. She's already approached Alex this evening – though, judging from his mood, I've an idea it didn't do her much good – which is probably why she introduced you to lisping George.'

Chloë shot him a very direct glance. 'What do you mean?'

'About what? Gresham?'

'No. I understood that. About Alex and Lady Sarah.'

'Oh that.' Danny grinned. 'I'd say she was casting her bread on the waters – if you see what I mean.'

She drew a long breath. 'Yes. I think so. And what about Mr - Alex's mood?'

Rupert had taught her a lesson she had not forgotten.

'Oh he's sickeningly cheerful. The way he always is when he's found someone to be bloody rude to.' He grimaced. 'Sorry.'

Chloë grinned. 'For what? It's the best news I've heard tonight.'

Danny steered her towards the side of the room but he had no need to tell her who the surprise visitor was for she saw for herself.

'Why – Freddy!' She smiled, holding out her hand.

Freddy, uncomfortably conscious of the elegance of his surroundings and company, the splendours of his new coat and the tightness of his collar, took it and smiled back nervously.

'Hello, Chloë. I say … you look different. Wouldn't have known you.'

'It's only skin deep,' offered Danny cheerfully.

Chloë ignored him. 'It's lovely to see you, Freddy. Is it just a visit?'

He nodded, relaxing a little. 'Tired of Oxford, you know. Thought I'd come and see how you all were. Which reminds me.' Gloom settled on his face. 'Got a message for you from Ashton. But it ain' the kind of thing one likes saying to a lady.'

Caught in the act of sipping his wine, Danny gave a splutter of laughter and choked.

Chloë patted him absently on the back and said, 'Don't worry, Freddy. My brother can stew in his own ill-humour all he likes but I don't have to hear it.'

'What she really means,' explained Danny, 'is that she's got enough problems. Alex has more humours than anyone. They're just different, that's all.'

Freddy shook his head dubiously. 'Can't – '

'Say that!' chanted Chloë and Danny in unison.

* * *

On the evening of May the twenty-third, Chloë gave a small, informal supper to which were bidden Lady Julia and Sir Thomas Blanchard, Giles, Danny and Freddy. She had tried to persuade Mr Lewis to join them but received only an acidulous grin and the information that he was engaged with a party of friends at the Swan in New Palace Yard.

No disaster occurred to mar Mistress Jackson's culinary skills and Chloë, exotic in peacock brocade, was able to sit serenely at table and enjoy with her guests a menu of roast chicken, venison, beef-and-oyster pie, Lisbon melons, syllabubs, fruit tarts and cheeses, all washed down with light Rhenish wine.

Afterwards they removed to the parlour where Julia, having been persuaded to bring her lute with her, played melodies by Dowland, Morley and Wilbye before turning her talents to more popular songs and encouraging them all to join in. The evening passed in pleasant conviviality until interrupted by a tap at the door, followed by Naomi's head and the intelligence that Mr Lewis had returned and expressed a wish to speak with the master.

Mr Deveril and Mr Beckwith exchanged a brief glance, then Alex said, 'He'd better come in then. Unless it's a secret.'

The hayrick head vanished and Matthew emerged through the doorway.

'It's no secret,' he announced tersely. 'I just thought you'd like to know that they say the French are about to drop on us like bugs at harvesting.'

There was silence. Finally, Alex rose and poured a glass of brandy which he gave to Matt.

'You were right. Sit down and tell us.'

'I heard it at the Swan from one of the Duke of York's lads. He said Charles Talbot brought the Elizabeth into Falmouth yesterday with a report of thirty-six French sail under Beaufort approaching the Channel.'

Mr Deveril's eyes narrowed a little. 'Does York believe it reliable?'

'Aye. And what's more, it seems His Highness thought it worth his while to make a little contingency plan for it before he joined the fleet.' Matt grinned sourly. 'It makes your heart bleed for them. By all accounts, York's staff and the commissioners have spent all day chasing their own tails trying to put it into operation. The King's sent an order to the Prince that he's to stop Beaufort joining de Ruyter's Dutchies and – '

'Wait,' said Alex. 'Do we know if the Dutch are at sea or about to sail or planning to holiday at home this summer?'

'No,' said Matthew, 'to all three. Lord Arlington hasn't got any recent news of de Ruyter's movements. If you ask me, the man couldn't get the juice out of an orange.'

'Quite,' said Mr Deveril bitterly. He looked at Giles. 'It seems our intelligence service is in perpetual hibernation. Christ! What the hell to they think they're doing?'

'What they believe is their best, I imagine,' said Tom Blanchard pacifically. 'Go on, Matt. How is Rupert going to deal with the situation?'

'The fleet's to be split,' answered Matthew without looking at Alex. 'Albemarle's to keep sixty sail in case the Dutch come out and the Prince is taking twenty-four and hoping to get ten more from Plymouth. They're moving the whole lot from the Nore to the Downs and His Highness will sail on south to intercept Beaufort.'

There was another long pause. Alex looked again at Giles.

'If Rupert doesn't get his extra ships he'll be two against three ... and if de Ruyter does come out, it won't be with less than eighty sail which gives Albemarle similar odds. I wonder,' mused Alex, 'how wise we are to put our faith in Captain Talbot?'

Daniel, who had listened throughout with an air of suppressed excitement, surged to his feet. 'Who cares? It'll be one hell of a fight – and I don't intend to miss it.'

Giles directed a lazy smile at him. 'In which case we can't lose.'

Danny grinned back. 'Glad you realise it.'

Freddy regarded him with interest. 'You ever been to sea, Danny?'

'Not really. I don't think just crossing the Channel counts.'

'Me neither. Tell you what ... if you go, I'll go.'

He was immediately impaled by six pairs of astonished eyes.

'You?' asked Julia, laughing. 'I don't believe it.'

'Are you serious?' asked Danny.

Freddy nodded.

'Are you sober?' asked Alex.

'No,' said Chloë crossly. 'Neither of them are.'

'Yes,' said Freddy simply. 'I am.'

Danny held out his hand. 'Done. We'll go together.'

'Done,' agreed Freddy, taking the hand. 'When?'

Daniel grinned sadistically. 'Tomorrow. At dawn.'

* * *

Chloë managed to seize a few minutes alone with Danny before he left.

'I wish you wouldn't go. You're sure about it?'

'Of course, I'm sure. I want to go. You can understand that, can't you?'

'Yes. It's just – oh, I don't know.' Then, irritably, 'Yes, I do. I'll miss you, damn it!'

'Because I'm the only one who dances the couranto without treading on your feet?' He paused and then pulled a face. 'I'll miss you too.'

For a second Chloë stood, still and demure in her blue-green gown and then, without warning she put her arms around him in a fierce hug. 'Good. Then you won't stay to fight the whole war.'

'No.' Surprised and rather moved, Danny hugged her back and kissed her cheek. 'Goodbye, my dear.' And was gone.

FIVE

On the twenty-eighth of May, the eve of both the King's birthday and the anniversary of his Restoration, the City of London planned to celebrate the double event with a Grand Banquet and Masque at the Guildhall. It was to be a memorably spectacular blend of food and culture, purposely designed to eclipse the similar function which would take place at Whitehall on the day itself and to which the Aldermen and Guild-masters had not been invited.

It was certainly to prove memorable and, even, in its way, spectacular. The first sign that the occasion might not go exactly to plan was when a corner of the embroidered awning fell on the head of an Alderman. Mr Deveril watched through the carriage window as the afflicted gentleman strove to uphold the canopy while the Lord Mayor finished his lengthy speech of welcome. By the time it was over, he had changed arms three times and Alex remarked that he was glad it was only the royal party under there.

Inside the banqueting hall, below the royal dais, chaos reigned as merchants and their wives jostled for the best seats. Alex glanced about him and then, looking at Chloë, said, 'I suppose we could shout 'Fire!'.'

'We could,' she agreed. 'But not while we're standing in the doorway. Let's just find a seat. Any seat.'

Mr Deveril took her arm and forged a path through the crush to a table where there were just two empty places. On one side sat the Earl and Countess of Falmouth ... and, on the other, Mr Simon Deveril and Lady Sarah Marsden.

'Wonderful,' said Alex, not quite under his breath. 'It's going to be one of those days when one should just have stayed in bed.'

'Speak for yourself,' said Chloë. And, choosing the seat beside Lord Falmouth, sank into it with a swish of cream shot-silk.

Alex bathed Simon and Sarah in a too-bright smile.

'How nice of you to save us a place,' he said. And sitting down, 'Let the games begin.'

Chloë, chatting lightly with Charles Berkeley and his wife, was trying hard not to listen to that other conversation on her right and finding it difficult. She smiled at the Earl and asked him when he would be rejoining the fleet.

'Tomorrow,' he said cheerfully, 'as early as I can manage it. I'd have returned today but that I'd rather face Albemarle's wrath than the scold I'd have had for failing to escort my lady here this afternoon.'

And Lady Falmouth, who was young, pretty and, in Chloë's opinion, quite the nicest of the Duchess of York's ladies, flushed and laughed.

'I should think so too! Heaven only knows when I'll see you again after tonight – and Her Grace released me specially so that we could come here together.'

Chloë made a suitable reply and came to the conclusion that, though maintaining a happy ignorance might do for an ostrich, it wasn't for her. With reluctant efficiency, she proceeded to lend an ear to what Cousin Simon was saying to Mr Deveril and promptly learned that what people said of eavesdroppers was true.

'But, of course, dear Chloë is so very … challenging, is she not? I know that Gresham finds her so.' The soft voice held a thinly veiled innuendo. 'And we all know how His Majesty admires her.'

'Do we?' asked Alex mildly. 'But you know … one could almost believe that you are jealous. The only question is – of whom?'

And that, thought Chloë, definitely took care of that.

Her husband, meanwhile, had turned to Lady Sarah.

'Still without your estimable spouse, I see?'

She shrugged. 'At home in bed. He hasn't been well lately – his heart, the doctor says.'

'Really?' The pleasant voice was reproachful. 'I'm surprised you chose to leave him.'

'I have nursed him,' returned Sarah grittily, 'for three days and now he's much better. He has his man-servant and he said I was to go and enjoy myself – so I have. Is there anything wrong with that?'

'You tell me,' invited Alex. 'But how fortunate that my cousin was able to escort you. What you might call keeping it in the family.'

The food began to arrive, borne aloft on silver salvers by line upon line of liveried servers. It wasn't that there was anything wrong with it;

on the contrary, it was well-cooked, artistically presented and carefully-served. It was simply that there was too much of it. For in an orgy of competitive pride, the butchers had striven to outshine the fishmongers and the pastry-cooks to demonstrate their superiority over the bakers – and the result was a menu of unrivalled variety and imagination. And in it came on relentless feet and in no particular order, scenting the air with an exotic blend of aromas and filling every available space until the boards creaked beneath the weight.

Alex surveyed it in fascination and said, 'They've catered for the five thousand.'

Chloë looked and felt her appetite disappear along with an impulse to giggle.

Sirloins of beef lay flanked by cheeses and jellies; the hams jostled the syllabubs and the lobsters lay cheek by jowl with strawberries and quails; roasted geese looked down on oysters and custards and a suckling pig, its mouth full of apple, glared balefully at a panoplied peacock; the mackerel breathed over the sweetmeats and the salmon slyly nudged the fruit tartlets, while delicately placed piles of oranges loomed ominously over venison pasties and cream darioles. There were chickens and melons, cakes, pies, rabbits, pears and flans – all arranged in flagrant and riotous disorder – and, not to be outdone, the wine-merchants had provided untold casks and bottles of their best wares. The City of London had surpassed itself.

Chloë drew a long bracing breath and turned to look at her husband, who grinned quizzically.

'Take your pick,' he said waving to the laden table. 'Choose the lobster and you'll upset the butchers – take the peacock and the fishmongers will never forgive you. Less a feast, you might say, than a competition.' He offered her a parsley-trimmed salmon. 'For what we're about to receive, may the Lord make our digestions sturdy.'

'Amen,' sighed Chloë, resignedly helping herself from the dish.

For the next two hours each of the City's two hundred guests tried (to a greater or lesser degree, depending on their capacity) to do justice to the banquet – and failed. Indeed, a few of them failed before that and were forced to retire to places less public. One of these, as luck would have it, was Simon Deveril and, smiling vaguely, Alex watched him go.

'He that eats and runs away... ,' he murmured.

With funereal pomp, the remains of the feast were cleared away and some of the boards withdrawn to make room for the entertainment. Chloë observed that, though by no means drunk, Mr Deveril was at that hazy stage some way removed from sobriety. She sat back to watch the masque.

'Oh Majesty enthroned with Sceptred Rod
Oh King in Might; Oh Crown, oh Throne - - '

'Oh God,' said Alex, looking across at Lord Falmouth. 'They didn't commission John Ogilby to write it?'

The Earl nodded. 'Bludworth liked his verse translation of Aesop. Personally, I'd call it an acquired taste.'

'You mean it's awful.'

'It's awful,' agreed the Earl, 'but perhaps this will be better.'

'I doubt it,' said Alex, settling back in his seat. 'So let's enjoy it.'

The narrator, meanwhile, had raised his voice to something approaching a shout.

'Our task tonight good Masters is to tell
In epic lines, a tale of danger fell
From which our King was plucked by Fortune's smile
To rise like Phoebus o'er his Foemen vile.'

'They're doing the King's escape after Worcester,' said Lady Falmouth gently. 'I think perhaps they've made a mistake.'

'Probably,' replied the Earl. 'But His Majesty will love it even if it's abysmal.'

'If you don't mind,' said Lady Sarah freezingly, 'some of us are trying to listen.'

'Good for you,' said Alex. 'It would be a shame to miss poetry like this.'

'O Woe, thrice Woe! The battle's roar is done
And all is lost beneath the setting sun.
The fated sky grows dim; the angels weep –

'And pinching Shakespeare's words is pretty cheap,' finished Alex, folding his arms. 'Are we in for spot-the-quotation time?'

'Well, if we are,' said Chloë repressively, 'I'm sure you'll be the one to inform us of it.'

Apparently tired both of listening and being ignored, Lady Sarah gestured to the six oddly-robed damsels ranged behind the narrator and said, 'Those women – what are they supposed to be?'

Leaning back between his former mistress and his titular wife, Alex glanced from one to the other and then, choosing Chloë, said, 'She wants to know who the six lovelies are and I don't know. Do you?'

'Well, I think,' said Chloë cautiously, 'that they are the Muses.'

'She says they're Muses,' he told Sarah. And then, again to Chloë, 'Shouldn't there be nine of them?'

'Yes. But do you really want three more?'

'Like these? No.' Mr Deveril eyed the Muses critically. 'I wonder why the one in blue has her finger in her mouth ... or no. Polyhymnia, do you think? Muse of Mimic Art?'

'Very likely.' Chloë was trying not to laugh and finding it difficult. She pointed to the five homespun-clad youths who had just come in. 'And those?'

'They're the Penderel brothers,' said the Earl, 'Oh Lord – is that meant to be the King?'

They all looked at the florid, beefy figure. Chloë stifled a giggle, Lady Falmouth hid behind her fan and Mr Deveril and his lordship dissolved into not quite silent mirth. Lady Sarah eyed them all with cold incomprehension.

Things got worse rather than better. The famous oak tree got wedged in the doorway and finally arrived minus a branch or two ... and Terpsichore executed an enthusiastic, rather than graceful dance around it while the King crouched symbolically beneath its painted boughs. The viols scraped and the noise level rose.

'I don't think I can take much more of this,' said the Earl a little wildly.

'You'll have to,' replied Chloë. 'The tree's stuck again.'

A large soprano accompanied by Euterpe's lute was making an ineffective attempt to be heard over the chatter. Chloë winced as the heavy voice wobbled through a flood of semi-quavers in the upper extremity of its range.

'That's Jane Lane,' Alex told her. 'The King posed as her groom and they rode pillion to Bristol. Those two would need an elephant. Oh good – they've got rid of the tree. Now the Roundheads can get in.'

Clinging grimly to the shred of her composure, Chloë watched the soldiers blundering down the hall. Two of them became inexplicably entangled and a third ended in the Earl of Rochester's lap. Meanwhile the Muse of History screeched verses over the din.

'Oh men of iron! Oh beasts of cloven foot!

In massy hordes come seeking blood to gloot – '

'Gloot?' asked Alex.

'Glut,' supplied Chloë unsteadily.

'Their hungry blades; oh woe and thrice, thrice woe!'

'Alas! Alack! Ah me! And thrice ditto,' finished Mr Deveril triumphantly.

'Stop,' gasped Chloë, sorely tried. 'They're doing their best.'

'Perhaps. But it's a comedy but they left Thalia out. She's wreaking her revenge. Look -they've got trouble with the doors again.'

'It – it's a ship!'

Alex nodded. 'The Surprise ... what a pity they bent the mast. It looks a little limp, don't you think?'

It did but it trundled on towards the beckoning Muse of Astronomy and narrowly avoided running her down. The King stepped cautiously aboard and the ship turned and set sail for France. Urania, brandishing her compass, lured it from a safe distance and Calliope boomed an epic farewell.

'And so adieu! Sail safe o'er waters blue

While England to itself rests all untrue;

For thou wert saved by God's Celestial hand

To rule restored once more in this fair land.'

It was not quite the end, however. As the Surprise rolled back down the hall, she raised her hatch-covers and out of them flew a cloud of white doves. Out and up they winged their way, blurring the high, painted ceiling and startling the well-dressed noisy gathering below into silence at last.

Mr Deveril watched them appraisingly.

'I don't think,' he said at length, 'that this was a good idea.'

'No,' agreed Chloë. 'One of them is sitting on the Lord Mayor's hat.'

'And that is the least of our worries. Birds have some nasty habits.'

The words had barely left his mouth when there was a loud splat from somewhere near at hand and turning, they saw that one particular nasty habit had been delivered on the table in front of Lady Sarah who was staring at it with picturesque revulsion.

It was too much. Their powers of endurance severely over-strained, Chloë and Alex collapsed into helpless laughter.

* * *

Later on, still hiccupping faintly, they said goodbye to Lord and Lady Falmouth and climbed into their carriage. It was a little after nine o'clock and, remembering that Mr Beckwith was supping with the Blanchards, Mr Deveril suddenly decided to visit his sister. He therefore ordered the coachman to take them to Wych Street and, sweeping Chloë with him, entered Julia's house happily chanting, 'Oh Woe and thrice, thrice Woe!'

One look at their faces was enough to prompt Sir Thomas into begging for a description of the evening's glories and, nothing loth, Alex proceeded to oblige him. By the time he reached the part played by the oak tree, Julia was helpless with laughter and her husband actually crying; but Giles, who at first had been equally amused, abruptly found himself watching Chloë. And Chloë, of course, was watching Alex.

He knew what she was seeing. He'd seen it himself countless times in the past but never in the last six years; never since they'd all returned to England and Alex had discovered that, despite his father having died for the King and he himself having spent half his life fighting to see Charles returned to his throne, his own birth-right had been handed over to Simon Deveril. Worse still, the King he continued to serve lacked the power to set things right. And so, since then, Alex's wit had always contained a thread of bitterness and was rarely completely free of mockery. The part of him that enjoyed the ridiculous and rejoiced in the absurd had been locked away behind impenetrable barriers ... and wouldn't have surfaced now, Giles thought, had the evening's debacle not been floated on a glass of wine too many.

Chloë sat very straight, her cheeks faintly flushed and a light in her eyes that Giles had no difficulty in interpreting. He felt as if a knife was twisting in his stomach. She was sensible and level-headed, yes ... but that was no protection against Alex at his most magnetic. He had tried to warn her not to be blinded by the good looks and easy charm ... but it was happening anyway, right now under his nose. He wondered if she realised it ... or if Alex had any idea what he had done.

Alex had just launched into a rendering of Oh Men of iron! and, though he glanced at Chloë, he didn't appear to notice the candle lighting her gaze. Giles wanted to shake him – to break the spell and make him stop. But Julia and Tom were still laughing and Giles was too well-bred to make a scene – particularly one he'd have difficulty explaining. He looked back at Chloë and saw a change. Her back was still straight but she no longer looked at Alex. Instead, her eyes stared down at her hands, gripped so tight in her lap that the knuckles glowed white. And Giles had his answer.

Chloë took a long breath and recovered her composure. It was hard, when one was no silly romantic girl, to accept that one could fall heedlessly in love at first sight. Common sense said that it was quite impossible; it warned that there was no future in it and that epic love stories belonged in poetry.

It made no difference. The fact remained that she had fallen in love with Alex Deveril at their first meeting and had known it from the second; and that was why she had allowed herself to be rushed into marriage. One might be twenty and practical but there were times, even so, when one's vision overcame one's judgement. In the space of a painfully exquisite moment in the frosty moonlight of an Oxford street, she had allowed herself a moment of hopeful indulgence and it had proved too strong a temptation.

With the morning had come a return to uncompromising reality. He had been drunk, she had been stupid and there was no basis for a relationship between them – now or ever. Furthermore, her feelings for him were unreasoning and she knew it. The only sane course was to terminate their crazy marriage and put aside the knowledge that she'd met the only man she wanted and that he was not for her.

But the marriage had not been terminated and gradually, over the weeks, had come some of the understanding she had lacked. His brusque, unexpected kindness on the day of Sarah's wedding when she had deliberately goaded him into losing his temper; the laughter in her sooty kitchen and the necklace at Whitehall which, she had later realised, had been given because he knew she was frightened. He was sometimes intemperate, often utterly provoking and always unpredictable. But he was never truly unkind or mean-spirited. He was like a fascinating puzzle that one could never quite unravel. And though she knew he did not love her and almost certainly never would, she also knew that her heart was given irrevocably – and that he must never know it.

From across the room, Giles still watched her and thought he understood. For an instant, his nerves felt raw and a blind anger consumed him. Abruptly, he rose from his chair, made an excuse and left swiftly before anyone could question him. There was a limit to his powers of endurance and concealment and he knew that he had reached it.

Walking to his lodging, he gave careful thought to the situation and, by the time, he entered his rooms, had reached the only possible decision. He'd tried to stay away from Chloë as far as it was possible but it hadn't done any good. It was time to put real distance between them. An hour later he was riding hard eastwards out of London, having left a brief, untruthful letter of explanation to be delivered to Mr Deveril. At Chatham he changed horses and, obtaining the information he wanted, rode on through the early hours of the morning.

By six o'clock he was in Canterbury and just before eight he reached Deal. He was only just in time. The Royal James and her squadron were under canvas and preparing to sail. Giles hired a ketch, instructed its owner to signal the flagship and had himself rowed out and taken aboard.

Having spent his last hours of preparation in the irritating half-expectancy of receiving fresh orders, Rupert was busy and not in the best of humours. He greeted Giles curtly and with some surprise but, having completed a feu de joie of orders, he took him below and announced that he could spare him just ten minutes.

'Two will do,' responded Mr Beckwith in level tones. 'I haven't come to bring you a report. As yet there's nothing to tell. I'm here because I want you to take me as a super-numerary.'

'I thought,' said the Prince crisply, 'that I had made it plain that you could be of more use to me in London.'

A tinge of colour stained Giles' cheeks.

'You did, sir. But Alex can handle it – and, if he finds anything, I can always go back. I'm not proposing to join your command permanently. Only for a few weeks.'

The dark eyes examined him thoughtfully. 'Why?'

'Because,' replied Giles concisely, 'I'm in love with Alex's wife.'

His Highness did not appear surprised. 'And?'

His attitude threw Mr Beckwith slightly off balance.

'And what?'

The Prince made a gesture of impatience.

'I'm presuming there must be more to it than that,' he said, 'because you already knew this when I saw you last month, didn't you?'

Giles drew off his gloves and turned them over and over in his hands.

'Yes. You're right, of course. The difference is that a month ago, I didn't know she cared for Alex – and now I do.'

'I see. And Alex?'

Mr Beckwith shook his head and, tossing his gloves on to a table, turned to look out across the Downs.

'If he felt anything for her, he would see it – just as I have. But he doesn't. Last night, quite by accident, she saw him at his best but that's a rare occurrence these days. Unless something changes and Alex starts to appreciate what he has, Chloë's going to spend her life hoping for something that will never happen. And I don't want to watch it.'

'Are you saying,' asked Rupert, 'that you would be happier if you knew you had no hope?'

Giles turned round and his eyes were bleak.

'I've none anyway. Alex is my friend.'

The Prince stared back for a moment, a wry smile touching the corners of his mouth.

'Quite,' he said at length. 'It's an impossible position – and by no means as unique as you may think. If it's any comfort, you may be assured of my sympathy.'

Somewhere in Giles' tired brain recollection stirred, only to be dismissed.

'Thank you, sir. Then I may stay?'

Rupert nodded and the smile became a grin.

'Yes. But you'll have to put up with cramped quarters. I've taken on eleven others as well as yourself – and Pepys will probably have a seizure when he finds out.' He opened the door to go back on deck and then, turning round added quietly, 'And you were quite right. Her name was Mary.'

SIX

By the time Mr Beckwith joined Prince Rupert and set off southwards to intercept the Duc de Beaufort's French flotilla, Danny and Freddy had already been assigned, separate and sad, to the fleet. Freddy lay aboard the Portland, while to Danny went the honour of serving under Rear-Admiral Sir John Harman in the Henry.

On May the thirtieth word reached Whitehall that, contrary to previous tidings, the French were fixed at La Rochelle with every appearance of remaining there. Having already divided the fleet, this was certainly irritating; but when further news told that the Dutch had put to sea on the twenty-ninth with some ninety ships, it was seen to be critical.

The King ordered the immediate recall of Rupert, and Sir William Coventry swiftly drew up the necessary papers and carried them to the Duke of York for signature. It was close on midnight and the Duke was abed but he dutifully appended his seal and, yawning, added the advice that Albemarle would do well to remove from the Downs to Gunfleet.

Desirous of despatching the orders by special courier, Coventry set off for Goring House only to find that the Secretary of State, Lord Arlington, was also in bed. Sir William wasted twenty precious minutes attempting to persuade his lordship's servants to wake him before giving up in furious disgust and having the papers forwarded by express post. By the time they were handed to Rupert on the first of June, he had reached the Isle of Wight.

Albemarle, meanwhile, had weighed anchor early that morning on a fresh, south-westerly wind and was starting for Gunfleet when his scouts fired a warning that the enemy lay to their leeward, mid-way between Dunkirk and North Foreland. He instantly summoned a Council of War and this proved a sore trial for everyone present. Sir John Harman and many of the other senior commanders expressed grave doubts about the wisdom of giving battle. The wind, they said, though in the right quarter, was too strong and would result in loss of formation and an elevation too acute for the use of their lowest gun-decks; and they were substantially outnumbered. Albemarle brushed their qualms aside and then when, tempers rising they persisted, came perilously close to openly ascribing their reservations to cowardice. The meeting was concluded in a mood of resentment and rigidly controlled anger.

At an hour before noon, the fleet formed into line of battle and bore down upon the disarmed and unsuspecting enemy who, caught in the act of weighing anchor, were forced to cut their cables in order to meet the attack. But, as Harman had said, the wind proved a mixed blessing and within minutes the English van had outstripped its centre while the rear became a uselessly straggling muddle. With no attempt to send in fire-ships, they sailed south-east down the Dutch line to engage its rear under Admiral Tromp; only then, with masterly aplomb, de Ruyter brought his van and centre into play.

The ensuing mêlée lasted for some three hours while the smoke-laden air was rent with cannon-fire and the screams of the wounded until, at about two in the afternoon, Albemarle tacked back to the north-east. This manoeuvre successfully completed their disarray by causing the van and the rear to change places, whilst carrying them directly into the Dutch centre. Not surprisingly, this reversal caused total confusion during which the Henry and the Swiftsure became isolated from the main force.

A feral gleam lit Harman's eye as he assimilated his position.

'Crass, bloody stupidity!' he swore, in what Mr Fawsley could only assume to be a comment on Albemarle's tactics. And then emitted a stream of orders to minimise their danger.

This was very great – and not only from the murderous cannon-fire of the Dutch rear-guard. The Swiftsure was already disabled and being boarded from every side and, swallowing a sob of impotent fury, Danny turned away to find a fire-ship blazing down on their port bow.

He did not stop to think. Even as the grappling-irons seized the Henry's side, he grabbed a rope and, leaping up on the gunwhale, swung himself aboard the roaring, crackling pyre. Smoke filled his lungs with choking agony and the heat scorched his skin as he sought swiftly for the grapnel bolts; and then, finding them, had to work by touch as his eyes streamed with scalding tears. The first iron fell loose and then the second. It seemed to take a lifetime. He reached the last hook and released it, his chest a raw and aching anguish and his hands burned and blistering.

He never knew how he got back aboard the *Henry*. And, lying on the deck in a paroxysm of coughing, he was equally unaware that, approaching on the luff, a second fire-ship had succeeded in setting light to their sails. He recovered in time to watch men frantically hauling down burning canvas; and by then the third fire-ship was on its way. Danny staggered to his feet and glanced at Sir John with a vestige of grim hilarity.

'Christ,' he said hoarsely. 'I'm sick of this. It's becoming damned personal!'

Harman's reply was to issue a calm order to his master-gunner. A minute later four of their demi-cannon blasted a quartet of thirty-pound shots straight into the belly of the approaching vessel and the Admiral's mouth exhibited faint signs of satisfaction.

'One to us,' he said laconically. And then, 'Evertsen's running up a signal ... well, well – he's offering us quarter.' He turned to order the signalling of a refusal. 'It seems a shame to disappoint him ... but it hasn't come to that yet. Mr Corwen – prepare a full volley and fire when ready.'

Mr Corwen did so and had the pleasure of seeing his guns cripple the Dutch flagship. Harman, meanwhile, cast an experienced eye over his damaged sails and rigging and regretfully announced that they had no choice but to put into Aldeburgh for repairs.

* * *

Woken at dawn next day by the sound of cannon-fire, Danny took himself off to attend to his duties and glean the latest news. It was around three in the afternoon when he was on the point of informing Harman that their repairs were all but complete that he sighted the *Portland* limping into harbour. Half an hour later, he and Freddy were eyeing each other over two welcome tankards of ale.

'Well?' asked Danny. 'What happened? Your starboard side looks as if someone took it apart then forgot where the pieces went.'

An expression of disgust crept over Mr Iverson's amiable countenance.

'We had a run-in with the *Guernsey*.'

Danny howled with laughter. 'You mean it was one of ours?'

Freddy nodded. 'Came off all right from the Dutch – and then some silly fellow tacks right into us. Makes you sick.' He appeared to dwell on this thought and then said, 'Any word of the Prince?'

'Rupert? No. Why do you ask?'

'Lot of talk,' came the succinct reply.

'What talk?'

'Kind you'd expect,' said Freddy with unaccustomed cynicism. 'Got to blame somebody, you know. Not that it makes any difference. Reckon we'll be in retreat in a couple of hours.'

Danny tried to work this out and failed. 'Why?'

'Wind's dropped. Our pilot says it might come up from the north and Albemarle won't like that. He's in a cautious mood today. Could have surrounded 'em this afternoon but he didn't. If you ask me, he's waiting for Rupert.' He shook his head dubiously. 'Silly, really – because it stands to reason he ain't going to be with us before tomorrow. Not without any wind.'

Draining his mug, Daniel bent a fascinated stare upon his friend.

'I can't quite believe it,' he said slowly, 'but I'm damned if you're not enjoying yourself.'

Freddy coloured slightly and grinned. 'Yes,' he said simply. 'I am.'

* * *

Re-joining the fleet late that afternoon, Danny swiftly discovered how accurate Freddy's conjectures had been. No sooner had the Henry come up with the rest of its squadron than word came to make a fighting retreat towards Gunfleet – an operation which was conducted with a panache that went a long way towards restoring Danny's faith in the Admiral-General.

The morning of Whit Sunday dawned on a flat calm which lasted till noon when a fresh easterly breeze sprang up and enabled the English to continue their leisurely retreat. And then, at shortly before one, the Henry was hailed by a fishing-trawler with the news that Prince Rupert's squadron had been sighted off the Goodwin Sands at nine that morning.

Harman received the tidings with a terse expression of relief and instantly sent Danny to the Royal Charles to tell Albemarle. 'For we'd best halt this retreat before we leave His Highness stranded on the other side of the enemy.'

The Duke apparently thought so too for he immediately gave the necessary order. Then, rather to Danny's surprise, he produced a wallet of letters and requested him to deliver them to Harwich before returning to the Henry.

'And while you are there,' said the Duke gruffly, 'I'd be obliged if you will look in on Clerke – Sir William, you know. Poor fellow lost his leg on Friday and he was unconscious when we put him ashore. One of York's young men who is serving as a volunteer offered to stay with him in case he wakes – but they're not hopeful.'

Danny cleared his throat. 'I'm a little acquainted with Sir William, sir – he's a friend of my uncle. Is there any message you wished me to give?'

'No – no.' Albemarle rose from his desk and limped painfully to the window. 'Damned leg of mine! Same shot that got Willie, y'know.' He paused, frowning out to sea. 'Just wanted him to understand I'd be there if I could. No. He knows that. Tell him – tell him to watch out for himself and not to worry. With His Highness come up to us, we'll have de Ruyter on the run in no time. Just tell him that.'

By the time Danny returned from Harwich the day's action was almost over and he found himself with little to do except consider the brief and wholly astonishing suggestions made to him by a man was clearly dying. He wished that Alex or Giles were there to be consulted; but, since they were not, he eventually decided that, for the present, the only useful thing he could do was remain silent.

Throughout the evening, the men celebrated Rupert's arrival and tried to forget that the day had seen the loss of their best ship which had unaccountably struck Galloper Shoal and been burned by the Dutch. In the light of Sir William Clerke's disclosures, Danny gave a great deal of thought to the fate of the Royal Prince; and found that sleep eluded him.

By morning the wind had veered back to south south-west and was blowing hard. At eight o'clock the fleet came in sight of the Dutch and formed line of battle; two hours later very little order was left and vessels lay to both windward and leeward side of an enemy whose artillery pounded them not only with all the usual missiles but also with a new device comprising of two smaller cannon-balls linked by a length of chain. It tore through sails, shrouds and rigging, wrapped itself around masts and snapped them and inflicted wounds the like of which Danny had never imagined. And by the time he had seen limbs shot off and bones shattered and a man breathing his last in excruciating agony having been caught in the stomach by this hellish invention, he was too numb even to be sick.

It went on until five o'clock when Albemarle and Rupert, their flag-ships severely damaged, could no longer maintain any semblance of order and were forced to make for shore. This time Danny did not wonder why de Ruyter neglected to move in for the kill; he was simply grateful for it – and even more so when he realised that the Dutch were apparently sailing for home.

It was past midnight before he was free to seek out Freddy and bear him off to the deserted deck of the Portland ... and even then he stared silently out across the dancing lights of the harbour for a full minute before he spoke.

'Freddy – you said you had a brush with the Guernsey. Do you think ... have you any reason to suppose it might not have been an accident?'

Mr Iverson gaped at him. 'What?'

'Think, will you? Could it have been deliberate?'

Freddy thought. 'Well, it could, I suppose. But it ain't very likely, is it? Didn't do any real damage and – '

'It put the Portland out of action for nearly twenty-four hours,' Danny reminded him.

'All right. But who'd go to the trouble for a fourth-rater? Be different if it had been one of the flag-ships – more point to it.'

Danny sighed. 'Yes. I daresay you're right. But what about the Royal Prince? Did you see what happened?'

Freddy began to feel that the horrors of the day had left Danny temporarily unhinged.

'Saw her burning, if that's what you mean. Didn't see her run aground though.'

'And it doesn't strike you as odd? I mean, wouldn't you expect a first-rate ship to have a first-rate helmsman and pilot and Captain, all of whom should be capable of avoiding Galloper Shoal? Or does it just seem as silly as disabling a sister-craft?'

Mr Iverson blinked owlishly. 'What's the alternative? That the Navy is riddled with enemy agents all popping out of the bulkheads like maggots out of a -- ' He stopped abruptly as Danny's hand closed tight on his arm. 'What the -- ?'

'Sh!' Daniel took a step away, anxiously scanning the dark and seemingly deserted deck. 'I could have sworn ... did you hear anything?'

'No. What's the matter with you? You're as jumpy as a rabbit.'

With a rueful grin, Danny came back and perched himself on a hatch-cover.

'I know. Sound thoroughly beef-witted, don't I? But this engagement's been one long disaster.' He paused, looking steadily into Freddy's face. 'First we get a false report on the French so the fleet's split – then we discover our mistake so Rupert's recalled. But someone must have slipped up with that as well or he'd have been with us much sooner. Your ship's crippled by one of our own and we lose our best vessel on a sandbank. Am I really an idiot to think that there may be more to it than just coincidence?'

There was a long silence, then Freddy said, 'Don't know. Someone put the idea in your head?'

'Yes. Willie Clerke – the Secretary at War,' replied Danny, half-reluctantly. 'And for God's sake keep it to yourself. I haven't told anyone else and I don't suppose I should be telling you. If it isn't nonsense, then I ought to go to Albemarle or Rupert – and if it is, then I should just keep my mouth shut. Only I think I need another opinion.'

Mr Iverson folded his arms, a frown of concentration creasing his brow.

'Sure mine'll be any use? Not clever, y'know.'

Danny grinned. 'Maybe not. But you've got common-sense and that's what I need right now.'

Colouring modestly at this tribute, Freddy asked hurriedly, 'So what did Sir William say?'

'That's the trouble,' Danny admitted wryly. 'He didn't say very much at all – and he died this afternoon. I saw him yesterday and he was in a lot of pain. Some fellow named Warner was with him and, although he left the room while I was there, Willie seemed convinced he was listening. To begin with I thought he was delirious but then I wasn't so sure. He kept saying he should have told the Duke – over and over again. Then he made me promise to do it for him. He said, "All these accidents and faulty reports – someone's behind them. Tell Albemarle or the Prince but not – '" A tiny sound caught his ear and he stopped, looking up.

Slightly baffled, Freddy followed his gaze but just a second too late. He heard Danny shout and then he was sent spinning by a hefty shove that carried him half-way to the poop as the yard-arm of the aft-mast came crashing down where he had been; and where Danny, with no time to do more than try rolling aside, still was.

Shocked by the suddenness of it, Freddy took an instant to start forward to the wreckage around the great, solid beam. Then a knife, thrown from above, missed him by inches to stand quivering in the deck and he recognised his danger.

Two weeks at sea had done a lot for Freddy and, without stopping to think, he wrenched the dagger from the planking and swung himself up on to the bulwark, his eyes searching the rigging for his would-be assassin. Already he could hear the sound of running feet and the voices of seamen, drawn from the wharf by the noise of the falling spar. Help was at hand; but beset, for the first time in his life, by cold anger, Freddy did not want it.

Then he saw the man high above him, silhouetted against the moon and rapidly descending the mast; and, gripping the blade between his teeth, Freddy raised his arms and began to climb.

His quarry reached a joist where the rat-lines would take him over to the mainmast and hesitated, glancing first at Mr Iverson in determined pursuit and then at the deck, now alive with sailors; then, evidently deciding on escape, he seized the ropes and started to traverse the cross-rigging.

Arriving at the first yard, Freddy saw his intention and realised that his chances of catching up were diminishing by the second. He steadied his position and took the knife from his teeth.

'Escape would you?' he said to himself. 'Well, not if I can help it.' And threw.

The blade took his adversary hard in the shoulder, impairing his grasp. He called out, tried to retain his hold and failed; then, with a single wild scream, he fell thirty feet to the deck below and landed with a sickening thud half across a capstan.

In the sudden silence that followed, Freddy did not even spare him a glance but went swiftly back the way he had come, down to the poop-deck ... and Danny.

They had moved the huge timber spar from where it had lain across his hips and someone had covered him up to the chin in a heavy boat-cloak. In the light of the lamps, his face was chalky-pale and the bones stood out in sharp relief against the hollows of his cheeks. Freddy dropped on one knee beside him, seeking his hand.

'Danny? You badly hurt, old fellow?'

The sandy lashes flickered slowly open to disclose eyes that, although beginning to cloud, still held a trace of their usual smile.

'Bad enough,' said Danny faintly. 'But I can't feel anything.' His eyes closed, then opened again. 'Looks like Willie had the right of it. Did you get him?'

Freddy cleared his throat. 'Yes. I think he's dead.'

'He's dead all right, sir,' volunteered a young midshipman behind him. 'His neck's broke.'

Danny's lips tightened a little. 'Pity. You could have asked him why ... ' There was a pause and then, with the ghost of a grin, 'Unless he just don't like redheads.'

It took an effort greater than any Freddy had ever made to grin back and reply in kind.

'Might've been aiming at me for calling him a maggot. Only you ... stopped him.' And there he halted, not knowing how to express what he felt.

The cold fingers gripped his hand weakly.

'Don't be an ass. You'd have done the same. It's just ... the luck doesn't last forever.' The lashes dropped again and he seemed to fall asleep.

A rustling stir ran through the small group of sailors at Freddy's back but he didn't turn his head until he heard a familiar voice, unfamiliarly crisp, saying 'What the devil's going on?'

And then he looked up into Giles Beckwith's grey eyes.

'Giles?' Rousing, Danny looked hazily up. 'Is that you?'

And the cool gaze was cool no longer as it rested on the pinched face beneath its mop of tangled, fiery hair.

'Danny!' Giles knelt swiftly beside him. 'What happened?'

'Freddy will tell you. I'm glad you've come ... thought you were in London.'

'No. I've been with Rupert.' Giles scanned the young face with a sinking heart. He had seen death too often not to recognise it in the dimming eyes and bluish pallor before him. Taking care to move him as little as possible, he slid an arm beneath Danny's shoulders and held him in a comforting grip. 'Are you in pain?'

'No.' Making a huge effort, Danny turned his head. 'Listen, Giles – it's important. Freddy'll explain ... only you mustn't tell York or ... or Arlington. Willie Clerke said so. Not York, not Arlington. Promise?'

Giles cast a frowning glance at Freddy and then looked back at Danny. 'I promise,' he said calmly. 'Don't worry. I'll take care of everything.'

He was rewarded by a faint sigh and the flaming head sank back. There was a long silence and then, in a voice that was now a mere thread, Danny said, 'Will it be light soon?'

Giles nodded. 'Yes. Very soon.'

Danny smiled. 'Good. I'd rather not go in the dark. But they say you see the sun ... afterwards ... so perhaps it doesn't matter.' His glance flickered to Giles's face. 'Explain to Chloë ... give her my love. Alex too.'

'Yes. I will.' A white shade bracketed Mr Beckwith's mouth but his tone remained level.

'And tell him ... he's lucky. Time he knew. Too damned clever to ... to see what's under his nose. Always was.' A laugh which became a rattle shook Danny's chest and for a long time he was silent, fighting to breathe. But finally, he said, 'I'm glad you're here ... you and Freddy. But I wish ... I wish there'd been more time.'

He lasted until sunrise, slipping peacefully away as the first fingers of dawn lit the sky so that in death, as in life, he was smiling. And Giles, without quite knowing why, would not cover the dead face nor suffer him to be moved until the sun was truly up, but sat quietly with Freddy, waiting.

SEVEN

For those at home, the first days of June dragged by in a ferment of anxious waiting. On the second, London was ablaze with rumours of an engagement between Albemarle and de Ruyter. On the third came news that Prince Rupert's squadron had been sighted off Dover and on the fourth, Alex took Chloë out to the gravel pits where they stood for half an hour listening to the guns.

As soon as she stepped from the carriage, Chloë regretted having asked to come. The persistent booming of the cannon, unaccompanied by news or any view of the action, was both frightening and macabre when you knew that each shot could mean the end for someone; for Danny, or Giles, or Freddy. She discovered she was standing beside Lady Falmouth, pale and heavy-eyed with sleeplessness, and without thinking, took her hand and held it tightly while they stood listening till they could bear it no longer.

On the following day Alex brought news that Rupert and Albemarle had finally joined forces.

Chloë looked up at him and tried to smile. 'Well, that's good isn't it? It may even be over by now.'

'Yes. They say the guns have stopped.' His manner was oddly unfamiliar.

'You're worried,' she said, wondering why this should scare her. 'Do you think we may have lost?'

'I don't know. Perhaps not. But we seem to have lost a lot of ships ... and men.'

She sat staring motionlessly down at her sewing. 'Anyone we know?'

There was a pause, then Alex said, 'Falmouth is dead.'

Chloë's heart sank. She swallowed and said, 'Oh God. When?'

'Two days ago.'

She looked up then, brown eyes wide and upset, sharing with him thoughts of the Earl's gaiety on the night of the banquet; and that, when they had stood at the gravel pits with Lady Falmouth, she was even then a widow.

Wednesday the sixth was the customary monthly fast-day for the plague. Again no gun-fire was heard and likewise no more news came from the fleet, except that the Duke of Albemarle was believed unscathed save for a minor leg-wound. The citizens of London assumed that the battle was not only fought but won and rang bells and lit bonfires in celebration.

Their joy was premature. On the following day came tidings that though the fleet had lost many ships, it had taken none; that the Navy had lost twelve commanders, several flag-officers and countless ordinary seamen; that it was not victory – but defeat.

It was not until the tenth that Mr Beckwith arrived in London, made his way reluctantly to Southwark and, for the first time, had Naomi formally announce him.

Alex stopped reading and his eyes sought Chloë's. Then, laying his book aside, he bade Naomi send Mr Beckwith in and rose from his chair to meet him. Chloë, filled with relief that this one was safe, folded her sewing with less than her usual care and waited.

He was as elegant as ever and apparently unhurt. Chloë smiled warmly at him and only then saw his face. It was tired and gaunt ... and the grey eyes held an expression that had nothing to do with either.

'My God,' said Alex brightly. 'You took your time. They say it's been over since Monday – but perhaps you were enjoying yourself?'

Giles, who for five days had been wondering how he was to tell them, promptly forgot every speech he had prepared and uttered the words that had been ringing in his brain since Tuesday.

'Danny is dead.' And then realised, through a haze of fatigue, that Alex had guessed there was bad news and deliberately made it easy for him.

Alex might have been prepared for it but Chloë was not. The room seemed suddenly dark and sounds became muffled. The blood drained from her face and she stared disbelievingly at Giles.

'He can't be,' she said. 'It's a mistake.'

He shook his head. 'No.'

'Were you with him?' asked Alex with a sort of detached calm.

Giles sat down and passed a hand over his face.

'Yes. Freddy was there too.' He stopped and tried to think. 'Freddy's all right. He's with the fleet.'

Alex glanced down at Chloë who was sitting like a stone, save for hands that couldn't keep still. He said, 'What happened? And when?'

Giles also glanced fleetingly at Chloë. 'I don't think – '

'Say it,' ordered Alex crisply, 'and get it over with. Quickly. She'll have to know.'

It was a moment before Giles answered. Then he said unevenly, 'It was in the early hours of Tuesday morning. A yard-arm fell. Danny pushed Freddy out of the way but – but didn't have time to move himself. It ... it crushed his spine and legs.'

Chloë made a tiny sound and clamped her fingers hard over her mouth. Alex drew a ragged breath but said nothing.

'When I got there,' Giles went on with an effort, 'he was still conscious but failing fast. He talked ... mostly rambling ... but some of it you should hear.'

Mr Deveril's face was completely colourless and as rigid as a carved mask.

'Yes,' he said politely, walking to the door. 'I expect I should. And if you will excuse me for a moment, I shall be entirely at your disposal.'

Somewhere in the recesses of her mind, Chloë realised that he was probably going to be sick. There seemed to be something odd about that but she wasn't sure what it was. Very carefully, she lowered her hands till they lay in her lap and looked down at them. She could not trust herself to speak yet for she knew that if she did, she would not be able to bear it.

A minute passed, then two. Finally Giles spoke.

'He wasn't in any pain, Chloë. He – he even joked a little. And he sent you his love.'

Before he had finished speaking she was on her feet and half-way to the door.

'Sorry, Giles,' she said. And fled.

Passing her in the hall, Alex let her go. He re-joined Mr Beckwith in the parlour, nudged the door shut with his foot and placed a bottle of brandy and two glasses on the table. Having filled them both to the brim, he handed one to Giles and then sat down, taking a large drink from the other.

'I think we'll both be the better for getting this over with as fast as possible,' he said. 'Tell me everything.'

Giles leaned back and closed his eyes.

'I was aboard the Royal James with Rupert,' he said wearily. 'As you've doubtless heard, we didn't catch up with Albemarle until the third – largely because no one had bothered to tell us that he'd moved to Gunfleet. You'll hear people blaming Rupert for his slowness in coming – but the truth is that he turned back as soon as he heard the guns. There's no point in going into detail – sufficient to say the action was heavy all that day and again on the next. Our losses are enormous – ten ships at least.'

He opened his eyes and took a sip of brandy.

'It was late Monday night before I had a chance to get to Harwich and look for Danny. He'd been aboard the Henry but when I got there Harman said he'd given him leave to meet a friend sailing on the Portland. So I went after him.' He stopped and frowned into his glass. 'If I'd arrived even an hour earlier - - '

'You might have died with Daniel or instead of him,' observed Alex impatiently. He got up and walked to the window. 'It's a useless, damnable waste but blaming yourself won't help.'

Giles drew a deep breath and the words came out with an effort.

'You don't understand, Alex. If Danny had fallen in battle, it would have been a waste. But he didn't and it's more than that. It's a tragedy.'

Even without looking, he felt Mr Deveril's shock.

'Are you saying,' asked Alex slowly, 'that it wasn't an accident?'

There was no way to soften it. 'Yes. Danny was murdered.'

For a second, Alex just stared at him. Then he dropped heavily on to the window-seat, his face driven into the cage of his fingers. 'Oh Christ.'

There was a long silence and Giles wisely left him alone. Then, rising, he poured more brandy into Alex's glass and pushed it into his hand.

'Drink that and pull yourself together,' he said harshly. 'Alternatively, if you're going to throw up again – go and get it over with. We've work to do.'

It worked. Alex looked up, white but with a glimmer of his usual astringence.

'It's all right,' he said. 'My guts are dismantled but I'll live. You can continue.'

'Good.' Giles paused and then said, 'Will you tell Chloë?'

Alex stared back blankly. 'In God's name, what for?'

'She might want to know the truth.'

'And will it make her feel any better? If she has a right, it's to be protected from knowledge that can only make her even more upset than she already is.'

'I'm glad,' said Giles simply, 'that you realise it.'

Alex contemplated him between narrowed lids, then said curtly, 'Very clever. But if you've finished testing my discretion, I think we should get on with the business in hand.'

'Very well. Then try this for size. The yard-arm was cut and Freddy saw the man who did it.'

The blue gaze sharpened. 'Did he catch him?'

'Oh yes. He caught him, all right. He killed him.'

'Freddy killed him? I wouldn't have thought he had it in him. In fact, I wish he hadn't.'

'So do I – but he had no way of knowing.'

Alex leaned against the window embrasure.

'Clearly. But if Danny was killed, it must have been for a reason and it would help if we knew what it was.'

'We do know. It was because of something he learned from Sir William Clerke.'

Alex frowned. 'Clerke? The Secretary at War?'

Giles nodded. 'His knee was shattered and they had to amputate. He didn't survive it but Danny was with him for a while before he died and he told Freddy that Clerke thought there was more than inefficiency to the consistently poor intelligence we'd received.'

'And that's all?'

'No. That's all Freddy knows.' He paused. 'I told you that Danny's mind was wandering and perhaps it was. But he said two things that made perfect sense.'

The muscles of Mr Deveril's jaw tightened. 'Well?'

'He said,' replied Giles, his voice level and empty, 'that Freddy would tell me what he knew so that I could deal with it. And then he made me promise not to tell the two most obvious people.'

Their eyes met and locked.

'Arlington and York,' breathed Alex, taking his thought. 'But of course it's not either of them ... and we've got to make a new list.'

'We have,' agreed Giles, 'but, if I'm right, it may be a shorter one than you think.' He moved away to the fireplace and leaned one elbow on the mantelpiece. 'I've done a bit of checking. The man Freddy killed was one Miles Warner and, like so many of us, he'd been taken on as a super-numerary. He'd also – so Danny told Freddy – been with Sir William at Harwich.' He paused. 'My guess is that Warner was a cut above the usual tools used by our anonymous friend. It's only supposition, you understand, but it seems likely that some hitch occurred which gave Clerke the suspicions he spoke of to Danny. He may even have known more than he was able to tell.'

'In which case, Warner was despatched to remove him?' suggested Alex. 'Yes. That would fit. Only, of course, he didn't need to because a combination of the Dutch and the Naval surgeons kindly did the job for him.'

'I think so. But he was probably watching Clerke, which is why he saw the need to ... ' He stopped, not wanting to say it.

'To get rid of Daniel,' supplied Alex inimically. 'Don't be diffident. Very well. If he was intelligent enough to work that one out and to act on his own initiative then, as you said, he may well have been a senior operative. And if he was sent by the principal to dispose of Clerke, I think we can assume he knew the principal's identity.' His smile did not reach his eyes. 'What a pity Freddy killed him. We might have cut out the paperwork.'

Giles was familiar with the technique Mr Deveril used to cover moments of weakness but on this occasion it made his stomach churn.

'If you're about to become facile,' he said coldly, 'I'm leaving.'

There was a pause and the pale, impervious gaze altered a little.

'In that case, I'll restrain myself,' said Alex by way of apology. Then, 'I take it you've checked on Warner?'

Mr Beckwith nodded. 'Superficially, yes.'

'And?'

'And he was employed by no one – openly. But he was known to be friendly with a number of gentlemen in the Duke of York's set. So that's where we start.'

Alex rested his chin on his clasped hands and stared abstractedly at Giles, a faint frown creasing his brow.

'This man ... he's clever. We both know how difficult it is to set up this type of operation and yet remain anonymous.' He hesitated and then went on, 'It sounds damned silly, I know – but the sheer perfection of the cover we're trying to break reminds me of something.'

'Go on,' said Mr Beckwith. 'Try me. I promise you I never felt less like laughing.'

Alex picked up his glass and turned it between his fingers, meditatively watching as the amber-coloured liquid caught and reflected the light.

'When we were working for the Knot, I had a certain amount of warning that exposure was imminent. I used that time to pass on the knowledge to as many of our people as I could reach. I also attempted to locate the sources of their information – one of whom was Wyllis, with his crassly indiscreet letters to Thurloe. The other was a cautious gentleman whose name I never discovered because I believe only Cromwell and Thurloe knew it. But he was good; he had all the attributes of the professional – careful attention to detail, an eye for what to report and a superbly-preserved incognito. Just,' finished Alex pensively, 'like the man we're looking for now.'

There was a long silence, then Giles said, 'Are you suggesting they're one and the same?'

'No. I'm suggesting it's a possibility worth considering. We're after someone who is as good as we are ourselves – probably better. With all due modesty, I'd like to point out that there can't be many candidates. And if it is the same man, we're going to need more luck than judgement if we're to catch him.'

Mr Beckwith sighed and dropped into a chair.

'On which cheering note, I suppose we'd better get to work.'

'In a minute,' said Mr Deveril, getting up. 'You spoke of two things Danny said that made perfect sense. What was the other?'

Giles looked up at him, fine-drawn with exhaustion. 'It wasn't important.'

'Nevertheless. I'd like to know.'

Suddenly too tired to care, Giles shrugged and said, 'He asked if it would soon be dawn – said he didn't want to go in the dark. He asked me to explain to Chloë and give her – and you – his love. Then he said, "Tell Alex he's lucky and it's time he knew it. He's too clever to see what's under his nose."'

Very slowly, the ice-blue gaze widened and filled with too-innocent enquiry.

'Dear me,' said Mr Deveril mildly. 'Dear me ... I wonder what he meant?'

Giles came swiftly to his feet.

'Do you?' he asked with bitter hostility. 'Then I think you must be suffering from necrosis of the brain.' And striding to the door, he wrenched it open and left.

Standing quite still, his back to Persephone and her dryads, Alex watched him go, a crooked and rather desperate little smile touching his mouth.

'Exit pursued by a bear,' he announced to the empty room. And laying his fingers carefully on the rim of the table, he stared down at them with an air of disciplined control.

* * *

Dry-eyed and face down on her bed, Chloë stayed all day alone in her room, her soul awash with numb desolation. The simple daily duties of her household were forgotten. Outside the bitter rawness of Danny's loss, her only remaining thought was that somewhere in the house, Alex suffered too but would have to hide it in public as she did not; that to him would fall the task of telling Matthew. She knew it but shrugged it uncharacteristically aside. She had no comfort to give.

The hours wore by; afternoon passed and then evening. The moon rose, sending pale bars of light through her window to lie in silvery pools on the floor. For a long time Chloë lay staring at them. Then, levering herself stiffly into a sitting position, she swung her feet to the floor. Her hair was clinging to her face and lying in tangled coils about her neck. She pushed it absently aside, all her attention tuned to listening. There were no sounds; the house was apparently asleep. Chloë got up.

Wraith-like, she moved down the stairs to the hall. There she hesitated for a moment, her head turned towards the open parlour door and then, obedient to an inner prompting she did not try to analyse, she moved towards it.

The room was dark but she knew without looking that it was not empty. She always knew when Alex was close by. She stepped inside, then stopped. He was at the window, one arm resting upraised against the frame and his profile silhouetted against the faint grey light as he stared pointlessly into the garden. Chloë stood for a moment, watching and then turned away, quietly so as not to intrude.

Restless now but lacking a purpose, she went to the kitchen, lit a candle and placed the heavy kettle on top of the dying embers of the fire. Then she sat down to watch it. Almost immediately there was a small sound behind her and she turned slowly. It was Mr Deveril, the planes and tangents of his face oddly changed by the poor, shadowy light.

'Hello,' he said quietly. 'Do you mind if I join you?'

The stark brown gaze rested on him dumbly then, shaking her head, she turned back to the fire. For a second, Alex stood still, then he picked up the solitary candle and began lighting others.

'I hope we're not economising,' he said. 'I realise that the price of candles is quite scandalous but I'm abysmally clumsy in the dark. Especially on unfamiliar territory. And I don't think I've been in here since the day you accidentally swept the chimney.'

Apathetically, Chloë turned again and discovered that the alteration in Mr Deveril's features had nothing to do with the light. He had discarded his coat and above the whiteness of the cambric shirt, his skin was the colour of parchment and stretched tight over bones which seemed suddenly too sharp for it.

'You look tired,' she said with what seemed a very great effort. Then, taking a deep breath, 'And I don't suppose you've eaten. You should have something.'

He smiled bleakly. 'Possibly. But I don't think I could.'

Chloë let her head fall forward. 'No. Neither could I.'

Alex looked thoughtfully at the veiling curtain of rose-gold hair. Then, 'The kettle's boiling. Shall I lift it off?'

'I'll do it.' She moved the kettle on to the hob and then stood looking at it as if she couldn't remember what she had wanted it for.

'I don't suppose,' said Mr Deveril gently, 'that we have any tea? Or that you know how to make it?'

'Tea?' repeated Chloë vaguely. 'Yes. The Queen gave me a box. Do you want some?'

He nodded and sat at the wooden table. 'It might do us both good.'

She eyed him blankly and said abruptly, 'I think I'd rather get drunk.'

'No, you wouldn't. It doesn't help – take my word for it.' He smiled again. 'Make the tea.'

So she did and, when it was poured, sat facing him from the other side of the table. She stared at the steaming brew and turned her cup round without speaking for a long time. Finally, she said, 'Have you told Matt?'

'Yes. Don't worry about it.'

She picked up the cup, spilled it badly and put it down again, withdrawing her hands to the safety of her lap. Then she stood up again and reached for a cloth.

'Leave it,' said Alex. 'It doesn't matter. Sit down.'

She looked at him a little wildly.

'I can't believe it. It's silly ... but I can't believe he's dead. Not Danny. He is – was – so full of life. And so young. It doesn't seem possible.'

'I know. Sit down, Chloë.' He waited till she had done so. 'You have to believe it because it is so. We both know what he was – and that it's unjust and cruel. And we know how much we'll miss him. But life isn't always fair ... nor does it stop when the unspeakable happens. Today has been about shock and grief. Tomorrow you have to try to go on with all the things you're thinking don't matter. And the next day and the next until it becomes easier. We all do.' He paused. 'You should cry. It might help.'

'I can't.'

His gaze on his untouched tea, he said expressionlessly, 'You loved him. I'm sorry.'

Chloë made a small helpless gesture. 'Of course I loved him. Who wouldn't?'

This time the silence stretched on and on.

'He spoke of you. Did Giles tell you?'

Her mouth tightened. 'Yes.'

'He sent you his love and Giles was to tell me I'm lucky. I imagine you know what he meant by that.'

'No.' She clenched her fingers.

'I think you do. He meant I was lucky to have you … so it's clear that –'

'Stop it!' She stood up, poised for flight. 'I don't want to talk about it!'

'That he loved you too,' finished Alex simply. And then, 'You could have told me.'

Chloë drew a ragged breath and her hands crept to her mouth. Mr Deveril had misunderstood and she probably ought to put that right. But the only thing that counted was that Danny had obviously known where her heart lay … had probably known for a long time … and said nothing. Until he lay dying.

'Please.' Her breathing was hopelessly disordered. 'I can't do this now.'

'No. But one last thing – which may comfort you later. You should know that Danny didn't die in pain, or alone, or in the dark. He died in Giles' arms as the sun came up.' Alex paused, his mouth twisting wryly, 'If go one must, there are worse ways.'

Outside, the bells of St Mary Overie were chiming midnight but Chlöe did not hear them. Her ears were filled with Danny's voice, bright and eager, on a cold February day at Queenhithe. Something about the East and the sun. And then the barriers broke at last. For Danny, for an unfulfilled life and dreams that had never been hers, Chloë dropped back on to the settle, buried her head in her arms on the table-top and burst into a storm of deep, painful sobbing.

For perhaps a minute Alex watched, before he rose and went to sit beside her. He did not speak but, reaching out, drew her firmly towards him and held her in steady, passionless arms. It lasted a long time. When it was over, he passed her his handkerchief and continued to hold her in silence. Chloë blew her nose, leaning exhaustedly against the damp warmth of his shoulder and only then becoming aware of his arms around her and the light pressure of his cheek on her hair. Yesterday such proximity would have sent all her muscles into spasm; today it didn't seem to matter.

'You did that on purpose,' she said huskily. 'Thank you.'

'My methods are often debatable,' he replied tranquilly. 'I'm sorry I couldn't find another way.' He was silent for a moment and then said, 'It will soon be light. Will you come walking with me?'

She shifted a little, turning her head to look into his face and felt his arms fall gently away.

'Yes. I – I'd like that.'

He studied the flushed, tear-stained face gravely. 'Come, then.'

Outside the air was cool and fresh but it was not cold. The streets were deserted and the cobbles gleamed with dewy dampness. Side by side without speaking or touching, Alex and Chloë skirted the west front of St Mary Overie and walked slowly towards the sharp tangy smells of the river. Reaching it, they stood for a moment looking at the bridge with its narrow arches and tall houses and shops; then, leaving it behind them, they turned left along the riverside.

It was quite different from the noisy, bustling place it became by day when the banks and stairs swarmed with watermen and porters, seamen and stevedores; now the water's edge was crowded with the anchored sleeping shapes of its usually busy traffic and further out the larger vessels lay, quietly lit and dreaming, under the moon. The taverns were shuttered, their music stilled and their customers gone, and the only sounds that broke the night were the rhythmic slapping of water on wood or the occasional snore of a boatman asleep on his barge. Alex took Chloë's hand and held it in a light, friendly clasp.

They walked along Bankside, past the emptiness of the Bear Garden and on till they came to the Upper Ground. There, as if drawn by some invisible thread, Mr Deveril turned again to the river and, drawing Chloë with him, descended the Falcon Stairs.

The steps were smooth and hollowed, worn away by the passage of feet and by the water which licked them with such deceptive gentleness. Chloë and Alex stood one rise above the river and gazed across at the shadowy warehouses of Puddle and Baynard's Wharves, behind which rose the high, gothic splendour of Paul's Cathedral, towering above the City like some vast guardian.

They did not know how long they stood but gradually the light began to change and, turning eastwards, they watched the pink glow of dawn rise slowly behind the irregular rooftops of the bridge and the grey, crenelated walls of the distant Tower.

Her mind far away, Chloë said, 'Danny dreamed of seeing the East. Do you think sunrise is more beautiful there?'

'I don't know. Different, perhaps.'

She let the river flow on at their feet for a minute and then, without looking at him, she forced out the words that needed to be said.

'You were mistaken before. It's true that I loved Danny and that perhaps he loved me. But as friends – nothing more. He … he was the brother I wished I'd had. So our friendship was precious to me.'

Something indefinable changed in Alex's expression; and simultaneously the mood between them shifted.

He looked down at her and watched as the breeze coiled a strand of hair around her throat to catch in the marigold chain she seemed always to wear. Her face, still turned away from him, looked as Rupert had drawn it; serene and pure but with an earthly reality of flesh and blood that woke a response that surprised him. Something platonic, born of the night's companionship; and something triggered by the drift of her hair and the line of her neck that wasn't platonic at all.

Her words had released him from the constraint of believing she and Danny had been in love with each other. Had he still thought that, he could never have acknowledged what he felt now. He wanted her; and that, of course, was foolish. What he wanted was no more than a little basic comfort and the price of finding it with the girl at his side was too high for either of them. Their hoped-for annulment was not something to be cast aside on the whim of the moment – especially when he knew that his desire was not, could not be, for Chloë herself. Or could it? Doubt stirred, clouding the surface of his mind.

Stretching out his free hand, he brushed the hair back from her cheek and waited as she turned towards him, her eyes dark and faintly questioning. He looked back at her, giving her time to read his intention, time to move away if she wished and then drew her slowly into his arms. His lips trailed lightly from temple to jaw and finally found her mouth where his kiss, at first gently persuasive, gradually deepened into something quite different; something deeper that hovered on the brink of something much more. And, beneath it, without even realising, Chloë let him know that what he wanted, he could have.

Of their own volition, her hands rose to tangle themselves in his hair; sparks rushed along her veins and sensations she'd half-experienced only once before and still hardly recognised flooded her body. There was no room for conscious thought. She simply melted against him.

In the end, ironically, it was her response which at once freed and betrayed her for Alex, who had sought one discovery, had found two. Lifting his head, he stared down into her dilated gaze, his hands sliding to her shoulders.

'It was you,' he said at last. 'That night in Oxford with the fellow who's name I've forgotten. It was you, wasn't it?'

Chloë looked back with a sort of random interest. 'Yes. How did you know?'

He shrugged slightly and, his mind not entirely focussed, said absently, 'Probably because you're the last girl I kissed.'

She stared at him. 'Oh.' A pause, and then, 'So you haven't been -- ?

'No.' This wasn't a conversation Alex wanted to have – particularly now. It was nothing to do with embarrassment. Simply that the celibacy that hadn't bothered him in the least for six months was suddenly becoming an issue. To divert her, he said, 'Why didn't you ever mention it?'

'It was just a bit of foolish mischief,' she said, flushing a little because although it was true, it wasn't the reason for her silence. 'It didn't mean anything and I didn't think you'd remember. Does it matter?'

And Alex, meeting the anxiety in her eyes, thought that it very probably did – as did her response to him and his to her – but that it was not the time, while their nerves were stretched and heightened with so many emotions, to attempt an analysis. He smiled reassuringly and drew her hand through his arm to go back up the stairs.

'No, Marigold. It doesn't matter. Come ... let's go home.'

And slowly, their faces turned to the dawn, they retraced their steps; and did not look back.

EIGHT

As lovely day succeeded lovely day in that cloudless, blazing June, Chloë cast herself into a frantic orgy of activity. She swept and polished, dusted and sewed – anything in fact, however trivial or unnecessary, that might occupy her mind or tire her body so that she would be too busy or too exhausted to think. It did not work and she wondered dully why it seemed to do so for Alex and Giles, once more taken up with Prince Rupert's mysterious assignment. For her, from the time she rose to the time she found herself unable to sleep, every day was a battle to avoid the only thoughts that held any significance. Like twin goblins, they shadowed her steps and turned her world into a dark place where she dwelt alone with the nagging ache of Danny's death and the soul-destroying void of a hollow marriage.

Alex had kissed her and she did not know what – if anything – that meant, since he had subsequently neither referred to it nor shown any inclination to repeat it. The only thing that she was certain of was that her feelings for him which, before that kiss, had been largely controllable, had now swelled to a tumult of longing that threatened to overwhelm her.

It was perhaps fortunate that across the river in Whitehall, Queen Catherine was also beset with troubles. The palace, as everyone knew, had been set by the ears when Lady Castlemaine had told the Queen that if His Majesty had taken cold from the night air, it was because he visited other ladies after departing from her house. Unfortunately, she had said it within the King's hearing and Charles, usually placid to the point of indolence, had actually been sufficiently stirred to deliver a stinging reprimand and bid her remove herself from Court.

Wild with anger, Barbara had gone to lodge in Pall Mall, leaving poor Catherine to indulge in the rosy hope that she was rid of her thorn at last. Alas, she was soon disillusioned. Within three days, Barbara was back, bolder than ever and boasting that she had brought the King to heel; and the collective, sniggering rumour that hurt Catherine more than her return was the widespread whisper that her ladyship had achieved this by threatening to publish Charles' letters to her.

Disappointed and sickened, Catherine felt she could no longer tolerate the hateful presence without the support of someone she both liked and trusted. With a sort of pathetic defiance, she offered Chloë a position in her household and Chloë, glad of anything that might fill her days, accepted and then walked out into the bright afternoon sun to find a boat which would take her home.

She had mistimed it, she realised, by about five minutes. Cousin Simon was just settling into a barge as she came down the steps. He hailed her with languid delight, informed her that he was going to Trinity House, and insisted that she allow him the pleasure of taking her to Southwark. Since it was on his way and no other craft was available, the watermen having gone into hiding again to avoid the Navy's latest large-scale press, Chloë was forced to stifle her polite refusal. Disdaining his arm, she stepped into the boat and sat down facing him. The waterman set out towards midstream.

Simon smiled benignly and Chloë was reminded of a cat when it stole a morsel from the pantry. 'I thought,' he said, eyeing her gown, 'that our period of full mourning was over.'

'It is,' Chloë replied stonily. 'Danny Fawsley is dead.'

The smile disappeared and his eyes narrowed slightly. 'Old Sir Roger's nephew? Really? I had not heard it. It must have been very sudden.'

'It was.' She looked at her hands and concentrated on keeping her voice steady. 'He died at Harwich on June the fifth.'

'At Harwich?' The drawling voice sharpened. 'But this is dreadful – I really had no idea. I can scarcely believe it ... the poor boy was so young.'

'If you don't mind,' said Chloë, 'I'd as soon not discuss it.'

'Yes, yes. Of course.' He dabbed his eyes with a lace-edged handkerchief. 'You must excuse me – I am somewhat overcome. The sudden anguish, you know. One really feels that one should go home and change.' He looked with a pained expression at his red velvet. 'But what can one do? I am expected.'

Chloë stared across the bright, rippling water, crowded with lighters and barges, to the imposing façade of Arundel House and wondered bleakly if Simon ever entertained a thought that did not come back to his raiment.

'My spirits,' he continued plaintively, 'are quite worn down. You can have no notion of the problems one is surrounded with – my tact and discretion are at breaking point. And now you tell me young Fawsley is dead. It is too much. I really believe I must seek the Duke's leave to go to the country for a time before I become quite ill. One does one's best and one hesitates to complain but with the Duchess about to give birth any day and the Duke so preoccupied with Lady Denham – she wants him to own her publicly as his mistress, you know – the burden of responsibilities falling on my shoulders is quite crushing. I have even,' he concluded pettishly, 'had to miss two fittings with my tailor.'

'What a shame,' said Chloë automatically. She turned to the waterman, told him to set her down at the Falcon Stairs and watched as he began to steer cautiously across the river, her interest in Cousin Simon's idle discourse registering at several points below zero.

Pausing, Simon eyed her with a measure of suave gravity and said, 'I hope you will feel able to offer my condolences to Alex. I hesitate to do it myself – out of motives of the purest delicacy you, understand – but one would not wish to be thought lacking in any attention.'

The barge slid to a halt at the stairs and Chloë immediately stood up.

'Don't worry. I'll tell him.'

'So kind,' sighed Simon. 'He must be quite downcast. I do trust that he hasn't allowed the news to overset him. But then, he is so very hardy, is he not? Not one to entertain sentiment. You have no idea how I envy him. My own sensibilities are so very strong.'

'Yes. I noticed that. But Alex, fortunately, is too busy to be overset.' She climbed out on to the steps and her voice became noticeably astringent. 'He hasn't visited his tailor either. Thank you for the ride. Goodbye.' And before he could reply, she had turned and was mounting the stairs.

* * *

At that moment, Mr Deveril and Mr Beckwith, having returned from a two-day expedition, were just entering the parlour. While Alex called to Naomi, Giles sat down by the empty fireplace and stared abstractedly up at the decorative over-mantel. Both men looked extremely tired.

'I don't understand it,' said Giles at last. 'Whether by sabotage or accident, it shouldn't have happened.'

'No.' Hands pushed deep in the pockets of his blue riding coat, Alex gazed out of the window. 'Chicheley thinks the same. He was virtually in tears.'

'Understandably,' agreed Mr Beckwith grimly. 'Quite apart from the wasted money, the replacement time will be considerable. The Loyal London was due to join the fleet within the week – but without guns she's less than useless. And if they wait to cast new ones, the fleet will be at sea before they're ready. If this is another attempt - - ' He stopped as Naomi came in bearing wine and glasses.

She set it down and hovered uncertainly, plainly wondering if she should pour.

Alex turned round and waved her aside with sudden, irritable impatience. 'Leave it – we can manage.' He watched her go and looked back at Giles. 'Go on.'

'I was going to say that if it is another instance of sabotage, it will prove uncommonly effective.'

'Quite,' said Alex dryly. 'And if not, then our gun-makers are hellishly careless. Either way, it's equally incredible. Castings occasionally prove faulty, we know – but not to this extent. And how, without leaving any clue of your activities, do you tamper with each of eighty guns so that every one appears perfect until it's test-fired?'

'God knows. But if it was deliberate, someone made a damned good job of it. They'd shattered like glass.' Giles sipped his wine and then went on, 'It was in the smelting – it has to be. The proportion of copper to zinc, perhaps – or maybe there were impurities in the metal. I doubt that, though. Every timber and nail of that ship is the very best quality – including, one would suppose, the gun-metal.'

Mr Deveril sat down and looked thoughtfully into his glass, the blue eyes shadowed with fatigue. 'So. We can rule out faulty materials – probably. Workmanship then ... also unlikely since no one man worked on all of them. Which brings us back to – '

The door opened again and Chloë walked in.

'Oh Christ!' said Alex. In one fluid movement, he was out of his chair and across the room. 'It's not bloody open day. What do you want?'

She stared at him. 'Nothing that can't wait.' And turned to leave.

It was Giles who stopped her.

'Don't go,' he said. 'He's just tired. We both are. Do you want me to leave?'

She turned back, shaking her head. 'No. It's merely that the Queen has asked me to join her household and I've accepted. She's going to Tunbridge Wells the week after next and wants me to go with her. I thought Mr Deveril might like to know.'

'At any other time,' drawled Alex, 'Mr Deveril would be fascinated. But not just now because we're really rather busy. So if there's nothing else?'

For the first time in months, Chloë lost her temper.

'Not quite,' she said unsteadily. 'I've a message for you. Your cousin sends his condolences and congratulates you on your lack of sensitivity. He wishes he had it. As it is, he's tortured with sartorial anguish because he'll have to appear at Trinity House in a red coat. I wonder,' she finished lethally, 'if your family has a monopoly on dramatic trivia?'

And she walked out.

Giles swung round to face Alex. The ice-blue gaze held a strange expression but Giles ignored it. 'For God's sake! I know you've had no sleep for the best part of two days but do you have to be so bloody nasty?'

'Apparently, I do,' snapped Alex. 'And I don't have to excuse myself to you. So now I suggest you try applying your brain to what she just said. Cousin Simon is on his way to Trinity House.'

'What's new about that?' Mr Beckwith's voice was tight with control. 'He's on York's staff.' And then stiffened as the significance of it dawned on him.

'Precisely,' said Alex. 'He's on York's staff.' He met Giles' eyes steadily and there was a long, heavy silence. 'It's like finding the last piece of the puzzle has been in your hand all the time.'

Giles turned away with a dismissive shrug.

'An over-statement, surely? As Chloë pointed out, Simon's mind doesn't function beyond the confines of his wardrobe. I agree that we should check on him, just as we're checking others – but I imagine he's no more likely to be our clever friend than one of the King's spaniels.'

'Don't under-estimate him,' said Alex. 'Remember that before '59 he moved in Parliamentary circles but had the wit and address to effect a perfectly timed volte-face.'

'And he holds your father's estates and you don't like him,' supplied Giles, 'so you'd find it convenient to brand him traitor.'

'I don't deny it – which is why I want us to discuss it very carefully.' Alex dropped his hands on the table and rested his weight on them. 'We know our man is close to York – and who is closer than Simon? He knows everything the Duke knows, has access to any document you care to name and is trusted despite a very dubious past. If he were really as effete as he seems, what use would he be to York? And his father was one of Richard Willys' closest friends.'

There was a pause, then Giles said, 'A lot of people liked Willys – Rupert, for one. And since the Sealed Knot was betrayed all of eight years ago, I'm inclined to believe your notion of a connection between that and the present situation is a trifle fantastic. I'm sorry, Alex. I think you've got to accept that you're just biased.'

With a violent twist, Alex wheeled to face him, eyes blazing with weary frustration.

'So are you – in the opposite direction. Why can't you trust my judgement for once?'

'Because you're too damned clever,' replied Giles truthfully. 'But it isn't your judgement I'm questioning. It's your motives and eventual intentions.'

'Why? Because I'm sometimes rude to my wife and undisguisedly jealous of my cousin? Because I don't serve honour the same way you do, you believe I don't serve it at all – never mind to the best of my ability?' Alex's mouth curled in something not quite a smile. 'So my temper and behaviour are frequently are not all they might be – I'm impatient, intolerant and generally not fit to live with – my God, don't you think I know that? But we've known each other for fifteen years, Giles. I may not have many virtues, but surely I have enough to be credited with at least some proper feeling. So why is it so bloody difficult for you to at least give me the benefit of the doubt?'

Very slowly, Mr Beckwith rose and looked at him.

'In the general way, it isn't. In this instance, however, I think you must admit that the facts are against you. Frankly, I think it's a combination of our useless efforts and wishful thinking. And I'm not helping you conduct a personal witch-hunt.'

'I see.' The moment of appeal gone and already regretted, Alex's tone became completely impersonal. 'Then I'll just have to help myself, shan't I?'

* * *

It was much later that evening before Mr Deveril finally found the opportunity for a quiet chat with Mr Lewis. He explained his theories in much greater detail than he had troubled to do for Mr Beckwith and when he had finished he looked into the shrewd black eyes and said with only faint mockery, 'So there you have it. My Cousin Simon – if it is my Cousin Simon – is sitting hidden, secure as Zacchaeus up his tree. What we have to do is shake him out of it.'

The seamed, weather-beaten face remained expressionless.

'And did you,' asked Matt, 'have any idea of how? Bearing in mind that if it's not him and you show your hand, the little maggot will take to the heather and leave you worse off than you are now?'

'Quite,' said Alex with a grim smile. 'You wouldn't also like to point out that I'm allowing my imagination to run away with me – that I'm merely prejudiced?'

Mr Lewis moved as though to spit and then thought better of it.

'No. Are you?'

The smile became a shade less grim. 'I don't think so. At least, I hope not.' There was a pause, then, 'Very well. I wondered,' said Mr Deveril invitingly, 'if you'd like to come house-breaking with me?'

Finally Matt spoke.

'Why not?' he asked with dour humour. 'Why not? It's about the only lunacy we haven't tried before.'

* * *

Five nights later, with cloud obscuring the waning moon, two black-clad figures in soft boots made their way discreetly to the Strand and scaled the wall of one of the houses there. Once inside the garden they stopped for a moment, apparently listening, and then separated without a word to circle the darkened house until they met again at the rear.

'Anything?' asked Alex.

Matt shook his head. 'No lights and quiet as the grave.'

'Right. My side, then – and into the library.'

Silently, they made their way round to the east wing of the house and then Alex led the way slowly along it, counting windows as he went. At the fifth one he stopped and, producing a slim but stoutly handled knife from his pocket, inserted it carefully into the casement and proceeded to work at the catch. Standing beside him, Matt kept a watchful eye on either end of the house and strained his ears for sounds from within. The click of the latch as it yielded to the knife seemed unnaturally loud in the stillness and he turned his head to find Mr Deveril grinning at him in the faint silvery light.

'Having broken, we can now enter,' he said with what Matt privately thought an inappropriate degree of levity. 'You know what to do?'

'Aye.' They'd been over it so often that Mr Lewis could have set it to music.

'Good.'

Turning back to the window, Alex began to prise it open with his fingernails until it swung outwards with a mournful groan. Then, drawing aside the heavy curtain, he peered in; the room was in darkness and apparently empty. He nodded curtly at Matthew, placed one foot on the sill and, grasping the frame, levered himself easily up and for the first time in eighteen years, entered the home of his childhood. Then he took the lantern from Mr Lewis so that he could follow.

When they were both inside, Alex signalled Matt to hold back the curtains while he trod quietly across to the door, placed his ear to it and then opened it to look briefly into the hall. It was blackly silent and, closing the door again, he turned the key in the lock and returned to Matt's side.

Mr Lewis pulled the casement to, drew the curtains closely together and only then did he light the lantern. A soft, golden glow illuminated the room, touching the heavily-carved furniture and high shelves full of books and rolls of parchment. Matt glanced swiftly around him, allowing his eyes time to become accustomed to the light. Mr Deveril was already standing beside a large oak desk, systematically discovering which drawers were locked and which not. Only the top left one appeared to have been secured, all the rest opening easily to his touch. Alex smiled to himself, beckoned Matt to join him and drew from his pocket a string containing an assortment of keys, specially collected over the last few days.

'I'll see to this one,' he said. 'You start on the rest.'

By the time he had found a key which, with only a little forceful persuasion, opened the locked drawer, Matthew had searched through the contents of two others, replaced them and begun on a third. Alex lifted out a sheaf of documents and laid them on the desk-top while he examined the interior of the drawer for false panels. He found none and turned his attention to the papers.

They proved extremely interesting and he subjected them all to a swift scrutiny, pausing every now and then to read, but when he reached the bottom of the pile he shook his head in response to Matt's enquiring glance, replaced them tidily and locked the drawer again.

'Fascinating,' he said regretfully, 'but not what we're looking for. I wonder if Arlington and Coventry know they're being watched.'

'Are they?' Matt's hands continued their methodical work.

'Oh yes.' Alex gestured to the locked drawer. 'Reports in minute and tedious detail. Where they go, who they see, who they sleep with – and so on. Perhaps Simon is writing their memoirs.'

'Aye. And perhaps he isn't.'

Alex did not reply. For a moment he stood, deep in thought, then said, 'There's somewhere else I'd like to try. You finish off here – I'm going upstairs.'

Matt looked up sharply. 'Have you gone daft? Simon's out of the way at Court but there are servants here somewhere.'

'I'll be careful,' shrugged Mr Deveril. 'And, if the worst comes to the worst, I can always bob them on the noll.' And was gone.

Cat-like, Alex crossed the hall and set his foot on the stairs, one hand lightly skimming the bannister and his mind engaged in summoning every submerged recollection of Deveril House. And, as he climbed, the details came clearly back so that he was twelve years old again, automatically stepping over the place where there was a loose board, adjusting his stride for the trip-step and raising his arm to avoid the carved newel at the turn in the staircase. Then he was at the top.

He paused for an instant, listening, then turned unerringly to the left, moving soft-footed along what he knew to be a wide corridor but of which he could see nothing. It was pitch-dark; black as total blindness but it did not matter. Alex kept close to the right-hand wall, running his hand along it to count doorways and then side-stepping around the place where a huge china vase had always stood. Idly, he stretched out his fingers and smiled as they met the cool, glossy surface of it. He moved on to the next and stopped, searching delicately for the latch; then he found it, lifted it, went in.

There was light here, a little, fading in from windows whose curtains had not been drawn but he knew without looking that the room was empty. Other senses, less defined but no less real than those of sight and sound, told him that there was no danger here; nobody in the vast bed, no one waiting in the shadows. Only emptiness.

He moved unhurriedly to the wainscoting covering the far wall and stood for a while staring at the intricate frieze-work. Then he ran his hands over the upper row of carved devices, counting again to find the section he wanted. A second later the long fingers closed on one of the bosses, twisted it to the left and Alex stepped back to watch as a portion of the panelling in the lower tier slid smoothly back to reveal a dark cavity.

He needed light now and drew from his pocket a small piece of candle and a tinder-box. Then, shading the flame with his hand, he stepped into the recess.

It was a priest's hole, small and cleverly concealed, its existence known only to the immediate family. The Deverils, so his father had said, had never had occasion to hide a priest in it; but they had used it for pretty well everything else – from mistresses to contraband. And it was just the place, thought Alex, to hide a dirty secret ... if you happened to have one.

There was nothing there save a shelf containing a miscellany of objects. Alex began sifting through them, sensibly leaving till last a small, battered and obviously locked casket. And then he heard footsteps; even, unhurried and approaching. In a breath, the candle was out and Alex was across the room to stand behind the door, listening. If this were Simon returning unexpectedly, he had no mind to be trapped inside the cache. But the footfalls passed on and receded. Alex allowed his lungs to relax and went back to work.

Three leather pouches of gold and some jewellery; a bundle of letters tied with fraying blue ribbon which proved to have been written by Alex's mother to his father. After the first, he did not read these but simply glanced through to check no other paper had been lodged amongst them. Then he sat for a time, turning them gently in his hands and forcing down his revulsion at the knowledge that he must leave them here in Simon's possession. Finally he laid them reluctantly back on the shelf and picked up the box.

As he had expected, it was locked – but not for long. Alex put down his collection of keys, the appropriate one thoughtfully segregated, and began to inspect the contents. More letters; this time from a variety of senders. He went through them, reading each with rapid concentration and laying it back in the box just as he had found it. They were all much the same; letters dating from the time of the Commonwealth, all of them showing clearly where Simon's allegiance had lain during that time and all of them perfectly useless.

He dropped a letter into the box and picked up the next, starting to read dutifully but without much hope. And then the air left his lungs and his stomach clenched. He stared at the signature, he re-read the letter; and then he stayed where he was, deep in thought, until the candle guttered and died, leaving him alone and blind in the dark.

He moved then, slipping the letter into his pocket and performing by touch the necessary actions that would leave everything as he had found it. He restored the remaining letters to the box, locked and replaced it; as best he could, he scraped up the warm, soft remains of his candle, then rose and stepped out into the room, closing the panel behind him.

When he re-entered the library, Mr Lewis was standing on a chair diligently inspecting the rolls of parchment on one of the shelves and it was not until Alex rose up beside him out of the shadows that he knew he was there. Matt's eyes, as he looked down, were full of relief but his words were at odds with them.

'I see you didn't rush. I wondered if you'd maybe found a woman up there.'

Mr Deveril grinned, his face aesthetically pale in the strange light.

'Perish the thought. These days I'm a damned monk – see my robes.'

'Or, right now I'm a damned burglar – see my noose?' Matt asked crossly. 'Let's go.'

'Exactly,' said Alex pleasantly, 'what I was about to suggest. Though not, perhaps, in those exact words.'

It was not until they were at the riverside looking for a boat which would take them home that Mr Lewis finally brought himself to ask the obvious question.

'Did you find anything?'

Alex gazed across the water in rapt contemplation of the Surrey bank.

'Something, you might say, and nothing,' he replied vaguely. And then, grinning, 'Come home and I shall light a candle of understanding in thine heart which shall not be put out.'

To which, thought Matt irritably, there was no answer at all.

* * *

Not surprisingly, Chloë knew nothing of these activities and, during the first days of July, was as busy as she could have wished – and far too busy to wonder more than seven or eight times a day what Alex was doing. It had been arranged that the Queen should leave for Tunbridge Wells on the ninth for a stay of at least three weeks and Chloë suddenly realised that this meant she would be unlikely to return to London until the beginning of August – and August, of course, was when she might expect to see The Black Boy again. Weighing the situation carefully, she came to the conclusion that, since she needed storage space for the merchandise, it would have to be found now.

Accompanied by Mr Lewis, taciturn and disapproving of her stubborn insistence on visiting the wharves herself, Chloë set off on a round of enquiry and inspection and finally found what she wanted; a dry, sturdy warehouse hard by the Three Cranes in the Vintry. Chloë paid its owner two months' rent and Matt heaved a sigh of relief.

On the eve of her departure, Mr Deveril sought her out to take a business-like farewell. The formality of his manner made him a stranger. Certainly, this was not the man who had lent her his strength, understanding and unspoken sympathy on the night they had learned of Danny's death. Nor was it the man whose mere presence could make her heart leap into her throat and whose kiss had made her blood sing. She wondered what he was thinking ... and realised she would never know.

As it happened, Alex's thoughts weren't entirely clear even to himself. When he'd kissed her that night on the Falcon Stairs, he'd wanted more than a kiss and known that he could probably have it. But Chloë was no Sarah, to be taken and then discarded; nor did she deserve to be irrevocably tied to him unless they were quite sure it was what they both wanted. And even then, what he had said to Giles was true; he was intemperate, intolerant and impossible to live with. Unless ... but he refused to entertain that idea. Only two things were crystal clear. These days, the curve of her mouth or the tilt of her head were suddenly a temptation they'd never been before; and Chloë's quick mind, forthright charm and innate kindness clearly made her deserving of a better man.

Hiding his doubts behind a screen of practicality, he began by asking a number of questions about the safety and comfort of her travelling arrangements before coming at last, and with some reluctance, to the point.

'You may possibly have been wondering about our annulment.'

Chloë, who had been trying not to wonder about the annulment, swallowed, met his gaze and found it unreadable. 'Yes.'

'Yes,' he repeated with a faint glimmer of his usual acidity. 'I've done everything I can – including signing the necessary papers – but, as I believe I warned you, the wheels of the Church grind exceedingly slow. Eventually they must ask to see you and when that happens I imagine the end will be in sight. Alternatively, they may place the matter before the King and if they do that – or have already done so – it might be possible for you to move things along a little by appealing to the Queen.'

'I see.' She thought for a moment. 'Is ... that what you want?'

Forcing down a sudden urge to admit that he had no idea, Alex shrugged and maintained his indifferent façade.

'Not particularly. You may do as you see fit. It makes little difference to me since I'm in no hurry to resume my bachelor status. But it occurred to me that – if and when your ship comes in and you find yourself financially independent – you might prefer to find yourself legally free as well.'

Chloë put a lot of effort into keeping both face and voice neutral.

'Thank you. Like you, I'm in no particular hurry ... and I doubt the Queen would help anyway. I know we're looking for an annulment not a divorce, but Catherine's so devoutly Catholic that she may not recognise the difference. However, I'll bear it in mind.'

'Do.' He paused and then, against his will, heard himself say, 'I'm likely to be rather busy while you're away - but when you come back we should probably talk.'

Just in time, she stopped herself asking about what.

'Yes. I imagine we should.'

'Then I'll see you in three weeks or so,' Alex finished pleasantly. 'In the meantime, don't do anything I wouldn't do. Or, in fact, a good many things I would.'

On which felicitous note, he took his leave of her.

* * *

For the next week after Chloë had gone, in day after day of scorching heat, Alex relentlessly pursued his enquiries. On the one hand, he continued to follow the existing lines of information which kept him in loose communication with Mr Beckwith and on the other, he and Matt devoted a good deal of time and energy to the observance of Cousin Simon. And then, on Monday the sixteenth, when the weather mercifully broke in a hailstorm of epic proportions, a letter arrived from Prince Rupert's secretary.

Alex read it thoughtfully, then went in search of Matthew.

'Do you think,' he asked, 'that you can keep up the good work without me?'

Matt surveyed him with mistrust. 'If I have to.'

'You have to,' replied Mr Deveril. 'I'm joining the Navy. Temporarily, I hope. I'm summoned to render an account of our progress to His

Highness. And since I've nothing whatsoever that I can usefully tell him, you'd better pray – as I shall – that I find him in a good humour.'

NINE

Chloë had gone to Tunbridge Wells hoping to find peace of mind and in the first few days there was tranquillity of a sort, brought about by the air of dawdling business that invested the royal household. You never, she discovered, had much to do but you always had to be there, formally gowned and smiling, as you chatted over your embroidery or accompanied the Queen in her carriage or walked with her in the gardens. And you were never, ever alone. Chloë settled in amongst the other ladies like a raven amongst peacocks and for a time the strange novelty of her life contrived to exercise a beneficial effect on her spirits. Then came the letter from her husband and she was carrying hods in Egypt again.

It was a cool, impersonal letter, written in flamboyant hand-writing and signed with his initials. Chloë had stared at it for a long time, disappointment in her eyes and anxiety in her heart, thinking how typical it was. Anyone else would use their name; anyone else, damn it, would stay at home in his slippers and leave the war to those whose job it was. Hadn't anyone, she wondered, blowing her nose, ever told Mr Deveril that the things you liked were usually bad for you?

Wednesday, the twenty-fifth, was the feast of St James the Apostle and Chloë, who had woken with a nagging headache, went quietly to Mass with Queen Catherine and moved through the rest of the day with a vague sense of unease. It was not until Friday, when news came that the fleet had been engaged, that she understood it; and then had to live through four long days before more detailed news arrived with the King and his suite.

They were only too pleased to talk of the late battle for this time Prince Rupert and the Duke of Albemarle had won a conclusive victory. Moving discreetly from one gentleman to another, Chloë discovered that the two fleets had finally converged early on St James' day after previously losing each other during twenty-four hours of gales and heavy seas. The opposing vanguards had gone into action first but the centres were soon engaged and Sir Jeremy Smith of the Blue Squadron had become involved in a confused struggle with the Dutch rear under Tromp; a struggle which Sir Jeremy had presumably had the best of, since he kept Tromp away from the rest of the Dutch fleet and then chased him all the way home.

Elsewhere, the Dutch van had been driven into retreat in some fierce fighting but the hottest action, so everyone said, had been in the centre. Rupert and Albemarle had conducted a furious mêlée, grappling with the enemy and firing broadside upon broadside against de Ruyter who, though weakened by the loss of his rear and vanguards, was still determined to fight on. No one mentioned Mr Deveril but Chloë gloomily thought that she knew where he would have been.

She joined the periphery of a little group about the Duke of Buckingham and listened while he described in hilarious terms how Albemarle had supposedly boasted that de Ruyter would give him but two broadsides and then run. This anecdote was greeted with a good deal of amused ribaldry from his audience. Chloë moved away and found herself confronting the King. She curtsied and waited for him to move on. He did not do so and the cynical gaze rested on her with disturbing knowledge.

'Mistress Deveril,' he said, raising her to her feet and placing her hand on his arm, 'you have been talking to all the wrong people.'

Walking at his side between the stately rose-beds, Chloë decided to say as little as possible. 'Oh?'

'Indeed,' nodded Charles placidly. 'That is – I presume that you want news of your husband? Or perhaps I'm mistaken and some other fortunate gentleman is the cause of this pallor?'

The pallor vanished beneath a deep flush.

'No,' said Chloë baldly. 'There isn't – he isn't – that is, I – '

'Quite.' His Majesty was laughing. 'You know, there is a question I should dearly love to ask you. And I imagine that you can guess what it is.'

'I - I think so, Your Majesty.'

'But since it isn't my business,' he went on, 'it would be churlish of me to inflict upon you the embarrassment of answering it. So I shall strive to content myself with telling you that, to the best of my knowledge, Mr Deveril is both alive and well and aboard the Royal James with my cousin.'

The sense of it took a moment to sink in and behind her black satin bodice, Chloë experienced a number of conflicting sensations. At length, she looked up and her mouth curled into a wide, irresistible smile.

'Thank you, sire.' She thought for a moment. 'How do you know?'

Charles raised one mocking brow.

'My dear – is it possible that Alex could take part in any campaign and not be mentioned in a despatch? As I understand it, when de Ruyter went into retreat there was insufficient wind to enable our fleet to overtake him – so your husband asked for, and was given, command of Rupert's small sloop, the Fan Fan. He took it up behind the Seven Provinces under oar and, with only two guns and good deal of impudence, proceeded to harry our Dutch friends for almost an hour. Much, I might add, to the delight of our own seamen.'

'And without getting himself blown out of the water?'

'And without getting blown out of the water,' agreed the King gravely. 'Not that they didn't try, you understand. But Alex has the luck of the devil.'

* * *

Five days later they were all back in London and Chloë, leaving the Queen to be settled in by her usual attendants, obtained her release and scuttled home to Southwark where she was received by Naomi with rapturous relief and the intelligence that Mr Deveril was still at sea. An enquiry as to the whereabouts of Mr Lewis produced a faintly disapproving sniff and the information that he was out and, as usual, no one knew where.

Matt returned just as Chloë was sitting down to supper and it immediately struck her that his normally imperturbable face wore signs of distinct harassment.

'I think,' she said conversationally, 'that you should tell me why Mr Deveril suddenly decided to join the fleet.'

Matthew took his time over a mouthful of beef and then said, 'Maybe I should – but Mr Alex'll gut me if I do.'

She sighed. 'It's to do with his work for Prince Rupert?'

'Aye.'

The food turned to ashes in Chloë's mouth and she laid down her knife.

'Was Danny involved in it?'

There was a long silence before Matt said, 'No. Only Mr Alex and Mr Giles – and me.'

The pause had given him away and her eyes widened with tired shock.

'But someone thought he was – is that it? And they – ' She stopped, pressing her fingers over her mouth, her stomach cold and every sense revolted by the smell of the food.

Matthew pushed his plate away with a jerk.

'Come on.' He rose and drew her out of her seat. 'You can't stay in here with this lot. Come away to the parlour.' Then, when he had her settled beside the empty fireplace, he sat down facing her and said roughly, 'As for Mr Alex's work for the Prince, you know I can't discuss it. It's not that I don't think you can keep your mouth shut … but the less folk that know, the safer we'll all be.'

Chloë looked across at him and for once didn't trouble to school her expression.

'I'm frightened, Matt. I wish he'd come home.'

And Matt, who felt much the same, scowled direfully.

'That's no way to go on, lass. Mr Alex can take care of himself well enough.'

'I know. I know … but it's hard just waiting and doing nothing.'

The sharp black eyes rested on her with sudden thoughtfulness.

'Well, worrying yourself silly is no help. But what you could do is keep your ears open at Court and tell me what you hear. Not the bedchamber gossip – but other things you'll hear a lot quicker on the inside than I will on the out.'

Chloë looked blank. 'What sort of things?'

Mr Lewis gestured vaguely. 'Anything at all – particularly if it's to do with the Navy.' He paused, then added casually, 'Or the Duke of York's household.'

* * *

Chloë's first item of topical excitement came three days later when she passed the Duke and some of his gentlemen in the Stone Gallery and observed that the royal nose and right eye were hidden beneath three separate dressings and around these the skin was covered in bruises and long, angry scratches. He looked, thought Chloë, as if he had been in a fight. Seeing Cousin Simon detach himself from the group and move in her direction, she dutifully slowed her pace to let him overtake her, then smiled encouragingly and tried not to stare at his ornate wig and lavender brocade.

'Is His Grace setting a new fashion in face patches?' she asked lightly.

Simon gave a delicate shudder. 'My dear – pray don't mention it! He is quite morbidly sensitive about it at present. Scars, you know.'

Chloë raised her brows. 'My goodness – has Sir John Denham taken exception to the Duke's pursuit of his wife? Or was it the Duchess?'

'Not at all – though it does look that way, don't you think? No. It was a hunting accident. He will ride so recklessly and this is the result. He rode straight into the branch of a tree and they say it almost cost him his eye. Dreadful, isn't it?' He waved a scented handkerchief languidly beneath his nostrils. 'I am so glad I wasn't there – I really cannot support the sight of blood. But fortunately I never hunt. It is so rough and noisy. And the company, my dear … positively reeking of the stables and so very tedious. All one hears are tales of "Courses I Have Run" and "Tosses I Have Taken." It really isn't for me.'

'No,' agreed Chloë amiably. 'I quite see that.'

Simon beamed with innocent pleasure. 'Do you? How charming!' He paused. 'One hears, by the way, that Alex is at sea. I am surprised he could bear to leave you again.'

Chloë's expression remained perfectly bland.

'In fact it was the other way about. I was with the Queen, you know – and Alex was restless and in need of some occupation and a change of air. I expect him back any day now.'

'Oh I see. Most understandable,' he drawled. 'I need a rest myself – indeed, I leave for Kent at the end of next week. And then, of course, the estates require attention.' He sighed gently. 'No peace for the wicked, as they say.'

Chloë smiled brilliantly upon him. 'Quite.'

Later, when she relayed this conversation to Mr Lewis he surprised her by listening with rapt attention and then annoyed her by flatly refusing to explain his interest. She threatened to keep anything else she found out to herself but he would not budge; and two days later she was back again with something much more promising.

'Lords Coventry and Arlington are accused of being in Dutch pay,' she told Matt briefly, 'and the King has spent all day looking into it.'

Mr Lewis fixed her with an unwinking black stare.

'Accused by who?'

Chloë shook her head regretfully.

'I haven't heard any names yet. There are four of them, I think; three who have been rather adventurous with Sir William's reputation and another who's done the same for Lord Arlington.' She looked at him eagerly. 'Is it any help?'

Matt laughed wryly.

'Oh aye. It's that all right.'

And would say nothing more.

TEN

After the success of the St James day battle, the whole of Holland had been thrown into a state of panic which the English were naturally at some pains to prolong. Rupert and Albemarle ordered a blockade which efficiently sealed up the Dutch fleet and then cruised serenely under their enemies demoralised gaze whilst planning a shore-raid on Vlie Island.

News of this small splinter action reached London some days later and was the cause of an official day of thanks-giving with gun salutes from the Tower and street celebrations of varying description. Sir Robert Holmes, it appeared, having been prevented by bad weather from landing at Vlieland, had fired one hundred and sixty Dutch East Indiamen at anchor in the Fly and then, with the aid of a renegade Dutch Captain, gone on to make a highly successful raid on Terschelling.

Early on Tuesday morning Chloë and Matt received a visit from Captain Pierce who, under cover of the blockade, had returned complete with tongue, larynx and lungs to report every imaginable detail of his voyage, his ports of call and his cargo.

At the end of two hours, Matt claimed a pressing engagement and fled, leaving Chloë to listen patiently to a glowing description of Genoa and Bizerta and then, over dinner, to a laborious account of the return trip. It was a quarter after two before she was able to bring the worthy Captain down to the mundane requirements of business and half past four by the time they had worked through The Black Boy's bill of lading and made all the necessary arrangements.

By the time Captain Pierce finally left the house, Chloë felt as though she'd been squeezed through a wringer and when Matthew came in with a conciliatory glass of wine, she didn't even have the energy to berate him for his perfidy. Instead, she sipped the wine and then leaned back with closed eyes before saying weakly, 'They're to begin unloading tomorrow – and I'm in attendance on the Queen. Thank God.'

Matt regarded her darkly. 'Are you saying what I think you're saying?'

The brown eyes opened and looked back at him with malicious enjoyment.

'Yes. Tomorrow, dearest Matt, Captain Pierce will be all yours while you check his surprisingly large cargo. Item: thirty bolts Genoese velvet, various. Item: four cases Neapolitan tortoiseshell, also various. Item: twenty bolts Bizertan silk - - '

'Various,' finished Matthew dourly. 'I think I get your drift. It'll likely take all day.'

'And that,' grinned Chloë, 'is only if you're lucky.'

It did, in fact, take all that day and half of the next one but by Thursday afternoon Matt was able to report that the bill of lading tallied perfectly with the goods stacked neatly in the Vintry and also to present Chloë with the various samples she had requested. Despite his undeniable irritations, Captain Pierce undoubtedly had a good eye for quality and Chloë, stroking a fragment of sapphire velvet, was unable to resist sending a length of it to a tailor to be made up for Mr Deveril.

The next day she concentrated on finding buyers for all the perishable goods – oranges, figs and almonds – and was surprised at how easily it was done. And on Saturday, having spent the morning at the palace, she returned to find Mr Lewis in possession of a pamphlet catchily entitled A True and Perfect Narrative of the Great and Signal Success of a Part of His Majesty's Fleet which related the events of what was now popularly known as 'Holmes' Bonfire'. Eagerly, the two of them settled down to peruse it – which was how Mr Deveril found them when, without a word of warning, he strolled calmly into the house some half an hour later. Indeed, the first they knew of his presence was when a cool, pleasant voice said, 'Happy the wanderer who, like Ulysses, is come joyfully home at last.'

They looked up then and came swiftly to their feet, the pamphlet falling unheeded to the floor, as brown eyes and black fastened themselves on his face.

Alex raised a mocking brow. 'Isn't anyone going to say "Welcome back"? You don't have to mean it – but the silence is making me nervous.'

'Welcome back,' said Chloë dutifully. Her voice split on the words and her eyes were suspiciously bright. 'Excuse me. I have to see Mistress Jackson about a fatted calf.' And she fled.

Faintly bewildered, Mr Deveril watched her go and then turned to Matt.

'Has something upset her?'

'Aye. You have,' snorted Matthew. 'You beef-witted idiot, she'd been going daft with worry over you!'

'Has she?' If Alex found this either surprising or significant, he hid it well, merely saying casually, 'Yes, I suppose she would be. It's a habit with her.'

Matt bit back a hasty reply. 'You look thin.'

'The whole Navy looks thin. It's been on short rations since the beginning of the month.' Alex sat down and picked up the pamphlet. 'And then, of course, some of us have been rather busy. Too busy, for example, to read adventure stories. But perhaps you've been enjoying a little holiday?' He smiled enquiringly.

'What else?' snapped Matthew sarcastically. 'You know I never do a tap if I'm not watched.'

A hint of colour stained the lightly tanned skin.

'Don't be an ass, Matt. You know I didn't mean it.'

Mr Lewis grunted, not visibly mollified.

'Aye. Well, if you're ready to listen, I'll tell you what's been happening here while you were playing with fire in Holland. I suppose you were with Holmes?'

'Yes. You know I can't resist a little rape and pillage.'

'I know you can't resist playing the fool,' snapped Matt. 'Did you make your report to His Highness?'

'Yes. And since the victualing service is so hopelessly adrift that he thinks he may be forced to abandon the blockade, he naturally found our efforts less than satisfactory. Which is why he sent me with Holmes.'

'I don't follow.'

'Subtle and appropriate punishment,' explained Alex coolly. 'I was given the troop "allotted to the Dutch Captain to preserve him from violence". And, as Rupert well knew, my personal preference was for handing the bastard over.'

Matthew grunted and produced an epithet seldom heard even in infantry regiments. Then he said casually, 'While you were away, your Cousin Simon went out of town.'

'Where?' Just one word but it assured Matt of Mr Deveril's undivided attention.

'Kent. And you needn't panic. I've set a good lad to watch him.' He paused. 'And then last week, Coventry and Arlington were accused of spying.'

The blue eyes narrowed, then widened again with growing satisfaction.

'Now that,' said Alex, 'is interesting. Tell me more.'

* * *

A couple of hours later and having shed his dusty riding clothes, Alex tracked his wife to the tiny room she used as an office and went in, closing the door behind him.

Chloë, who had been staying out of his way because she couldn't trust herself to be careful – or, at least, not careful enough – looked up from her desk, startled and despairing. She wondered why it was that disadvantages, like troubles, never came singly. Surely it was enough that relief at his safe return had caused her to behave like an hysterical hen without having to face him at inescapably close quarters with her face flushed and shining and her hair hanging untidily around her shoulders?

He, of course, appeared entirely unaware of the heat. The loose cambric shirt, left open at his throat, was snowy-fresh and the raven's-wing hair fell lightly curling to his shoulders. He looked cool and alert and diabolically attractive. And if he had sought her out to tease her, Chloë thought she would probably start to howl.

'Hello,' he said simply. 'Are you busy – or can I disturb you for a moment?'

'Oh.' For a second, she almost blurted out that he disturbed her all the time. 'No. That is – yes. Of course.'

The merest hint of a smile tugging at the corner of his mouth, Alex perched on the edge of her desk. 'Matt tells me that your ship is back. Is the cargo all you hoped?'

She nodded. 'Yes. We expect to make a good profit.'

'I'm glad. Don't you want to say "I told you so"?'

'No. But it's very noble of you to give me the opportunity.'

'Yes. I thought so too. And, having re-established my credit, I hoped you might care to accompany me to the King's reception tonight.'

This was unexpected. Chloë allowed her gaze to wander to his hands. They lay loosely clasped on his knee, their usual grace overlaid by the crude marks of five weeks at sea. Inevitably, Mr Deveril had been doing more than give orders.

'Yes,' she said, with a calm she didn't feel. 'If you wish.'

Abruptly, he rose and turned away and when he spoke it was almost in answer to her thought. 'It was necessary, Chloë. But if you were worried – then I'm sorry.'

'Worried?' She managed a brief laugh. 'My goodness! As if I didn't know you can take care of yourself.'

'I'm pleased to hear it.' He looked back at her, obliquely considering. There was a short silence while he leaned against the door and folded his arms. 'I seem to recall that you have a rather splendid gown of cream shot-silk. I'd like you to wear it tonight.'

And that, thought Chloë, was so cunning that it nearly worked.

'Why?'

'To please me?'

'It's a lie,' she said flatly. 'You just want me to stop wearing black.'

He sighed. 'No. Wear black because it suits you, by all means. But don't wear it for Danny.'

She toyed restlessly with a sheaf of papers.

'Are you asking me to stop mourning him?'

'No. I'm asking that you stop cheapening a very genuine sentiment with the kind of conventional observance he would have laughed at.'

Chloë discovered that her hands were shaking and gripped them together.

'You're probably right,' she said slowly. 'Very well. But will you tell me something in return?'

'If I can.' His expression was guarded.

She drew a long breath. 'Was Danny murdered?'

Some of the colour drained from his skin.

'Oh God,' he said wearily. 'How did you find out?'

'I guessed. It – it doesn't matter. And you are looking for the man who did it?'

'No. That man is dead. I'm looking for the man who paid him.'

'I see.' She looked into his face. 'It's much more than Danny, isn't it? It's this thing you're doing for His Highness.' She paused, thinking. 'And this man you want … does he know that you're looking for him?'

A grim smile touched Mr Deveril's mouth. 'No. Not yet.'

Chloë's eyes widened suddenly. 'You know who he is.'

'Yes.' He sat down again on the side of the desk. 'I know who he is but that's not enough. I need proof; cast-iron, incorruptible proof. Or, because he is who he is, no one is going to believe me. Not even Giles.'

And because she was beginning to know him now and knew how to listen, she heard the almost imperceptible bitterness in the apparently level tone. She said, 'Matt believes you. And so would I.'

He smiled again but differently and stood up to go.

'Would you? I can't think why you should.' He laid his hand on the door-latch and then looked back. 'And will you also accept my word on the subject of mourning and wear the cream silk tonight?'

'Yes,' said Chloë. And to herself, 'And give you my heart on a plate. You need only ask.'

* * *

Whitehall was more than usually crowded and, having been delivered there by Julia on her way to visit friends, Chloë and Alex found themselves jostled in the press of people moving slowly inside.

'Oh dear,' sighed Mr Deveril mildly. 'It's jam-making night and we're going to be crushed, boiled and reduced to pulp. Hell!' This as he was hailed loudly from the steps by the Earl of Chesterfield and then, rather closer at hand by Lauderdale, the Scottish Secretary.

'Well, Deveril. They're saying we've taken a dozen ships of hemp and flax,' said Lauderdale with the soft lilt that masked a uniquely unscrupulous mind. 'Is that so?'

'A slight exaggeration,' replied Alex, bored but courteous. And then wheeled suddenly, aware that a hand was sliding into his pocket.

Mr Deveril was quick but the hand and whoever it belonged to was quicker. Even as he moved to grasp it, it slid supple as an eel through his clutching fingers and, as he turned after it, it's owner – a child of no more than ten – darted swiftly through the crowd and was gone.

'Well?' demanded his lordship tetchily. 'I asked ye how slight an exaggeration?'

Alex looked absently back at him, the light eyes frowning slightly.

'We took only one,' he replied. And, ignoring Lauderdale's tut of disapproval, looked back across the courtyard in the direction the child had taken.

For an instant, he debated forcing his way back through the crush but then dismissed the notion. It would take too long – and for what? To catch a child who'd tried to pick a pocket and gone away empty-handed? Lunacy. Pushing the incident to the back of his mind, he tucked Chloë's hand through his arm and said, 'Take a deep breath, Marigold. We're going in.'

Except in its large attendance, the reception that night was the same as any other; the wide, elegant chamber and the faces of the glittering throng all belonged to other evenings, other seasons. Only for Chloë, her hand on her husband's arm, was the music sweeter, the lights brighter, the colours sharper. And then he left her to report to the King and the occasion lost its charm.

She spoke to Lady Chesterfield, then to a number of other acquaintances and managed to avoid Lady Sarah Marsden, ravishing as usual in blue; but quite how she came to end up tête-á-tête with Lord George Gresham she had no idea. It wasn't the first time he had attempted to single her out but previously she had managed to defeat him by summoning some innocent third party to her side. Tonight, crowded as the room was, she could see no one to fulfil this function and realised that, for courtesy's sake, she would have to bear patiently with his lisping lordship's particular brand of double-entendre until he either tired of the game or some method of escape offered itself.

What she did not realise was that Gresham, taunted by Sarah Marsden and piqued by the knowledge that he had been weighed in the balance and found wanting, had resolved to change his tactics. He bowed over her hand and smiled at her.

'Mistwess Devewil – I had begun to fear I should not find you. Whitehall is so cwowded tonight.'

Chloë agreed that it was.

'His Majesty,' he continued smoothly, 'asks that you join him – and, of course, your husband – in the yellow saloon and has sent me to escort you there.' He offered his arm. 'Shall we?'

Chloë hesitated, her mind racing. The room he spoke of was not one she knew but, when you considered the size of Whitehall, that wasn't particularly surprising; and it was true that Alex was with the King. What troubled her was an innate distrust of George Gresham coupled with the notion that the only reason she could think of why her presence had been requested was the trifling matter of her annulment. Slowly, painfully, her breath leaked away behind her cream shot-silk bodice and the hand she laid on his lordship's velvet-clad arm was not quite steady.

He led her out into the corridor, along it a little way then across a gallery and into another, all the time chatting pleasantly. Intensely preoccupied, Chloë heeded their direction not at all and his lordship's conversation scarcely more so, though she occasionally responded to it with brief monosyllabic answers. And all the time a voice in her head was saying foolishly, 'Please, God, let it not happen ... please, God – let it not be now.'

Gresham opened a door and waited for her to pass through it. She entered without thinking, heard the latch click gently shut behind her and only then realised that they had arrived.

One of the palace's smaller chambers, the yellow saloon was panelled in yew and hung with curtains of gold-coloured silk. It was furnished with small inlaid cabinets, a high-backed couch and three carved chairs. And, except for themselves, it was quite empty.

Her brain functioning normally again, Chloë swept round to confront his lordship and said, 'Unless His Majesty is hiding under the sofa, we seem to have made a mistake.'

The worldly eyes examined the room with faint surprise.

'Perhaps he has been delayed.'

'Or perhaps,' returned Chloë astringently, 'he got lost on the way. I should be obliged if you would conduct me back to the Great Hall.'

He smiled then, raising his brows a little.

'Why certainly – all in good time. But there is no huwy for I doubt we'll be missed.'

Though aware that she had been tricked, Chloë felt too relieved to be either angry or afraid. 'Possibly not. Nevertheless, I want to go back.' And she moved to walk past him to the door. His arm shot out, barring her way.

'Why so cold?' he asked, amused. 'I won't eat you.'

Her brows soared derisively. 'I know. You won't get the chance. Now let me pass.'

'Pwesently, my dear. You see, you are such a cold little fish that I weally must discover if you have any warmth in you at all.' His arms closed round her. 'Or is it,' he murmured provocatively, 'all weserved for Alex?'

'Well at least he doesn't need to resort to trickery,' snapped Chloë. 'And if he did, I feel sure he'd think of something more original. Now – stop being ridiculous and let me go.'

His answer was to swoop on her mouth in a long, fierce kiss and Chloë, who had been expecting it, neither struggled nor responded but remained passively inert, waiting for an opportunity to hit him where it hurt. Lifting his head, Lord Gresham said nastily, 'If that's how you tweat your husband, I'm not surpwised he went to sea.'

'Aren't you, my dear?' said a pleasantly mocking voice from behind him.

With an oath, Gresham released Chloë and wheeled to confront Mr Deveril, his face flushing with annoyance.

'What the hell - - ' he began hastily and then stopped.

'Am I doing here?' finished Alex, his mouth curling unpleasantly. 'Saving my honour, it seems.' He walked up to Chloë who closed her mouth and tried not to blush, 'And yours. I thought I warned you about lonely antechambers?'

'You did,' she replied weakly. 'But I expected to find the King in this one. And you.'

He tutted reprovingly. 'Some people will believe anything. And some other people,' he said, looking at his lordship, 'can only be glad of it.'

Gresham, who already felt both foolish and alarmed, made an effort to recover his dignity. Blustering a little, he said, 'It was less than nothing. A little flirtation, nothing more. But if you want to make an issue of it, there are accepted civilised standards.'

Allowing regret to seep into every syllable, Alex said, 'But I, being a nasty common soldier, am not civilised at all. My inclinations are really quite crude … and the one I feel at the moment is to knock your teeth down your throat.' He drew Chloë gently to the door and then looked back. 'I'll restrain myself because I don't want my wife edified by the sight of me pasting you to the wall. But if you ever lay a hand on her again … if I hear you've been discussing her in any terms but those of purest courtesy, I'll do it. In fact, I shall enjoy doing it.' And before Gresham could think of a reply, they had gone.

Retracing their steps along the endless corridors and galleries, it was a long time before either of them spoke and Chloë, her soul awash with unholy glee, was not sure that she could. Finally, after they had collected their cloaks, she looked up at him rather shyly and said, 'Did you mean it? About pasting him to the wall, I mean?'

His glance was mildly surprised. 'In essence – though perhaps not literally. Of course. Why not?'

She drew a long breath. 'Oh. Thank you.'

He was amused. 'For what? Not offering to fight a duel on your behalf – or preserving the sanctity of our annulment?'

Chloë's joy evaporated with unpleasant rapidity.

Unaware of it, Alex went on blithely, 'Not that it would have come to that. Gresham may be a fool and a libertine but I never heard him accused of rape. Or alternatively,' he grinned, 'you could have consented and then summoned him as principal witness for the defence. He'd have loved that.'

It was more than Chloë could tolerate and, pulling her hand free of his arm, she stalked quickly away from him and out into the still, starry darkness. Without even pausing to think, she moved with a swift flurry of skirts across the court and through the chequered arch into King

Street. Then a hand closed firmly round her wrist and Mr Deveril swung her round to face him.

'Chloë, I'm sorry. That was in poor taste. Forget, if you can, that I said it.'

She looked at him, her eyes wide and bleak.

'Just tell me one thing. Did you mean that as well?'

His hand fell away from her as if burned. He said quietly, 'No. But if you need to ask, then I doubt my saying so will convince you.'

Revulsion became repentance and, feeling a lump hardening in her throat, Chloë hunted fruitlessly for her handkerchief and gave a wail of prosaic anguish.

The tension vanished. Alex dug deep into his pocket and pulled out, not a handkerchief, but a folded piece of paper. For a second, flicking it open, he stared at it faintly puzzled; then Chloë sniffed despairingly and he pushed it away, fished in the other pocket and produced a piece of soft cambric which he placed in her hand.

'I seem,' he said dryly, 'to be making a habit of this.'

Chloë mopped her face, blew her nose and then shook her head.

'I'm sorry. It's been a difficult day - but I don't suppose yours has been any better so it was unfair of me to enact you a tragedy. Of course I know you didn't mean it.'

'Chloë, no.' He swung round to face her and, taking the damp handkerchief from her to shove it back in his pocket, grasped her hands. 'The fault was wholly mine and you should have slapped me. In fact, I wish you had. I wouldn't feel such a bastard.' A glint of humour reappeared in his eyes and he raised her right hand towards his cheek, 'Shall I show you how? It might come in useful.'

She shook her head and managed a watery chuckle. 'Next time, perhaps.'

'There had better not be a next time.' He examined her face. 'Am I forgiven?'

'Yes.' She couldn't quite resist laying her palm briefly against his face. 'Of course.' And then, trying to hide the tell-tale impulse by withdrawing her hands from his in order to pull her cloak about her, said thoughtlessly, 'It's only that you spoiled the moment.'

'Moment?' He looked bewildered. 'What moment?'

'You coming to find me and arriving just when I needed you – then threatening Lord Gresham the way you did – and not saying a single word about how stupid I'd been.' She stole a glance up at him and was surprised by the sudden grimness of his expression. 'I know I shouldn't have believed – '

'Stop. I know I'm a bastard – I already admitted it. I open my mouth and say things I shouldn't. I'm always doing it. And I know I deserve to be made to grovel but there's nothing you can say that can make me feel worse than I do already.'

Chloë stared at him blankly. 'That wasn't what I was doing.'

'I know it wasn't. That's the trouble.' Alex drew a long breath and then, loosing it, said, 'Enough. Let's walk ... before I decide to fall on my sword and have done with it.'

Unsure how to take this, Chloë merely nodded and took his arm.

It was late and the wide, cobbled thoroughfare of the Strand was deserted as they walked silently past the New Exchange and the Savoy Palace. After a time, they held a desultory conversation about Alex's time at sea and Chloë's cargo lodged in the Vintry. At Temple Bar they joined Fleet Street and moved on past St Dunstan-in-the-West and up Ludgate Hill into the City. It was as they entered St Paul's Court that a very faint sound reached Mr Deveril's ears; the sound of metal scraping stone. He grasped Chloë's wrist warningly and stopped for a second to listen. One slight, muffled clink and then nothing.

Moving on again, Alex released Chloë and loosened his sword in its sheath. Then he looked down at her, laid a finger against his lips and gave a brief, reassuring smile.

'Footpads?' thought Chloë, her ears straining to hear sounds beyond the gentle rustling of her skirts. Then she caught something; a low whistle from in front of them. And glancing quickly at Mr Deveril, saw that he had heard it too.

They had reached the end of the south transept and Chloë was wondering, with a sort of academic interest, why she wasn't more frightened, when Alex stopped again. She had just time to be aware that there were shapes emerging from the shadows of the houses to their right when his hand closed on her arm like the jaws of a trap and propelled her behind him with a force that spun her hard against the wall of the cathedral. Then, in two fluid moves, he tore off his cloak and drew his sword.

Eyes alert, Alex held the cloak to one side while his blade swept a gleaming arc in front of him, causing the would-be assailants who emerged from the shadows to falter. Then they were on him – one holding a sword and the other two armed with cudgels and knives. Alex twisted to engage the first man while deflecting a cudgel blow to his head with his cloak-swathed forearm. He lunged and there was a grunt as the first man crumpled and then, wrenching his blade free, Alex stepped back to make another steely sweep at the pair in front of him. A billet took him hard on the shoulder making him stagger but then the sword drove home again and the second attacker dropped back clutching his arm and turned to run. Alex caught the third man's blade in the folds of his cloak, ducked to avoid a swinging blow to his ear while at the same time making a hard, upwards thrust of his sword arm. There was an unpleasant choking sound and the man dropped like a stone, his throat pierced below the jaw.

For an instant Mr Deveril remained poised, gazing in the direction taken by the second man, then, shaking his arm free of the cloak, came slowly back to Chloë.

'Are you all right?' His breathing was a little fast but he sounded perfectly calm.

'Of course. Are you?' She was pleased to find that her voice was as steady as his.

Alex nodded briefly. 'Stay here for a moment. I won't be long.' Then he turned and went back to the two corpses.

Watching him wipe his blade clean of their blood, Chloë shivered a little. She had always known that Mr Deveril was a swordsman of some ability; what she'd never fully appreciated was that he was a professional.

He came back to her holding a dagger taken from one of the bodies and closed her fingers round the hilt. 'Only a precaution. I doubt we'll be attacked again but, just in case, I'd like you to carry this for me. Don't worry – you won't have to use it. Now, keep close to me but don't talk. Ready?'

She smiled and nodded.

'Good girl. Everything's going to be all right.'

They moved on between the massive, crumbling wall of the cathedral and the shadowy houses. At the end of St Paul's Court, they crossed the lower end of Old Change into Watling Street and were just approaching the junction with Canning Street when they heard the sound of running feet from somewhere not far behind them.

'Damn,' said Alex. And, grabbing Chloë's hand, dived headlong down Dowgate Hill.

Cloak billowing behind her, Chloë somehow managed to keep pace with him. He swerved off to the right, then left towards the Skinners Hall and she realised that they were heading for the river somewhere around Queenhithe. Then he turned right again, plunging into a labyrinth of alleyways and finally came to an abrupt halt, pulling her hard against his side in a doorway. His teeth gleamed in a smile.

'We haven't lost them for long. They know we have to cross the river.'

'They're not footpads,' gasped Chloë, 'or they wouldn't be following us. Do you think it's to do with -- ?'

'Unlikely.' It was a lie but he didn't want to frighten her unduly. 'Get rid of the petticoats. You can't run weighed down by twenty ells of taffeta. I won't look.'

'Why not?' she asked, fumbling with her skirts. A sinuous wriggle got rid of the discarded garments and, kicking them aside, she looped her now over-long silk skirt over her arm.

'Not ideal but the best I can do. Now what?'

'A boat, if we can find one. Give me your hand and do exactly what I tell you.'

This time it was easier. Without the extra weight and with her feet reasonably free, she was almost as nimble as Alex. They came to the river at the Three Cranes and flitted along the waterfront looking for a barge or small boat. Then, without warning, there were figures rushing at them from the Steel Yard and Alex dodged back between the warehouses in the direction of Thames Street.

The next ten minutes was a sort of wild-goose chase. They climbed stairs and ran down alleys, circled buildings, zigzagged, then doubled back, eventually ending up by St Lawrence Poultney from whence they could hear runners approaching from the direction of All Hallows the Less. Alex stopped, pulled Chloë close and hissed, 'Enough of this. Let's hide.'

'Where?' she gasped, looking around them wildly.

'There.' He pointed to an aged and over-full laystall, behind which ran a ledge some five feet off the ground. He grinned suddenly. 'Oh yes. That's perfect.'

For some reason Chloe couldn't identify, he tossed the handkerchief from his pocket down on the ground a few feet in front of the trough. Then, towing her with him, he ran to one side, briefly eyed the height of the ledge and, placing his hands on top of it, hauled himself up until his knee met the surface. Turning, he leaned down and reached towards Chloe.

'Give me your hands. Quickly!'

With no time to think, she did as he asked and found herself pulled swiftly upwards until she arrived, her feet tangled in silk, into the safety of one steely arm.

Alex slid to the other side of her and pushed her along the ledge, behind the steaming pile of ordure-laden rubbish. The stench was horrendous.

'Get down,' he whispered. 'As low as you can.' And grinned when, having done so, she smothered her nose and mouth in a handful of skirt. 'I know. Don't cough. They're coming.'

Crouching down on one knee beside her, he surveyed the trough and its framework appraisingly. The thing was already virtually groaning under the weight of the refuse inside it and the props beneath it were rotten with age. Alex gave it an experimental push and felt it give just a little. At the same time, their three would-be attackers ran into the square and then stopped, presumably looking around for their quarry.

Hidden from view up above, Alex dragged the skirt from Chloe's hands and laid them silently against the side of the trough. Then, smiling maliciously, he signalled her to wait.

One of the fellows below them said, 'Where did they go?'

'Dunno,' replied another. 'Bugger. I hope we ain't lost 'em or he won't pay. Maybe they didn't come this way.'

'Yes, they did,' said a third voice, triumphantly. 'Look!'

There was a sound of swiftly approaching feet and then, 'Bastard dropped his hankie, careless sod. Question is – which way was he running?'

And, hoping for the best, Alex looked at Chloe and hissed, 'Now!'

They shoved with all their might and the laystall simply gave up the fight. Quicker even than Mr Deveril had hoped, it gave a massive creak and toppled over with a crash which almost, but not quite drowned the yells of those below it. For a second, there was silence and, looking down, Chloe saw that one of the men must have got trapped directly beneath the trough, while the other two had been knocked flat by half a ton of horse-dung.

Laughing, Alex drew her to her feet and said, 'Well, that makes up for some of the running. But we don't have time to gloat. Let's go.'

He sat down, swung his legs over the edge and, using one hand for support, dropped neatly to the ground. Then he held up his arms to Chloe. 'Jump, Marigold.'

Without a shred of hesitation, Chloë sat down, swung her feet over the edge and propelled herself into his waiting arms.

And, holding her hard against his chest while meeting the laughter in her eyes, Alex made a discovery; a discovery that stopped his breath and set every nerve vibrating with shock. His gaze widened and his grip on her tightened. Then, because they were still in danger, he put the knowledge to one side and stepped back, releasing her. Just one random instant to create a truth from a myth, hope and purpose where there had been none; to change a life. 'And what a stupid time,' he thought, 'what a stupid bloody time for it to happen.'

He drew a steadying breath and caught Chloë's fingers. 'Come on!'

Once more zigzagging through alleyways they'd already seen once tonight and which he hoped never to see again, he led her back towards Thames Street and the river. If they could just make it on to the bridge, he reasoned, they might have a chance of out-running their attackers. If not, he'd have to fight them off yet again – this time leaving nothing to chance. The alternative didn't bear thinking about because the smallest miscalculation on his part would leave Chloe unprotected. 'And if she gets hurt because of me,' he thought, 'that will be the last damned straw.'

They reached the Fishmongers Hall, swung round a corner and found themselves face to face with the fellows they'd left buried under the noxious contents of the laystall. The smell was overpowering. Alex pulled Chloë behind him and said, 'Get ready to run.'

'Now,' said the burlier of the two with gloating anticipation. 'Now we've got you.'

'Not quite,' returned Mr Deveril. 'You still have to take me. If you can.'

'Oh we can,' said the bravo. And emitted a loud, piercing whistle.

Uncomfortably aware that there was a third man somewhere behind him, Alex hurled himself at the two in front with a suddenness he hoped would disconcert them, sent the smaller man hurtling backwards with a vicious kick to the stomach and whirled on the other with a twist of his sword arm. It nearly worked but not quite. The blade glanced off the man's shoulder and Alex found himself threatened with a dagger. He parried it just in time and, expecting to be attacked from the rear at any moment, tried to alter his position so that the wall was at his back. He wasn't as successful as he'd hoped and, realising that there was no time to waste, he lunged at the fellow with dagger and dropped him with a thrust to the heart.

Meanwhile, the third man advanced stealthily through the shadows. He stepped past the posts into the road, the light glimmering palely on his dagger as he raised it, preparing to strike at Mr Deveril's unprotected back. But he never achieved his aim nor knew whose hand held the knife that plunged deep and true into the base of his neck, cutting off his life with a surprised gurgle.

Chloë stepped back and watched him fall to the cobbles, his body twitching and pumping blood. Her stomach heaved and, turning away, she vomited helplessly and painfully against the wall.

Aware that the man he'd kicked was scrambling to his knees, Alex felled him again with a second kick – this time to the side of the head – and whirled round to face the third assailant. And saw the fellow on the ground in a pool of blood, with Chloë a couple of steps beyond being violently sick.

He had intended to keep just one of their attackers alive in order to ask a few pertinent questions. One look at Chloë changed that. All that mattered now was to make an end – and that meant leaving no survivors to call up reinforcements. Without wasting any more time, Alex drove the point of his sword through the fellow's throat and ran to his wife.

Shuddering uncontrollably, Chloë wiped her mouth with one shaking hand and turned to find Mr Deveril's arms closing about her.

Her voice raw and muffled against his shoulder, she said, 'I've killed him.'

'Yes. Don't look. Just come away.'

'He was c-coming up behind you.' It hurt to speak and she thought she was going to be sick again. 'I had to.'

'You had to.' Firmly leading her away from the scene of carnage, he wondered how much more of this hellish night she could stand. Then he said, 'We should go. Hopefully, there's no one left to follow – but we shouldn't linger. We're nearly at the bridge so it's not far now. Can you manage?'

She nodded and swallowing her nausea, said, 'Yes.'

'Good girl. Now!'

They were off Fish Street Hill and on to the bridge in a flash. By the time they were half-way across it and with no sign of pursuit, Mr Deveril – seeing Chloë clutching her side and breathing in painful gasps - judged it safe to slow their pace a little. She stumbled and he steadied her with a firm arm about her waist. Then they were across, past the Bear-at-the-Bridge-Foot and St Mary Overie. Alex stopped to listen and then, apparently satisfied, looked down at Chloë, leaning against him and still sobbing for breath. His own chest was heaving but he managed a weak laugh as he lifted her up into his arms and set off to carry her home.

The house was quiet and the only light a single candle on a table beside the door. Alex left it where it was and trod noiselessly up the stairs to Chloë's room. It was only when he laid her on the bed that the brown eyes, dark with stress, flickered open and followed him while he lit a candle and crossed the room to close the curtains. Then, as he turned back to her, she propped herself up on one elbow and looked at him.

His hair was wildly disordered, his coat ruined, his hands grazed and filthy, and the expression in his eyes was one she had never seen.

Making a huge effort, she said, 'If you look like that, I hate to think what I must look like.'

Smiling a little, Alex remained where he was, contemplating her from head to foot.

'Your face is dirty, your hair is a disaster and you'll never wear that gown again. But you're in one piece – and, thanks to you, so am I. Consequently, in the only ways that matter, you've never looked better.'

Chloe sat up, pushed her hair back with shaking hands and, her voice a mere thread, said, 'I've killed someone.'

The smile faded. Alex came to sit beside her and took her hands in his.

'I know. I also know it's pointless asking you to forget it. But try, if you can, to remember why it was necessary ... and what might have happened if you hadn't.'

Her fingers clung to his but she nodded and drew a long, ragged breath.

Alex saw in her eyes the plea she wouldn't make but, inwardly cursing, pretended he didn't. Even though it was clear that she needed him, he couldn't stay with her because he was afraid of what might happen if he did.

Releasing her hands, he said, 'I'm sorry – so very sorry – that this happened. But if it helps, I know of no other woman who either could or would do what you did tonight.' He moved unhurriedly to the door, then looked back, the blue gaze suddenly intense, and said, 'You are quite remarkable. Try to sleep, Marigold.' And was gone.

Alex had walked into his room before he realised that, although aching in every muscle, he had no intention of sleeping. Absently, he drew off his coat and washed his face and hands; his shirt was sticking uncomfortably to his shoulders so he removed it and put on another. Somewhere at the back of his mind, he knew he ought to be trying to figure out what had just happened ... why and on the orders of whom, they'd been attacked. Instead, he stood for a time gazing out of the window, wanting to go back to Chloë and seething with rebellion because he couldn't trust himself not to say or do something for which this was unquestionably not the right time.

He sat down, gathering and absorbing the night's other cataclysm before facing the all-important question. The question of how you convinced the girl you'd married while magnificently drunk that, after eight months of a marriage that was not a marriage, you had fallen irrevocably in love with her; and were afraid that you had left it too late.

ELEVEN

Alex sat deep in thought for perhaps half an hour, then stood up and stretched his rapidly stiffening muscles. The shoulder that had taken the cudgel-blow was now a screaming ache. He suspected that, within a few hours, it would be black and blue and seriously affecting the use of his left arm. He was just wondering, vaguely, whether the short time left before dawn justified the trouble of undressing and going to bed when a sound reached his ears; a faint sound, but loud in the stillness of the house. Out of the habits of fifteen years came the conditioned reflex to listen. But that was all for his mind was still elsewhere. And then he heard it again; the distant betraying sound of movement downstairs. Alex was abruptly restored to himself.

Four legitimate possibilities; Chloë, Matt, Naomi, Mistress Jackson – all of them equally unlikely and leaving only one logical alternative which, after the murderous chase home, wasn't so hard to believe. The only question was, were they being burgled or invaded?

From a drawer, he drew a small serviceable dagger and then slipped out of his room. The landing was in darkness and no light showed under any of the doors. Alex crossed swiftly to the stair-head and quietly made his way down. A few steps from the foot he paused, realising that although he had left a candle burning, the hall was dark. Then the smell of it reached him; warm wax, recently extinguished. He moved on, listening and finally isolated the sound.

Beneath the door of Chloë's office lay a ribbon of light and from behind it came the unmistakeable rumble of drawers and the crackle of paper. Someone was conducting a thorough search. Alex looked down at the knife in his hand, then laid it gently on the floor against the wall. Just one man it seemed, and this time he needed him alive. This time, he thought, grimly smiling, we'll find out what the hell is going on.

His fingers closed on the latch, lifting it silently, then he flung the door wide and was face to face with the intruder who looked back at him, startled, one hand just withdrawing from his pocket. And then he jumped.

The fellow was heavily-built and his hands were like bill-hooks. Less your average burglar, thought Mr Deveril as he side-stepped, than a wrestler – or, scenting the odour of tar, a sailor. And apparently unarmed which, given the smallness of the room, was probably just as well. Then the enormous hands were on him, spinning him round and wrenching his arms behind his back with a knee to the kidneys as leverage. Alex grunted as his bruised shoulder flamed with agony; then, delivering a savage kick to the other man's shin, he bent sharply, broke his grip and hurled him to the ground in a sea of papers.

The candle went out. Prepared for it, Alex was on his opponent before he had time to move and already engineering a knee lock. It was answered with a hard chopping motion which he caught half-way to his throat. Altering his grip, Alex twisted and, holding the arm at an unpleasant angle, said breathlessly, 'I wonder what's in your pocket. And if you can be persuaded to give it to me.'

He felt, with surprise, the fellow's muscles relax and then, too late, understood why. With sudden, unexpected venom, the man spat hard in his face while simultaneously jerking himself free; then a fist like Thor's hammer took him in the stomach and his left arm was seized and twisted viciously against the socket.

Through the white-hot anguish that was his shoulder, Mr Deveril recognised that he had committed a major miscalculation. After a month of continual work on poor food, followed by twenty-four hours without sleep during which he'd already received a fairly comprehensive battering, his physical capabilities were at an unsurprisingly low ebb. He rammed his elbow into the man's side and inflated his lungs to do the only sensible thing; yell for Matt.

He never managed it. Even as he opened his mouth to call, his arm was given one final, excruciating jerk and, in the haze of burning pain that followed, released so that the burglar could spin him round and deliver a flailing blow to the jaw. Alex's head snapped back, hitting the desk and, without a second's delay, the other man was up and off through the door.

By the time Alex had recovered sufficiently to haul himself dizzily to his feet, the front door had slammed and his intruder was long gone. He dropped heavily on the edge of the desk, allowing his left hand to fall loosely at his side while using his right to delicately explore the damage to his shoulder. It screamed to the touch but mercifully did not appear to be dislocated. He closed his eyes, controlling faintness and frustration with every ounce of his will.

When he opened them again Chloë was standing in the doorway, candle in hand, her eyes wide with anxiety and one arm thrust into a blue chamber-robe over her night-rail. Then she moved slowly through the wreck of her office to stand before him.

'Some people,' she said severely, her voice not entirely steady, 'will do anything to enliven a dull Friday.'

'Saturday,' Mr Deveril corrected weakly. 'It's Saturday. You've had a burglar.'

'So I see. And you've had a fight. Another one. What's wrong with your arm?' She did not touch him but set about using the candle to light others.

'Nothing that won't mend.' He eyed her consideringly. 'I'm sorry to be tedious – but he took something and I need to know what.'

Chloë sought her straying sleeve, then tied the ribbon at her waist with a business-like air.

'What you need,' she replied, 'is to go to bed. All this will wait and you've done enough for one day. Come on.' She reached out to take his hand.

His fingers closed over hers but he did not move. 'It's important, Chloë.'

'Really?'

'Really. It can't wait ... but I can't do it alone. Help me?'

She drew a long breath and said, 'All right. But I don't need you – I can do it on my own. You get some sleep and when I find out what's missing, I'll wake you.'

'No. But if it will make you happy, I'll do no more than sit and watch.' His brow was faintly furrowed but beneath it the translucent eyes gleamed with the same expression they had held earlier and which Chloë still could not interpret.

She frowned crossly. 'You think that's a compromise? You're hurt and you're tired – and if you weren't so stubborn, you'd admit it.'

'I'll admit it willingly – but I won't go to bed.' He stood up with an effort that made Chloë grit her teeth and then looked down at her, smiling a little. 'Please, Marigold?'

And that, of course, settled it.

Chloë pushed her hair behind her ears and knelt down on the carpet amongst the lists and costings before he could see that tears were stinging her eyes.

'Sit down,' she said irritably. 'And if you lift a finger, I swear I'll go back to bed.'

'Don't do that,' begged Mr Deveril, meekly doing as she said and concealing the acute relief it brought. 'The truth is it's just an excuse because I like to share my insomnia.'

Head bent over a sheaf of papers, she retorted, 'The truth – as someone once said – is that you don't know when to recognise a piece of good advice and take it.'

'Or how to tell it from interference?'

'Quite.' She sifted a handful of documents on to various piles and collected more from the litter around her.

Alex forced down the temptation to say things for which this was definitely not the time and fell silent, watching her. The fall of shining hair brushed the floor where she knelt and the narrow, arched brows were drawn together in concentration as she went through the papers, filing them one by one. He leant his head against the chair-back and his eyes grew heavy as he followed the small, capable hands.

He fell asleep very quickly and, through an hour of sorting and collating, Chloë glanced up from time to time to assure herself that he had not woken. Then she became absorbed in her task, checking and re-checking the piles until there was no doubt at all that only one document was missing. She sat on the floor, frowning thoughtfully, and then, hearing sounds that told her it was day and the servants were up, rose stiffly and went in search of Naomi.

When she returned some half-hour later bearing a tray of warm medicinally spiced ale, Mr Deveril had not moved. Chloë set the tray on the desk and stood for a moment, seething with resentment. Then, because she had promised, she blew out the candles and opened the curtains. Sunlight came flooding in but still he didn't stir and looking at his face, fine-drawn and bruised, Chloë wasn't surprised. Then, hating the necessity, she set out to wake him.

Eventually he sat up, wincing as the movement jarred his shoulder and rubbing a hand sluggishly across his eyes while Chloë put the ale in front of him and tried not to watch.

'I need a shave,' he said stupidly.

'Yes. Never mind. Drink that.' She paused, then added, 'It's still early – just past six. You only slept for an hour or so.'

Alex took a drink and then looked up, the blue gaze focusing slowly. 'I've kept you up all night. I'm sorry.'

Chloë repressed a desire to scream. 'It doesn't matter. I've found what you wanted to know.'

He was suddenly wide awake. 'And?'

'There's only one thing missing. The Black Boy's bill of lading.'

'What?'

'The bill of lading,' she repeated. 'The list of the cargo on – '

'Yes. I know what it is.' Alex stared at her with worrying intensity and then hauled himself to his feet. 'Wait here, will you?'

Chloë watched him go and then sat down, wondering if her control would last as long as she needed it. Then he was back and holding a piece of paper out to her.

'A bill of lading, you said. Like this?'

She looked and then, with surprise, into his face. 'Yes. Only this is for the Arabella – Captain Vine's ship. How did you get it?'

'I rather think that it was put into my pocket by mistake last night at Whitehall,' replied Mr Deveril slowly. 'This man Vine ... do you know anything about him?'

'Not much. Captain Pierce thinks he's either smuggling or breaking bulk.' She stopped abruptly. 'Put into your pocket? By that child?'

He nodded and watched her, a curious smile touching his mouth.

'Then somebody discovered their mistake and came to get it back but took mine instead,' she went on in growing disbelief, 'And we were chased all over the City and five men died ... for a bill of lading?'

'It looks that way, yes.'

'But why?'

'That's what I have to find out.' The smile grew into one of enormous charm and, taking her hand, he raised it to his lips. 'You may not realise it, but thanks to you I believe I may have the key. All that remains, is to find the door it opens.'

'I knew it,' said Chloë, covering confusion with gloom. 'You're going to tell me to forget what I know and ask no questions.'

'I'm afraid so. But not without gratitude.'

She rose and walked wearily to the door, saying flatly, 'The only thing you need thank me for is waking you up just now. Compared to that, the rest was nothing.' And she went out.

For a minute, Alex stared after her then, picking up the bill of lading, examined it carefully. He read every word, looked closely at both sides, held it to the light and found nothing that gave a clue to its importance. He tapped it thoughtfully against his hand. It might, of course, just be coded but he did not think so; which left only one other possibility. Reaching for the flint, he lit a candle and proceeded to warm the paper gently by the flame. And then smiled as, between lines of open script, new ones in faded ochre began to appear.

The cipher was moderately complex but it presented few difficulties to one experienced in the art and half an hour later Mr Deveril was writing it neatly on to a fresh sheet of paper. Then he decoded the message which was brief and consisted of just three lines.

Send detail sail power and planned movement.

Submission re. Beverweed approved. Proceed.

Urgent you increase victualing disruption.

Alex drew a long breath and considered the words. Then, 'Eureka,' he said, without visible signs of rejoicing and, going to the door, shouted for Matt.

By the time Mr Lewis made an appearance, Alex was sitting at Chloë's desk assembling various writing materials in front of him and did not immediately look up, thus giving Matt the opportunity to make a comprehensive survey. He noted the marks on the face and hands and the tell-tale stiffness of one shoulder, then said, 'She must have been a sturdy lass. What happened? Did you forget your money?'

Mr Deveril raised cool blue eyes.

'Sit down. If I had the time, I'd ask where the hell you were last night – but as it is, we need to hurry.' He tossed the bill of lading across the desk. 'Last night that was put in my pocket – a mistake it's owners later tried to rectify by attacking us on our way home and then burgling this house. As you see, there's an extra message in code.' He flicked his translation in the wake of the original. 'I'm about to make a copy which you'll deliver to Captain Vine aboard the Arabella – make sure you put him off the scent with a quantity of naïve chatter. It's vital he thinks this document is the original and myself entirely unaware of its hidden contents. Clear so far?'

'I think I can just about follow you,' said Matthew, annoyed.

'Good. Once he has the paper, watch him and if – as I think likely - he sends a messenger out of London, follow him. I trust you've still got someone watching my cousin?'

'Yes. He's at Sandwich and looks like staying there a while longer.'

'Then we must hope Captain Vine changes that. Unless we're very unlucky, he'll send the bill to Simon – who will then need to visit the Naval Office.'

'You're sure,' asked Matt, 'this it's meant for Simon?'

'Quite sure,' said Mr Deveril smoothly. 'The second instruction refers to Isabella van Beverweed who is not only Dutch but married to Lord Arlington. As we know, Simon has failed to discredit his lordship in other ways and so has presumably decided to try doing so through his lady.' He paused. 'Also, we have the not unimportant question of why that paper was put in my pocket.'

'Well?'

'A fortuitous coincidence. Their arrangements and information were, for once, poor – and presumably I was where Simon was expected to be. Someone hailed me loudly by name and the obvious mistake occurred. Truly,' finished Alex pleasantly, 'God works in a mysterious way. And now, if you'll excuse me, I have work to do.'

* * *

Some three hours later, having furnished Matt with an artfully contrived forgery, then shaved, bathed and changed his clothes, Mr Deveril stowed the original carefully in his pocket and set off for Mr

Beckwith's lodgings in King Street. Giles greeted him civilly but without warmth and then waited to be given the reason for his visit.

'I want you to come with me to Goring House,' said Alex, without preamble. 'I have a certain matter concerning our mutual endeavours to lay before Lord Arlington and it will save time if you're there.'

'What matter?' asked Giles, unimpressed and irritated by Mr Deveril's abrasive manner.

'Come and you'll find out. It won't take long.'

The dark grey eyes examined him impersonally.

'You look somewhat the worse for wear.'

His mouth curling at the understatement and his hand on the door-latch, Alex said, 'You know me … never a dull moment.'

Their journey to Goring House, situated on the edge of St James' Park at the far end of the Mall, was accomplished in a short time and in total silence. Even when they stood in an antechamber waiting for the Secretary of State to receive them, they neither spoke nor looked at each other but maintained an air of studied relaxation. And then they were called in.

In his late forties, Henry Bennet, first Baron Arlington, was distinguished from his fellows in two respects; the scar on his nose gained twenty years ago in a skirmish at Andover and the extreme formality of manner acquired during an exile spent at the court of Madrid. Both were in evidence as he rose from his desk and bowed slightly.

'Good morning, gentlemen. Please be seated. My assistant informs me that your business is urgent and so I have agreed to see you. However, I am expected at Whitehall within the hour so I would be obliged if you will come directly to the point.'

'The point,' said Mr Deveril, 'is that, at the request of Prince Rupert, Mr Beckwith and I have spent five months trying to discover and identify a traitor within the Naval service. We are now, I hope, in a position to do so – subject to your lordship's approval and a small amount of official help.'

There was a long silence while Arlington looked at them narrowly. Then he said, 'And why was I not told of His Highness' suspicions before?'

'Because suspicions are all they were,' replied Alex. 'Our orders were to furnish both the Prince and yourself with proof.'

'Which you now have?'

'Yes.' Rising, Mr Deveril produced two folded sheets of paper and handed one to his lordship. 'This bill of lading came into my possession yesterday. As you can see, it contains more than is at first apparent and is, in fact, the means by which our man receives his orders and relays his information. A simple device – but it works.'

'And the message? I presume you have decoded it?'

Alex nodded and, without speaking, passed over the second sheet.

Arlington read it twice, a frown mantling his brow. Then, looking up, 'If you are aware of the significance of the second of these instructions, I would be glad to know it.'

'Yes. I thought you might.'

Giles, who had possessed himself in patience up to this point, rose and crossed to where his lordship sat.

'May I?' he asked coolly, extending his hand. 'Mr Deveril likes surprises and I know as little of this as you do, my lord.'

Arlington passed the papers over, his eyes fixed on Alex. 'Well?'

Alex sat down again. 'You are right in believing that it refers to your wife. The person for whom the message is intended presumably has some plan to discredit you through her. Indeed, he has already tried something of the sort which resulted in the unsuccessful accusation you faced last month.'

'How do you know the two are connected?' asked Giles sharply.

'Because the gentleman in question holds detailed reports on both Lord Arlington and Sir William Coventry.'

'How do you know?' It was Giles again.

His lordship stood up. 'I assume you came by this information in an unorthodox manner that you would prefer not to disclose,' he said shrewdly. 'But the little I have seen of you, Mr Deveril, leads me to suspect that – having found these files – you then read them. Am I right?'

Alex smiled. 'Quite right, my lord. But you know as well as I that they contained nothing remotely treasonous ... and, for the rest, you may depend on my discretion.'

'I am obliged to you,' said Arlington sardonically. 'And would have been more so if you had seen fit to warn me. However. There remains only one question to be asked. The gentleman's name.'

There was a pause while Mr Deveril surveyed them with an air of chilly amusement.

'I'm afraid,' he said gently, 'that I don't propose to tell you.'

'You what?' snapped Arlington, startled out of his usual punctiliousness. 'Why not?'

'Because I prefer to give you the man himself – in flagrante, as it were.'

'I might have known,' said Mr Beckwith acidly, 'that you'd find a way of turning this into a drama. You're enjoying it, aren't you?'

'Yes. I am.' Temper flared briefly and then was gone. 'I'm also, if you can believe it, trying to ensure there can be no mistakes – and no need for further proof.'

'That is all very well,' said Arlington, 'but there are other considerations. If your traitor is in a position to fulfil the requirements on that paper, he holds a post of some responsibility. You must realise that it is my official duty to determine the political implications of publicly arresting such a man.'

'I do realise it,' replied Alex, 'but in this case I think you will find that your problems lie less with the man himself, than in the doubtful light his actions will cast on his innocent patron. And that, Sir Henry, is your affair not mine. What I require right now is a little help from yourself to enable me to complete the necessary arrangements.'

His lordship sat down again. 'Since you are perfectly aware that I need this person caught as quickly as possible, you may be sure of my complete attention.'

'Thank you.' Alex paused. 'Very well. I've traced a copy of this bill of lading – complete with additions – and by now it will be in the hands of the same Captain Vine who mistakenly allowed it to stray into mine. We can only trust that he doesn't notice the difference. His movements are being watched and, when he sends a message to his principal, I'll know.'

'This man, Vine,' interrupted Arlington. 'I want him as well.'

'Naturally – and you'll have him once he's performed his function. But he's just the carrier-pigeon. First we have to make sure of the vulture.'

'Go on,' said Giles. 'So the vulture receives his orders and tries to fulfil them.' He stopped and gave a brief, humourless laugh. 'Of course. The Naval Office.'

'Exactly,' agreed Alex. 'The Naval Office – where our friend will go quite openly, expecting to be given the information he asks for. Only this time he won't get it. And that, Lord Arlington, is where you come in. Can you secure the relevant files and ensure that Pepys and his staff tell all comers that they've been locked away on the King's command and can only be seen with his permission?'

His lordship nodded slowly. 'Yes. But I don't see - - '

'You will,' smiled Mr Deveril. 'We're going to make it impossible for our man to get what he wants legitimately and thus force him to try other methods. So long as he believes the documents are still there but inaccessible to him, he'll have no choice but to break into the Office to take them. And when he does, we'll be waiting.'

'We?' queried Mr Beckwith.

The blue eyes filled with restrained exasperation.

'I am not,' said Alex, 'inviting spectators, if that's what you think. You can come, or not – just as you please. Lord Arlington's presence, on the other hand, is vital. Because, from this point on, I want all proceedings blessed with official sanction.'

Lord Arlington nodded approvingly but Giles wasn't satisfied. 'Why?'

The exasperation was no long restrained and, in one smooth movement, Alex was on his feet. 'Because I don't want to have gone to all this trouble for nothing and will expect some recognition. Why else?'

* * *

Within the space of three hours, Mr Deveril received word that Matt had successfully accomplished his mission and was currently travelling south-east out of London in discreet pursuit of Samuel Vine. He would, so his message said, advise Mr Deveril further in due course.

It was at this stage that Alex discovered the flaw in his arrangements for he now had nothing to do but sit at home and wait for news. And with time on his hands, he did little but indulge in bitter recollections that were totally unrelated to the task ahead. Instead, it was his own voice that came back to taunt him with an eight-month catalogue of mistakes; the stupid jibes and pointless remarks he'd doubtless thought so clever; the off-hand way he'd given her that bloody trinket she now wore as if it were some sort of talisman; and worst of all, his callous, flippant reaction when she'd volunteered to undergo what had to be the most horrible of physical intrusions in order to secure the thrice-damned annulment. All of these things and more, all said without care or thought, to the girl he had been falling in love with; and all of them waiting now, like snares to trap him.

She wasn't stupid, his Marigold, and she knew too well what he was. Try to woo her now with all the arts he possessed but had never thought necessary to practise with her and she would see through them. So he was left with no alternative but simply to declare himself, which – after all that had gone before – would sound either fatuous or highly improbable. And even if, by some miracle, she believed him, what had he ever done to deserve more than tolerance or mild liking? Neither of which was enough. For his love wasn't mild and she would not stay if she couldn't return it. Nor, in truth, would he want her to.

He tried to tell himself that thinking was pointless since he couldn't do anything about it yet. Afterwards, when he could tell her that Danny was avenged – that was the time to speak. But he found, for the first time in his life, that he could not help himself. The house was empty when she was not in it and, when she was, he avoided her.

He felt lost. And when he tried to find relief in reading, even the poetry betrayed him. For it was too late; the damage was done and spreading, mockingly, through the words of Suckling's verses.

"Out upon it, I have loved three whole days together;

And am like to love three more, if it prove fair weather."

And then, at the end of his three days, came the message he had been waiting for.

TWELVE

'You look ill,' said Mr Lewis, by way of greeting.

'I've felt better,' agreed Alex, shrugging. 'I take it you've come to tell me that Simon is on his way?'

'Aye.' Matt sat down, irritably noting the signs of fatigue and strain on Mr Deveril's face. 'You need to calm down. You're living on your nerves and, by the look of you, they won't stand much more.'

Surprisingly, Alex neither denied it nor grew impatient.

'Possibly. But they'll serve a few days more – long enough, anyway.'

'What is it?' asked Matthew bluntly. 'The job?'

'No. Leave it, Matt. I'm not about to fall apart. Tell me about Simon.'

Mr Lewis snorted but knew better than to enquire further. He said, 'I trailed Vine to Sandwich and, when he set off back, I left my lad to keep an eye on him. Cousin Simon started out this morning – but he's coming by coach so he won't be here before tomorrow. I passed him on the road.'

Alex thought for a moment before he spoke.

'So. Tomorrow night should see the end of it. Arlington will have to be warned .. and Giles, if he cares. Can you - - ?' He stopped abruptly. 'Or no. I'll go myself. I need some fresh air and you've earned a rest.'

Eyeing him sardonically, Matt got up. 'I'm not so old I can't cope with a bit of a ride and trip across the river both. I'll go – and, if you'll take my advice for once, you'll go to bed with a glass of brandy for company.'

Mr Deveril smiled crookedly.

'I can't. If I start to drink, I might not stop.' He paused. Then, 'I suppose it might be as well if you went. If I see Giles, I'll probably let him provoke me. Again.'

'Will he try? It doesn't sound like Mr Giles.'

'No. My fault, I expect. And he has a slight handicap. I've told neither him nor Arlington that our man is Simon.' Alex looked into his friend's shrewd black eyes and added, 'So it's all going to be a beautiful surprise.'

* * *

Next morning saw Matt up with the lark and off to Seething Lane, hard by the Tower, to watch the Naval Office. Shortly after noon he was back in Southwark, his relief that Alex's prediction had proved accurate hidden beneath a mask of dour satisfaction.

'He came,' he told Alex dryly, 'then after no more than ten minutes, he was away again. And he wasn't smiling. Almost, you might say, as though he'd had a nasty disappointment.'

'Very well,' said Mr Deveril. 'Goring House and King Street again for you. I imagine we can count on Simon waiting until it's completely dark – but Arlington and Giles should be inside well before then. And myself, of course.' He paused, then said, 'See Arlington first. I hope he'll have arranged it so we don't have to break in – and then, when you have the details, you can inform Giles of them on your way back here.'

'You're certain,' said Matthew, 'that the daisified beau-trap'll go himself?'

Alex smiled faintly. 'If I read the situation correctly, he has no choice. You don't build a cover as good as his by confiding in your underlings. It's possible that Vine is the only one who knows his identity. And that,' he concluded, 'brings us to your part for tonight.'

Matt folded his arms. 'I'm to have one, then?'

'Naturally. Did you think I'd leave you out? While I am dealing with my cousin, you will be picking up Samuel Vine – but not until you know that Simon has entered the Office. I leave the details to you but get some men from Arlington. I doubt Vine and his crew will give up peacefully and whichever of them broke in here nearly tore my arm from its socket.'

Mr Lewis did not look impressed.

'You mean you gave him the chance? Damn me, but I thought you were better than that.'

* * *

It was half past eight that evening when Chloë, just back from her spell of attendance at Whitehall, walked wearily into the parlour to find Mr Deveril preparing to go out – and not, if appearances were anything to go by, to a social engagement.

He had dispensed with all the trimmings of fashion and was soberly attired in a coat of serviceable blue cloth over a shirt worn open at the neck and without a vest; soft boots of supple leather had replaced the usual silver-buckled shoes and, although he wore no sash, thirty-five inches of double-edged steel lay across his palms as he stood examining it carefully in the light from the window. He looked tired, but his face was grimly purposeful in a way that she had never seen and matched the sword which, despite its latticed and scalloped basket-guard and its copper-wired grip, was anything but a toy.

Chloë walked towards him, her throat constricting.

'Don't tell me,' she said. 'It's the gardening season and you're off to hack down a few weeds?'

He raised his eyes and his expression lightened a little.

'Something like that.' He restored the sword to its sheath and laid it on the table before picking up two folded sheets of paper which he stowed carefully in his pocket. 'But not in our garden, I'm afraid.'

Able to hazard a guess as to his plans for the evening, if not his destination, and knowing equally that it was pointless to say so, Chloë smiled and concentrated on keeping her voice bright. 'And Matt is going too – armed with a hoe?'

'Not quite. He's hoping to catch a pigeon.' He gave a sudden, brief laugh. 'It's Giles who is bringing the hoe. He uses it for sorting out principles – usually mine.' He paused as though searching for words. 'I caused you some trouble the other night – on top of a rather unpleasant few hours during which you displayed quite uncommon fortitude for no thanks that I can remember making. I wanted you to know that - - '

'I do know. It's all right You thanked me quite adequately.' She stretched out a hand to touch the swords voluted quillons, discovered that it was shaking and withdrew it again. 'I haven't seen this before.'

'No.' Alex looked down at the weapon, his eyes hooded and unreadable. 'It belonged to my father. I rarely use it.'

'But tonight is a special occasion?'

'You could say so.' He picked it up and stood staring at it as if unable to make up his mind to go.

Chloë looked at his hands, their hard beauty outlined against the dark scabbard, and wished she had the right, just this once, to storm the barriers and say what she meant. Then the silence was broken by Matt's voice from the doorway saying, 'Mr Alex – you haven't forgotten the time?'

The air of indecisiveness vanished and Mr Deveril nodded.

'I'm coming.' He looked at Chloë and smiled. 'I'm sorry. I have to go.'

'I know.' She tried to think of something witty to say but couldn't. Instead, she heard herself saying, 'You'll be careful? I think I'd sooner be annulled than widowed.'

An oddly desperate look lit the blue eyes and was gone.

'Don't worry,' he said lightly. He strolled to the door, then turned back to fix her with an enigmatic smile. 'Time shall moult his wings away ere he shall discover, In the whole wide world again, such a - - ' He stopped. 'Or no. You wouldn't believe it, would you? And who could blame you? Goodbye, Marigold.' And on this cryptic note, he was gone.

* * *

With the gathering dusk, the small-windowed rooms of the Naval Office were already dimly shadowed as the Secretary of State ushered Alex and Giles swiftly in through the rear entrance.

His lordship, thought Mr Beckwith, watching him peer through the door before he closed it, was experiencing a precarious pleasure in his adventure. Having arrived at the end of the lane in his own blazoned carriage, he had stepped out into the stifling August evening with his hat pulled low over his eyes and a heavy black cloak enveloping him from chin to ankle and then made a nervous beeline for his destination, jerking his head every few seconds to see if he was being followed.

'And after behaviour furtive enough to give any qualified spy an ague, ' thought Giles irritably, 'it's a miracle that he wasn't.'

Mr Deveril was engaged in checking that the building was empty while simultaneously amassing a collection of candles and lamps. Giles perched on the edge of desk and let him get on with it, thinking that here was someone else who was enjoying himself. Then Alex came back and in the deepening light Giles looked into his face and knew that he was wrong.

There was no levity there – no enjoyment, no anticipation. Only tiredness and a fixed, single-minded resolve that blocked out everything except the things that had to be done and that made Giles realise suddenly that if one of them was blinded by mistaken attitudes and motives, then it was not Alex, but himself. Not a pretty thought – and still less so if one acknowledged that its root lay in sickening, pointless envy.

'It seems that I owe you an apology,' he said lightly. 'I think I may have been misjudging you.'

For a second, Alex looked at him and then, quite suddenly, he smiled.

'No more than usual. And I expect I deserved it.' He held out his hand and, as Giles took it, said with a rare note of sincerity, 'But it's good to know that I don't have to face this thing on my own.'

Mr Beckwith eyed him searchingly. 'What is it you're afraid of?'

'That I'll kill him,' replied Mr Deveril flatly. 'You were right not to trust me, you see.' He glanced to where Arlington was flattening himself against a wall to squint into the street and then looked back at Giles with a tremor of uncertain laughter. 'Oh Christ! He's like a child playing at soldiers.'

'Just be grateful his disguise didn't run to a false nose.'

'I am – oh, believe me, I am. And will be more so when he stops flitting about like a gadfly. Are you going to tell him – or shall I?'

Mr Beckwith politely explained to his lordship that since they would be given no warning of the gentleman's arrival, it was necessary to make their preparations and then wait in silence if they were not to scare him off. To this, Alex added a couple of tersely-worded instructions of his own before they disposed themselves in the positions he requested. Giles stood to one side of the window, obscured by the curtain; Lord Arlington occupied a tall-backed chair in the remotest corner of the room; and, behind the door, Mr Deveril leaned negligently against the wall in the shadow of a large cupboard.

The time passed slowly while they watched the twilight gradually fade into darkness; and then their test of waiting truly began as the interminable minutes ticked by, became an hour and moved on into the next. Alex and Giles remained silent and motionless. His lordship, at first nervously excited, became rapidly bored and finally irritable. From time to time he stirred, altering his position in the chair and once he got up, intending to walk about the room.

'Sit,' came Mr Deveril's voice, soft and disembodied in the gloom.

Lord Arlington sat and did not get up again.

It was Alex who first caught the faint sound of a footfall on the stair and, with one precise snap of his fingers, warned his companions that the end of their vigil was at hand. Then he took no more notice of them but stood poised and alert, his eyes fixed on the door-latch and his ears on those light, approaching footsteps.

They reached the door and stopped. Then, very gently the latch quivered to the touch of a hand and was quietly raised. The door swung slowly back in front of Alex, obscuring his view, and then the footsteps moved on into the room. It was all he had been waiting for. Gently, unhurriedly, he shut the door and leaned against it, arms folded and smiling coldly at the visitor as he wheeled sharply to face him.

'Welcome, Cousin,' said Mr Deveril.

And as if on a signal, light flickered from a flint as Giles began to light the candles.

Simon Deveril, resplendent in violet satin and silver lace, looked back at Alex; he was a little pale and breathing rather fast but he said nothing. Then, in the next instant, his opportunity was lost as Lord Arlington erupted violently from his seat.

'My God!' he said, stunned. 'Deveril! I wouldn't have believed it!'

Without removing his eyes from his cousin, Simon answered him composedly.

'Dear me. I seem to have stumbled on a plot. But just what is it that your lordship would not have believed?'

'That you are a traitor, sir!' snapped Arlington. 'A paid agent of His Majesty's enemies.'

Simon turned then and smiled slowly.

'Not I, my lord,' he said significantly. 'It seems that His Majesty should have investigated you more thoroughly. I wonder what you are doing here now – gathering information perhaps? And you, Cousin.' He glanced back at Alex. 'Seeking to build a fortune and a career in Dutch employ since you have failed to do either by honourable means? You should have put away your resentment and come to me, you know. Pride is a luxury that beggars can't afford. And yours is about to send you to the headsman.'

'Well done,' said Alex cordially. 'You're as good as a play. Unfortunately, it won't work. We've been waiting for you.'

Simon laughed but his eyes were watchful. 'Really? And on whose authority, may one ask?'

'On mine,' said Arlington.

'And on that of Prince Rupert,' added Giles, 'who five months ago asked us to find him a traitor.'

In a waft of heliotrope scent, Simon produced the inevitable lace handkerchief from his pocket and shook it, his gaze resting meditatively on Mr Beckwith.

'Well, if that is so,' he said at length, 'you have a made a very poor job of it – for I am not he. I know no harm of you, sir, and am therefore willing to believe you honest – but you are plainly misguided for you have confided in the two persons that it appears you set out to unmask.'

'No,' said Giles simply. 'Not so.'

'Check,' said Alex. 'My move, I think. Perhaps you would like to tell us why you came here tonight?'

Simon turned languidly to face him, sighing slightly.

'Certainly. I have an urgent report to prepare for the Duke and was careless enough to leave one of my files here.'

'I see.' Alex smiled. 'A report on the victualing service, perhaps? Or on the fleet's sail-power and projected movements?'

The breath hissed faintly between Simon's teeth but his manner retained its urbanity.

'You are very importunate, are you not? And all because of childish jealousy. I know – everyone will know – what it is you want.'

'You would think that,' replied Alex calmly. 'Unfortunately, it's not true. I'm afraid you will have to do better than that.'

'Not I, Alex – you. I have served York faithfully for seven years and I have his regard. At best you will be thought merely vengeful – at worst, guilty of treason. But either way your pathetic plot is doomed to failure because it is a matter of your word against mine.'

'It is a matter,' countered Alex, 'of hard fact. We've had the accusation, the denial and the counter-accusation, so let's move on to the evidence. For you have sold and betrayed your King, your country and your fellows ... and I can't wait to hear you try to prove otherwise.'

For a long moment, Simon met the cold, steely eyes and then he yawned delicately.

'I don't need to prove anything to you – nor will I try. But if nothing will content you but that I listen to your co-called evidence, then make haste and get on with it.'

'By all means. Let's begin with your presence here at this hour. You may be wondering why we were expecting you – and for that I must refer you to this.' Sliding a hand into his pocket, Alex produced the Arabella's bill of lading and flicked it open for his cousin to see. 'Perhaps Captain Vine did not feel in necessary to tell you that he'd committed the great mistake of delivering this to me instead of you?'

This time Simon said nothing and his eyes narrowed fractionally.

'It wasn't very difficult,' continued Alex, 'to discover its secret or to make a copy of it, return it to your accomplice and allow him to take it to you at Sandwich. And naturally, we can prove that he did so. At this moment, I imagine that my friend Mr Lewis is arresting the good Captain ... and once in custody, it's only a matter of time before he tries to save his skin by naming you.'

'This is quite ludicrous,' said Simon, a slight edge creeping into his drawling tones. 'I do not know Captain Vine and I have received no document such as the one you have there.'

'Destroyed it, have you? I thought you would.' The smile touching Alex's mouth faded along with the pleasant timbre of his voice as he opened out another sheet of paper. 'A wise man would have destroyed this too – but I'm so glad you didn't, for it provided the solution to a puzzle I'd almost given up hope of solving.'

'I should be obliged,' said Simon frostily, 'if you would keep to the point.'

'If you are patient,' replied Alex, 'you'll find that I am keeping to it. First, I must confess that I took the liberty of searching your house – and very illuminating I found it. It was interesting, for example, to discover that you were compiling dossiers on my Lord Arlington and Sir William Coventry – but more interesting by far was the letter I found in the priest's hole and which I can only suppose you kept because its congratulatory tone appealed to your vanity. Old Noll was pleased with you – and for good reason.' Alex paused briefly and then went on. 'So far you stand arraigned for the treasonable selling of information and the disruption of His Majesty's fleet; you are also guilty of murder, for Daniel Fawsley died by your agency as surely as if you'd struck him down yourself. But more than all of that,' finished Mr Deveril, with lethal clarity, 'this letter proves you responsible for the capture and execution of a number of loyal gentlemen when, together with Richard Willys, you betrayed the Sealed Knot to Cromwell. And I would suggest that it is your death warrant.'

There was a long, heady silence and then Giles crossed the room saying abruptly, 'Let me see.'

Without taking his eyes from his cousin's face, Alex handed over the letter and Giles moved away, reading as he went. Then, passing it to Arlington, he looked back at Simon, his eyes filled with disgust. 'You bloody Judas,' he said contemptuously.

Simon, his attention fixed on Alex, did not bother to look round.

'Dear me,' he said mildly. 'What a meddling nuisance you've become, Cousin. I believe I really must relieve you of those letters.'

'You think I'm going to give them to you? And to what end? Three people in this room have read them and a fourth outside it.'

'I don't consider that an insurmountable problem. But first ... first dear Alex, I seem to have no alternative but to clear you from my path.'

Alex smiled. 'Ambition should be made of sterner stuff .. but, since the way to the door lies through me, I was rather hoping you might like to try.'

The effete face flushed and changed so rapidly that it might have belonged to another man.

'Try?' echoed Simon gratingly, as he drew his sword. 'Try? I'll do more than try. I'll cut off that prying nose and rip out your heart. But first let's even the odds a little.' And with a swift, unexpected movement, he was at Arlington's side, twisting the hand that held the incriminating letter high against his spine whilst laying his blade close along his lordship's throat. Then, gesturing to Giles, 'You. Take off your sword.'

'Or what?' asked Mr Beckwith, unmoving.

'Or I slit his lordship's gizzard. Take off your sword and throw it into that corner. Now.'

Arlington swallowed and a thin line of blood followed the bright edge of the blade.

'Do it, Giles,' said Alex quietly. 'This was always going to be my fight.'

'He's bluffing,' said Giles. 'He won't do it.'

'He will.' Anger flared in the light voice; anger directed, not at Giles or Arlington, but at himself for not foreseeing this eventuality. 'He doesn't care who dies - and he has nothing to lose. So just do it.'

'How wise,' purred Simon. 'How very wise.' He watched Mr Beckwith reluctantly discard his sword and slide it along the floor, then looked back at Alex. 'I wonder, my foolish failed hero, where you have put your sword ... for I am very sure you didn't come here without it.'

'No,' agreed Alex. Two seconds were all he needed to snatch the weapon from its resting place in the shadows of the aumbry but, as long as Simon held Arlington, it was useless to him. 'No. And it's at your disposal.'

Simon laughed softly and was about to reply when the unexpected happened. With a brief, muffled moan, the Secretary of State grew suddenly lax in his hold and he found himself supporting what was swiftly becoming a dead weight. Lord Arlington, it appeared, had fainted.

Simon did the only possible thing and let him fall, the tip of his sword sweeping down to maintain its threat. But even as he moved, Giles seized the moment to hurl himself forward and Simon, startled, whipped up his guard and side-stepped. Off course and unable to do anything about it, Giles crashed harmlessly past him; something ice-cold seared his left arm and he hit the floor harder than he had expected before rolling less than gracefully to his feet. Then he smiled.

As an attacker, he had been an unqualified failure; but as a diversion he had achieved all he had hoped. Thirty-five inches of steel gleamed in Alex's hand and Arlington, remarkably spry for a fainting man, had seized the chance to scuttle crab-like to safety. The wheel of advantage had turned full circle. Then he heard Alex say, 'Well done. But you're making a terrible mess on Mr Pepys' carpet.' And looked down, vaguely surprised to see blood trickling over his fingers from a deep gash in his upper arm.

Alex's light, compelling gaze rested on his cousin with a remoteness that was mere illusion. He said, 'Your leverage is gone and your path still lies through me. Will you fight?'

Simon smiled and his fingers flexed on the hilt of his sword.

'Trial by combat, Alex? How archaic of you. But yes, my winsome cousin. Of course I'll fight.'

Despite his reddened throat and dishevelled appearance, Arlington suddenly became every inch the Secretary of State.

'I find the case against Simon Deveril proven beyond any reasonable doubt and, as a trusted confidant to the heir presumptive of this kingdom, consider him a serious political threat. The Duke of York's popularity is too weak to withstand the scandal of this sort. It is therefore necessary to dispose of the matter privately – here and now. But the law states that every man is entitled to stand his trial and, in view of this, I grant Alexander Deveril the privilege of defending his sovereign in single combat against this traitorous felon. My only proviso is this. That since Simon Deveril's life is forfeit to the Crown, Alexander Deveril shall justify the honour granted him by claiming it.' He paused, for it was a huge risk and he knew it. Then, 'Are my terms accepted?'

Simon laughed derisively but said nothing.

Silence stretched out on invisible threads before Alex said crisply, 'They are accepted. Giles – shove that desk out of the way; my lord, pull your chair into the corner and get yourself behind it. We're going to need some room.' And when it was done, with a slight bow, 'I believe we are ready, my lord.'

'So eager,' murmured Simon. 'So full of confidence. What a shame it's misplaced.' And immediately opened the attack with a thrust in high tierce which Alex met without apparent difficulty, stepping back to disengage and following through with a riposte that forced Simon into a swift, sideways parry.

Giles found himself watching Simon's sword-play with professional interest. He was good – very good, in fact – which was surprising for, since he must practise in secret, it was hard to know where and with whom he could have done so. But practised he undoubtedly was, for his wrist was flexible, his footwork neat and his knowledge of strokes and techniques remarkably extensive. Indeed, he once produced a sweeping pass which Mr Beckwith had never seen before and which nearly cost Alex the tendons of his left wrist. Giles frowned a little, wondering what Alex was doing; and then, thinking that he knew, smiled to himself whilst trying to stop his arm dripping on the carpet.

'Finger by finger,' purred Simon, 'and hand by hand – like so.' And he sent his blade skimming along the till its point reached the guard and slid off to score the back of his cousin's knuckles.

Alex did not even glance at it. With a swift hard, flick, he forced up the attacking blade and in the same fluid movement, delivered a low thrust that forced Simon to retreat part-way across the room.

'I could maim you or I could kill you,' mused Simon. 'Which would you prefer, I wonder?'

He made a sweeping cut that might have sliced through Alex's thigh had he not seen it coming in time to avoid it.

'I'd prefer that you stopped talking,' returned Alex dryly. 'Unless you want to bore me to death?'

Relentless, untiring, the fight went on. Simon attempted a daring flanconade and his point slit Alex's sleeve before it was deftly parried. There was a confused scraping of blades and Simon disengaged to recover his guard. He was panting a little from the exertion of delivering a constant attack that he plainly hoped would provide him with an opening but somehow never did.

Blood began to drip steadily from Alex's arm but the sword remained an extension of his body and his defence never wavered. Simon lunged, Alex replied with a counter-disengage and Simon was forced to retreat. He circled, his point darting playfully at Alex while he strove to recover his breath.

'Is this the best you can do?' he taunted. 'I expected better of one of Rupert's puppies.' And, leaping forward, his blade slashed down towards the bones of Alex's hand.

Alex snatched it back and forte met foible.

'The stars move still, time runs, the clock must strike,' he said quietly.

'Oh please.' Simon's teeth gleamed in a feral grin. 'How tediously predictable.'

'Not exciting enough for you?' asked Alex. 'Really? Perhaps I can help with that. The devil will come and Faustus must be damned.'

And with the words, a change came, as Alex finally chose to exert the full sum of his skill. Suddenly hard-pressed, Simon lunged and met an opposition of such force that it drove him breathlessly down the length of the room.

The light eyes were brilliant and Harry Deveril's sword was wielded with supple dexterity in the hand of his son as it pushed Simon back and back down the room. Simon had no breath now for words, none even to waste in attack; he could only parry automatically to protect himself.

And then, as Alex feinted inside the arm, he thought he saw an opening and lunged. It was a mistake – his last, he thought, reading his death sentence in the cold purposeful eyes. He saw the thrust coming, in high quarte and destined for his heart; then, strangely, it checked briefly before fractionally altering its direction. Simon looked again into the pale gaze and then Alex's point bit deep into his shoulder. His sword dropped and very, very slowly, he followed it to the floor.

His hands shaking a little, Alex wiped the sweat from his eyes and looked down at Simon lying crumpled at his feet with the blood soaking through his elegant violet satin. But it was Giles who went to kneel at his side and, after a brief examination, removed Cromwell's incriminating letter from his pocket.

'Congratulations,' he said, glancing up at his friend. 'An inch lower and you'd have killed him.'

'I know.' Alex's voice was oddly muffled. 'I know.'

'Do I understand that he isn't dead?' demanded Lord Arlington frigidly.

'You do,' replied Giles, busy trying to staunch Simon's bleeding.

'Why not? Why isn't he dead? I made my instructions quite plain.'

'Because I'm not an executioner,' said Alex. He looked down at Mr Beckwith. 'And because I wanted to kill him. More, in fact, than you can possibly imagine.'

'I did congratulate you,' Giles reminded him. And to his lordship, 'You don't have to bring him to trial. There are any number of ways to be rid of him.'

Lord Arlington was not visibly mollified.

'It is not at all satisfactory – and I am sure Prince Rupert will agree with me when you report to him.'

'Prince Rupert,' said Mr Beckwith, coming to his feet, 'is realist enough to find it quite sufficient that his services return to normal.'

The Secretary looked sceptical and turned back to Alex, now engaged in a somewhat unsuccessful attempt to bind his forearm with a handkerchief. Then the door opened and Mr Lewis walked in. His face was marked and his knuckles badly grazed but his expression was unusually cheerful.

'God,' he said to no one in particular, absorbing the fact that everyone in the room was bleeding from somewhere. 'The mammet must've been a hell of a fighter.'

Mr Deveril abandoned his attempts to tie a knot with the aid of his teeth and held out his arm for Matt to deal with.

'Moderate,' he said and his voice had recovered its usual tone. 'Did you get Vine?'

Matthew finished bandaging and looked up.

'Aye. It was easy enough – though we'd a bit of a scuffle. Queenhithe's littered with battered sailors and I doubt Captain Vine's feeling so well either.'

Laughter stirred remotely in the light eyes and Alex said, 'I'm glad you enjoyed yourself.'

'And I'm glad,' said Lord Arlington tartly, 'that something has gone according to plan.' It had been a long night. He felt tired and old and he looked on Alex with vague discontent. 'I shall need the written evidence to show to the King when I report this affair. I imagine that you can explain to Prince Rupert without it?'

Mr Deveril gazed back with an expression that boded ill for the civility of his reply. Then the blue gaze travelled to Giles.

'I rather think it's my turn to do some work,' said Mr Beckwith pleasantly. 'I'll go to His Highness.'

'No.' The Secretary's voice was sharp. 'Mr Deveril can make a much more accurate report and I wish him to do so. The fleet is still in Sole Bay but it may put to sea any day now so the matter will not wait.'

Alex stared at him wildly but, before he could speak, Simon drew attention to himself by moaning feebly.

'If he's not attended to,' observed Matt in a tone that suggested he didn't much care either way, 'he'll die of blood loss.'

'Or old age,' snapped Alex acidly. He ignored his lordship and looked at Matthew. 'It seems I'm going to Sole Bay.'

'Do you want me to come with you?'

'No. I want you to stay with Chloë.' He paused, an odd look crossing his face and then said, 'If she asks about tonight – and I expect she will – you can tell her everything. In fact, I'd like you to. And tell her - -' He stopped again, his mouth curling crookedly. 'Or no. Perhaps not.'

'No,' agreed Matthew all-too-knowingly. 'I'll make your excuses and your explanations. But that's my limit. And you'd a tongue in your head last time I looked.' He grinned. 'So get yourself home and use it.'

PART THREE

THE SONG

London
August and September, 1666

'Yet we will be loyal still
And serve without reward or hire,
To be redeemed from so much ill
May stay our stomachs, though not fill:
And if our patience do not tire
We may, in time, have our desire.'

THE CAVALIER
Alexander Brome 1620-1666

ONE

At about the time that Mr Deveril took the decision to ride to Sole Bay, his wife – who had retired expecting to pass a wakeful night – was just falling asleep. It was therefore not until just after eight when she came downstairs to find Mr Lewis awaiting her in the parlour, that she discovered that Alex had returned briefly for a change of clothes, prior to setting off at first light for the coast.

Heavy-eyed and anxious, Chloë stared at Matt.

'You mean he's gone? Just like that? Without even an hour's rest? He's mad! Does he think nothing can be done that he doesn't do himself?'

Matthew grinned. 'Yes. But he didn't want to go – that pot-faced Secretary made him.'

'Arlington? What has he to do with it? I thought you and Mr Deveril went after the man who – who – '

'We did. And caught him too. You'd better sit down. It's a long story.'

'You mean I'm allowed to know? Really? I'm honoured!'

'And cheeky,' retorted Matthew. 'Sit down.'

Rather to his surprise, Chloë listened without interrupting while he described the suspicions and events that had led up to the previous night's successful capture. The brown eyes widened when he named Simon Deveril but still she did not speak, allowing him to continue his narrative undisturbed; and even when he came to the end, she sat for a long time without saying anything.

Then, 'He – he's all right, isn't he?'

Matt did not pretend to misunderstand. 'Aye. A bit of a scratch, no more.' He did not tell her what he had learned from Mr Beckwith – that Alex had been lucky not to lose the use of one of his hands. 'You don't think that Mr Alex can't deal with a mere dog in a doublet like Simon, do you?'

She smiled. 'No. What I think is that, since Simon isn't what he seems in any other way, it's reasonable to suppose that he might also be rather more of a swordsman that one would have thought.'

Mr Lewis regarded her with bitter satisfaction.

'He might be. I wasn't there.'

'But you know.' It was not a question.

The seamed face split in a curious grin.

'Aye.'

'Well?'

'God,' said Matt disgustedly. 'You're a bone-headed lass. Why can't you ask a normal question like why Simon isn't dead?'

'Because I know why he isn't dead. And I'm glad.' She looked into the shrewd black eyes. 'And so are you. Because the truth is that if Mr Deveril had killed him, he'd have spent the rest of his life wondering whether he'd done a service for his country or committed murder. And he'd never have been free of it – or of Simon.'

Matt looked back thoughtfully, pleased with her but unwilling to say so.

'If you really want to know,' he offered at last, 'Mr Giles says Simon's swordplay was good but dirty – and that he was no match for Mr Alex when he chose to exert himself. You'll know that Mr Alex is pretty fair with a blade.'

'I do know. I've seen him.' Chloë sighed and the smooth brow creased in a frown. 'How long do you think he'll be gone?'

'Hard to say.' Matthew watched her, thinking it was a pity that Alex had gone at all because it was high time the two of them put an end to the nonsense between them. 'Five days, maybe. It'll depend on His Highness. Meantime, I don't doubt you've plenty to do.'

'I shan't pine, if that's what you mean. I'm in attendance every afternoon and evening for the next week and I've the arrangements to finalise for selling the silk and velvet. Fenton's on Cheapside are taking most of it and Bennett's the rest. I sent a length of the sapphire velvet to Mr Penny at Saint Dunstan's to make up for Mr Deveril – and I thought to send some of the black brocade as well. What do you think?'

'I think,' said Matt caustically, 'that you should remember the profits – but that you'll send it anyway and probably some more besides.'

Chloë tilted her head and surveyed him consideringly.

'It's funny you should say that. There's a bolt of white watered silk I thought might suit him – and it's very much in vogue just now.'

Matthew got up, shaking his head and tutting reprovingly.

'Send the pink satin,' he advised acidly. 'He'd look a treat in that.'

* * *

The Queen and her ladies strolled across the sun-baked lawns, their silks rustling on the grass and the ribbons of their wide-brimmed hats fluttering gaily.

'It's so hot!' moaned Frances Stuart as loudly as she dared. 'Surely Her Majesty must go in soon?'

'She likes the sun,' said Elizabeth Chesterfield. 'It reminds her of Lisbon.'

Frances dabbed a wisp of cambric surreptitiously over her brow.

'I know. But look what it does to your skin – so brown.'

Chloë glanced round at her and smiled. 'Well, if you stopped fanning yourself with your hat and put it on your head, you wouldn't need to worry.'

'And you know she won't turn back yet,' said Lady Chesterfield. 'She's hoping to meet the King, poor thing.'

Poor thing, indeed, thought Chloë, her eyes dwelling compassionately on Queen Catherine who was walking a little ahead of them, chatting quietly with the Countess of Penalva and the little Buccleuch heiress. But at least she's learned to be content with half a loaf – which is what I ought to be doing myself.

'I hear,' Lady Elizabeth was saying, 'that your husband is out of town again?'

Chloë nodded but said nothing.

Frances giggled and looked slyly at the Countess, whose topsy-turvy relationship with her handsome lord was a by-word. 'What? Are you jealous, my dear?'

Elizabeth shrugged elegantly. 'Nothing so fatiguing. Though I own it would be pleasant if Philip were to remove himself occasionally.' She eyed Chloë speculatively. 'Now you have every opportunity to amuse yourself as you wish but no inclination to do so – while I have the inclination but very little opportunity. Odd, isn't it, how one always wants what one can't have? Take Philip for instance; when I loved him, he loved Barbara Castlemaine – and now I'm largely indifferent, he wants none but me.' She paused. 'You should remember that, my dear – because they're all the same.'

'Are you saying I ought to provide Alex with a rival?' laughed Chloë.

'Stolen waters are sweet and so on,' came the light reply. Then, 'Did you know that Graham Marsden is dead?'

Chloë's breath caught and she felt suddenly chilled despite the heat of the sun.

'No, I didn't,' she said. 'When did it happen?'

'Two days ago – on Friday. It's not entirely surprising because he's been ailing for years. But he might have lasted longer without Sarah coaxing him to take her rowing on the river in this heat. They say he just collapsed and died.'

'So Sarah's a widow again,' said Frances. 'Two husbands and she's still only ... how old do you think?'

'She's twenty-eight,' replied Lady Chesterfield. 'Though to be fair, no one would think it to look at her.'

'Twenty-eight, twice widowed, rich and beautiful,' chanted Frances artlessly. 'I wonder who she'll marry next?'

The Countess looked expressionlessly into Chloë's eyes. 'I wonder?'

And that, supposed Chloë, was meant as a friendly warning.

'Oh here's the King,' cried Frances, patting her hair. And more quietly, 'Thank heaven! Now we can go back indoors.'

Charles was accompanied by his dogs and a small group of friends, amongst whom was the Earl of Chesterfield. Chloë caught herself watching the way his lordship's eyes followed his wife and then rebuked herself sharply.

'Next I'll be looking around for somebody to flirt with,' she thought derisively. And quoting Mr Lewis, 'That's no way to go on.'

The two parties joined and turned back in the direction of the palace, laughing and talking as they went. With an ease born of long practice, the King dropped back to seek out Chloë and detach her from the other ladies for a moment.

'It seems that Alex has rendered his country a signal service,' he said easily. 'Although my lord Arlington is of the opinion that it would have been significantly greater had the gentleman in question perished.'

Chloë looked back uncompromisingly.

'If Your Majesty will forgive me saying so, it's all very well for his lordship to think that – but quite unreasonable to expect Mr Deveril to do the deed. He's not an assassin.'

Charles was amused. 'My dear, I entirely agree with you. When he returns, you must send him to me so that I can express my gratitude.' He gave her a sleepy smile. 'When a knight has achieved his endeavour, it's customary for his liege to offer some reward – though it cannot, I fear, be one of money. I wonder what little thing Alex would most like me to give him?'

'I really can't imagine,' replied Mr Deveril's titular wife. And wished, very much, that it was not a lie.

* * *

Chloë did not tell Mr Lewis of Sir Graham Marsden's death. It wasn't that she didn't want him to know; he was sure to hear of it elsewhere anyway. But she preferred not to contemplate its possible consequences or allow Lady Sarah's golden image to invade her thoughts – for both seemed to give her a headache. So she resolutely banished them from her mind and was glad that she had plenty to occupy her.

Monday the twenty-seventh passed quietly and without incident save for a rumour that the Dutch had put to sea again. On Tuesday morning, she decided to set Alex's bedchamber in order in case Wednesday should see him home again and was just crossing the hall in search of a duster when the pealing of the bell summoned her to the front door. She opened it and then froze as she identified her visitor.

Ethereally fair beneath a floating black veil, Sarah Marsden looked back at her mockingly.

'My poor child – don't you even have someone to answer the door?'

'No,' said Chloë sardonically. 'I do it myself in between scrubbing the floor and scouring the cooking-pots. If you came to see Alex, he's not here.'

The delicate brows lifted.

'I know. He rarely is, is he?' responded Sarah sweetly. 'No. It's you I came to see. Are you going to let me in?'

Chloë stepped back, holding wide the door. 'By all means.'

Lady Sarah drifted into the parlour, trailing widow's weeds and the scent of cassia and, putting back her veil, examined the room critically. Then, quite unhurriedly, she turned to face Chloë and eyed her in much the same manner, while the beautiful mouth curved in a pitying smile.

'He's never touched you, has he?' she asked, her tone liquid with sympathy. 'Not once in all these months. But you mustn't blame yourself, you know. It isn't that you're unattractive – although not at all Alex's style. It's simply that he only kept you to annoy me. He hoped to make me jealous and might have managed it if he'd taken you to his bed. You've no idea what a spectacular lover he is.' She sighed languorously. Then with a tiny ripple of laughter, 'But of course you haven't. How could you? And that's the point. Alex should have known I'd never be jealous unless I thought he'd made love to you – and one only has to look at you to know that he hasn't.'

'Is there a point to all this?' asked Chloë. 'Only I'm rather busy.'

'The point is that I'm sorry for you. It's very naughty of him to keep you tied to him when he knows he'll never want you.'

Chloë's eyes remained completely without expression. Folding her arms and keeping tight control over her voice, she said, 'Let's dispense with the trimmings and cut straight to the crux of the matter, shall we? You've come to tell me that now you are available again, Alex will want to take advantage of the fact. There are two very large assumptions there; first that Alex and I are not truly man and wife - and second, that he's still in love with you. You might take a moment to think about that. You might also try to remember that Alex likes to make his own decisions.'

'Well, of course, you silly girl. That's what I'm telling you.'

'No. You're talking as if it's a fait accompli. Perhaps you're assuming that I'll make everything easy by vanishing nobly into a fog of obscurity?'

'It's a matter of complete indifference to me what you do,' replied Sarah carelessly. 'Go or stay – you won't change anything. I merely came to warn you.'

'Thank you,' said Chloë politely. 'And do you plan to marry him this time? Because, if you do, then he'll need to divorce me first.'

Lady Sarah laughed again. 'Not divorce – annul. I don't foresee any difficulty.'

Somewhere deep inside Chloë a spark of anger flared into being.

'Don't you?' she asked dulcetly. 'I can think of several – quite apart from the obvious one which you are so determined to believe doesn't exist. And even supposing you're right and our marriage hasn't been consummated – what then? Are you so sure that Alex will be willing to say so? It would make him appear rather foolish, wouldn't it? And then, of course, there's me.' She paused and smiled dangerously. 'Perhaps I'm not willing to say so.'

The cornflower eyes widened in astonishment.

'But why ever not? Surely you can't have imagined that you could keep him? The most you can do is to make it hard for him to re-marry – which is rather petty, don't you think? For married or not, he'll still be mine.'

Never in her life before had Chloë encountered an ego to match Lady Sarah's and for a moment she stared at her speechlessly while trying to force down a gust of pure temper. Finally, as calmly as she was able, she said, 'You talk of him as if he were a lapdog. I don't believe you've the remotest idea of what he really thinks or feels or wants. All you know is what you want – and at the moment, you want Alex. But want is the word. You don't love him. You can't. You're too busy worshipping yourself.'

A faint flush stained her ladyship's cheeks.

'That is ridiculous – but one sees why you'd wish to think so,' she said scornfully. 'After all, who is ever going to worship you? Not Alex, certainly. Why, you stupid creature – if, after eight months of living in the same house, you've failed to share his bed, what do you think you can possibly have to offer him?'

Chloë was rather white but she looked back stubbornly. 'Understanding, perhaps.'

Sarah laughed. 'You understand him? You? You don't know the first thing about him! He only married you because he was too drunk to care. Had he been sober, he'd never have given you a second glance. Look in the mirror, my dear. You don't seriously suppose yourself my rival, do you?'

'No,' said Chloë with bitter honesty. 'But this isn't about that. What you don't seem able to grasp is that he needs more than a body – no matter how beautiful. If he loves you, he'll want your heart. And I don't believe you have one.'

'I think,' said Lady Sarah smugly, 'that I'm rather better placed to know what Alex wants than you are.'

'Well, you should be,' retorted Chloë with grim pleasure. 'You've quite a lead in the realms of age and experience, after all. But I wouldn't have thought it was necessarily an advantage. "At twenty-five in women's eyes, Beauty fades – at thirty dies", you know.'

For the first time an expression crossed Sarah's face that was neither becoming nor confident. Then she let down her veil and walked to the door.

'You are impertinent and very stupid. Are you telling me you'll refuse to release Alex?'

'I'm not telling you anything,' said Chloë, 'except that I'd like you to go.'

Sarah cast her a glance of venomous dislike and swept past into the hall. At the door she paused and, producing a sealed billet from her reticule, placed it defiantly on the table.

'I'm leaving this for Alex. If you open it or destroy it, you'll simply appear childishly jealous – which, of course, you are.' She smiled maliciously. 'I really wouldn't stand in his way , if I were you. When he is crossed, Alex can be quite unpleasant.' And she flung open the door and went out.

Very calmly, Chloë closed the door behind her and then marched resolutely away to get rid of her breakfast. Aside from the obvious, hurtful question of Alex, the whole conversation had been made worse by the knowledge that Graham Marsden had been dead for only five days. Just five days and already his widow had forgotten his existence and was planning to replace him. It was incredible to Chloë that anyone could be so ruthlessly self-absorbed. Lady Sarah was utterly beautiful – and rotten to the core.

The Queen found Mistress Deveril pale and absent-minded that afternoon and finally insisted that she go home to rest. Chloë went without protest but she did not sleep. Instead, she lay flat on her bed in wordless communication with the embroidered tester and thought of all the things she'd tried so hard to suppress.

Soon, tomorrow even, Alex would return and the pattern of all their lives could be changed in a single hour; or it could be if she let it. Long ago she had offered Alex an annulment. It had not been offered lightly but in reparation for her mistake in marrying him. She had promised to set him free because she'd owed him that much - and still did. And though he had seemed indifferent, she had always known that the day would come when he would cease to be so and that she would go then to the King and ask him to cut the knot. Or so she had thought until today when Lady Sarah had cast her into a limbo of doubt.

'It isn't that I want to hold him,' she told herself, 'or at least, I do – but not like this. If it were a question of freeing him for his own sake, I wouldn't mind ... or not so much. But I can't – I don't think I can free him to marry that woman.'

Driven to a point where stillness was intolerable, she got up and walked restlessly about the room. She caught sight of her reflection in the glass and stopped, examining critically.

'Well, she was right about one thing anyway,' she thought wryly. 'He'd have to be drunk to prefer me. But that's not the issue. The point is what I'm going to do if I find he wants Sarah and whether I've the right to interfere in the only way that would work. Because if he wants to go, he will. All I can do is stop him marrying her right away in the hope he'll see her for what she is.' Her stomach coiled like a snake. 'He'd never forgive me, though – and I'm not sure I have the courage to look him in the eye and say I'm going to tell the one lie that would make an annulment impossible. He'd be furious – and have every right to be. Because no matter what the circumstances, a promise is a promise. And the truth is that I can't even be sure I'm not still hoping for a miracle.'

And that, of course, was the most painful thought of all.

* * *

The following day Chloë resumed her duties at Whitehall with all the outward appearance of her usual calm good sense. She did not, however, attend to the matter of her merchandise and the bolts of cloth lay undisturbed in the Vintry while her prospective buyers sought an appointment with her and Mr Lewis began to worry.

Wednesday passed without any sign of Mr Deveril and Thursday gave every indication of doing the same. Chloë completed her spell of attendance and went out into the darkness where, at the Queen's order, a carriage always waited to take her home. She climbed inside it and found herself facing Mr Beckwith.

'Hello,' he said simply. 'I couldn't get near you at the palace so I thought perhaps you'd allow me to escort you home.'

'Of course. I'm glad to see you – it's a long time since I last did. You don't visit us any more.'

'No. I've been busy.' It sounded lame and he knew it.

'Yes. You must be glad it's all over.' She smiled politely. 'Was there something particular you wanted to say to me?'

'Yes,' replied Giles. And, to himself, 'I love you. I always have. Leave Alex and come with me and I'll spend my life trying to make you happy.' But he could not say those things – would never be able to say them. He tried to remember what he had planned to say to her and then, in the flare of a torch, caught sight of her face and promptly uttered the words that had been ringing in his mind all evening. 'My dear, what's wrong?'

It was his tone that succeeded in piercing Chloë's detachment and lump rose and hardened in her throat.

'Don't, Giles,' she said, with an effort that could be heard. 'Don't be kind. I can't cope with it right now.'

He did not reply immediately but finally said, 'It's Sarah, isn't it?'

Her mouth twisted wryly. 'Am I so transparent?'

'Only to those who know you best.' He paused again. 'I've known for some time that you ... have grown fond of Alex.'

Chloë looked down at her hands, glad of the darkness.

'I see. Then you know what I'm afraid of.'

'Yes. I'm sorry.'

'Don't be. I always knew that something like this might happen.' She looked up at him and her voice was utterly logical. 'For he's never pretended to love me, you know – or ever given any sign that one day he might.'

Giles forced down an impulse to take her in his arms.

'I know,' he said gently. 'I know. But that doesn't mean he won't stay with you.'

She gave an odd little laugh. 'Lady Sarah wouldn't agree with you.'

'You've seen her?'

Chloë nodded. 'She visited me on Tuesday. To warn me that Alex would be seeking an annulment. Of course, she doesn't know that he already has been.'

There was a long silence. Giles felt his fingers begin to ache with the strength of their grip on each other but they were the gauge of his control and he dared not release them. He drew a long breath and when he spoke it was in his usual level tones.

'And if he gets an annulment ... what will you do?'

She gazed unseeingly out of the window into the dark. 'I don't know. What would you suggest?'

A muscle moved in his cheek and then was still.

'That you accept it. Not for Alex, but for yourself. You shouldn't waste the rest of your life. You're worth more than that. I can understand what you feel for Alex – but it will pass. And there will be someone else one day. Someone who loves you as you deserve to be loved. All you need do is give yourself some time.'

'You're suggesting I might marry again.' Her voice was flat. 'And I daresay you are right – I could. But not to someone who loved me.'

'Why not?' There was an intensity in the question that he couldn't quite subdue.

'Because all I have to offer is friendship – and that could only hurt a man who loved me. You see, I know how it feels. And it wouldn't be fair.'

'If he loved you,' said Giles evenly, 'he might not mind. And things change, Chloë.'

The coach drew to a halt and the driver climbed down to open the door. Chloë gathered her skirts and then fixed Giles with a gaze of austere candour.

'Some things do – and some never can.' She managed a crooked smile. 'Stupid and useless and my own fault. Unfortunately. Goodnight, Giles.'

And she was gone, with no idea what she had said or the hurt she had left behind her.

TWO

It was a little after seven on Friday, August the thirty-first, when Mr Deveril finally arrived home again to find the house deserted, save for Naomi. He stood for a while in the hall, sternly reminding himself that he had been away for a full week and had sent no warning of his return so it was therefore childish to feel disappointed. He looked round at Naomi and willed himself to speak normally.

'Do you know where Mr Lewis is?'

She shook her head. 'No, sir.'

'And my wife?'

'At Court, sir. She'll be home around midnight.' Naomi felt a sudden twinge of sympathy for her intimidating employer and then thought of something that might cheer him and remove the strange, blank look from his eyes.

'There's a letter for you, sir. It's been here since Tuesday.' She held it out to him.

Alex glanced down without much interest and, for a moment, Naomi thought he wasn't going to take it. Then he stretched out his hand and received it while his expression grew, if anything, even more withdrawn and he walked wordlessly away to the parlour.

He stood before the empty fireplace staring absently at Persephone.

"Thou art fairer than the evening air, clad in the beauty of a thousand stars."

For the first time, the words meant something to him and he turned sharply away. His head felt light with fatigue and he supposed that it would be sensible to go to bed; but his need, as it had been through all this interminable week, was to see Chloë so he sat down, preparing to wait. It was only then that he saw Sarah's letter still in his hand and, because there did not seem to be anything else to do, he opened it.

It was quite short but he found he had to read it twice before its meaning reached him – the reward, he realised, of inadequate sleep – and then he simply tore it across and dropped the pieces in the empty hearth. If there was anyone, thought Alex grimly, that he did not want to see just now, then it was Sarah. Sarah with her airs and graces, her insincerity and her monumental self-conceit; Sarah, with her shallow heart, her vapid brain and her flaunting, deceptive beauty. Sarah – with whom, incredibly, he had once thought himself in love.

He looked down at the torn pieces of paper. She'd made it sound urgent ... but that only meant she wanted to see him and was determined, as always, to have her own way. Well, let her wait. He did not want to go – couldn't think of any reason why he should; except that she was the most ruthlessly persistent being he had ever met and would continue disrupting his peace until she got what she wanted.

'Oh damn it to hell!' said Alex to himself, wearily quitting his chair. 'Better to get it over at once, I suppose. But this time ... this time had better be the last.'

* * *

'Alex! My dear!' Lady Sarah flew across the room in a swish of pearl-grey satin and then stopped, ludicrously unable to cast herself against his chest as she had intended. 'But you are so dirty! Whatever have you been doing?'

'Riding,' said Mr Deveril succinctly.

'Oh!' Sarah brightened. 'You've come straight here to see me without even stopping to change? But how gallant! I'm flattered.'

'Don't be. I hadn't even thought of it.' He looked at her and his eyes matched his voice, cool and faintly impatient. 'I haven't much time so perhaps we can come to the point. What do you want?'

Some of the vivacity drained from the lovely face and she eyed him petulantly. Then, recovering, and managing a melting sigh, she said, 'You don't know then. I had thought that someone must have told you – your wife, perhaps?'

'I haven't seen her,' he replied briefly. 'What is it?'

The cornflower eyes rested on him mistily. 'It's Graham. He's dead.'

It was the last thing he expected and it threw him slightly off balance.

'Oh. I'm sorry,' he said politely.

'And I,' continued Sarah with restrained emphasis, 'am a widow. A very rich widow.'

Alex appeared to give this a modicum of thought. Then, 'Well, I expect you'll enjoy that. It's what you always wanted, isn't it?'

There was a pause and then she said carefully, 'You're mistaken. I don't want to be a widow at all.'

'Don't you?' Boredom was beginning to creep into Mr Deveril's face. 'Then I don't suppose you'll have much trouble finding someone to help you change that. Only take my advice, Sarah – choose somebody young and healthy with safe habits this time – or you may find your suitors wondering if your fatal charms aren't rather more fatal than charming.' He smiled perfunctorily. 'Why did you want to see me?'

And for the first time, Sarah – who thought she'd already told him – was lost for words.

Alex looked at her, remotely indifferent; then something in her face penetrated his mind and stirred it into life.

'You didn't,' he asked with slow incredulity, 'think that I might become Number Three? Did you? Is that why I'm here – to lay my heart at your feet and offer you my name?'

She did not reply but two spots of colour began to burn high on her cheekbones.

Mr Deveril stared at her with an oddly desperate expression in his eyes. Then, his voice not entirely steady, he said, 'My compliments, Sarah. You are unbelievable!' And dissolved into helpless laughter.

'Stop it!' shouted Sarah, stamping her foot. 'Stop it this instant! I will not be laughed at. How dare you?'

With an effort, Alex pulled himself together.

'I apologise. But you must see – or no. You can't, of course.' He was conscious of a crazy wish that Chloë was there to share this priceless moment and then pushed it aside. 'But you do appear to have forgotten that I'm already married.'

'No, I haven't.' Her voice was sulky. 'But that's nothing. Any fool can tell you've never bedded her – don't try to deny it! – so you can easily have it set aside.'

Alex was suddenly very serious indeed.

'It's an interesting concept – but what makes you so sure? I doubt Chloë has told you so.'

Sarah had recovered her poise and was aware of a need for caution. It would be as well not to mention her visit to Chloë or their conversation.

'She didn't need to. One can tell simply by looking at her. And it's hardly surprising. She is dreadfully commonplace – with absolutely nothing to attract you.' She smiled with teasing malice. 'Except her brain, of course.'

Mr Deveril smiled back. 'So you thought I'd be glad to be rescued from such mediocrity – and would get rid of Chloë in order to marry you?'

Lady Sarah took his hands and peeped seductively into the silver-blue eyes.

'And won't you?' she asked huskily.

Alex allowed his hands to remain passively in hers.

'No, Sarah. I won't,' he said flippantly; and felt the shock run through her body to her fingertips. He disengaged himself then and took a step away from her and when he spoke again his voice was hard and cold. 'This farce has gone far enough and it's time we made an end of it. You have miscalculated. I will not annul my marriage for you for the simple reason that I don't want to. To be frank with you, my egocentric little leech, I'd as soon choose a wife from Bridewell or from any street corner.'

'But you love me. You've always loved me!'

'No.' His gaze was frigidly implacable. 'It's true that I once thought so – but that was long ago and I now know how wrong I was. I neither love you nor want you and I wouldn't care if I never laid eyes on you again. In fact,' he said clearly, 'I should prefer it.'

Sarah stared at him as though he were speaking a foreign language and then the beautiful mouth curled back over the small white teeth.

'You stupid bastard! You're nothing – do you near me? Nothing! So go home to your tedious little wife and I hope she makes you as miserable as you deserve – because you'll never forget me – never! Unless,' she finished with blistering sarcasm, 'you're going to tell me that you are in love with that plain, sorry creature?'

A slow, strange smile lit the sculpted face.

'But I am,' replied Alex. 'Completely and totally in love with her. And for my life-time.'

There was a long silence and then Sarah laughed derisively.

'You're losing your mind. You've been married for eight months and your wife is still a virgin - and you say you love her? What is it, Alex?' she asked vindictively. 'Won't she have you? Or aren't you capable?'

Mr Deveril shrugged. 'I don't expect you to understand – only to believe that it is so and accept that there's no more to say.' He looked for a moment into her stunned, silenced face and swept a deep, formal bow. 'Life, you should know, is full of small disappointments. But I'm sure you'll soon get over it. Goodbye, Sarah.'

And he left without waiting for her reply.

* * *

Back in Southwark, with the clock of St Mary Overie just striking half past nine, there was still no sign of Matt or Chloë. Alex went upstairs to wash and change, then returned to the parlour. It was still only a little after ten; two hours to wait; an eternity. He poured a glass of wine, picked up the first book that came to hand and sat down to read. Ten minutes later, when the glass was empty and he had not turned a page, he got up irritated by his own restlessness and walked over to re-fill his glass.

Completely and totally ... and for my life-time, he had said; and it was true – though he wasn't sure why he had said it to Sarah. Alex stared into the ruby-coloured liquid and came to the conclusion that there was a terrible tyranny in words. Just a collection of syllables with no meaning except what one chose to give them, no life until they were uttered. They could say anything or nothing – be a bridge or a chasm; and once spoken, they were inviolate, existing indestructibly in one's mind.

You've been married for eight months and your wife is still a virgin. The annulment, he recalled hazily, had been Chloë's suggestion and never once had she given any sign of having changed her mind. She had never sought his company nor tried to bring herself to his attention in any way; in fact, she had seemed almost unaware that he was both masculine and her husband – merely offering him a placid, sexless friendship where there was no need for pretence, no room for shyness. And that, he now realised, was as unusual as it was depressing.

So why, since she did not even seem to regard him as a man, let alone as a potential lover, had she never treated him as she did Danny?

Because, came back the uncompromising reply, you never gave her the chance – any more than you treated her as a woman. So what you got was precisely what you asked for. Except once; on the Falcon Stairs, when you thought you only wanted a body and she offered you the moon in a kiss.

A ray of light; the only one. What is it, Alex? Won't she have you? Trust Sarah to find the thing that could really hurt – but she was wrong. She had to be wrong for there was the kiss to prove it. Chloë might not love him but she had undoubtedly responded to him in a way which suggested that it would not be very difficult to seduce her.

And there the thought stopped, leaving him feeling ashamed of himself.

He filled his glass again and was about to drain it when he realised what he was doing.

'Oh God! I'm drunk – or as near as makes no matter. I must be or I wouldn't be thinking this way.' Through the silence came the sound of a carriage rumbling to a halt outside the gate. Alex stood up and then, rising, extinguished the single branch of candles.

'Oh Marigold,' he said, vaguely rueful. 'I meant well .. but I really don't think I'm fit to talk to you after all. And it won't help if you find me cup-shot.'

On entering the house, Chloë's eyes went automatically to the place where, for four days, Sarah's letter had lain. She saw that it had gone and felt her breath leak away. He was back, then; she had half-expected it. Taking off her cloak, she dropped it over a chair then stood for a moment, staring at the parlour doors, trying to compose herself. At length, she took a deep breath and went in.

There was no light but every sense told her he was there.

'Hello,' she said quietly. 'Have we run out of candles?'

The silence seemed to stretch out to infinity and then Alex stirred and spoke, his voice disembodied in the gloom.

'No,' he said to the sound of scraping flint. He re-lit the candles and looked across at her. 'How did you know I was in here?'

'Instinct.' Her eyes rested on his face as if she had never seen him before. 'Is everything all right? You look ... strange.'

He smiled and came out of the shadows towards her, saying pleasantly, 'You mean, more so than usual? No. You're just seeing me as a hero for the first time.'

'No, I'm not.' Chloë managed a creditable grin. 'The only difference is that now it's official. I just hope you won't let it go to your head.' And to herself, she added despairingly, 'You're bone-tired and tense and not very sober. Again. Why must I pretend not to notice?'

The light gaze dwelt on her intently. 'I think I can promise that. Matt told you about it?'

'Yes. I think he was sorry he missed the grand finale, though. Was it spectacular?'

'Very. A worthy rival to the City of London's Royal Birthday Party.'

Chloë smiled. 'But without Muses or doves?'

'We didn't need them. We had Giles doing acrobatics and me supplying the verse. Faustus, in fact. It seemed appropriate.'

There was something in his expression that Chloë found disturbing and she turned away to escape it, feeling rather confused. It was as if they were conducting their conversation in code. Her own part she understood; she was doing what she always had to do, when all she really wanted was to ask about Sarah. But the baffling thing now was that he seemed to be doing it too; forcing himself to say things he cared nothing about as a shield for those he did.

She sank gracefully into a chair and started the nightly ritual of pulling the pins from her hair while she said hesitantly, 'I can see why you said you had to have solid proof. It's quite hard to believe Simon was behind all the things Matt told me about. He was always so ... efféminé.'

With an effort, Alex tore his attention away from the delicate curve of her neck and summoned a reply. 'Quite. Unfortunately, he's also vain, avaricious and vindictive – not to mention dangerously clever. I don't know what they'll do with him but I hope never to hear of him again.' He paused for a second and when he spoke again, his voice was faintly unsure. 'Perhaps I should have killed him. I intended to.'

Chloë looked round and met his eyes.

'You intended to and you wanted to – which is why you didn't. And you were right. Wasn't Prince Rupert satisfied?'

He smiled a little. 'Eventually.'

'Well, I should think so too. And the King is not only satisfied but grateful. In fact,' she said, a shade less buoyantly, 'he wants to give you a reward. Anything, I gather, except money or Frances Stuart.'

As she hoped, Alex laughed. 'What a shame. We could have done with the money.'

'And Frances Stuart?' asked Chloë, unable to help herself.

'Is she His Majesty's latest?'

'About to be, I think.' She dropped the last of the pins on the table, shook her hair loose and ran her hands through it.

'I can take her or leave her,' Alex said, staring and wishing he could touch. 'And then, of course, I'm not looking to establish a seraglio.'

And this time, Chloë couldn't think of an answer.

Alex watched as she bent her head thoughtfully over her hands. The candlelight touched the rose-gold hair with flame and shadowed the artfully darkened lashes lying downcast against her cheek. Her face was thinner than he remembered and she looked pale – as if, beneath the composure, lay a strain at whose cause he could not even guess. Something he couldn't name rose in his chest and it hurt to breathe. He forgot that it was late, that he wasn't entirely sober, that he'd meant to wait for a better time. He forgot everything except that, though uncertainty was killing him, the possibility of a rebuff was worse.

With some vague idea that an oblique approach might be safest, he said lightly, 'I've been wondering whether our annulment is worth the trouble of continuing to pursue it.'

Chloë's throat closed with shock. 'Oh?'

'Yes. One becomes ... accustomed, after all. And Matt is strongly averse to change. It seems a pity to upset him necessarily. What do you think?'

What she thought was that she didn't know where this might be leading and why he was choosing to say it now right after, presumably, reading Sarah's letter. She said carefully, 'I – I think it seems a rather drastic step to take for Matt's peace of mind.'

'Not just his. I too have grown comfortable with our life.' And thought wildly, 'Comfortable? God, what a bloody stupid thing to say!' Then, striving for lightness, 'And who else will sew on my buttons?'

There was a tiny tremor in the insouciant voice that Chloë, with her back to him, took for laughter. It never occurred to her that quick-witted, sharp-tongued Mr Deveril was so completely out of his depth that he had no idea what to say. Something inside her shrivelled and when she spoke again, her voice matched his. 'I'm sure you'll think of someone. And buttons aren't everything.'

'True.' He laid one hand gently on the polished table and contemplated his fingers. 'You haven't answered my question.'

'Haven't I?' Chloë kept her gaze on her lap. 'I didn't think I needed to. I thought you were joking.'

'No,' he said. And thought, 'Not joking, Marigold. Just afraid I'll make myself ridiculous by drenching you in emotion.' Then, aware that it was not going well, he said in a tone stripped of all levity, 'No. In fact, I wasn't. It simply occurred to me that we have been waiting eight months for our marriage to be declared null – and we may wait another eight. It seems an inordinate amount of inconvenience for something that I, at least, do not particularly want.' He hesitated and then ploughed on. 'We're not strangers any more – indeed, I hope that we've become friends. And so I wondered if we might not bow to the inevitable and allow our marriage to stand.' Another pause while he forced out, as unemotionally as possible, the words that had to be said. 'Unless, of course, you find me distasteful in any way or have ... formed an attachment for someone else?'

He waited for what seemed a very long time before she turned slowly towards him.

'Are you suggesting,' asked Chloë, her eyes wide and dark, 'that we go on just as before?'

The ground shifted beneath Alex's feet, bringing him to the edge of the precipice. He managed a crooked smile. 'Not quite, my dear,' he said, so casually that he astounded himself. 'I hoped you might consider sharing my bed.'

For the second time that evening, Chloë's breath froze in her lungs. Then, because his words made no more sense than anything else in their conversation so far, she rose mechanically from her seat and heard herself say, 'Did you? Why? Because the annulment is troublesome and

Matt dislikes change? Or because your life is beautifully ordered and I don't disturb it? I'm sorry – but I don't find those reasons adequate.'

A rare flush stained Alex's skin and his eyes glittered strangely.

'Don't you? Then forget them and I'll give you another,' he said before he could stop himself. 'I love you.'

Hope blossomed at the words but was instantly withered by the flatness of his tone. For a tiny instant Chloë thought she was going to be sick and then the feeling was washed away in a wave of anger. Again, the notion that he was sincere but so unsure of himself he was afraid of being laughed at, never occurred to her.

'Really?' Well, that is a surprise!' she snapped. 'You must think I'm an idiot!'

Burningly aware of his own clumsiness, Alex proceeded to make matters worse.

'No! I didn't mean it to sound like that – I never meant to say it at all just yet.'

'That I can believe!' she retorted furiously. 'Won't you ever learn not to make these sort of proposals when you're three sheets to the wind?'

An oddly shaken laugh escaped him. 'Not true – or not entirely. I know I'm making an unholy mess of it – but I mean what I'm saying. I love you.'

'So you said. Roughly translated, that means you need me to sew on your buttons and save you from your wealthy widow. Oh – how is Sarah, by the way? Still pining for you?'

'Not any more, I hope.'

Chloë stared at him, a knife twisting in her stomach. 'You've seen her?'

He nodded uneasily. 'Yes. I wanted to – '

'Spare me,' said Chloë coldly. 'At least it makes some sense of the last ten minutes. The only thing I don't understand is why you should think it necessary to endure the tedium of making love to me. After all, with a little address and careful planning – both of which are supposed to be your speciality – you could have the best of both worlds.'

There was a sudden deathly hush, then Alex gave a reckless little laugh and advanced towards her smiling.

'You're quite wrong, you know. Utterly, spectacularly wrong. I have the best of all worlds, here in this house with you. I want nothing else. But I need you to tell me that I may keep it.' The wide, silvery gaze held hers. 'Please.'

The saving wrath fell away from her, leaving her defenceless. She stared into his eyes, still unable to trust him and seeking to discover what lay behind the words. He rarely said what he meant – and frequently said things he didn't. She had always known that. So what then did he mean? His eyes didn't tell her. Instead, they warned of his immediate intention but a fraction too late to avoid it.

In two strides, Alex was at her side, capturing her hands and holding them deftly behind her. It was Oxford all over again and brown eyes met blue in a moment of shared recollection. Then Alex said softly, 'Forgive me, Chloë. But it's the only weapon I have left.' And his mouth found hers.

Too startled to resist, too shaken to engage her brain, and wanting beyond reason to have this one moment, Chloë simply gave in. Her hands relaxed and her mouth opened to the warmth of his. Alex released her wrists and gathered her against him, gliding one hand up into the waterfall of her hair to cradle her skull. The kiss deepened and her arms slid round his neck. She was lost. They both were.

Aeons later yet still too soon, Alex released her mouth to look into her eyes.

'I want you,' he breathed. 'Say you want me too.'

Reason returned. It would be so easy ... so very easy to just say 'yes' and let it happen ... and God knew, she wanted to. It would make the lie she had been prepared to tell a truth and the annulment an impossibility. And yet ... and yet ... if she did that, she might never know if this moment had been real. He had been drinking and, though not drunk, neither was he completely sober – and they had been here before. She couldn't let it – didn't dare let it – happen again. Summoning up every ounce of will, she brought her palms to his shoulders and tried to push him away.

'We can't do this,' she said as firmly as she was able. 'You have to let me go.'

Her chin was taken in one long-fingered hand and she was forced to meet his eyes.

'Why?' he asked, his other arm still holding her fast.

'Because you need to think what you're doing – and what it means. This ... isn't clever. And you – you've no right.'

'Yes I have,' responded Alex, with that rare beautiful smile, 'I've had the right for eight months. But don't worry. I'm not going to ravish you. I think – I hope – I don't need to.'

And then his mouth was on hers again, shamelessly invoking her senses. Flames licked along her veins, heat spread to every nerve and sinew and her bones melted. His hands framed her face, trailed down her neck and explored the soft skin of her shoulders. With hunger threatening to over-take him and his arms still holding her hard against him, Alex raised his head. Looking into half-awakened brown eyes, he gave a small unsteady laugh as her fingers brushed his cheek.

'Do you find me distasteful, Marigold? Do you?' he asked, his lips skimming her hair, her eyes, her throat. 'Can you say I don't attract you? Just a little? Tell me!'

And driven beyond her defences, Chloë at last replied with the simple truth.

'No – no. And you know it.'

His arms tightened around her and the silver-blue eyes blazed with an unmistakeable demand which mingled oddly with a sort of desperate pleading.

'I know it,' agreed Alex, almost beneath his breath. 'I just don't know if it's enough.'

And it was then, with the words of total admission hovering on her tongue that Chloë realised what their result would be if she uttered them now. She wanted to hold him close and tell him she loved him ... and she wanted to cry because this wasn't the way and neither of them could afford any more mistakes. Anguish rose, choking her voice so that she could only lay frantic hands against his chest and try to push him way.

Alex said, 'Chloë – don't. It's all right. Be still. I won't do anything you don't want.'

Past words and coherent thought, she only knew she had to get away from the terrible temptation of his arms. She twisted her head round only to feel his lips against her ear and it was then that she caught sight of the wine-bottle on the table beside her. Mindlessly, she seized it and brought it down on her husband's head.

Alex dropped to his knees, clutching his skull and dripping claret.

'What the hell ...?' He looked up, his gaze blurred. And then, typically, 'My dear girl ... you only had to say no.'

Chloë fled – out of the parlour, up the stairs and into her bedchamber. And for the first time ever, she locked and bolted her door. If he came in now, she'd either end up strangled like Desdemona – or naked in bed with him; and wasn't sure which would be worse.

THREE

People said that the night brought counsel and Chloë, finally slipping from an uneasy doze into sleep, hoped it was true. When she woke, later than was usual, she was surprised to find that she felt marginally better. For five days she had felt as if a stranger was inhabiting her body; a stranger who walked and talked and had managed to appear rational – until last night. She shuddered. She'd been tired and overwrought, of course – but that was neither an excuse nor a comfort. Nor did it help her to figure out how on earth she was going to face him.

But despite all this, she discovered that she didn't feel unhopeful. Mr Deveril had, after all, shown no inclination to exchange her for Lady Sarah – quite the reverse, in fact. Chloë wondered why that was … and exactly how much of what he'd said last night was actually true. Then she decided that what really mattered was that, although Alex might not love her, he did apparently want her; and even if that was only because he'd been living like a monk for eight months, it didn't alter the fact that it was her and not some other he'd tried to seduce. Chloë's mouth twisted wryly. She didn't care why he wanted her – only that he did. For the one thing last night had taught her was that half a loaf was definitely better than no bread at all.

So there was hope then, of a sort and all she had to do was decide how it could amount to anything. The thing which had held her back last night and which would continue to do so was her fear of trapping him; of removing his only escape route from a marriage for which she had always considered herself responsible. And therein lay the key.

Her brain reeled at the sheer, breath-taking simplicity of it. She wanted to lie with him and he seemed to want that too – but her conscience was standing in the way of it. So what they needed – what they had always needed – was the thrice-blasted annulment. All she had to do, it seemed, was go and ask the King.

Chloë laughed at the irony of it, then embarked on the most careful toilette of her life whilst considering the possibilities. It was a gamble, of course – but for high stakes. Hold on to her marriage and it was stalemate; jettison it, and they could begin afresh.

'God gives and God takes away,' she told her reflection firmly. 'Everything has to be paid for.' Her reflection looked back, neat as wax and elegant in tawny silk. Chloë hoped it would do.

At the foot of the stairs she encountered Mr Lewis. His shrewd black eyes held a knowing gleam she could have done without so she said cautiously, 'Have you seen Mr Deveril yet?'

'Aye.'

'Did he ... do you know if he got any sleep last night?'

'Damn,' said Matthew, cheerfully. 'I clean forgot to go and tuck him in.'

She sighed. 'You know what I meant. Just tell me how he is.'

'He's well enough – saving a lump on his head and his good shirt covered in claret.'

'Oh.' Chloë crossed her fingers behind her back. 'Did he say how it happened?'

'You mean you don't know?' Matt grinned and, when she flushed but said nothing, added, 'Don't worry. He wasn't very talkative this morning. And then he went fishing.'

'He what?'

'Went fishing,' repeated Matt. 'Or that's what he said. If you ask me, he's gone off on his own to think. And about time, too.'

A significant glance accompanied this remark and Chloë flushed slightly. Then, in order to avoid deep water altogether, she said, 'I'm going to call on Mr Fenton and Mr Bennett on my way to Whitehall. It's time I finalised the sale of the cloth so that I can pay Captain Pierce. It will be too late to arrange to move it all today and tomorrow is Sunday – so do you think we can be ready by Monday morning?'

'We've been ready for a week,' replied Matt. Then, 'I didn't think you were due at Court today.'

'I'm not – this is something else.' She smiled suddenly. 'Mr Deveril's not the only one who's been doing some thinking.'

* * *

It was the first day of September and, though a fresh easterly breeze blew through the City, it was still very hot. Chloë's errands to Cheapside and Paternoster Row were quickly discharged and she continued serenely on her way through the sunshine to Whitehall only to discover that the King was playing tennis.

Chloë refused to be deterred. She informed His Majesty's equerry that she would wait in the Stone Gallery and asked him to beg the King to grant her a very brief but private audience at any time to suit his convenience. Then she retired and, with complete calm, proceeded to pass the time in idle conversation with various acquaintances.

It was almost six o'clock before she finally received a summons to the King's closet where she found him engaged in winding his collection of clocks. Charles greeted her with his usual charm, apologised for keeping her waiting so long and begged her to be seated.

'And while you tell me why you wanted to see me,' he smiled, 'I hope you won't mind if I finish setting my time-pieces. Like your delightful but capricious sex, they require a good deal of attention.'

Chloë perched on the edge of a chair, wondered how he could bear the busy, incessant ticking and tactfully remarked that the clocks were very beautiful.

'I think so,' replied the King. 'But you didn't wait all day to discuss chronometry, did you?'

'No, Your Majesty. I came to ask you to dissolve my marriage. I once told you that there was no hurry but that's no longer true. I need to be set free – today, if it's possible.'

Charles set down a small, silver clock and eyed her with lazy interest.

'I see. At the risk of appearing vulgarly intrusive, may I ask why?'

She had anticipated the question and decided that only the truth would serve. She smiled a little, reflecting that the nicest things about Charles Stuart were his lack of formality and his total unshockability, and said, 'I think Your Majesty has long suspected that I've never been ... indifferent ... to Mr Deveril, which is one of the reasons you delayed the annulment. And I'm glad of that because it seems that his feelings for me have changed – though I don't yet fully understand how. All I'm sure of is that last night he wanted to make love to me and that, as long as we're married, I can't let him.'

The heavy gaze dwelt on her with amused fascination.

'Are you saying that you would let him if you weren't married?'

'Yes. That's it exactly.' She paused, face and voice suddenly very serious indeed. 'You see Alex was drunk when he married me - and his desire for me now may be as temporary as his intoxication was then.'

'And you don't want him to discover that the hard way … yes, I see. But perhaps,' suggested Charles, 'you should take advantage while you have the chance?'

Chloë smiled bitterly. 'I can't. I can't let him take that risk. I'd never forgive myself.'

The King picked up another clock and wound it thoughtfully.

'Alex is fortunate,' he said at length. 'I take it there is no question of you wishing to … resist his blandishments?'

'No. I don't think I can. I only managed it last night by knocking him down.'

He gave a choke of laughter. 'Indeed? Then you have managed what a good many men have wanted to do but never succeeded in.'

She grinned. 'That's all very well, sire. But I can hardly make a habit of it, can I?'

'I suppose not,' agreed Charles, amused. 'My dear, I can't imagine why Alex isn't hopelessly in love with you – but if you want your annulment, you shall have it. Excuse me for a moment while I send for the necessary documents.' And he left her alone with the clocks.

When he came back, he was holding a sheaf of papers which he laid on a table at her side, saying, 'It appears that Alex signed these some time ago. So all they require now is your signature – and mine.'

Chloë accepted the quill he offered her and carefully wrote her name in the places he indicated, then watched while the King scrawled his own name and appended his seal.

'I – I'm truly grateful,' she said. 'I can't tell you how much.'

Charles merely cast her a quizzical glance and then watched as she fingered the folded sheets with the only sign of unease that she had shown so far. Sighing, he said, 'I have the feeling that you are about to ask something more of me.'

She looked up into the dark, clever eyes.

'Yes,' she admitted ruefully. 'I would be glad if this matter could remain secret for a few days. I … well, I'd prefer Mr Deveril not to know about it for a little while yet.'

For a moment he surveyed her in silence. Then he said, 'I wonder if you realise what a dangerous game you're playing? What, for example, if Alex beds the lady he believes is his wife but doesn't feel it necessary to re-marry her when he learns his mistake?'

Chloë stared back in astonishment. 'But I don't expect him to do so. To be honest, my worst fear is that he'll be completely furious with me for going behind his back.'

'Your worst fear? What about your reputation?'

'Will be lost. I shan't mind. Only I'll have to resign my post with the Queen ... and I don't know how to explain it.'

Charles accepted without a blink the implication that what would do for the King would not do for the Queen.

'I'm sure,' he said dryly, 'that, between us, we'll think of something. For now, it would be a kindness if you spent this evening with her – as it may be the last time. And I wish you luck with Alex. If he's lived with you for eight months without learning that you are utterly unique, I think you're going to need it.'

* * *

Mr Deveril did not return home until early evening. He didn't bring any fish with him but, seeing that the strain had largely faded from the blue eyes, Matt forbore to comment on it. He also forbore to mention that, though Chloë was at Court, it was not because her duties commanded it; and Alex, restored to an acceptable level of composure, did not trouble to ask.

He ate a light meal, washed down with a single glass of wine and then, removing himself to the parlour, spent an hour attending to various pieces of correspondence. There was no urgency now, no torment of doubt or impatience; only a quiet thread of hope, nurtured all day and not to be relinquished now. In the end, when you thought with your intellect instead of your emotions, the truth of the matter became amazingly simple. Either your wife was a wanton who would respond to any man as she did to you – or she wasn't. And since you knew she wasn't, that left only one possible alternative. Or so it seemed.

Sealing the last letter, he contemplated the thought, by no means new, that he had made a complete botch of the whole affair in a way that not only showed a lack of back-bone but also made him wonder what had happened to his so-called artistry. Except, of course, that it wasn't easy to make pretty speeches when one was in deadly earnest.

The door-bell rang and Mr Deveril swore gently beneath his breath, hoping that his visitor, whoever it was, would not stay long. Then the doors opened and Mr Beckwith walked in.

'Good,' he said. 'I hoped I might find you at home.'

Alex stood up, smiling.

'Well, it's always nice to be wanted,' he replied lightly and then stopped, his eyes resting narrowly on his friend's face. 'Sit down. You look as if you need a drink.'

Giles dropped his hat on the table and seated himself on a high-backed chair while he watched Alex pour a glass of burgundy. He said, 'I haven't much time. But I thought you'd like to know that Simon is still alive and aboard a ship, about to embark on a new career as a bond-servant in the Caribbean.' He took the glass that Alex handed him but made no move to drink. 'Vine is still in the Tower and, in all probability, they'll tactfully forget about him. I take it you haven't seen the King yet?'

'No.' Alex sat down and eyed him thoughtfully. 'I suppose I must go tomorrow. How did York take it?'

Giles frowned into his glass as if concentration was difficult.

'As you'd expect. He blustered his way through the full gamut of emotions and ended by feeling sorry for himself.' He glanced across at Alex. 'You're not drinking?'

'No.' A transient smile touched the sculpted face. 'Not tonight.'

There was a long pause, then Mr Beckwith said expressionlessly, 'That's a pity. I thought you might like to wish me bon voyage.'

The light gaze widened suddenly. 'You're going somewhere?'

Giles gave a wry smile and drank his wine. 'Yes. I'm sailing from Gravesend at dawn.'

'For where?'

'Jamaica.'

The word exploded between them.

'Jamaica?' asked Alex incredulously. 'What the hell for?'

Mr Beckwith shrugged. 'The same reasons that take a mercenary anywhere.'

'That wasn't what I meant and you know it,' replied Alex. 'Why go at all?'

'Because,' said Giles, with an effort that was beginning to show, 'I've been appointed Simon's official escort to Port Royal. I'm to get him there in one piece and give a full explanation to Governor Modyford.'

'In which case,' said Alex blandly, 'you won't be staying.'

'Why not? I'd like to recover my skills but don't particularly want to sell my sword to a foreign power and this seems a reasonable solution. There's a Welshman, Henry Morgan, who is making something of a name for himself out there and to whom I'm to deliver letters from the King. His exploits are no more piratical than were Rupert's during the Commonwealth and the rewards are rich – so you might call it a career of sorts.'

'A career,' said Alex sardonically, 'amidst all the outcast scum of Europe? I can't think of anything that would suit you less. So I'll ask again. Why Jamaica?'

Giles set his glass down with unnecessary violence.

'Because,' he snapped, 'it's about as far away from England as I can get.'

Alex surveyed him through narrowed eyes.

'And why would you want to do that?'

'Various reasons – none of which concern you.'

'They do if they're going to be the cause of you ending up stuck like a pig in some stinking Port Royal pot-house,' responded Mr Deveril caustically. 'Don't be an ass, Giles. I may play merry hell with my friends from time to time – but do you honestly think I'm going to wave a cheery farewell without at least trying to understand?'

Mr Beckwith stood up and picked up his hat.

'I appreciate that you mean well – but I'm afraid that, in this instance, the only service you can do me is to take my hand and wish me a safe journey. My reasons, even if I explained them, wouldn't help either of us.'

'Try me. I might surprise you.'

'I think not.' The grey eyes were hard. 'My mind is made up and I've a barge waiting at the Irongate Stairs. The only way you can stop me is by laying me out and I don't recommend that you try it.'

'I don't intend to,' Alex replied mildly. 'It would take all night and reduce the furniture to matchsticks. A pointless exercise and Chloë wouldn't like it.'

Giles' lost what little colour he had. 'Are you going to divorce her?'

The dark brows soared. 'Why do you ask that?'

There was a tiny pause and then, 'I just wondered if you were thinking of filling Graham Marsden's shoes.'

Alex frowned. 'Hardly.'

'And Chloë?'

'Will remain my wife,' he said. And thought, 'I hope.'

Mr Beckwith's fingers clenched on the brim of his hat.

'That will be nice for her. Does she know?'

A faint flush stained Mr Deveril's cheeks.

'What the hell is this? My relationship with Chloë is none of your business … but you surely can't have thought I'd go back to Sarah?'

'What I think doesn't matter,' replied Giles. 'But since Sarah believed it strongly enough to come here and tell Chloë that – '

'Stop!' snapped Alex, startled. 'She did what?'

'You didn't know?'

'No. Who told you?' The blue eyes were faintly dazed.

'Your wife.'

It was the tone rather than the words that gave it away but, before he realised it, Alex said, 'Chloe?' And then, blankly, 'Oh. That's it, isn't it?'

Giles said nothing. And Alex, who felt as if a bottomless pit had just yawned at his feet, didn't dare speak in case the words tipped him into it.

After a long, catastrophic silence, Giles said, 'I should go.'

'No.' Alex drew a harsh breath. 'Does she know?' And then, immediately, 'Or no. Of course not. You'd never tell her.'

'And neither will you.'

Mr Deveril's skin was entirely without colour. He said, 'Perhaps you should. She might … she might be glad.'

'She won't.'

'You can't know that.'

'Yes I can!' came the furious reply. 'What are you suggesting – that we let Chloe chose between us? What the hell for? Do you honestly think that if she'd ever given the merest hint of looking on me in that way I wouldn't know it by now? And she's your wife!'

'But you love her.'

'Yes. All right - I love her. Now, for God's sake, leave it.'

Alex said flatly, 'So do I.'

Caught in the act of replacing his hat, Giles stopped short. 'What?'

'I love her too.' He paused, then added, 'But I don't know if she'll ever return it.'

'Oh.' Giles hesitated, put aside what Chloe had told him because it wasn't for him to reveal and, instead, said bitterly, 'Well, at least you've the right to tell her.'

'I tried.' Alex's mouth twisted wryly. 'I made a complete mess of it. You'd have laughed.'

'I doubt it. There's very little in this that I find remotely funny.'

'No. I suppose not.' Another pause. 'So you're leaving.'

'I am leaving,' snapped Mr Beckwith, 'not because I'm in love with your wife but because I won't stay here to watch what happens next. You'll either sort out your marriage – or you won't. That's up to you. But I'm going to Port Royal - and you're going to forget we ever had this conversation. Because, for all the good that's come of it, we didn't.'

'I can't forget it,' returned Alex simply, 'because you're not just my oldest friend but also, possibly, a better one than I deserve. If you weren't, you wouldn't be stepping aside like this.'

'Don't cast me in the role of a martyr,' said Giles, finally putting on his hat. 'I've no taste for sackcloth and ashes. I'm merely doing what needs to be done. And now I have to go or I shan't make Gravesend in time.' Then he stopped, suddenly realising that, whatever else lay between them at this moment, some of what Alex had said was true. They had been friends for fifteen years and, after tonight, might never meet again. He turned slowly and looked across the room with a rueful, fleeting smile. 'I'm sorry. It's a poor way to say goodbye, isn't it?'

For an instant, Alex gazed back grimly and then, crossing to his side, dropped a hand on his shoulder. 'So would any other be – but we're not saying it yet. I'm coming with you to Irongate. Unless you'd rather I didn't?'

Some of the tension left Giles' face and he flushed a little.

'God, Alex – I'd welcome it.'

It was a little after eleven as the two men quitted the house and set off for Bankside and the bridge. For a long time neither spoke, then Mr Deveril broke the silence and opened up a channel of light conversation which lasted them all the way along Thames Street. Then, as they started up Tower Hill, Alex said abruptly, 'Do you realise that if you'd suggested this a couple of months ago – crazy scheme though it is – I might have gone with you?'

Mr Beckwith glanced obliquely at him. 'So what's changed?'

'I have.' He gave a brief laugh. 'It's ironic, don't you think? Having wasted five years in bitter resentment, Simon's banishment means no more to me than the end of a task I'd begun to find irksome. The truth is that he was never important – nor even the house and land; and the things that do matter were always quite outside his reach.'

It was a full minute before Mr Beckwith made any answer and his face wore a curious expression, as though he were contemplating an absorbing problem. Finally he said, 'We each have our choices to make. Mine, for the time being, is exile and has the merit of being as temporary as I wish it to be. What of yours?'

They passed the postern and then turned south towards the river. Alex smiled in the darkness and said quietly, 'Mine is for my lifetime … if she'll have me.'

Even more than the words, his tone was an avowal and Giles at last fully understood – and did not know if he was glad or sorry. He heard himself say, 'You said you made a mess of telling her. What went wrong? Didn't she believe you?'

'Not at all. And I made such a fool of myself that she hit me over the head and nearly knocked me senseless.'

'She what?' Giles was shaken by an unwilling laugh. 'How?'

'With a half-bottle of claret, if you must know.' He paused, then said, 'I haven't known how to tell her because, as with yourself, she's never offered me anything but friendship and I'm uncomfortably aware of how little I've ever done to deserve anything more.'

Mr Beckwith wondered why Alex's lack of conceit always managed to surprise him and why it was suddenly so easy to believe him; and then realised that it didn't matter. He said, 'If you'll take a piece of advice for once, you'll start by undoing any harm Sarah may have done. And then, instead of using twenty words where three would do, just say it.'

They arrived at Irongate on the stroke of midnight and at their feet the steps fell gently away where the water lapped rhythmically against the side of a barge, its lanterns lit and its oarsmen waiting.

'I'll try,' agreed Alex. 'And, if she'll let me, I'll do my best to look after her.'

'You'd better.' Giles descended the steps and then, turning, smiled a little and held out his hand. 'You're probably the most annoying fellow I ever met - but I suspect I'll miss you.'

'Bad habits are always the hardest to break,' said Alex, gripping the outstretched hand. Then, 'Don't fall off the map, will you?'

'Never.' For a moment, grey eyes met blue and then Mr Beckwith stepped quickly into the waiting barge. 'Make my farewells to Chloë ... but don't, whatever you do, give her my love,' he said as the oarsmen untied the ropes.

'If that's what you want.' Alex looked down at him and smiled. 'It's Boot and Saddle – or whatever the nautical equivalent is. Good luck, Giles.'

The barge was sliding away now, out into the current where it gathered speed.

'Au revoir,' called Giles in reply, his eyes on the dark, diminishing figure on the steps. 'Take care.' And then, since he could no longer see him, he turned his face to the east and sat back, letting the barge carry him swiftly to the sea and the start of a great journey.

* * *

For a long time after the lights of the barge had vanished beyond his sight, Mr Deveril remained on the steps, staring thoughtfully in the direction it had taken. The wind was full on his face but he was hardly conscious of it except to think that Giles would have a slow ride to

Gravesend. Time passed ... and the clock of St Katherine's was chiming half past one before he finally stirred to go.

Without haste, he retraced his steps to the top of Tower Hill and there an unexpected sight met his eyes. Ahead of him and not far away, the sky was lit by a fierce, red glow and streaked with trailing smoke. Just for a second, Alex stood still, staring at it and then he was off, racing with all possible speed along Tower Street. Somewhere on the far side of St Dunstan-in-the-East was fire; and in that location, after a four-month drought and in a freshening wind, it was a recipe for disaster.

Fire-bells started to toll as he passed the church and he could hear shouts and screams issuing from the afflicted neighbourhood; great tongues of flame leapt up behind the houses in Botolph Lane, silhouetting them in brilliant orange light and he could smell smoke. Then he reached the top of Pudding Lane and stared in disbelief at the pandemonium that reigned there.

The old, closely-built, wooden houses were as dry as tinder and the fire fed on them greedily, spreading from one to another with astonishing rapidity. Even as Alex watched, the wind tossed a shower of sparks cascading down on a house so far untouched and within seconds it was alight, as if composed of touchwood. Half the street was furiously ablaze and the flames were gaining strength with every second – while, as far as Alex could tell, no move was being made to halt their progress.

The lane was thronged with people whose sole aim appeared to be the preservation of their property. Goods and furniture of all kinds were being thrown from windows or carried from doorways into the narrow street, effectively blocking the way and providing a powder-trail to the houses opposite. With a mocking gust, the wind veered suddenly, sending sparks and flames across the road and then immediately shifted back again. But too late – for already the far side of the street had been ignited.

His face tingling with the heat and his ears deafened by the crackling roar of the flames, Alex crossed to a group of watchmen who were observing the conflagration with an air of helpless melancholy.

'Buckets, fire-hooks and ladders!' he bellowed. 'From the churches, you dolts. St Magnus, St Margaret's and St Andrew's. Move!'

FOUR

Chloë's first waking thought was the recalled disappointment of Mr Deveril's absence the night before. Then she became aware of a cacophony of bell-ringing that seemed excessive even for a Sunday and, getting swiftly out of bed, she ran to the window to look.

Across the river from Botolph's Wharf to Dowgate the sky was black with smoke, swirling in vast clouds from the area around Fish Street Hill and so dense that it completely hid the flames that were its source. Chloë stared at it incredulously and then, realising from the smoke-drift that the wind was blowing the fire steadily westwards to the wharves and her precious cargo, she began to dress in frantic haste.

Ten minutes later, still engaged in tying her hair back in a scarf, she flew out of her room and collided violently with Mr Deveril.

Alex caught her deftly by the shoulders, subjected her to a quick, keen scrutiny and then asked crisply, 'And where do you think you're going?'

'The Vintry,' replied Chloë, equally terse and eager to be off.

He shook his head and released her. 'Oh no you're not.'

She stared back in annoyance.

'I am. The silks and velvets are still in the warehouse and I'm going to move them.'

'Unnecessary. Matt set out half an hour ago.'

'Oh.' For a second, she felt faintly nonplussed, then she said stubbornly, 'Well, I'm going anyway. It isn't fair to leave it all to Matt – and that cloth represents five months planning and work. It's worth nearly fifteen hundred pounds.'

'I don't care if it's worth fifteen thousand,' replied Mr Deveril inflexibly. 'You're going to do as you're told and stay meekly by the hearth.'

Chloë's brows rose to impossible heights.

'And what,' she asked politely, 'are you going to do?'

A gleam of humour lit the silver-blue eyes.

'Play with a fire-engine,' he replied, heading for the stairs.

'I might have known,' said Chloë gloomily following. Then, 'How bad is it?'

'It's critical,' said Alex over his shoulder. He reached the door and turned to face her with a sudden smile. 'Which is why you're staying at home like a good girl. D'accord?'

She smiled meekly in reply and watched him stride to the gate. Then, as soon as he was out of sight, she shut the door behind her and wasted five minutes walking round the garden before setting off for the blazing north bank.

By the time she had fought her way to the middle of the bridge, she was beginning to realise that her magisterial ex-husband probably had a point. The narrow, shop-lined road was choked with laden carts and, between these, the poorer people jostled their way south, their arms full of whatever possessions they had managed to save. Bruised and battered, Chloë ploughed doggedly on to the far side and it was only then that she felt her resolve weaken.

The fire had reached the church of St Magnus and was sweeping down towards the river with horrifying speed while the air, acrid with smoke, was charged with a deluge of sparks and fragments of burning material. It was a matter of minutes before the bridge itself would be ablaze – and the knowledge drove Chloë on. Tearing the scarf from her hair to hold it over her mouth, she darted an erratic course through the press of noisily frightened refugees and dived headlong down the side of the Fishmongers Hall towards the Old Swan. She raced through the Steelyard without attracting a second glance, all the men there busy tipping combustible loads of wood, coal and tar into the river; and at length, her chest heaving, she reached the Vintry and Matt.

Mr Lewis stared at her crossly. 'Didn't Mr Alex tell you to stay at home?'

'Yes,' panted Chloë. 'What are you doing?'

'Trying to get a boat. I've paid a couple of lads to move the stuff but as yet we've no transport. You can't do anything so you might as well go back. Unless you fancy the rough side of Mr Alex's tongue?'

'I'm staying,' she said obstinately. 'And Mr Alex won't know anything about it unless you tell him.' She surveyed the chaotic waterfront where a spotty youth in a small boat was desperately trying to find a space to tie his craft. 'This couldn't be one of yours, could it?'

Matt looked and gave a grunt of satisfaction before marching into the warehouse where his other assistant stood waiting. 'Jump to it, lad – we'll start with the velvets.' He turned to Chloë. 'If you're set on helping, go across with Tom. You'll have to find somebody to carry the cloth to the house and they'll need watching if you don't want to be robbed.'

Chloë went to pick up a bolt of crimson velvet and had it taken unceremoniously from her hands. 'Leave it. Wait by the boat – you're only in the way here. And I doubt we've more than an hour.'

Having, as he thought, despatched Chloë safely back to Southwark, Matthew was considerably irritated when she returned with the boat and announced that she'd left the business of supervision in the capable hands of Mistress Jackson.

'The bridge is on fire and people are throwing things out of their windows into the river,' she said, following as he carried more velvet to the boat. 'And the Fishmongers Hall and the Old Swan are ablaze. It's moving quite fast, isn't it?'

Mr Lewis' reply was to accelerate his efforts but, even so, by the time they were ready to set off again, the air was thick with smoke and nauseous fumes from a warehouse of resin and pitch in the Steelyard.

Matt ordered Chloë to go home and stay there; Chloë, despite streaming eyes and intermittent bouts of coughing, refused. There followed a brief but pungent exchange at the end of which Tom rowed off alone and Mr Lewis took the liberty of informing Mistress Chloë that she was a damned stubborn nuisance.

Chloë spent the next twenty minutes in a mounting fever of anxiety. From the edge of the wharf she was able to see the fire engulf All Hallows the Great and pass on to All Hallows the Less; a warehouse of wine and brandy sent huge flames soaring high into the air and the wind was carrying burning debris closer and closer to where she stood. Then the roof of the building next door but one caught light and Chloë was flooded with a sense of bitter frustration. She thought of all the things that this cargo was to have bought – fresh hangings for Mr Deveril's bed-chamber, new rugs for the parlour – and her eyes filled with tears that had nothing to do with the choking air.

'What the bloody hell are you doing here?' a furious voice demanded.

Chloë jumped and swung round to meet a wrathful stare.

'I thought I'd made it clear that you were not to come?'

'Yes. Well. You did,' replied Chloë weakly. 'Only I thought – '

'What you thought is perfectly plain,' snapped Mr Deveril, 'and you're a little fool. Where the devil is Matt?'

'Inside.' She swallowed and her gaze dropped from the frowning, sweat-streaked face to the ruin of yet another coat. 'He tried to send me home.'

'Well, I'll do more than try and I don't have time to argue. I have to demolish your warehouse – and quickly, if it's to be any use. You may go voluntarily or the other way – but go you will. And this time you won't come back. Do you hear me?'

An ache filled Chloë's chest and she gazed desperately across the waterfront. 'You can't pull it down. More than half the cloth is still inside. Can't you - -?'

'No I can't.' Seizing her shoulders, Alex spun her to face the fire. 'Look at it. We've ten minutes – possibly less. Do you want to sacrifice the City to a few ells of silk?'

The roof that had caught a few minutes ago was now angrily ablaze and the fire was roaring and crackling its way to the next one.

'No. I'm sorry.' A sob tore at her throat. 'You're right, of course.'

Mr Deveril pulled her back to face him and his smoke-reddened eyes examined her narrowly. 'Oh God! All right – wait here. I'll see what I can do.' And he raced into the warehouse.

Five minutes later when Tom brought the boat back, Alex and Matt had a mound of silk waiting on the quay while the demolition crew started work with axes at the rear. Within seconds, Mr Deveril had hurled the cloth into the boat and turned to grasp Chloë's hand; then, very swiftly, he pulled her into his arms and dropped a light kiss on her hair. 'I'm sorry, Marigold – but the King wants us to hold it at the Three Cranes. Try to understand – and don't cry. It doesn't matter.' And before she could reply, he handed her into the waiting boat.

Chloë sniffed and stared wetly up at him as Tom pushed off from the bank.

'You're tired,' she said.

'A bit.' Alex smiled at her. 'I'll come when I can. Don't worry.' Then he strode back to his work.

They moved fast, bringing the loosely-jointed wooden structure down before the flames touched it – but to no avail. Although they were able to remove the debris by flinging it into the river, the fire continued to fasten hungrily on the next building; Alex swore with rare fluency, tossed a stream of orders to Mr Lewis, now ably assisting, and raced, coughing, through the smoke in the direction of Thames Street.

The conflagration had already spread this far and was burning patchily north towards Canning Street whose inhabitants were busily loading their goods into a myriad of vehicles which almost totally blocked the road. Alex sped through a gap and cannoned into Mr Pepys of the Naval Office.

'Have you seen Bludworth?' demanded Mr Deveril, pitching his voice over the din.

Mr Pepys shook his head and then, suddenly pointing to the far side of the road, 'Over there!'

Alex shot off, forging a path, with the Naval official hard on his heels.

If the Lord Mayor had seen their approach he might well have striven to escape, for he had a great dislike for forceful young gentlemen of Mr Deveril's stamp; but, as it was, the first he knew was when his arm was seized in an iron grip.

'We can't go on like this,' Alex shouted. 'It's too damned slow. What fresh orders have you given?'

Sir Thomas quivered with indignation.

'Lord – what more can I do? I'm spent and the people won't obey me. I have been pulling down houses – but the fire overtakes us faster than we can do it.'

'I know that!' snapped Alex. 'Pulling them down isn't enough – we need to use gunpowder.'

'What? The people would never tolerate it.'

'His Majesty,' said Mr Pepys primly, 'has commanded that demolition should proceed with all possible expedition – to which end, the Duke of York offers soldiers if you should need them.'

Sir Thomas mopped his brow with a large handkerchief and said peevishly, 'Well I don't! We are doing everything that can be done and I have been up all night.'

He tried to move away but was detained by Mr Deveril's hand on his arm.

'Have you called out the Militia?' he demanded. And then, 'Obviously not. So you'd best do it before you go off to put your feet up.' And finally, with an explosion he could not control, 'You bloody fool! How long to you expect to fight this thing with volunteers? For Christ's sake, use what little sense you have and call out the troops!' And leaving the Mayor goggling apoplectically and Mr Pepys staring with faintly scandalised satisfaction, Alex shot back towards the wharves.

Within the hour the City Militia took over demolition work at the riverside, one detachment going to stop the blaze at Botolph's Wharf and another relieving Mr Deveril's crew west of Dowgate. The river, by this time, was speckled with barrels, boxes and items of furniture that had been cast into it and were floating up with the tide to bob gently amongst the profusion of loaded barges and lighters. The bridge was burning fast and its terrified occupants descended the pier stairways to boats tied below in which they embarked with everything they could carry. Like their human neighbours, the pigeons were also loth to leave and flew round and round until, their feathers scorched by the fire, they dropped into the water.

Water had become Mr Deveril's most immediate difficulty. Having left Dowgate, he and Matt took their men northwards into the City only to discover that the pumping mechanism at London Bridge had stopped working as soon as the flames attacked it and that all the pipes and sluices had been cut by panicky fire-fighters to fill their buckets. Consequently, though he now had access to the cumbersome 'suck-and-squirt' fire-engines, the sole water supply was a quarter of a mile away and the process of obtaining it made even slower than necessary by the press of carts, refugees and gleeful plunderers thronging the streets.

As the afternoon passed, the fire seemed to spread even faster. Two by two, Mr Deveril sent his little force off to rest while he himself worked on. Darkness fell and the night sky glowed red from the immense blaze as Matthew went with unwilling fury to Southwark; and still Alex stayed, his brain clogged with fatigue and his body responding with mechanical slowness. Only when Matt returned shortly before four in the morning did he finally yield to the inevitable and leave for home himself.

Fully dressed and dozing fitfully in the parlour, Chloë was jerked awake by the sound of the front door closing and, running into the hall, she found Alex – filthy, dishevelled and swaying with exhaustion. Summing up the situation at a glance, she flew to his side and, rapidly revising her plans, flung a series of orders at Naomi whilst guiding Alex firmly towards the stairs. He tried to say something but was overtaken by a fit of coughing. Chloë's grip on him tightened.

'Don't talk,' she said. 'You'll be better when you've slept.'

She pushed open the door of his room and made him sit on the bed while she pulled off his boots – which, like the rest of his clothing, looked beyond repair. Then she untied the laces of his charred and blackened shirt, wondering stupidly what had become of his coat.

'I'm afraid,' said Alex in a hoarse whisper, 'that I'm going to make a terrible mess of your sheets.'

'It doesn't matter. You can bathe later. Lift your arms so I can take your shirt – ah, good. Thank you, Naomi.' This as the maid entered to place a mug beside the bed. Chloë handed her the ruined shirt. 'This can be thrown away. But can you see what – if anything – can be done with Mr Deveril's boots?'

Naomi curtsied, picked up the boots with a dubious air and withdrew.

Chloë put the mug in Alex's hand and closed his fingers round it.

'Drink this,' she said, frowning at the numerous small burn-marks that adorned his torso. 'It's warm milk and honey to ease your throat.'

Alex did as she asked and gave back the mug with a hazy smile.

'I've been talking too much.'

'You still are.' She watched him lie down and cast a light woollen coverlet over him before crossing the room the close the curtains.

'Chloë?' His voice was a mere thread.

She moved back to the bedside. 'Yes?'

'Don't let me sleep more than four hours. Promise?'

If she hesitated, it was only for a second. 'I promise,' she said. And left him.

When she went back shortly after nine he was still sound asleep – which, after forty-eight hours of continued and strenuous activity, was hardly surprising. Chloë set down her tray, watching him; his face was turned into the pillow and he lay with one arm outstretched, its fingers lax and curved inwards towards the blistered palm. A great wave of emotion welled up inside her, so intense that it robbed her of every thought but one and, sitting lightly at his side, she enclosed the beautiful, desecrated hand in hers for a long moment before raising it to her lips. Then, laying it gently down again, she drew a long, unsteady breath and set about rousing him.

As she had expected, Alex was too tired to wake easily but eventually he rolled over and propped himself on his elbows, his face driven into his hands. Chloë left him rigidly alone while she opened the curtains and poured warm, honey-spiced mead, then she sat down again on the edge of the bed and put the cup in his hand.

'Naomi will be up in a minute with hot water and there's some salve for the worst of your burns on the wash-stand,' she said, as if it were perfectly normal to sit on his bed while the City was in flames. 'I've laid fresh clothes on the chair and we've done the best we could with your boots. Is there anything else I can do for you?'

Mr Deveril set down the cup and sat up with a smile that was plainly an effort.

'No. Thank you. Can - - ?' He stopped and Chloë set her teeth and waited. 'I'd like to talk to you. Later, when I'm thoroughly awake. Will you be here?'

She got up and smiled back with flawless, if superficial, composure.

'I'll be here,' she promised, walking to the door. 'Indeed, I've no intention of going anywhere – or of letting you go anywhere – until you've had a proper meal.'

When Alex joined her in the dining-parlour half an hour later, he was largely restored and able to do justice to a plate of chops whilst rendering an astringent account of the situation across the river. Chloë made a pretence of eating an apple she didn't want, her eyes never leaving his face.

'... and add to that the fact that, in most cases, the buckets, ladders and axes stored in the churches are either rotten with age or have been pilfered,' he said, 'and what you have in not only a disaster – but a stupid disaster.' He laid down his knife and fixed her with a sudden, penetrating gaze. 'None of this is what I wanted to say to you – but, as usual, this isn't the time. It seems that I owe you a great many apologies and explanations and thanks – not least for your patience. Is it asking too much for you to bear with me till this is over?'

Chloë flushed a little. 'No. And you owe me nothing.'

A vagrant smile lit the intent face as he got up and walked towards her.

'Not even for the warehouse?'

She shook her head. 'You had no choice.'

'No, I didn't. But you mind – and I'm sorry for that.' For the space of a heartbeat, brown eyes met silver-blue and then he said abruptly, 'I have to go.'

Chloë stood up and discovered that her knees felt like jelly.

'Yes. But don't work so long without rest this time,' she said, striving for her usual tone. And finding it, 'Or I'll be forced to use drastic measures. Again.'

* * *

Alex picked his way through the smouldering wreckage of what had once been Fish Street Hill towards the so far untouched reaches of Gracious Street and Cornhill. Fenchurch Street was choked with carriages and frightened pedestrians scurrying to deposit their belongings on Tower Hill, while Leadenhall Market swarmed with people haggling noisily over the possession of a cart – the cost of which had risen from ten shillings to twenty pounds.

He came upon Matt just east of St Mary-le-Bow and, without preamble, asked what new measures had been taken in the last few hours. Mr Lewis responded with a grimy, sardonic grin and the information that the Duke of York, now officially in charge, was attempting to quell the panic by riding about with his guard.

'Wonderful,' said Alex. 'And that's all? No gunpowder? No soldiers?'

'God, no! They think they're going to douse it with those daft bloody machines,' snorted Matthew. 'Man – you'd as well try to do it by spitting!'

Mr Deveril smiled grimly. 'All right. You carry on here. I'm going to see York.'

It was not hard to convince the King's brother that stronger measures were necessary; he had realised for himself that their only hope lay in the use of explosives but, with the Aldermen against him, his power was limited. He did, however, call out the troops – and after that Alex had a very busy afternoon.

While Mr Deveril dashed from one fire-post to the next, Chloë stood at Bankside in a crowd of strangely silent onlookers and watched the blaze gain in strength until she could bear it no longer. It was then that she became aware of the large number of refugees sitting huddled along the waterfront, pitifully clutching their few belongings and too dazed to move further. Chloë stopped, looking at them. There seemed to be a great many children, some of them very young and all of them hungry, holding fast to mothers who stared blankly out of dark-rimmed eyes filled with shock. Her heart wrung with pity, Chloë did not hesitate. She walked straight home to her kitchen and confronted Mistress Jackson.

'Pack up as much food as you can and take it to Bankside. There are people with nothing but what they stand up in and the children are starving. Get Naomi to help you.'

'But Madam, we can't feed them all – there's too many of them!'

'I know that,' replied Chloë tersely, 'but we can at least try. Take everything you can spare and divide it into small parcels to make it to further. Go on!'

* * *

As Monday night drew on the fire raged with greater and greater intensity, filling the sky with a brilliant, blazing light visible for forty miles. By daybreak on Tuesday, Cheapside was in ashes and the fire was moving north to Aldersgate and west to encompass the decaying, gothic splendour of Paul's Cathedral. It was also spreading towards Tower Street … and it was this that, around noon, finally produced the order Mr Deveril had been seeking since Sunday.

Although the wind had begun to show signs of abating, the fire continued to burn towards Cripplegate and the Tower; and the White Tower was London's main arsenal, containing enormous supplies of gunpowder. So when the flames reached Tower Street, His Majesty hesitated no longer but issued an order for the necessary demolition to be accomplished with explosives.

Receiving the news, Alex remarked that it was about bloody time and set off eastwards to lend a hand. He arrived to find the King personally supervising the unloading of the gunpowder, his wig lightly dusted with ash and his well-kept hands engrained with dirt. He surveyed Mr Deveril with unaccustomed gravity and said, 'They tell me you've done sterling work so far. But do you know how to lay a fuse?'

Alex nodded. 'Yes. I'll see to it. But you should move back beyond Water Mark Lane, sire. You're in too much danger here.'

Charles replied, 'So are many of my people. And if these men can hazard their lives, the least I can do is to be here with them. Now – the barrels are ready. Shall we begin?'

So begin they did, His Majesty assisting with his own hands and only retiring when Alex and the men working with him flatly refused to proceed until he did so. After he had gone, Mr Deveril lit the first slow-match, watched with clinical interest till he was satisfied that it would achieve its objective and then moved very fast indeed, stopping just once to scoop up a small dog that strayed across his path.

He made cover just as the explosion occurred, hurling himself violently around a high wall to land, complete with dog, on top of Charles Stuart – while, behind him, the houses came down with a deafening roar and filled the air with slivers of flying timber. Over the head of the dog – which was trying to lick his chin – the King's dark eyes met Mr Deveril's light ones.

Charles said, 'This is a particularly ugly little dog.'

Alex stood up and examined the dirty bundle of fur.

'It is, isn't it? Fortunately, my wife has a fondness for waifs and strays.'

An odd smile crossed the swarthy face. 'Has she? But I was under the impression that you wanted to be free of her.'

'Once, sire.' Alex looked back steadily. 'But it was a mistake. And now, if you'll excuse me, I should get back to work.'

The King nodded slowly. 'When this is over, come to Whitehall. I'm in your debt.'

Mr Deveril smiled, his teeth gleaming white against the smoke-blackened skin.

'Then perhaps Your Majesty would be gracious enough to have this conveyed to Southwark.' And he held out the dog.

* * *

Alex worked on till just after four in the afternoon and then, when the wind was almost gone and he could scarcely keep his eyes open, he set off home. This time Chloë was too busy doing what she could for the refugees to do more than attend to his immediate needs of food and hot water and, having slept for five hours, he was wakened by Naomi with the gloomy news that the wind had risen again. Alex cursed wearily and started to dress.

At the foot of the stairs he came upon Chloë, her face drawn with fatigue and her hair in riotous disorder. He examined her for a moment in critical silence, then took her hand and led her out into the garden.

'Come on. You've been doing too much.'

She frowned irritably. 'And you haven't?'

'Shrew,' said Mr Deveril unemotionally, tucking her hand through his arm. 'Which reminds me – what happened to the nice present I sent you?'

'It's in the kitchen, sulking because I gave it a bath.' She looked up at him. 'You know there's hardly any food to be had? They say most of the corn was lost.'

'It was – but there should be new supplies by tomorrow. The King has ordered food to be brought in from the country.' He steered her along Bankside and then said with suppressed violence, 'Damn this bloody wind! I thought we were free of it.'

'Is the Tower safe? They've been blasting round it all afternoon.'

'I know. And I hope it's safe. I'm sick of playing with matches.'

The pit of Chloë's stomach fell away and she said, 'Of course. I should have known you'd have something to do with it. Some people have all the fun.'

Alex glanced sharply down at her pale face and would perhaps have spoken had not his attention been diverted by a sudden, stunned gasp issuing from the group of spectators gathered just ahead of them on the Falcon Stairs to watch the last blazing hours of Paul's Cathedral.

'The roof! The roof's melting!'

And indeed it was. Flames burst from the belfry and from the lofty, pointed windows beneath, flickering round the crumbling buttresses and curling through the framework of the once magnificent rose window; and the vast expanse of roof, its wooden rafters aflame from within, assumed an exquisite sheen of shimmering silver as the six acres of lead were transformed into a state of molten fluidity. Then down it came in a terrific, shining cascade; every gargoyle and gutter spouted a gleaming shower to fall down the hill, while the timber frame gave way with almighty groan and the stone pinnacles and transom beams began to split and crack like volleys of artillery.

Chloë's fingers clenched tight on Mr Deveril's arm and her eyes were utterly stark.

'But it's stone! How can it burn like that?'

'It's stone,' agreed Alex dryly, 'but the Paternoster Row merchants are using the crypt as a safe storehouse for their wares.'

She stared at him. 'What wares?'

'Books. They've crammed it with books and manuscripts. Enough to burn for a week.'

* * *

By dawn on Wednesday the wind had mercifully dropped again and by noon, the blaze was finally under control and in a fair way to being put out. Leaving others to douse the last few pockets of flame, Mr Deveril turned his attention to the depressing necessity of clearing up the mess and it was this, now the danger and frantic activity were over, that revealed the awful extent of the desolation.

'I hope to God,' said Alex bitterly to Matthew, 'that when they re-build, this time they'll do it in brick.'

Meanwhile, streams of food-laden carts were trundling their way to the fields around London where the refugees camped and, in Southwark, Chloë found her burdens eased by the establishment of special markets. Forced to pay six shillings for a pair of eels that a week ago would have cost but two, Mistress Jackson produced a lengthy diatribe against profiteering. And then Matt returned and Chloë asked where Mr Deveril was.

'God knows,' came the dour reply. 'The last time I saw him, he was at Newgate. He's doing the things nobody else is bothering with. You know he can't help himself.'

And although it was the truth and she knew it, it did not bring any comfort; so that she toiled dispiritedly on, too tired to think and too nervous to rest, until finally at just before ten o'clock, Alex came home.

FIVE

Chloë had just reached the foot of the stairs when the door opened to admit Mr Deveril and for a second she remained poised while, across the space of the hall, her eyes met his. Then, without stopping to think, she crossed the tiled floor to enclose him in her arms and lean her brow against his shoulder.

Bemused, startled and too tired to trust his own judgement, Alex held her in a light clasp and said a trifle unsteadily, 'I apologise for the smell.'

The rose-gold head moved in denial.

'Must you hurry back,' she asked, her voice muffled against his chest, 'or have you time to rest properly?'

'All the time in the world. I'm purely an emergency service – and, God willing, the emergency would appear to be over.'

He felt the tension seep from her body.

'Thank God. All those poor people ... Alex, some of them have nothing left.' She paused and stepped back, eyeing him guiltily. 'What am I doing? You'll be asleep on your feet if I keep you standing here much longer.'

Alex retained one of her hands and, smiling a little, said, 'Do you know ... I think that's the first time I've ever heard you use my name.'

A faint flush stained her cheeks.

'Yes. Well, one way and another it seems a bit late to be upholding the formalities,' she said. And then, seeing the question in his face, added hastily, 'But we can't talk about it now. Go away upstairs while I see about some hot water and meal for you – and then I don't want to see you up again before tomorrow evening at the earliest.'

Laughter stirred in the compelling eyes. 'As you wish. But on one condition.'

'What?'

'That you'll sup with me tomorrow – before Fate can devise any new catastrophe to prevent it.'

And because it mattered so supremely, Chloë stopped trying to pretend and offered him the unvarnished truth.

'You know that I will. You had only to ask.'

* * *

After a deep and dreamless night's sleep, Chloë awoke charged with vitality and full of plans. She began her day with a visit to the kitchen to discuss the evening's all-important menu with Mistress Jackson – a proceeding which, due to the depredations on the larder, was not particularly easy. Then, passing Mr Lewis with a cheery greeting, she stepped out into the untamed garden in search of flowers to grace the table. Matt watched her go with a satisfied gleam in his eye and then took himself off to see what help might still be needed on the ravaged north bank.

Chloë returned with her arms full of wild roses and assorted greenery which she spent a pleasant hour arranging in vases to set around the dining-room and parlour. Then, that done, she bade Naomi bring up some hot water and vanished into her bedchamber to begin the most vital preparations of all.

First she washed her hair, rinsing it in lavender-scented water and wrapping it tightly in a towel. Then she took a long bath. Surprisingly, she was neither nervous nor afraid – only excited and eager, like a child on its birthday. The knowledge that the annulment papers were locked safely in her drawer gave her confidence and a sense of freedom; she could do what she wished and it would hurt no one. The only thing that mattered was that she should look her best for this, the most decisive night of her life.

Choosing the right gown was difficult but she finally settled on the glowing peacock brocade and spread it across a chair while she attended to her hair. This she left loose, simply brushing it back from her brow and confining in beneath one thick plait.

By the time she was ready it was nearly half past five. Chloë cast a last searching glance at her reflection, raised her fingers fleetingly to the delicate marigold chain around her neck and then went downstairs to check that all was well in the kitchen and discover if Mr Deveril was awake.

He was; and not only awake but already down and awaiting her in the parlour, one foot on the window-seat and his gaze resting on the garden. Then he turned to face her and most of Chloë's blithe confidence trickled away.

Though still a little fine-drawn, he had recovered all his usual poise and air of self-containment; and he was, as Chloë had known from the first, the most spectacularly – and therefore alarmingly - good-looking man she had ever seen. The blue-black hair fell in waves to his shoulders and, against the snowy linen of his shirt, his skin was faintly tanned; his black brocade coat was unlaced and his only ornament, the heavy signet ring that habitually graced his left hand. But it was his eyes that commanded her attention; aquamarine over steel ... clear, alert and faintly smiling.

Alex bowed and raised her fingers to his lips.

'Hello,' he said simply. 'You look beautiful.'

Chloë coloured and fixed her gaze on the hand that held hers.

'Th-thank you. Have you been waiting long?'

'A life-time,' he said, lightly ambiguous. And then, as her eyes flew back to his, 'But it was undoubtedly worth it.'

Unable to decide how to take this, Chloë cast desperately around for something to say that would steer the conversation into safer channels until her nerves settled. Mr Deveril watched in some amusement and then helped her out.

'I know what you're thinking,' he said, releasing her hand. 'You're surprised that I still have a decent coat to my name.'

That produced a tiny laugh. 'Is it the only one?'

'Not quite – but it's by far the smartest. I was hoping to impress you.'

'You succeeded,' she replied truthfully. 'So well that I hardly know what to say to you.'

There was a moment's pause, then Alex said, 'Am I so formidable? I don't mean to be.'

An almost indiscernible note of appeal threaded the charming voice but, before Chloë could respond to it, Naomi was at the door informing them that supper was ready. Chloë thanked her, then looked dubiously back at Mr Deveril. He bowed again and offered his arm with a bitter-sweet smile. 'Well, my lovely wife?'

And that, of course, set the final seal on her confusion.

Facing her across the polished table, Alex sensed her unease and set out to dispel it with a gentle flow of talk. Adroit and skilful, he chose topics of mutual interest, drifting from one to another and avoiding potential pitfalls with an ease that gave no hint of the very real concentration he was having to employ. He spoke of Giles' departure for the Caribbean – but nothing more than that - and, for a time at least, felt her relax as she shared his own sense of loss; and then a casual reference to the King set her on edge again and left him wondering what he'd said.

The meal seemed never-ending and he began to wish that Naomi would stop bobbing in with some additional delicacy. Chloë was merely toying with her food and he could cheerfully have tossed every carefully-chosen dish through the window; but while his own glass stood virtually untouched at his elbow, he watched Chloë absently sipping from hers and started to hope that perhaps Candy wine might succeed where he was apparently failing.

Naomi made her final entrance to place a dish of sweet-meats on the table and then withdrew, regretfully closing the door behind her. Both she and Mistress Jackson knew a good deal about the state of affairs between Mr Deveril and his lady and both were romantically curious. Mr Lewis, of course, knew more than either of them – but was close as a clam.

With an imperceptible sigh of relief, Alex leaned back and looked at his wife.

'What's the matter, Marigold?'

'Nothing,' said Chloë untruthfully. 'Would you like some brandy?'

'No.' His tone was mildly amused. 'You're looking at me as if you expected me to pounce on you – or say something outrageously unacceptable. I think I can promise not to do either one. And I'm not drinking because – as you said yourself – we can't hold a proper conversation if I'm never entirely sober. But if I've said something to upset you, I'd really like to know what it is.'

'I'm not upset,' she said absently. And thought, 'Why can't you just pounce? I never realised how difficult this was going to be – and pouncing would solve everything. But that's not going to happen, is it? Firstly, because this is all too restrained and polite and we're sitting here like people in a play; and secondly, because – for all you know to the contrary – I might hit you over the head again.' Aloud, she said, 'I think I'm nervous. You said we should talk and you were right. But I don't know where to begin – so perhaps you should do it.'

'I'm not sure I know where to begin either,' he said quietly, 'but I can try.'

He thought for a moment, aware that there was really only thing he wanted to say but that if he said it now, he risked a similar reaction to when he'd blurted it out before. This time he had to get it right. This time, nothing could be left to chance. This time she had to believe him. And that meant clearing the ground first.

He said, 'I think perhaps we might start by exploding a few misconceptions – if you don't mind humouring me?' Chloë nodded and, leaning back in his chair, hands clasped lightly on the table, Alex said, 'That night on the Falcon Stairs, I told you that you were the last woman I'd kissed. Did you believe me?'

Her brows rose. Whatever else she'd expected, it wasn't this. 'Yes.'

'Why? Forgive my bluntness, but I basically told you I hadn't had a woman for at least six months and you believed me?'

'Yes. You may not always tell the whole truth – but I don't think I've ever known you to lie. So of course I believed you.'

'Thank you.' He smiled crookedly. 'At least you know I'm not a rake, then.'

'That's true.' She tilted her head and smiled back at him, suddenly calm. 'I hadn't quite thought of it that way.'

'No.' He paused, struggling to find the words 'And the other evening when I made a lamentably clumsy attempt to ... how shall I put it? ... when I -- ?'

'Pounced,' supplied Chloë before she could stop herself.

Alex gave a tiny choke of laughter. 'Very well. When I pounced on you ... did you wonder if that was a result of a sudden and overwhelming fit of non-specific lust?'

'You mean did I think you were desperate and I just happened to be handy? It crossed my mind, yes.' She eyed him amiably. 'But I decided that, after eight months of celibacy, you were entitled to a small lapse. Then again, if you really were crazed with lust, I imagine you'd probably have come straight to the point, as it were. So I decided it wasn't worth worrying about.'

This time Alex stared at her as if he couldn't quite believe his ears. Finally, he said, 'And people think I say outrageous things.'

'And so you do. Sometimes.' She grinned. 'Perhaps it's catching.'

'God, I hope not!' Rising, he pulled off his coat and tossed it aside, then moved round the table to take the chair beside her. 'If it wasn't worth worrying about, why did you crack a bottle over my head?'

This was also unexpected but Chloë kept her nerve and, shaking her head, said, 'If you don't know, you can't have thought about it properly.'

'I've thought about it,' he said, his eyes suddenly serious, 'but the only reason I can come up with is the one I don't want to talk about just yet.' He hesitated and then said abruptly, 'Giles told me that Sarah came here. What did she say to you?'

Chloë drew a long breath and released it. 'She said you would marry her.'

'And did you believe her?'

'I – I don't know. I thought that perhaps you might.'

Silence stretched out on invisible threads before Alex spoke with careful detachment.

'And if I did ... would you mind?'

She looked him in the eye. 'Yes. I would. She's selfish and vain and downright nasty.'

'I know. But is that the only reason?'

'Not entirely. Matt would never stand for it,' she replied as flippantly as she was able. And then, realising what he'd said, 'What do you mean – you know?'

Alex shrugged. 'I know what she is. I've known for a long time. And if she was the last woman in the world, I'd join a monastery. But she won't trouble us again. That's why I went to see her that night – to put an end to her importunities once and for all.' Reaching out, he took Chloë's hand and toyed with her wedding band. 'Your remark just now about Matthew ... I recall saying quite a number of stupid things to you the other night – but, as you very well know, I wasn't particularly sober. So it really isn't very kind of you to throw my idiocies in my teeth.'

Chloë frowned. 'I wasn't. And I'm perfectly well aware that you weren't drunk, just bone-tired – and that you're not an habitual sot. I've only ever seen you hopelessly drunk once and that was - - ' She stopped short.

'And that was on the night of our wedding,' he finished pleasantly. 'Quite. Do you despise me for it?'

'No! How could I? It is I who should never have agreed to it.'

Alex continued to turn her wedding ring on her finger, his eyes never leaving her face.

'So why did you?'

'W-what?' Chloë wondered how she'd failed to foresee this question.

'Why did you marry me?'

'We've been through this before. You know why.'

A strange smile crossed his face. 'All right. Why did you suggest the annulment?'

'You know that, too,' she said evasively.

'Perhaps – perhaps not.' He released her hand. 'Chloë ... I'm sorry, but we can't go on ducking the issue. We have to discuss it.'

She stared at him forebodingly. 'Now?'

'Yes – now.' Unable to sit still any longer, he rose and crossed to the fireplace. Then, turning he said, 'I tried to broach this subject a week ago but with a crassness for which I can only apologise. Forget, if you can, the reasons I gave you then – for only one was the absolute truth. Everything else was an attempt to test the water without committing myself and none of it came out right.' He paused and dragged his eyes away from the curve of her throat and the silky perfection of her bare shoulders. 'But before we go any further, you have to tell me if you still wish to proceed with the annulment.'

For one very good reason, Chloë found herself unable to comply with this request so, avoiding his gaze, she made yet another attempt at evasion.

'I don't understand why you want to know.'

'And I don't understand why you won't answer me,' he responded tartly. 'It's a simple enough question, after all. Yes or no, would do.' He paused and then said, 'I'm sorry if I sound sharp but this has to stop. There is only one reason for two people remaining needlessly tied to one another and it has to be mutual. If one is the victim of the other's overwhelming passion, the situation would become impossible.'

'Oh God,' thought Chloë. 'He knows.' And leaving her seat, she turned blindly away to the dresser. 'Yes, I can quite see that – and of course I'll release you. Have some brandy.'

Swift and soundless, Mr Deveril followed her, one flawed but still beautiful hand imprisoning hers around the neck of the squat, green bottle. He was so close that Chloë could feel his warmth against her back; she stared at the hand enclosing hers while every nerve in her body demanded what it now seemed she would never have.

'Chloë, no.' The pleasant voice was brittle. 'It's not I that am trapped – it's you. What I'm trying to tell you is that, for me, this half-marriage of ours is no longer enough.'

Her mind was working very slowly and his meaning escaped her but she grasped at the small ray of light which offered her the only thing she'd ever realistically hoped for.

'You mean you want me to go to bed with you?'

'Christ!' he said raggedly. 'You have no idea.'

'If that means yes, you could seduce me,' she suggested helpfully. 'You already know you wouldn't find it very difficult.'

'Yes. Perhaps.' Alex drew a long, unsteady breath. 'But that's not enough. I love you.'

There was a dizzy, earth-shaking pause while the words filtered dimly into Chloë's brain. Then, 'What did you say?' she asked faintly.

Releasing her hand, Alex swung her round to face him.

'Look at me,' he said. And when her eyes rose to his, 'Look at me and try to believe me. I said that I love you. And I do – in every way it's possible. Beside you, every woman I ever knew is but a shadow, a phrase, a single note; you are the flesh and the poem. And my heart's song.' He paused and then resumed carefully. 'I asked what you wanted in order to spare you an outpouring of possibly unwanted emotion – but it's too late for that now. You should understand that I don't want to give you up but I don't think I can go on as we are. My feelings for you are not mild – and I'd be less than fair if I didn't point out that I can't promise to stick to our original bargain. I'm no catch, I know; I'm intemperate and often bloody impossible. And if ... if you let our marriage stand, I can't even promise that you'll never regret it – only that I'll try not to give you cause. If you loved me, that might be enough. If not ... oh God, if not then say so now and let's get the sodding annulment.'

Seconds ticked by in silence. Chloë neither moved nor spoke but remained as if frozen, staring into the anguished candour of the blue eyes. Then, just when Alex thought he'd lost, she laid one hand gently against his cheek and said, 'I don't want an annulment. I never wanted it. I only wanted you. That's why I hit you over the head. I thought you'd have realised.'

He frowned and said slowly, 'I must be very slow - because I still don't.'

'If we'd gone to bed together that night, there'd have been no question of an annulment. And I had to be sure you still had a choice.'

A tiny flush touched his skin and the bright gaze widened, searching her face.

'And now?'

She smiled. 'Now it doesn't matter. You wanted the truth. And the truth is that I loved you from the first time we met – and when you kissed me in that horrid alley, I knew that I did.'

Alex stared at her, his hands tightening on her shoulders.

'I've tried so hard these past few weeks to think that you cared for me just a little – but I never dreamed ... ' He stopped. 'Perhaps I've been blind – but I can't imagine what you could have seen in me. Are you ... are you quite sure?'

'Utterly, totally, irrevocably sure.' Touched by his lack of vanity, she slid her arms around him and leant her head against his shoulder; and, as he gathered her closer, she said, 'As for what I saw in you that first time, I really don't know. I didn't for quite a long time even though what I felt didn't change. It was only later, when I came to know you that I understood – and by then it was too late.' She looked up, drowning in the warmth and scent of him. 'If a hundred or even a thousand well-behaved men queued up to offer me their hands, there would still only be you. Always and forever. I love you and I want you and ... and are you ever going to kiss me?'

Alex smiled down into her upturned face, for once beyond words. Then he slid his fingers into her hair and, bending his head, forged a trail of tiny kisses from cheekbone to jaw before finally seeking her mouth like a man parched. Drowning in sweetness, Chloë gasped and twined her hands around his neck to press herself even closer. He had kissed her before and it had been enough to steal her heart ... but not like this. Never with a passion that out-rivalled her own and sent sparks racing through her veins.

Eventually and with extreme reluctance, Alex released her mouth and looked deep into dilated brown eyes. There was no fear in them, no constraint; only an echo of his own need. He said, 'Chloë? If it's too soon – if you want to wait – '

'No,' she said with a smile that stopped his breath. 'No. We've waited long enough.'

'Come, then.' And lifting her easily in his arms, he carried her, laughing a little, into the hall and was just setting foot on the stairs when he spied Mr Lewis emerging from the kitchen. Pausing, Alex said, 'Repel all boarders, Matt. I don't care who they are. Even if it's the King himself, just send him on his way.'

Matthew grinned and settled himself on a chair in the corner.

'Right you are, then,' he said. And pulling a bit of wood from his pocket, embarked calmly on some serious whittling.

Alex, meanwhile, had sailed on up the stairs and into Chloë's bedchamber.

'It's tidier than mine,' he murmured absently, 'and it has both a lock and a bolt.' He set Chloë on her feet and let his hands stray lingeringly over her shoulders. Then she was in his arms again.

He kissed her hair, her eyelids, her throat while his hands unhurriedly smoothed away the ribbons and laces. The peacock gown slithered to the floor allowing his mouth to explore her shoulders; then, a little later, her petticoats followed it and he lifted her out of them before taking his time over the curve of her waist. Shaken by pulses and clad only in her shift, Chloë slid her hands beneath his shirt until Alex pulled it off over his head and tossed it aside, leaving her free to discover the hard contours of his chest. He paused for a moment, the intense ice-blue gaze resting on her mouth with an expression that sent heat flooding through her body; and then, sliding the shift slowly from her shoulders to leave her wearing only the marigold chain, lifted her on to the bed and spoke for the first time.

'For you are fairer than the evening air ... and my only love.'

Her breathing wholly disrupted and her bones melting in a maelstrom of desire, Chloë reached out to him. And shedding the rest of his clothes without once taking his eyes from her, Alex took the hand that she offered and lay down beside her. Flesh met flesh and Chloë gasped, stunned by the sudden explosion of sensation; and when he kissed her again, the sparks in her blood became wildfire.

After so long an abstinence and with the only girl he wanted in his arms at last, Alex had to exert iron control over his own desire – and simultaneously use all the skills he owned to make sure that she would not know it. Slowly, tantalisingly, he explored her body with his mouth and with light, questing hands ... rejoicing in every tremor of response and leading her, with every grace and care at his command, towards the ultimate delight. And Chloë, intoxicated by the muscle and bone beneath his skin, driven beyond all thought and consumed by a hunger greater than anything she could ever have imagined, said two words without knowing what they were.

Alex looked at her, his control all but gone yet still needing to be sure. And then, at long last, gratefully forsook his exquisite courtship and entered the fire and silk she offered him.

Much later, he smiled down into her cloudy brown eyes and stroked tendrils of hair from her cheek. Gradually, her eyes focused on his, their expression one that stopped his breath for a moment. Then he said, 'Well, my heart?'

She stirred slightly. 'Alex ... I didn't know.' Her mouth found his hand. 'I love you so much.'

'And I you. Always and forever.'

They slept then till the sun rose, filling the room with a rosy glow and it was Alex who woke first. For a long time he was content to lie still, holding her against his heart and looking down into her sleeping face and at the bright hair spread in gleaming disorder across his arm. Then, unable to resist any longer, he set about waking her with the lazy drift of his hands.

Her eyes opened slowly and she smiled up at him. And this time it was she who drew his head down to hers and, sliding a slender foot along his calf, said simply, 'Oh yes. Please.'

They slept again to wake far into the day when Mr Deveril roused his love by tickling her face with a strand of rose-gold hair. Propped lazily on one elbow, he lifted one eyebrow and said, 'Hello. I've married a turnip. Do you realise it's already tomorrow?'

Chloë started to laugh and then thought returned bringing recollection flooding in its wake. Her eyes flew suddenly wide and she made a small, incoherent sound.

Alex eyed her quizzically.

'In general, I rather like the profound effect I appear to have on you. But just what have I said this time to deprive you of breath?' He waited, idly tracing the line of her jaw with one finger until, when she didn't reply, 'Well, Marigold?'

A tide of colour washed over her and Alex watched its progress with interest. Then she swallowed and said weakly, 'You just reminded me of a little thing I forgot to mention.'

'I did?'

'Yes. You may perhaps feel that I should have recalled it earlier.'

'Oh I shouldn't think so,' he replied vaguely, his finger descending to investigate her clavicle and beyond it. 'You've been somewhat occupied, after all.'

'Only somewhat?' She hoped keeping the mood light would help. 'You mean you can do better?'

'We can try to find out, if you like.' He sounded amused and deceptively casual. 'Now. What was it that you wanted to tell me?'

Knowing that the sooner it was done the better, Chloë shut her eyes and said flatly, 'We're not married.'

The straying finger was abruptly stilled and the silence grew to monumental proportions. Then, with careful precision, Alex said, 'What did you say?'

She opened her eyes on a wide, blue and quite unreadable gaze.

'We're not married. We haven't been since Saturday. I – I got the annulment papers from the King.'

'Did you?' His tone was still level, if mildly strained. 'Why?'

She'd known he would ask but had never planned an answer. Averting her face from the penetrating eyes, she said, 'I thought it was a good idea.'

With one gentle, economic movement, Mr Deveril turned her face back towards him.

'Why?'

Even if she could have thought of a convincing lie, Chloë knew better than to suppose that she could fool him now. She sighed. 'Because I should have refused to marry you in the first place – and I could have done. And because I didn't want to make a habit of hitting you over the head.'

For a second, he stared at her so oddly that she wondered if he'd understood. Then he said, 'Oh God, Marigold – my delightful, wanton darling – my only mistake lay in giving you the chance.' And burying his face in the pillows, he dissolved into helpless, gurgling laughter.

It was a long time before he recovered and then, still hiccupping faintly, he said, 'There are times, this being one, when you scare the hell out of me.'

'Really? I'm flattered.'

'Don't be.' His skin was flushed and his eyes brilliant. 'The only reason I'm not beating you is that I'm rather taken with the idea of you lusting after my body.'

Chloë sat up in mock indignation and was pulled flat again with a lazy sweep of one arm.

'Also,' continued Mr Deveril, 'I'm aware that you did it for me – no, don't argue. I'm just coming to the crux of the matter.' He smiled with singular charm. 'I never proposed to you, did I, Chloë? Nor courted or wooed you as you deserve?'

She flushed and laid her hand against his chest.

'I've had my courtship. All I ever wanted.'

He took her hand and held it.

'I'm glad.' He paused, the blue eyes suddenly very serious indeed and went on simply, 'My name is Alex Deveril and I've nothing to offer you but a rather shabby home and a great deal of love. Will you marry me?'

Chloë's vision blurred with tears.

'Alex ... you don't have to ... there is no need.'

His fingers tightened on hers. 'For me, there is. I love you and I want you as my wife. Do you think I'd have taken you if I'd known?'

She shook her head, blinking. 'No. I know that you wouldn't.'

'Which is why you didn't tell me until today.'

'Yes. But you - - ' She broke off, shaken by unwilling laughter. 'Alex, you can't propose to me in bed!'

'Why not? If you consider the key moments in our relationship from the first day we met, this seems fairly consistent. But you haven't answered me and we're not going anywhere until you do. So are you going to marry me or not?'

And put like that, in a manner so typically Alex, there was only one answer.

'Yes and yes and yes. Of course I'll marry you,' she said, half-laughing, half-crying. And was swept into the crushing embrace that Alex could no longer deny her … or himself.

'Good,' he said a little later. 'Now let's get dressed and go and see if His Majesty can undo what's been done. He said he was in my debt - so now he can prove it.'

* * *

Hand in hand, they stood before Charles Stuart while his cynical dark eyes moved from one to the other of them and began to twinkle with amusement.

'Let me guess,' he said. 'You want me to annul your annulment.'

'No, Your Majesty,' replied Mr Deveril calmly. 'We want to be married. Tonight.'

The King raised one mocking brow and started to laugh.

'I'm relieved to hear it. There's far too much laxity at Court.'

Stifling a laugh, Chloë said demurely, 'I knew we could count on your understanding, sire – so we have Mr Lewis outside, ready to support Alex through the ceremony.'

Alex cast her an oblique and very private smile.

'It seems a small enough reward,' Charles observed, 'for unmasking a traitor and helping preserve poor London.'

'It's enough, sire. Everything, in fact.'

The King surveyed him thoughtfully.

'It doesn't appear to have occurred to you that I might have some ideas of my own as to how best to recompense you,' he remarked dryly, taking a large sealed document from his desk. 'But your reasons are clear ... and, moreover, not unpleasing since it's rare enough that I can give more than is asked. On this occasion, however, I can not only make the reward I would wish, but one poetically just. This.'

Very slowly, Alex accepted the parchment and, with a hand that was suddenly a little unsteady, broke the seal. Then he drew Chloë close within his arm so that they could read it together. The language was heavily ornamented with legal aphorisms but the sense was plain enough. The Crown was restoring to Alexander Charles Deveril and the heirs of his body, the properties lately held by Simon Robert Deveril – to wit, certain estates in Kent and a town house on the Strand.

Two pairs of eyes stared dazedly at their sovereign and then turned meditatively to each other.

'Well, well,' said Alex, with careful restraint. 'It seems I've something to offer you after all.'

Blinking back tears, Chloë said softly, 'You always did have.' And then, for His Majesty's benefit, 'But three houses? What on earth are we going to do with them all?'

A slow, beautiful smile lit Mr Deveril's face and his arm tightened about her waist.

'I'm sure,' he replied cheerfully, 'that we'll think of something. But first I'm going to take you to Kent for our bridal trip. You'll like it.'

'Kent?' she asked gently.

The radiant eyes laughed tantalisingly back at her.

'Naturally. What else?'

EPILOGUE

LONDON September 1666

In the end, as in the beginning, silence hung over London. Three-quarters of the City, from Custom House to the Temple and as far north as Cripplegate, was now nothing but a smouldering wasteland of wreckage; and the loss was immeasurable. Houses by the thousand, public buildings by the score and the only bridge spanning the Thames. The craft and heritage of centuries reduced, in four short days, to ashes.

Alone in his office, the young Surveyor-General, Mr Wren, burned with the fires of enthusiasm and opportunity as he joyfully tore up his recently completed plans for the re-modelling of what, a week since, had been the existing structure of Paul's Cathedral. For quite a long time he merely sat, chin in hand, and gazed far into the future to the grand new design that was only a part of his vision for a gleaming, orderly city of stone.

And then, smiling, he drew a sheet of parchment before him and picked up his pen.

Printed in Great Britain
by Amazon